The Wafer

Joseph T. McFadden

To Ralph Powers as promised
Joseph T. McFadden

Angus Publishing
National Writers Press

Also by Joseph T. McFadden

Herme's Viper

Fulton's Monkey and Others a Collection of Short Stories

Angus Publishing
Vail, CO
anguspublishing@aol.com
www.anguspublishing.com

In Conjunction with
The National Writers Press
3140 South Peoria Street, #294
Aurora, Colorado 80014
www.nationalwriters.com

Cover Design by
NZ Graphics

Artwork by
Dawn Knutson

Published in the United States of America.

Library of Congress Cataloging-in-Publication Data

McFadden, Joseph T.

The Wafer / Joseph T. McFadden
p. cm.

1. Transplant 2. Donors 3. Cannibalism 4. Human Sacrifice 5. The Eucharist 6. Heart Surgeon 7. Courier 8. Wafer
ISBN 0-88100-124-4
Library of Congress Card Cataloging Number 2002102646

ACKNOWLEDGMENTS

My thanks go to Dr. John Hess of the Department of Anesthesiology at Eastern Virginia Medical School for editing the drugs; to Dr. Hormoz Azar of the surgery department at EVMS for his help with the bypass surgery, and to Dr. Jack Crumley, Division of Cardiovascular Surgery, University of South Carolina, for letting me in on a heart transplant, especially the explant.

Bill Anderson and his staff at Life Net Transplant Services provided invaluable information. Many friends helped with their criticism, and I am especially grateful to the editors Mary Tuttle of Tattered Cover in Denver, and Sandy Whelchel, executive director of the National Writers Association.

They tore out the great bull heart and offered the heart to Shamash, bowing before the God, two brothers.
GALGAMESH -- as translated by David Ferry

The

Wafer

Joseph T. McFadden

Angus Publishing and
National Writers Press

CHAPTER 1

He jammed the accelerator, barely missing an oncoming car, and swerved across to the curb and slowed alongside her running feet. Alarmed blue eyes met his gaze. The door swung open — a silent offering. Without missing stride she leapt across the grass divide and plunged into the back seat. "Get out of here fast ... they almost had me this time, and they will get you, too."

He burned rubber to avoid an oncoming truck. "Where to? Where do you live?"

"Oh, no! Not there ... hide me somewhere," she gasped, the bellows sound of breathing rising from the floor where she lay.

A gust of misty wind swirled the water-laden Sycamore limbs arboring Olney Road in the cold dusk, and showers peppered his windshield with raindrops and springtime buds. A flurry of seagulls rose on wing from the inlet and screamed upward in erratic flight. He veered down a side street and turned back into Stockley Gardens Boulevard.

He slowed to a dignified speed, and cruised the streets to his own garage, his window shut now against the salty smell of the tide and warm dampness of coastal lowlands.

The garage door came down and he helped her out of the car. She stood, breathing calmly, poised and regal, leggy in tapered slacks. She had to look up to meet his gaze. Her hands trembled and she appeared weakened and vulnerable. Her perfume wafted clean and delicate, her eyes upon his face with quiet regard, the pupils big, the blueness intense.

"You are safe now."

"Thank you. And where are we?"

"In my house."

"Thanks for the hospitality."

"No problem, but we have to decide what to do with you, and perhaps me if they saw us together."

"I don't think they did," she said. "I escaped by jumping two brick walls and taking another street."

"Are they driving or on foot?"

"Driving ... A new black BMW M5."

The silken swish of a speeding automobile on wet pavement approached in the street. He went to the door and looked through the view glass as the sound peaked and diminished in passing. "They just went by at breakneck speed. I counted three, all wearing hats." As he spoke, tires squealed on a curve at the intersection down the street.

She closed her eyes and cringed. "Hoods. God! They are too close."

"Who are they?"

"I don't know."

"Nor why they are chasing you?"

She shook her head. "Not really, and I'm afraid to guess."

He turned from the door and crossed the garage. She looked up, watching his face, looking into his black eyes. She had seen this man before, many times, but never up close. Now she stood within touching distance of the red curly hair, his lanky and muscular leanness, his angular masculinity, and legendary appeal. A warm sensation stirred in her belly, a dissipation of the driving fear riding her heart. He said, "I'm Eric Stuart."

"I'm Joan Pully, and I know who you are — a fellow in heart surgery at Sentara. You have been pointed out to me in the hospital where I go often, working for LifeChain."

"Oh."

"And you are thirty or thereabouts, and single, and ... "

"How do you know?"

"All the girls talk about you."

"Who?"

"Nurses, laboratory technicians, hospital secretaries, single women, married women, volunteers — the pink ladies, all dreaming."

"I can't imagine why."

"You want to hear? It goes like this ... heart surgeon bar none, card expert, magician better than amateur, sleight of hand master who did his first triple bypass when he was still an intern and did it faster and better than seasoned guys training him, six foot three, handsome and desirable and gives no one a tumble, completely trusted by every woman who knows him, could have anybody he wanted, the talk of the town, the most desirable, the most eligible bachelor, dreamboat." She looked at him steadily, an eyebrow raised, a bemused smile, teasing.

"Hold it, hold it, hold it."

She laughed, "There's more."

"It can't all be good."

"Well, apparently no one has been given a chance to see the other side, if there is one. What are you, a street angel and house devil?"

"Frankenstein, maybe, or Dr. Jekyll." His face had flushed and he changed the subject. "What do you do for LifeChain?"

"Mostly carry live organs from one city to another."

"Well, a commendable operation, and nice to meet you."

"Meeting this way is a Godsend. Thanks for the rescue."

"How do you know who to trust?"

"Oh, I have no doubts about you. And how did you know to stop?"

"A tingling premonition, I suppose something like the way animals know violent weather beyond a cloudless sky."

"Not just a hunch?"

"A silent message in the winds of unspoken warnings. And you were beginning to wobble."

"Well, if you're psychic, thank God for it."

"Anyway, so here we are. I was planning to cook for myself tonight. The kitchen is right above," he said, turning toward the stairs.

She followed. As they passed behind his car, she said, "A

new Mercedes 400. Not bad for a fellow in training."

"It didn't come from medicine, and before you guess wrong, nor family money, either."

"Did it yourself?"

"Yes. I'm lucky at an interesting sideline."

"When do you complete your fellowship?"

"Little more than a month. June of this year."

"Then?"

"Several offers, but no decisions. I want to go where I'm needed, and where politics and complacency and commercialism don't impede progress."

"You think you will find such a place in this country at the beginning of the twenty-first century?"

"It's worth a try."

"Well, yes, but now tell me this ... Why did you pick Norfolk to be trained in the most gratifying of all surgery? You could have gone to more renowned and tonier places with your obvious talents."

"Thank you. To tell you the truth, I came to look at the place just on a fluke, and I was amazed. Every heart surgeon here came from high academia and surgical schools famous for their refined skills, and each of them is dedicated to the highest quality. They, one and all, are here to escape the tyranny of those places, and I could not have fallen into better hands."

"Well, they certainly have my admiration, too."

They ascended one flight, passed down a railed balcony paralleling the wall above the garage, and entered his kitchenette through a rear door. He crossed to the living room windows, and peeked out. Thunder rumbled behind a black cloud boiling out of the west, and a flash of sheet lightning blipped the landscape in stark outline. Twilight had deepened; streetlights were on in the drizzling rain, the park across the street hidden in darkness.

As he closed the curtains and reached toward a lamp, the

same muted sound of a speeding car swished down the street and she said, "Please don't turn the light on for a moment." And she collapsed on the couch. In the dim light she appeared to loom into a new depth of reality. Her shocked exhaustion enfeebled her like the spent flight of a defenseless creature rescued from a rapacious stalker. She covered her face with both palms and her bobbed black hair fell over her hands. She said, "Oh God ... I was so terrified I thought my heart would burst."

He crossed the room and stood looking down at her, thinking, and not knowing what to say or to do. He asked, "Would you like wine, or a cocktail?"

"No, not just yet, but water; I could drink a gallon of water."

He returned from the refrigerator with pitcher and glass, and she drank while he waited, watching, wanting to help. Uneasily, he said, "I will start dinner in a few minutes. When you feel up to it, come sit at the breakfast bar while I work."

"Okay. But right now I want to enjoy this moment of being alive and free. Thank God you recognized my predicament."

"Just followed my impulses. You can tell me about it when ready." He had known when he saw the pall of fatigue and exhaustion overcoming the agile leaps.

"After I catch my breath and rest."

He hesitated; then sat on the edge of the couch beside her. She nestled back, rested her head on a pillow, and closed her eyes. He half turned and watched. The last few minutes were difficult to believe, this beautiful woman suddenly there, like a dream still dreaming — an alabaster beauty, a regal and delicate woman of uncommon loveliness. Yet he sensed a robustness and strength hidden behind a beguiling litheness. Everything seemed very right.

She drifted into sleep, twitched, cried out, and awakened briefly, then drifted back into sleep. Drowsy himself from forty hours on duty without sleep, and sweaty and muggy, he needed bath, food, and bed. He eased off the couch and went to the shower.

When he reentered the room she aroused and looked up in surprise, recovered her bearings, and moved to rise. He snapped on a lamp and reached for her hand, and pulled her up. He guided her by an elbow to a barstool then crossed into the kitchenette and began dinner preparations.

"You've bathed while I was sleeping. I like your leisure suit."

"Yes. Feel free to do the same. Pick what you like from clothes in the bedroom ... first door on the right."

"Thanks. I will directly, but I could use wine now. May I pour for you, too?"

"Chardonnay and champagne in the refrigerator, glasses above the sink. You choose."

She poured champagne. They clinked rims, and she said, "Here's to being alive."

"And to staying alive."

"By all means."

"Do you think, by any chance, the people pursuing you might be trying to steal the organs you carry?"

"Perhaps, but there is more to it. They could grab the container and run, but they don't. And this afternoon I had already completed a mission when they began chasing me."

"Who could they be and what do they want?"

"I don't know, and I can only run."

"Your job?"

"The job can wait. It will have to."

"You work for Marcus Mann?"

"Yes. You know him?"

"I do. No one is more respected in the community for the quality and the readiness of his banked tissue, and his handling of live organs from the brain dead."

"The community, the country, the whole world."

"The country? The world?"

"Oh, yes! He founded LifeChain, one of the largest tissue and organ distributors in the world, and he has grown with the transplant era, a pioneer working to perfect the science of tissue and organ salvage."

"Well, I know what he does to help us get organs here, but I never stopped to think he might be doing the same for others elsewhere."

"Known the world over for it — the most giving person I have ever known, almost totally altruistic."

"Does he know you are in danger, for whatever reason?"

"He knows something is amiss. During the past two months, each of the other ten regions of UNOS has lost at least one courier. They disappeared while making runs with live organs. Ours, number eleven, is the only one not to lose a courier yet. But it's beginning to look like open war on the national system and I'm afraid our luck will run out. So far, the media is paying scant attention. As to Mann's concerns about me, he knows I feel harassed."

"I've heard rumors of trouble with the couriers, but apparently it's being hushed up. Something seems to be happening behind the scenes."

"Oh, yes. I suspect there is a spy in the LifeChain system selling information."

"What information?"

"Two avenues of deception — one would be the identity of potential donors with the right qualifications, such as blood type and body build, to fit the specific needs of a dying patient waiting for a heart or another organ."

"And the result?"

"The right person could be kidnapped, rendered brain dead, and used as a donor by the purchaser."

"Betraying well-intentioned people who have agreed to donate at the moment of some distant and unlikely personal tragedy, a tragedy they don't actually believe will ever happen."

"Oh, indeed, and who never suspect lurking deception."

"Well, the time is certainly ripe for something of the sort."

"Meaning what?"

"Nine out of ten cardiacs die while waiting for a suitable donor on our service, and I'm sure the same is true in all major centers. This is a tragic and frustrating situation in any affluent society and will sooner or later lead to unconventional sources for the needed organs."

"Then the inevitable begins to happen while we complacently hope it won't."

"And probably Marcus Mann expects it, too."

"Perhaps, since he so readily told me to hide if the need arises. He knows my dedication to the cause."

"The other deception ... you mentioned two."

"The stealing or robbing of live organs from the brain dead, by betraying the organ couriers en route to the dying recipient. And for the betrayal, there would almost surely be a spy in the operating rooms at Sentara General, locally, and in similar situations in other cities."

"You suspect this?"

"Yes. It could happen this way: The hospital lookout calls the spy at her desk in the LifeChain building and alerts her to the presence of a donor as the organs are about to be taken. The sale is then made to a pirate somewhere."

"You said *her.*"

"There are no male employees inside LifeChain headquarters dealing with the distribution of live organs."

"So the person betraying you or other couriers would have to be a woman."

"I think so."

"Has Mann tried to protect you?"

"He has tried to stop me from delivering organs."

"And?"

"I refused."

"Won't he fire you?"

"He can't fire me."

"Wooooah!"

"I do not need the employment financially, and I work for a dollar a year."

"Oh?"

"Have you heard of the Pullys, down on the Carolina coast?"

"Joseph Mixter Pully?"

"My father. He has contributed more money than any other one person to financing the startup of LifeChain, and I sit on the board in his place."

"Holy God, everybody in this community talks about him. One of the first tales I heard upon my arrival here eight years ago — richer than Cresus, and more powerful than the Mafia in his own bailiwick."

"Right on every count, but he is not mean for meanness' sake, nor for money, but meaner than mean for principle's sake, *when the principle of it arises,* if you know what I mean."

"Yes. He's awesome but not really bad. Does he know about your situation?"

"Oh, no. And I wouldn't dare tell him. Not yet anyway. Subtle or cautious he is not. If we pinpointed a definite target and needed help, then I would tell him."

"Great backup."

"In every way, but a dangerous crusader."

"I like his potential."

"I may come to need it one day."

"Deadly pursuit. Did you provoke it in any way?"

"No. My pattern of activity has not changed."

"Would you recognize the people chasing you?"

"Locally, always a man in a gray well-tailored suit with proper shirt and tie, and always wearing a fedora. I have distinguished several different faces and figures so outfitted."

"Who owns them?"

"I have no way of knowing with certainty."

"Perhaps from other suppliers of organs and tissue besides LifeChain?"

"We know of two competitors locally, one outfit called Legation, the other called Mercury. Have you heard of them?"

"No."

"Everybody's getting into the business these days, too much of it borderline or worse. Legation supplies banked tissue and live organs, both ostensibly for altruistic reasons under tax-free status, for huge profits, but with little or no quality control. It's a big outfit, started locally by an unschooled evangelist named The Reverend Lotte, with phenomenal success from the beginning. The Legation operation has spread to other cities."

"Legation is a peculiar name for an organ outfit."

"Not when you understand the owner. The Reverend Lotte considers himself to be, or at least claims to be, a legate, a missionary on a mission from God to supply organs and tissue to those in need."

"How do you know?"

"He proclaims *divine mission,* with messianic fervor to the members of a grieving family when he's trying to get permission to reap the live organs and the tissues of a dying or brain-dead relative."

"Well, well. What do you think of his claim?"

"He may have led himself to believe it. Anyway, it's an excuse for unbridled behavior."

"I had no idea. Why have we not heard of him?"

"Because Sentara hospital would never buy from him, nor would he sell most of his stuff to any qualified hospital. In live organs, he deals only with faraway third-rate hospitals, usually across a southern border, unless he has a legitimate local donor. Then he makes a great show of his benevolence."

"I see."

"The second outfit, Mercury, is owned and operated for profit by Ivan Prescott, a recognized biblical scholar, a Yale divinity school graduate, and a man with the highest scruples. But Mercury supplies only banked tissue ... no live organs. It was founded in New Haven, then established in New York, and it, too, has had great success, with an impeccable reputation, and has spread to numerous cities in this country. Prescott recently moved his headquarters to Norfolk. He has been criticized because he sells for a profit."

"Then Mercury would have no interest in you?"

"I have guessed not ... but there is one more."

"Here?"

"Operational worldwide, under the name SamuelS, headquartered somewhere in mid-Africa, at a place called Xanadu. The hospital there has the same name and it takes donor material of all types, mostly for its own use."

"Its quality?"

"By reputation above reproach."

"Then neither Mercury nor SamuelS would supply material not up to standard."

"Emphatically, not."

"Who owns and runs SamuelS?"

"It's run by a man named Kahan, and belongs to SamuelS, an organization financed by the oil cartel of the Middle East, and by European money. After its successful start up, other big money appeared from countries and people around the world who want to be assured of transplants when needed."

"American money, too?"

"From the wealthy for a place to turn when all else fails."

"Then Xanadu is the biggest outfit in the business."

"By far and away."

"Do you know its exact location?"

"Kahan built the hospital into the side of a mountain in equatorial Africa."

"Why?"

"Isolated, and protected, and apparently transplants can always be had there. It could never happen here because of federal regulations."

"Joan, how do you know about these organizations?"

"From my position on the board of LifeChain. There, these matters are discussed in meetings. I have one of the highest and one of the lowest positions in the organization — delivery boy and board member, both without pay. Ivan Prescott, though a competitor and the owner of Mercury, serves on the board too, believe it or not, because of his expertise and his altruism. He contributes his time to help LifeChain because it's nonprofit. He knows Kahan, and sells large quantities of banked tissue to Xanadu. He has visited the hospital and Kahan several times, and always brings back the news from Africa. Of course, locally, we know something about Legation, some of it hearsay, but all very troubling."

"Money."

"Yes, I'm afraid you're right. And I also think we are in danger of losing someone to this end in our own region very soon."

Eric thought for a moment, shook his head, and said, "Well, this is all very intriguing. But to more immediate concerns — why don't you bathe and change while I finish getting a meal together? It will be light and small."

"Great idea." She went toward his bedroom, and in a moment the shower came on. In the distance, muted thunder rolled, and rain began to drum heavily on the roof.

CHAPTER 2

As the plane climbed over the Chesapeake Bay, Chester Williams kept his right arm around the canister strapped in the middle seat. He would protect this precious cargo with his own life if necessary, and certainly not disappear like the other couriers.

Marcus' warning had been stern. "Banner is still missing, and so is one courier from each of the other ten zones of UNOS. We don't know what's happened, but we have to assume the worst, so be careful. Don't let the heart out of sight for a second until delivered."

When the plane reached cruising altitude, the man in the window seat politely introduced himself, Dr. Edward Wilson, a heart surgeon from Memphis. They shook hands. Imagine, riding in a plane with such important people, and carrying a living heart to save another person's life, already mingling with doctors, distinguished doctors, the best. Dr. Wilson said, "I know what you are carrying and to whom it goes."

Gosh no! According to Marcus Mann all courier missions were top secret. "Really?" he asked.

"You are wondering how I know?"

"Well, yes."

"It's quite simple. We all are very close knit in the world of heart surgery. I called Baptist Memorial just before boarding the plane, and the staff was in a high state of excitement, and so surprised at getting a heart at last for Jacob Tollins, all the way from Norfolk. They are setting up right now to implant the moment you arrive. We've fought long and hard to keep Tollins alive while waiting. Down in Memphis they know who you are and you're their hero, our deliverance."

Chester relaxed in the warmth of his importance. Dr. Wilson's cufflinks flashed as he pulled the telephone out of its bulkhead rack, and gave his chauffeur instructions. He hung up and said to Chester, "Best chauffeur I've ever had. Always reliable."

"Must be nice," Chester answered, trying to be polite.

"Indeed it is, and come to think of it, why don't you just ride in with us since we are all going to the same place."

"Well, I appreciate the offer, but we have our instructions you know ... never to accept favors en route."

"You are entirely right. In this day and time, I'm sure it's best not to trust anyone. No telling who might be up to something devious." He turned to his computer and began working again.

At the airport Chester could not find the hospital van assigned to meet him. Dr. Wilson appeared at his side and again offered a ride. Chester relented and got in the limousine. Blinds had been drawn in the rear compartment. "Take us to the Baptist, Fred," said Dr. Wilson. The chauffeur did not answer. They rode across town at high speed and stopped inside a building.

Hugging the canister against his front, Chester swiveled his feet out the door and stood. Wilson took him by an elbow and guided him forward. Two large white doors swung open and two men in long white gowns rushed toward Chester. My goodness, men in white were eagerly rushing to meet the important delivery. He started to speak, to shift the canister to one arm so he could shake hands as the introductions went around, but they were too serious. The need for the heart must be truly urgent. Each grabbed an elbow and propelled him forward. They were in a terrible hurry, and he knew a moment of embarrassed regret for being so slow.

"Whoa!" he shouted as the rope came down out of the ceiling and a hand slipped the noose over his head. With the canister in his embrace he lost the split second opportunity for defense. Too late, the rope choked out the next protest. As the hangman's knot tightened, strange hands rescued the canister, and the taut rope lifted Chester up and up, swinging in a forward arc, his arms flaying, his legs kicking until they snapped limp. The pendulum reversed. Other hands grasped his heels and flopped him on his back to the top of a rough wooden table. All breathing had stopped. The rope came off the now brain-dead courier, a tube went down the windpipe, and a respirator began with oxygen under pressure to keep the other organs alive.

Busy hands cut off his clothes, leaving him naked upon the rough wet wood. A team drained his blood through a large cannula thrust into a leg artery. Then rapid hands cut out the still beating, struggling heart along with the lungs, then the liver and the kidneys and digestive system. A second team moved the shelled-out body to another room where other technicians took bones, corneas, skin, and lesser parts. The team dumped the formless remains into a kitchen garbage bag along with his clothes and all his belongings except his watch and money. The bag went into the furnace. In less than half an hour, Chester Williams had disappeared from the face of the earth, leaving no trace. The technicians hosed down the table and floor, and brought in the next donor, in this case the driver of the hijacked hospital van.

—

Even before the rope went taut, Fred had begun backing the limousine out onto the large concrete apron beneath the signs, THE MERCY BLOOD BANK, and THE SAVIOR FUNERAL HOME in bold letters across the front of the old warehouse. Smets still sat on the front seat beside him, staring ahead, his immense neck and shoulders cramped in the limits of the limousine. Dr. Wilson had returned to the passenger compartment and joined Martin. The curtains had been raised. Fred drove past two other massive overhead doors and into the street, through a few curves and onto I-55.

As the car approached the Mississippi River Bridge from the Arkansas side and picked up speed, Dr. Martin addressed

Dr. Wilson. "Well, Dr. Wilson, congratulations on your brilliant surgery. The distinguished doctor has done himself proud. The Reverend no doubt will be immensely pleased."

Wilson reached forward and pushed a button to raise the glass partition behind Fred and Smets, both formal in the front seat. Fred smoldered. The nerve of a two-bit shyster talking down to him and giving orders, showing off to a guy he's leading to slaughter. Smets, too, despised the attitude and fought an impulse to lower the glass partition and turn to the two shysters on the back seat. Instead, he controlled himself and reached forward and flipped a hidden switch beneath the dashboard.

Wilson leaned back in the seat and said, "I don't trust The Reverend. The likes of Williams are chicken feed to him. He's more interested in the fear and terror the disappearance will stir up than he is in just another heart. More important, he's really sore because we didn't get Joan Pully on the Chicago run two nights ago."

"Man, she was cunning."

"Yeah, but we can't find a daydreaming dolt like Williams every time. God, he was stupid. He didn't have a clue."

"Yeah, just a green kid ... it was almost too easy, like killing sheep. What's the big deal with the woman, anyway?"

"Ten million dollars for her heart. She's the perfect donor for a very rich buyer."

"How do you know?"

"Never mind where I get my information. But you can count on it."

"I'm not sure I want to know."

"Well, I'm not supposed to, but I do."

"So, what's next?"

"We go back to Norfolk for further orders. The Reverend is determined to have Joan Pully. The crew he hired locally is a joke. Barney, Ned, Joe, and Willy are nothing but ex-hoodlums who turn to their bungling and brutal traits under pressure. The Reverend's got to have good help, and I expect to be sent on another mission to bring Joan Pully in."

"Well, she got a good look at both of us on the plane to Chicago, so she will be harder than ever to fool now."

"He will make the decision. There are eleven UNOS areas to be worked. He intends to increase the removal of couriers until he paralyzes the entire organ donor system across the nation."

"UNOS? What's UNOS?"

"United Network for Organ Sharing. The Reverend thinks it's doomed to failure because it's voluntary, and because donor organs are so priceless to the people who need them in order to live."

"How exactly will he halt the network?"

"After so many couriers disappear, no one will deliver an organ."

"Then?"

"After he moves in and takes over, anyone who wants an organ will have to buy or beg for it from The Reverend's network across the country through huge donations, of course."

"The idea seems both crazy and impossible to me. But who am I to know?"

"Well, nobody ever accused The Reverend of being sane. Crazy bastard makes me uneasy."

"You want to keep on doing this?"

"Where else could a lawyer like me, who doesn't even like the law, make ten thousand dollars in a single night? And where else could a paralegal like you make five — in cash, no taxes?"

"Right."

"I'm not ready to quit yet. Soon as I stash a bundle, I will be on my way with enough to live on."

"Oh?"

"Yeah. I think The Reverend will be most generous when I offer to keep quiet and disappear for a nice little settlement.

But first we have to keep up the scare tactics across the country, especially since they are making an enormous profit for The Reverend. And I'm going to get Joan Pully if it's the last thing I do."

Fred stopped the car at the departure gates of the Memphis International Airport and stared angrily ahead. He had pulled an enormous black hat over his big bald head down to his big flabby ears. His bulk over-filled the driver's compartment. Wilson and Martin got out and proceeded toward the Delta counter. As Fred drove into traffic again, Smets flicked another switch on the dashboard. A hissing tape rewound and played back every word uttered by Wilson and Martin.

"Will we be giving this to The Reverend?" asked Fred.

"You're damned right we are," said Smets. "I can't wait to lead uppity smart-assed Wilson to Chiron's reception."

CHAPTER 3

The Reverend Lotte, owner and boss of Legation, sat hunched over a microphone with his elbows planted atop his desk, both hands palm down on his wig of curly black hair, his tiny blue eyes squeezed shut behind wire frame spectacles. Electronic surveillance through concealed cameras and closed-circuit television and planted bugs provided the greatest power over people. He listened to the talk coming from the BMW. Infuriating! They had missed again, bumbling fools. Joan Pully would bring him ten million dollars, and when he handed her over she would be his first delivery of a living brain-dead donor.

So much money would finance the further development of Legation to make it the biggest and most successful supplier of organs and banked body tissue in the world, and would put the major local competitor, Mercury, out of business because finicky Mercury insisted on such foolishness as blood typing and cross matching, sterile technique, testing for existing diseases, and the like. The owners of Mercury simply had no faith in the will of the Lord, and lack of faith would be their undoing. Any organ, like all other organs, came as a gift of God, untainted except by the sins of the receiver. The donor had already paid a price and forever established his innocence because he had atoned to God for his sins in the sacrifice of his beating heart, the very essence of belief. And God had mandated Legation, while Mercury came from only the ambition of an educated pretender, an Antichrist without the fire of faith.

And LifeChain! Doomed to failure, fooling with a voluntary supply, as silly a notion as voluntary gold, or voluntary diamonds. And donor organs were far more priceless. People just hadn't caught on despite the publicity, like the revelations in *The Orange County Resister*, the *Chicago Tribune*, *USA Today*, and others, and he hoped they wouldn't catch on. Imagine the money! $2400 for a cornea, $7000 for a liver, $2500 for a knee tendon, $7000 for a valve from an otherwise worthless heart, nearly $900 for two teaspoonfuls of bone paste, $8000 for processed skin to make a bigger penis, $37,000 for four square feet of skin, twenty bags of human bones worth $680,000 stored in a New Jersey basement ... all together, $500 million a year from 20,000 dead Americans.

People would pay anything rather than die or see a relative die, and they would forfeit all their diamonds and all their gold every time in the face of certain death. And the chosen soldier of God would procure and guard the most priceless of all the world's treasures, a life-sustaining living organ. God would put the entire godless and pagan voluntary system out of business by killing and crippling the organ couriers until they all quit out of cold fear. LifeChain needed to be forced out of his way.

Then Legation would supply an organ for every person needing one, not only from the entire donor pool as it now existed, but a growing supply from the unlimited horde of sinners crawling the darkness of nightlife. Oh yes, Legation had been created for a purpose — to rescue God's children from death and to clean the world of the wicked. God would have the ten million from the sale of Joan Pully.

And only Smets, his manager, could control the thieves, spies, hoods, retired detectives, former policemen, and the maverick electronic experts who made his operation possible. But Smets should have known he could not train the likes of these stooges to imitate the ways of Mercury's diplomats. They cringed in his presence, fearful of his immense muscularity, his flashing angry eyes, the flattop military haircut, his short-tempered impatience. But even his terrible threats of retribution, could not stop them from reverting to type under pressure. And a voice dare not be raised against Smets, the manager of all national operations, including the directors of the Western, the Northern, the Central, and the Southern districts of Legation, bossing every branch in other major cities, each as well hidden as the Norfolk headquarters. And Smets would lead the war on LifeChain.

Legation displayed no signs and no logos to the outside world, hidden in a renovated waterfront warehouse behind a sign reading THE SAVIOR FUNERAL HOME across the facade, and around one corner of the building a second sign, MERCY BLOOD BANK. Those in need knew or heard sooner or later. Charity served as the facade, a funeral home for the deprived and the destitute. No matter how poor, the family could get some type of funeral for the deceased, and those headed to Potter's Field could retain their identity. These meager expenses came out of the profits from the sale of human parts taken from these same bodies, leaving further profit for Legation. And the profits had become enormous. Nominal fees went to blood donors, mostly winos who needed the cash for more drink.

The operation never provoked interference from the curious. The first of the three large overhead doors served as a service entrance for the heavy funeral home traffic. Through the second, bodies solicited from grieving families by Legation were brought into the laboratories for retrieval and processing of tissues to be sold at enormous profit, and these bodies usually went on to a free funeral. The bereaved, gaping into an open casket, could not know all skin below the collar had been removed, and all the bones replaced with old discarded PVC pipes to reshape the body for viewing. The destitute, with no relatives to ask questions and cause trouble, provided greater profit; anything could be buried in a closed casket funeral, without a funeral.

Recently a new idea had become tempting. Even more lucrative, cremations would allow totally unrestrained retrieval. Under the right circumstances the entire body could be used for its parts, and something else burned in a sealed paper box as long as it produced enough ashes to satisfy the waiting relatives. The finality of handing a vial of ashes to the bereaved brought them down to the ultimate resignation, and nobody analyzed ashes.

Through the third door the donors of most of the live organs entered his laboratories unsuspecting and exited the world unwittingly, in the hands of Smets, Fred, Chiron, and carefully chosen technicians, who knew better than to talk. Here many of the unwary victims came in of their own volition, seduced to it by the infamous Ralph Green, who lived in the twilight zone of bars and the borderline underworld, and worked for anyone, and belonged to no one. If only there could be a productive agent like him in every city. Ralph knew all the ropes, all the tricks, and could be counted on to bring in a steady supply of vulnerable people who lost their reserve in his presence and came willingly to his apartment or another chosen destination, and from there to Chiron's table, two or three a week, even more on demand, but how galling to depend on Ralph who could not be trusted when it came to ten million dollars.

Ralph would sell anybody for a price. And he would have been in touch with the LifeChain spy, Gladys Gleason, who had sold to everybody, including Ralph. She had no scruples; she would get her share of the ten million regardless of who finally caught Joan Pully, but Ralph used very clever and uncanny means when he seduced people to the sacrifice. He should be fed into the system himself for all of his foulness, but not just yet, because the terrible sinner, despite his evil ways, had become Legation's most effective ally. And Ralph knew and associated with the very people who deserved to become donors, the wicked of the night who habited bars and the underworld of darkness, and for these sins his little world would come full cycle some day, in the wrath of the Lord, after outliving his usefulness.

And how gratifying to watch the sinners pay for their transgressions, to watch the blood flowing and the beating heart surge from the opened chest, the alarmed and swelling cone retching itself in desperate heave and twist, to appease the wrath of God for the perfidy of these failed night crawlers, the divine hunger satiated only by the sacrifice of the beating heart, like the triumph of bullets tearing the life out of God's enemies in the heat of a Vietnam battle.

On this occasion, the bugs transmitted the words loud and clear from the BMW.

"Jesus Christ, Barney, you let her slip by again."

"Lissen to me Joe stupid, and lissen good ... this goddamn Kraut cock wagon won't go through hedges or jump brick walls five feet tall ... see buddy! You so fuckin' smart, you catch her."

Another voice cut in, "The Reverend is gonna' kill us for this one. Smets told us we got to have her. I happen to know she's the only one they've found yet good enough for somebody's special wife, some super rich Saudi named Moha. And The Reverend not only wants her, he wants her quiet, too. He thinks she knows sumpn' she don't need to know. Sumpn' about her threatens the whole operation."

"How you know, Willy?"

"How you think he knows ... his darling Gladys," said Joe's rasping voice, "deadly, sniveling LifeChain spy."

"Well, we ain't got her and we ain't even come close, and this is the third try. Too bad, asshole, you ain't a tall woman with a big young heart and type B, and a virgin. Then it would give me the greatest pleasure to haul your smart ass into the *laboratory,* Willy Boy, and let The Reverend's grinnin' idiot, Chiron, take care of you. A virgin! Ha, ha, ha ... imagine you a virgin with hot little snoop Gladys Gleason, baby."

"Likewise for you, *racer.* You oughta' be driving at the Indianapolis 500 where you don't have to catch nothin — jist outrun it — where you don't need no brains."

"We would have had her if she hadn't of dived through

them hedges."

"We would have had her anyway if you hadn't of been parked in the wrong direction when she come out of the grocery store ... wastin' too much time turning around."

"We wasted the time rescuin' pore Ned after she nearly killed him."

"Yeah, well, you know Smets' orders ... never leave anybody to get caught and forced to talk."

"Smets ain't said nothin' about goin' in the wrong direction."

"Lissen, and I ain't gonna tell you but one more time. I — "

The phone rang. Barney picked it up, and listened, then said, "Yes sir," and hung up. He turned and said in a state of wonder and in terror, "God, how does The Reverend know everything even before it gets through happening? He knows already she got away again."

"It's like he was right here listenin' to us," said Willy.

"Well, he knows all right, and he probably also knows you know too much. If he hears you talkin' about Moha, and type B, and big woman, and virgin, and laboratory, and all the other stuff you ain't supposed to know, and you at the same time screwin' around with his spy, you liable to be supplying somebody with your own spare parts."

"Well, if you think Legation can get nasty, jist think what would happen if the great Kahan's outfit SamuelS gets wind of us," said Willie.

"What do you mean?"

"I mean Kahan's outfit is smarter than the Mafia and has all the fire of them Arabs at its command. If SamuelS goes to war with Legation ... no more Legation."

"How do you know?" Willy asked.

"How you think he knows? Precious little Gladys again."

"How does she know so much?"

"Nobody in LifeChain is on to her, and she eavesdrops on

board meetings where everything is talked about."

"How does anybody there know about SamuelS and Kahan?"

"From a guy, some egghead from one of them fancy schools up East ... Ivan something or other. He goes to visit Kahan in Africa, and he tells about it in meetings."

"Yeah, yew are worse than I thought. Yew do all this talk about Moha's wife, and The Reverend wanting Joan Pully quiet, too, when yew ain't even supposed to know the preacher's name, yet yew know it all ... and yew know this ain't no time to be fightin' each other. And speaking of The Reverend, I wonder whatever happened to Roger," said Barney.

"The Reverend sent him out of town to track down a special supply of organs."

"Yeah, but Roger ain't back yet after three months."

"Well, he might have left town a organ at a time, in them white buckets."

"You think so?"

"I don't trust The Reverend."

"You don't even know him. You've never seen him."

"Nobody's seen him. They jist hear from him, hid out somewhere down below in the guts of the building."

"Better you don't hear from him."

"Yeah. Well, you know what I do hear? I hear the reward for this cute little bundle of live organs we been chasin' is ten millions dollars," said Willy.

"Who told you, Willy?"

"Who do you think told him? His little woman again, precious little spy. Pillow talk."

"Well, okay. And just who the hell is this Moha?"

"Like I said, a Saudi, rich as all get out, and he's desperate for the right donor for his wife."

"Then what the hell. Let's get outa' this lousy outfit and take Joan Pully our own way, then collect the ten million ourselves."

"Better yet, let's stay in and use their equipment then tell The Reverend nothing."

"Hey, not a bad idea."

"Quiet and subtle. What does a preacher know about taking people? We take this Joan Pully our own way this time. She is somethn' else and I ain't gettin kicked in the balls like old limp Ned here. Quiet and subtle my ass."

"Okay, what's next tonight?"

"Another assignment. Ralph Green's got a drunk over at Tony's Bar to be picked up. He will have her in a taxi, but we got to follow to see nothin' happens. Old Ned can lay right where he is till he comes to or till we get back."

"Ralph! God, what a creep! When he looks at me with them blank, pale eyes, my flesh crawls," said Willy.

"Well, he don't have the same effect on lonesome ladies 'cause they come a crawlin' and trustin'."

"Yeah, and if I know Ralph, he's after the ten million dollars, too."

"So is everybody else, I'll bet."

CHAPTER 4

Walter Exum, who operated the Norfolk headquarters of the renowned tissue bank, Mercury, sat in his office with the owner, Ivan Prescott, and demonstrated the newly installed equipment for listening to The Reverend's own snooping devices, and to The Reverend himself. Ivan had just returned from another visit to Xanadu in Africa, and more conferences with Kahan. SamuelS had expanded operations to include all major cities of the United States and had placed The Reverend's activities under surveillance.

"Why are we listening to this, Walter?" asked Ivan.

Walter studied Ivan, a quiet giant with black hair and a black beard, for a moment and said, "The police have not been willing to engage religious defenses. The Reverend screams out invectives about the persecuted even though he has never been questioned. So SamuelS agents took matters into hand and bought the equipment to tune in on The Reverend's bugs, and they also bugged his private office. Kahan, through the local SamuelS agents, insisted on giving us receiving equipment here at Mercury headquarters. He wants us to hear it for ourselves."

"Why is it our business, Walter?"

"Just listen to The Reverend in action," said Walter as he turned up the volume. The conversation continued to come from the Legation men in the BMW until The Reverend's listening device snapped off, and he shouted at Smets, giving him instructions for kidnapping donors and for taking Joan Pully, and for ignoring all scientific facts related to donor organs and tissue. The Reverend finally congratulated him on the successful kidnapping of Chester Williams and the use of Chester as a donor. "Wilson worked out just fine," he added.

The voice of Smets replied, "Smooth for a defunct, unemployed lawyer."

"Never mind his past as long as he takes the couriers and

the organs they are carrying, without street violence. But he didn't do as well with Joan Pully on the run to Chicago. How did he let her get away?"

"Joan Pully is no greenhorn, like the late Mr. Chester Williams."

"Yeah, well, use another method, but get her."

"Not Wilson."

"Why not?"

"I got a tape here, Reverend. We recorded it while returning Wilson and Martin to the airport in Memphis. You might be interested to hear Mr. Wilson in action."

After a click and a hissing noise, the entire conversation between Wilson and Martin came through clearly until The Reverend's voice interrupted. "Cut the damned thing off."

The Reverend's voice continued. "Smets, I want this war on UNOS escalated, and I want it done to scare the daylights out of all couriers the country over."

"You have something definite in mind?"

"Yeah. Keep taking them but step up the pace in all zones, and in addition to those who disappear altogether, send back a few screaming in pain without their corneas. Arrange for the rescue of an occasional open bleeding flank with only one kidney missing, and an occasional one with both flanks sewn up but both kidneys missing. The dead don't scream; the dead don't tell it; the silence is not terrifying. But those who return will terrify. Put the pressure on. All courier activity will stop when they become too scared to move."

Smets spoke again. "Reverend, ain't you afraid this will stir up the whole country and bring out the law in full force, the locals, the feds, the whole works?"

"No. We will quietly go about supplying organs. When UNOS stops, we move in. No patient then will be deprived of life while awaiting an organ, something UNOS could never do. Then we will be in control, and the people will be behind us. It's the Lord's will."

"And where will we get an unlimited supply of organs?"

"From the families of the brain-dead. We have a better way of convincing them. People would rather give to God than to an unknown. And we also will collect from the sinners of this world, from the wicked of the night, hordes of them now going unpunished. Not only will we have all the organs we need, but we will also clean up this wicked world."

"And if the supply is still too small?"

"Smets, greed. Token money with the right words can buy anything, the very reason all volunteer endeavors fail sooner or later. And don't ever forget, the world turns on profit, Smets. Money turns all wheels directly or indirectly. "

"Yeah, you're right about human nature, as usual, but we will need more people to do this job."

"Use everyone you have to the fullest."

"Wilson and Martin?"

"Oh, yes. I almost forgot, Smets. Take both of them to Chiron."

"And these three fools in the BMW?"

"Harvest time, Smets, harvest time ... and speaking of that, I want you to find us a nice little crematorium."

"What for, Reverend?"

"Buy it, even if you have to pay too much."

Ivan said, "The Reverend Lotte is totally irreverent in the world of medicine."

"Yes, a fanatic. A raving ignoramus, giving the whole transplant business a bad name. Already, his lack of quality control has brought a greater illness to some, and death to others, among those who seek help. He refuses to believe the germ theory, the facts of blood and tissue typing, or anything to do with immunology. As far as he is concerned, diseases such as AIDS, hepatitis, cancer, syphilis, tuberculosis, and Creutzfeldt-Jakob are not transmitted in transplanted organs and tissue, and he has no respect for the critical ischemic time in transplanted organs. He regards these facts as mere impedimenta thrown up to block his headlong and heedless enterprise. Any condition can be cured with *faith* according to his thinking, and any means is justified in the name of his church to the benefit of its ends. He sells body parts to anyone who pays, and we know he actually has sold frozen hearts thawed just for the sale. And the organization is in cahoots with numerous renegade funeral homes where the material for the tissue bank can be stolen outright, along with such items as gold inlays and the personal belongings some families send to the grave with their dead.

"For this reason alone we must know what he is doing. But this development, his grandiose idea of paralyzing UNOS, brings a new urgency. He must be stopped. And SamuelS wants us as allies because The Reverend will have to go down soon. What the fake Dr. Wilson said is true. The Reverend intends to destroy the voluntary system as it exists."

"And Kahan says he does not want to be the only legitimate supplier left standing in the world of live organ transplants. He wants to see a universal acceptance of the donor concept by grieving families. For this they have to be put at ease. The Reverend's mischief will do the opposite, ultimately. For this reason you have my blessings," said Ivan.

"Now why would Lotte want to buy a crematorium?" asked Exum.

"He will pass it off as charity, but the purpose will be devious."

Ivan savored and cultivated his commitment to SamuelS. Kahan, had been his best customer, buying large quantities of banked tissue from Mercury during the startup phase of Xanadu in Africa. Just three years ago, Kahan had sent a SamuelS agent to bring Ivan to Xanadu. There, Kahan had wasted no words. "We know your history. We have come to appreciate your practical view of donor problems."

"Within our limited scope we can reliably supply the needs of many people."

"With products of the highest quality," said Kahan.

"Yes, we can provide a much more commendable product on a more reliable schedule when we run our company as a business, working for profit and paying for our resources, than we could if we had to rely on favors done in the name of altruism."

"Altruism too often is the vain pursuit of importance and power which money can't buy," said Kahan.

"Then you do understand the vanity of the unaccomplished. Charity tolerates no critics. As the old saying goes, *beggars can't be choosers,* or hold still while I am doing you a favor."

"Indeed," Kahan said. "But not to worry. The giveaway system will not last."

"We ourselves are not hobbled by having to await gifts of either money or body parts, not since we began compensating people for this commodity."

"Precisely what I wish to discuss with you. After the basics, then perhaps we could go on with progressive ideas to expand our horizons," Kahan said.

"How may I help?"

"We need someone to monitor the tissue bank here and give it the same high quality you have in yours. This will be the world's largest hospital, and it will be devoted entirely to transplants and reconstructive surgery. Here we need your guidance, your expertise, to set up a laboratory and tissue bank in a class with yours at Mercury."

"Yes. I can send you someone. Whether he stays or not will depend upon the circumstances, I'm sure."

"No one has left yet."

"I can see the temptation."

"Are you tempted?"

"I have no talents other than zeal and a certain organizational ability."

"Well?" said Kahan.

"I have a commitment already, but I thank you for the offer. I may come to need it. In the meantime, I will send you someone."

"We will make your man happy when he arrives."

"He may wish to be temporary."

"I will wager you he will be eager to stay once he sees the surgery we do."

"Then you will get one of the best, one we cannot spare."

In this manner he had become a consultant to Kahan and Xanadu hospital, and indirectly a part of the vast SamuelS organization. Back home he recruited a tissue bank technician, John Bryant, who had a wife and four young children, and immediately accepted the offer, delighted with the high salary and all the perks in a foreign country.

Walter Exum paced the floor, his head of bushy, curly hair bent forward studiously, his hands folded behind his back, his body as spare and light as a small bird, with the same alertness. And he suffered a compelling enmity for the Reverend Lotte and his ways.

Ivan turned down the volume on the receiver and said, "Kahan is waiting for Moha to find a legitimate donor, but he does not intend to deal with anyone who places the lives of people like Pully in danger. He expects Moha to find a brain-dead victim of a tragedy, not a victim of deliberate homicide to an innocent and valuable person."

"Why does Moha himself have to find a donor? Kahan has greater access," said Walter.

"He has set notions about what he wants."

"Like what?"

"It has to be a woman, a white one, a virgin ... and of course the standard requisites: the same body build and the same blood type as his wife, six feet and type-B, already brain-dead and available," said Ivan.

"A hard bill to fill."

"Moha made many mistakes in his hysteria to find a donor. He phoned every branch of LifeChain, everybody in the business, and through his underworld contacts called Legation for help. The Reverend contacted the LifeChain spy for a donor. The spy, of course, had already heard, and she does not care who captures Joan Pully ... the reward will be the same, so the spy betrayed not only Joan Pully, but the entire effort. Kahan is very unhappy about Moha's bad judgment."

The phone rang. Walter Exum answered, talked briefly, and replaced the receiver. He turned to face the room. "Joan Pully disappeared a few minutes ago without a trace, while Barney and his crew were giving chase."

"SamuelS is still trailing Joan?" asked Ivan.

"In an effort to protect her, on Kahan's orders, of course, and man they are everywhere."

"Good."

"I suppose Moha has withdrawn his offer for a donor."

"No," said Ivan

"Why doesn't Kahan force his hand?"

"Moha alone gave two hundred fifty million dollars to Xanadu this year, and a much bigger sum in startup funds. Kahan does not want to offend the Saudis. Besides, Moha's wife may indeed need help."

"Reason enough. But Joan Pully is in grave danger. The Reverend Lotte, with all the resources of Legation, is determined. And the word is not only out, it is out of control. She will be kidnapped and very likely killed if SamuelS doesn't find her first."

"Virtually impossible until she shows up again. She is tough, and runs scared, alerted, and very leery."

"And the Pully qualifications?"

"Well, besides her height and blood type, she is a virgin yet, reputedly," said Ivan.

"Choosy fellow, Moha."

"Indeed unusual, to say the least."

"Extreme, perhaps?"

"Only in regard to his ailing wife, of whom he is very protective."

"Which has what to do with the virginity of a person seven thousand miles away?"

"AIDS. And there is another more fascinating reason. I will explain later," said Ivan.

"AIDS?"

"Yes, and other diseases. Virginity assures him no contamination has occurred."

"Naive concept, in more ways than one. So, what problem bothers him?"

"First, the problem with his notions — he thinks his wife needs a new heart, and he thinks it should be a *pure heart,* as he calls it, thus the virginity."

"I don't get the connection."

"A heart not altered or contaminated by experience."

"Tell me more."

"He reads about medicine. He's into glands. As he seems to understand, the endocrine system under control of the brain drives the functions of the body. But he also knows about the paracrine system in the individual organs themselves, and has put his own imagination to work. While the brain controls the hormones fed to target organs, such as the heart and the pancreas, each organ in turn feeds back its own chemical communications to influence the brain's control. So, in his concept, once the heart has had the experience of love, its paracrine system becomes forever altered and will then feed the brain a different type of information in the future. After the heart experiences love outside of wedlock, it can never be faithful to one man only. So the new heart for his wife must not have known love," said Ivan.

"This implies a certain intelligence in the organs."

"Yes, indeed it does."

"Which means all mentality is not at the brain level."

"Certainly not. We live by a vegetative wisdom of nature, say in the kidney, or the liver, the most complicated chemical factory in existence, manmade or otherwise."

"And the gut."

"Oh, yes. Imagine a poor helpless human being having to plan his own digestion," said Ivan.

"Not a chance. We take too much as our due."

"Ahh, yes, and Moha, whether he knows it or not, is into chimerism," said Ivan.

"What?"

"A new twist to an old mythological tale, a unique animal put together out of parts of others: for instance, a lion's head, a goat's body, a dragon's tail," said Ivan.

"A person who has had multiple transplants?"

"Yes, precisely, but the parts live together, and cells from the transplanted parts migrate and thrive and reproduce all over the body, and the total animal is like no other. The concept has taken on a new living reality in the transplant world," said Ivan.

"Thought provoking, isn't it?"

"Absolutely fascinating, and there could be something to his notions. The living being is the sum of its parts ... Okay. So be it."

After a moment Walter said, "It's time to go talk to donors' families." And he and his men left Ivan in his office with his books, and his thoughts.

Alone, Ivan dwelt on the predicament of organ and tissue supplies and the growing menace of Legation. As part of his divinity school training ten years past he had gone into the New Haven hospitals to practice religion on the sick and dying. Confused and desperate families looked to the novice, Ivan, for answers.

"We don't believe our little boy is dead, but the doctor says he is."

"Tell me about your feelings."

"His heart is still beating, so we know he is alive even if he doesn't recognize us ... even if the machine has to do his breathing for him."

"Did you tell your sentiments to the doctor?"

"Yes, and he says the child is legally dead."

"Did you tell your preacher the same?"

"Yes, and he agrees with the doctor."

"How can I help?"

"Explain it to us. They call him brain-dead, and legally dead, but we think not *really* dead."

"I have to agree with you in every way."

"Then why don't they tell us the truth?" asks the grieving mother.

"They are trying to save themselves difficult explanations as well as legal entanglements, and at the same time spare you the torment of a troublesome decision."

"We are intelligent enough to understand, and compassionate enough to want to help other people."

"I commended you for caring and for your concerns. But simply put, your child will never regain consciousness, and his heart would last no longer than five minutes with the respirator turned off."

"Pulling the plug, they call it."

"Yes. And there are hundreds of people waiting for a donor heart, and hundreds others needing livers, intestinal tracts, kidneys, lungs, just to name some of the live organs."

"We understand, but we want to be sure about our child. We will have to live with our decision for the rest of our lives. What if prayer or a miracle could give him back to us? What if we really killed him with the wrong decision?"

"I understand your concerns and your hopes."

"And our doubts about death, the way it has been presented to us?"

"Yes, I agree. But I also understand the other side of the problem."

"Yes?"

"All the studies have been done, and carefully repeated. He has no blood flowing through the hemispheres of his brain, and the human brain can live only four minutes at normal body temperature without a constant supply of sugar and oxygen fed to it by a high volume of blood. Your son's brain has been dead for days and can never regain its function, and his heart cannot survive much longer, despite all treatment."

"We can handle the finality, but the doubt, the confusion, and the subterfuge defeat us."

"This standoff carried to its logical conclusion will deprive some desperate person of a heart. What a shame it would be to waste a good heart this way, and deprive it, too, of a continued life. The time has come for you to decide who you can trust, and to make your decision."

"We trust you."

"Giving would let parts of him live on in other people awhile before entering eternity, the gift of life in more ways than one. You could look at it this way ... you are actually finding shelter for organs with a life of their own to be saved, in bodies needing to be saved. Could there be a more intimate love than this union, this marriage of an organ with a life of its own to a body in fatal need, the life of the organ saved while it nestles in the body it is saving, a new home, the rescue from certain death for both?"

"Oh, we could never have thought of it in such reality. I guess we are all blind to the hidden miracles supporting our lives, and I never thought of each organ as a separate life," said the mother.

"Yes, each has a life, and each is extremely intelligent in its silent chemistry, remote from human awareness, far removed from our will."

"Then we could truly think of Billy in the future as being alive in other people, a far better imagery than all of him in the dark grave."

"Yes."

"All right, let us sign the necessary permits."

As he moved to present the consent forms, he asked himself *why*? What justified his being the go between? Then he thought the answer could be in the doing, the path his religion had taken without his realizing it, a purpose beyond himself."

After signing, the mother said, "Another problem sets badly with us."

"You want to tell me about it?"

"The people who are coming to us for other parts of our little boy."

"Who?"

"We have been approached by at least three separate groups, each wanting to take his body parts for a tissue bank. They want bone, corneas, tendons, skin, and I am sure they have not told us all of it. They seem to be fighting over the remains, like jackals after the lions have been satiated — in this instance the heart surgeons and the liver and kidney transplanters."

"I would advise you to make your donations to the tissue bank affiliated with this hospital."

"We will follow your advice, but we would like to know your thoughts under the circumstances. Somehow, the word *harvest* offends us," said the mother.

"It infuriates me."

Puzzled by these revelations, Ivan began an investigation. Until then he had had no idea how little the system could supply, only a tiny fraction of the tissue needed by waiting patients. He found even more disturbing conditions: Tissue banks had sprung up like cottage industries, and to his dismay, none of them worked under any type of standard or regulation. They all got their supplies from donations made by grieving families under duress, and they all claimed to be non-profit. Suspicious, Ivan delved further. Nonprofit meant the families were being paid nothing, but the tissue banks were making substantial, even huge, profits, tens of thousands of dollars per cadaver, disguised as *preparation* fees. Now more suspicious and getting angry, he looked further and found funeral homes operating tissue banks, using parts stolen from the bodies entrusted to them. This meant, even to his mind untrained in medical principles, some patients were receiving diseased and damaged tissue implants at great cost.

This raised the question: What would he need to start a quality tissue bank? He called a friend, an investment broker on Wall Street, for an answer. Damned little, less than ten thousand dollars. And let us finance you.

"No," said Ivan. "I will do this on my own."

"Why?"

"Because I want total control. I don't want a board or a boss or a bank telling me to sacrifice quality for profit."

"Well, Ivan, angry again for the sake of principles?"

"Right, and this time for principles more than ever. I have an idea this will change my life entirely."

"And the lives of many others, no doubt."

"Yes, an adventure in reality larger than life or immediate death."

"We wish you good luck. Call us if you need help."

CHAPTER 5

After dinner Joan said, "Such a delicious meal and now I really do need a good night's sleep."

"Dessert and brandy first. You take the bedroom and I'll sleep on the couch."

"No way. I'm sleeping in your bed with you, snuggled as close as I can get. Security is my greatest hunger, and I'm not letting it wait any longer."

Her boldness surprised him, but he recognized a certain grace in her demeanor, more like guileless candor than indiscretion. "I'm honored and flattered."

"Well, before we go any further, I should tell you something else about me. It might be important to you."

"What?"

"I'm still, at the advanced age of twenty-three, a virgin."

"Oh, for God's sake. I never thought of your past, but under the circumstances I shall honor your status quo."

"Oh, I don't know. I think it's getting to be rather tiresome."

Eric studied her quietly: A brunette with muted freckles, the blue eyes, the regal bearing, the tall litheness, the breasts just understated, the slender hips, the forthright innocent approach, the serene beauty — fate had handed him a handful all at once. And real, he would bet on it, and too damned good to be true. He would know soon.

He served sorbet, and poured brandy. As he sat down again he said, "So, we need to talk more about the reasons for the chase."

"Two reasons possibly; someone could need my heart, and also want me silent, in other words dead."

"One certainly goes with the other, but why dead, why silent, and who are *they*?"

"Remember, I told you a person within LifeChain might be leaking information about donors, and potential donors. If the spy is a reality, perhaps the men chasing me want to protect their most valuable source of information hidden in our operation."

"You suspect someone in particular?"

"Yes."

"How did you find out?"

"My nose for rats, and just out of curiosity and on a hunch, I checked donor records on file in the LifeChain archives against the names listed on police records of missing persons. Twelve of the missing people had useful donor information in the UNOS files, here or in other cities. She could have sold information matching them to patients who were bidding for organs. Then these people could have been kidnapped and used as donors."

"Remarkable coincidence. What exactly is a donor record?"

"Consent signed by a person willing to become an organ donor in the nebulous future, if the consenting person through injury or stroke should become brain dead."

"Why would you be suspicious of her?"

"She's always in the offices, very late every night, hundreds of hours overtime without pay, as though she is vital to the entire organization. And the mood to her presence — something seems to seethe from her being ... secretive, silent, hostile."

"A hunch."

"To a certain extent, but everything adds up. I know she came to work for LifeChain with no money. She had to borrow to get through to the first payday. Three weeks ago she bought a sixty thousand dollar gas-guzzler, only high test, seven miles to the gallon. She bragged about it."

"Uhh ohh."

"Yes, sizable chunks of money have come her way recently."

"Why do they suspect you of knowing something?"

"She has a particular aversion to me. Then she saw me go into the files when I researched the missing persons list."

"Isn't all such information in the computer?"

"Because of gaps, I went to the old files and found the names of several people who had disappeared, but the names were not in the computer file. Only she could have withheld this information when the LifeChain staff loaded the new computer system."

"And you think she betrays data on potential donors to the people who bribe her, so to speak?"

"I suspect so, and in my case, my blood type, height, and medical history all gleaned from my employment and health records."

"Who is this spy?"

"Remember the name in case I disappear ... I suspect Gladys Gleason."

"Remember it, indeed I will."

She stood, reached for his hand, pulled him up, and started to speak. The phone rang.

Eric answered, spoke for a moment, hung up, and turned to Joan. "We have to make a house call. You can wear one of my fishing hats and sit low in the car."

En route, she slid down in the seat, slumping, with the hat pulled low over her eyes, and said, "I've never been on a house call."

"Not too many myself, but the circumstances are so unusual as to justify the trouble. The donor was a young police officer named Jim Byron."

"Oh, Eric ... from Nashville. I flew down while they were removing the heart and brought it back for ... let's see, a young cardiac. Oh yes, Edward Jennings."

"Right, two months ago."

A man in his mid-thirties sat on an ottoman in the middle of the living room, his pajama top unbuttoned. A pretty young woman knelt at his side, her left ear pressed against his naked chest below the left nipple, listening intently. Curls of her clean brown hair hung over a purple sensitive scar lined down his breastbone from neck to belly. Mrs. Jennings stood aside patiently. She said, "Dr. Stuart, you know Rachael Byron, of course."

"Yes, and this is my friend, Joan Pully," he answered.

"Hello," said Mrs. Jennings.

Mrs. Byron removed her ear from Jennings' chest and said, "Hello. Dr. Stuart, I couldn't sleep, and I haven't slept since Jim died and you took out his heart. I used to go to sleep every night listening to his heartbeat and now I can't sleep unless I hear his heart. He is alive in Edward's chest, I know he is alive in there, and I have to listen or I can never again go to sleep, so I have to be here every night at bedtime to listen, or I will just die. You wouldn't want me to die would you? I have three little boys to raise."

Eric said, "I'm so sorry, Mrs. Byron. Why didn't you let me know?"

"Know? Everyone knows Jim is alive. You said so yourself. You said mankind has never called it death until the heart stops beating. And Jim's heart is still beating, so Jim is alive."

"Oh my God," said Mary Jennings. "By the same logic my living husband is dead, and has been since his dying heart was removed and forever ceased to beat. This is beyond me."

"And beyond me too, and I've been afraid to tell anyone. They might think me odd, or even crazy."

"Oh no, not at all," said Eric.

"But I couldn't stand it any longer. I'm exhausted, completely exhausted, you understand, so exhausted I can hardly breathe, so I had to come here. It's the only relief I can get. I'm ready to die from exhaustion. I could sleep only if I heard his heart."

"We will put you in bed between us tonight and you can go to sleep listening to Jim's heart now beating in Edward's chest," said Mary Jennings.

"You are so kind, but what of tomorrow night, and the night after, and all the terrible nights in succession yet to come? I will have to live through them, too."

Eric spoke. "Mrs. Byron, with Edward's kind consent, we will make a heart-sound recording tomorrow on a digital tape, and get a Walkman with earphones for you to wear in bed every night."

"But a recording is not the real thing."

"And we will get some help for you."

"What kind of help?"

"Counseling. Psychologists trained to handle grief have been able to help many mourning people. Your situation is not unique, and your reaction is perfectly normal."

"What a relief to know. I thought I was just crazy with heartache."

En route home, Joan watched the diminishing rain and the growing mist. She said, "Jim Byron was killed on duty, I seem to remember."

"Yes. He had stopped a car for speeding, and as he approached the driver's window on foot someone in the car shot him twice in the head. After he arrived at the emergency room, only the respirator kept the heart going until he became a donor."

"What a shame."

"Indeed, the tragedy of the times. Ours is a violent society."

"Aren't you tired of it, Eric?"

"Discouraged, to say the least."

"Have you ever thought of going to another country?"

"To live?"

"Yes, to live in greater safety and tranquility."

"Well, to tell you the absolute truth, yes, in distressing moments I have. But where?"

"Some imaginary place, I suppose."

"Maybe some nonexistent place."

After a quiet moment Eric asked, "Where do you live, Joan?"

"Clayton Street, seven ten. Why?"

"Perhaps we should drive by."

"Okay, it's only a few blocks ... do you know the area?"

"Oh, yes." He turned a corner and drove two blocks into Clayton Street. Joan slumped in the seat beside him, the hat pulled down to her eyebrows. Suddenly, she gasped and ducked lower. Eric saw it at the same time, the black BMW parked along the opposite curb across the street from an apartment house.

"Is this where you live?"

"Yes." She flattened herself on the seat, her head against Eric's knee.

"Three men, all wearing hats," said Eric, looking straight ahead as he drove by with the high beams on. "Ahh yes, gray suits and neckties."

"Oh God, Eric! They're still looking for me. Take me home and hide me in your house."

As Eric and Joan entered the house, she said, "Come, let's go to bed. I can't stay awake any longer. Are the doors latched?"

"Double locked and bolted on the inside, back and front."

"Security, thank God."

In the bedroom, she slipped out of her robe and slid under the covers. He pulled open a drawer and took out a pair of pajamas. She said, "Put them back. I don't want anything ever to come between us." He laughed, slid out of his clothes, got in bed, and turned to reach the lamp. Her nipples and belly touched his back, the brush of exuberant hair against his buttocks. She shivered. The light went out and she snuggled, her arms reaching around, her palms against his chest, the soft texture of her warm front draped snugly all the way down his spine. And she said softly, "Eric, I think I have found a haven."

"And I believe I like being your haven."

Distant thunder rolled and rumbled and the murmurs of the misty night turned to steady rain again. She said, "This is so cozy, I feel so safe. I love the sound of rain. Don't you?"

"I love the sound of water. I would like to live by a rapid river, where running water babbles through the nights."

"On the side of a mountain, by a fresh stream rushing down to a peaceful ocean just steps away."

"Ah, yes."

"Dreamland."

And they drifted to sleep.

Eric awoke before dawn, his bladder full, his penis erect, Joan still against his back, sleeping quietly. He stirred, worked his way out of her embrace, slid off the bed, and went to the bathroom. When he returned, she took her turn. She walked stark naked, unashamed across the room. She came back the same way, and slid under the covers. They lay face to face, entwined in each other's arms, and the raw sensuality of her naked and beautiful presence did its work at another level and his penis prodded against her belly. She said, "Oh God, Eric. I am so ready."

Eric propped on an elbow and said, "Not now. I will not hurry this. I have to be at the hospital in half an hour, and I have to work all night tonight. Tomorrow night, when there is plenty of time to love you along with the rest of it."

Joan laughed. "Eric, you are real. I've waited this long. I can wait now for the right moment."

"Ahh, sweet heaven!" Eric got out of bed, showered, and

dressed. As he got ready to leave, he said, "We should let Marcus Mann know something of your whereabouts."

"Don't try to phone him or to make contact at LifeChain in any way."

"I won't. I plan to find him in the hospital within the next few hours.

CHAPTER 6

Marcus Mann, President of LifeChain, sat in his office alone studying Joan Pully's computer profile. She had disappeared two days ago; her concerns should have been taken more seriously. A search through the national roster of recipients showed no matches: *Six feet tall, 125 pounds, blood type B, age 23.* The international roster revealed the profile of Moha's wife. *Six feet tall, weighs 128 pounds, type B, age 25.* Had someone deliberately withheld the information?

He needed advice, but not from anyone on the scene. He picked up the phone, then remembered Joan's suspicions, and put it down. He left the building and drove to Piedmont Aviation, the private airport. At the hangar he called from a pay phone to a friend and confidant, Lind Nunnally, the regional director of UNOS in Philadelphia and arranged a meeting.

In flight he thought of his Sundays and the church pews, long before his legs grew to reach the floor. The shouting and the incomplete sentences never fulfilled. He sought the answers elsewhere and in adolescence turned to the lower echelons of Medicine. Among the sick he became an orderly, and the right eyes soon found him and he went to a laboratory and found the newborn science of tissue transplants. Here the evangelistic fire flamed with a destiny. In the right place he could do for thousands, not just one on one. He pioneered one of the first major tissue banks, and the retrieval of live organs.

As the plane taxied in, his emotions sought to deal with modern reality. An organ black market now loomed as a deadly intrusion into his altruistic world. But he should have been prepared. It would be stupid to expect people to line up complacently for something they might never get, only to suffer and die while waiting. The unlimited supply of donor organs, held back by only the restraints of man-made conventions and laws, in the presence of an unlimited amount of money, would sooner or later break these tenuous bonds. And when such a market arrived, it would arrive to stay. As in all human endeavors, a part of this market would supply reliable products, but another part would thrive without scruples. Events now came close to the point of forcing him either to close his eyes to reality, or to help the side striving to offer the same quality offered by LifeChain.

He would have to face the quandary with a sophistication surpassing the simple concepts of right and wrong, and the man-made restraints of lawless versus law-abiding. He would have to shut his eyes to the difference between right being done the wrong way, and wrong being done the right way.

Lind Nunnally entered the restaurant, bareheaded, hurrying, his tall thin frame draped in a trench coat wet at the shoulders, wire-framed glasses spotted with raindrops, thin sandy hair disheveled. He had always lived up to his scholarly appearance — intelligent, reliable, industrious. Marcus had trained and then placed him in charge of the Philadelphia branch of LifeChain. "Sorry to be late," he said.

"Not at all. We had a tailwind."

They went to a back booth. Marcus began at once. "I needed to talk to you about missing couriers."

"We've lost two within the past month. And you?" said Lind.

"One, besides those crippled by the removal of an organ, and maybe a second. Joan Pully has been missing for two days."

"Oh."

"You know about Moha, of course?"

"Oh God. Yes! Is he after you, too?"

"Well, the word is out, and I wondered if you knew anything about his needs."

"Do we ever! It's his wife, his fifth, and he happens to be crazy about this one. She needs a new heart; at least he thinks she does. His physician placed her way down on the waiting list below many sicker people. But Moha is impatient and afraid to wait, and refuses even to consider an ordinary donor."

"How do you know this?" asked Marcus.

"Moha himself phoned me, and I suspect he contacted all other suppliers as well. Didn't he phone you?"

"If he phoned the call was not brought to my attention."

"Unlike him to miss anybody."

"He means business, I guess," said Marcus.

"Yes, and we suspect that bad medical advice lies at the root of his impulses. His offer has climbed to ten million dollars for the right donor, and it will keep climbing, no doubt," said Lind.

Marcus grew silent. Lind stopped talking, and turned toward him, waiting. "You said ten million dollars!" Marcus finally exclaimed. "Ten million damned dollars! Christ ... Why the hell have I not heard this?"

"Moha made the offer to me himself on the phone. He surely made the same offer when he phoned Norfolk."

"If he did I was never told. Oh God, this does put a different light on things."

"As you say, he means business."

"So, the black market has arrived," said Marcus.

"Exactly, and when the need becomes a matter of life or death, supply methods can become deliberately violent."

"Well, we've had it too good for too long without the inevitable human viciousness surfacing somewhere. It had to happen sooner or later. And if it is not happening right now, it will in time," said Marcus.

"Oh, yes. A subtle approach could ignore both real and artificial concepts of death, and procure whole living specimens, create no disturbance, arouse no suspicion, and destroy all evidence. Its victims would simply vanish from the face of the earth. Eventually their remains could be found only as living parts of other living human beings, a remarkable burial ground, with no exhumations, indeed," said Lind. "And chosen carefully, the supply could be predictable, dependable, and always available for a price."

"I'm afraid you are absolutely correct. Now, I gather you are familiar with other competitors," said Marcus. "Two in Norfolk, and you know about them already?"

"Yes, Mercury and Legation."

"Prescott's Mercury is committed to excellence and profit. He pays no attention to his critics." Marcus hesitated a moment in thought, then continued. "But the heat is rapidly diminishing now. His activities have come to pale by comparison to recent developments."

"You are referring to the bone entrepreneurs and others ... I'll bet Horace Willy."

"Right. I fired him for not being a team player and for taking cuts. So did the next guy who hired him. Now, despite these setbacks, he has just sold the rights to a patent on a bone dowel for six million dollars, then his company went public. He is suddenly worth thirty million on paper."

"And he was a service station attendant when he came to you for training?"

"Right. And look at him now," said Marcus.

"This is the death knell of the volunteer system. It's too unfair for families to give, and these guys to make fortunes off the processing. The families should be receiving the bulk of the profits, if profit is made. A family can in a moment of grief give the body away, and it can bring in almost a quarter of a million dollars in so-called processing fees. This will change."

"Yeah. It will have to happen sooner or later."

"And what else now?"

"The other competitor, Legation, is owned by The Reverend Lotte, the evangelist. Some of his products are below standard, and he may well be the cause of a leak of information from LifeChain."

"We do know about him. There is a Legation in Philly."

"A branch of the same outfit."

"Yes, and it has a bad reputation among legitimate transplant surgeons."

"As it does elsewhere."

"Where does he sell?"

"Through both legitimate and forbidden channels. Most of his live organs go to second-and third-rate hospitals, many of them in Mexico as well as Latin American countries, we suspect."

"What can you do about him?"

"We are watching. And speaking of vigilance, I need to get back to Norfolk."

"Come along. I'll drive you myself."

Marcus boarded the Lear for the return flight, strapped himself in, and watched the ground as the plane maneuvered for takeoff. He felt entirely at home in the air. He had taken many hair-raising chances as the early transplant era developed along with the advent of longer-range jets and the discovery of cyclosporin and other modern drugs. But there had been few political obstructions then and no unscrupulous competitors in the beginning. Now the changes had started.

In Norfolk, Marcus went to his desk in mid-afternoon, expecting to finish a pile of paperwork. There, atop a stack of charts, lay a subpoena. A suit had been filed against LifeChain for unfair distribution of live organs, specifically hearts.

CHAPTER 7

After Eric left home, Joan lay under the covers thinking about her narrow escape three nights ago while doing courier duty. She came close to being fooled. As soon as they became airborne, the man in the window seat said, "Please let me introduce myself. I'm Dr. James Bendon. I'm a heart surgeon from Chicago on my way back. I've been at Virginia Beach for a brief vacation. My five o'clock flight got canceled because a thunderstorm closed the airport. Of course, I missed my reserved seat on a flight home. Boy, will I have a rough time trying to do the scheduled surgery later tomorrow with so little sleep."

"Oh." She stopped the impulse to give him her name.

"Well, I don't have to ask you about your traveling companion here," he said, while laying a hand on the white container. "I have implanted many a one in the unfortunate people who need them."

"Then you know the importance of my mission. And you know the rules of the game. We are not allowed to discuss the contents of the packages we carry, nor the origin, nor the place we are going."

"Oh, I know already. You are from LifeChain, and you are carrying a heart for our patient, Adams Simpson, who has been in desperate need of a transplant for months. We have had a tough time keeping him alive while waiting. And we were beginning to despair of ever finding a heart in time. Thank God for the new federal law."

Peculiar indeed! A stranger knew the correct details of her business. She would follow the rules and divulge no information. Finally she asked, "Where would you get such ideas about my business?"

"Oh, no offense and no intention to meddle. I have been in touch with our unit, Northwest Heart, out in Chicago tonight. And everyone is very excited by the find, although we are saddened because a young man has lost his life in a motorcycle accident. We of course feel for the unfortunate people who are being skipped over and who may well die while waiting for a heart. I will be there when they are doing the transplant, but operating in another room, three bypasses tomorrow ... I mean later today." He looked at his watch. Before you go to sleep, I would like to offer you a ride to the hospital when we get to Chicago. My chauffeur will be meeting me on arrival and there is plenty of room in the limousine."

"No thank you. I have my travel orders." His limousine. She had never heard of a modern doctor with a chauffeur-driven limousine, especially one who did academic surgery. They had relatively low incomes compared to the successful ones out in practice, and any one of these would know better than to arouse the enmity of other doctors with this show of affluence. And he didn't look like a heart surgeon who worked in a big university hospital, one of the world's best, the worn, haggard, fatherly look. His clothes were a bit too sharp, with at the same time a functional appearance, like he might belong to the FBI or the CIA, or a more urbane element of the Mafia.

As she began to drowse again she became aware of a presence to her left, across the aisle, and briefly looked. Two men, well dressed like the man to her right, carefully looked down at work in their laps.

Her ears awakened her as the plane began its descent.

Dr. Bendon smiled and said, "Good morning. It's past midnight now and you had a nice long nap."

She simply smiled.

He took out his wallet, removed a credit card, and inserted it into the telephone in the seatback in front of him, and punched out a number. He began to speak, a little loudly, as though he might be aware of distances. "Hello, Jake. Where are you? How far down? Oh, then you are about forty-five minutes away ... Good. Good. No. No. It won't be necessary. I will meet you at the limousine stand outside United. And

Jake, we have to hurry. Yes, and something else ... we may have a passenger, a young lady carrying a heart for our dear patient, Adams Simpson, who probably is already in surgery."

Off the plane first, Bendon caught up with her and offered to carry the container. "Oh, thank you so much, Dr. Bendon, but you know I am not allowed to relinquish my grasp on this until I have delivered it."

"Well, I certainly admire your dedication, and respect it." They walked on into the main lobby and he said, "My limousine will be right downstairs, waiting, and I can have you at Passavant quicker than you could ever make it in a taxi."

She hesitated and changed her mind. Her body language said *why not?* "Okay, the ride certainly would be a great favor to us. But I must stop at the ladies' room first, then I will be down. Have the door open so I can jump right in." She smiled at him and gave his arm a little squeeze with her free hand, then turned and hurried into the ladies room. She disappeared around the corner of the entrance, dashed to the exit, and peeked from behind the wall. Bendon entered the descending escalator. She ran down a back staircase to a pay phone, perused her list of restricted numbers, and called the Passavant operating room secretary.

"Northwest Heart, Chris speaking."

"Hello, this is Joan Pully from LifeChain. I'm at the airport with the heart for Adams Simpson."

"Oh, great! We are all set up and waiting. When will you be here?"

"Very soon, but I need to know this: Do you have a Dr. James Bendon on your staff, who is scheduled to do three bypasses today, starting at seven-thirty?"

The secretary gasped and after a long pause she said, "Oh my God, why do you ask?"

"Because Dr. James Bendon sat beside me on the plane coming out here and he has offered me a ride to the operating room in his limousine."

"My dear, something is not right here. Dr. Bendon died a year ago from lung cancer, a heavy smoker. And he was not a heart surgeon anyway. He was an internist, and no one had ever heard of him outside Passavant. I would wager he was never in a limousine in his entire life. What does this Dr. Bendon look like?"

"J. Edgar Hooverish: short, heavy, muscular, and very serious, and well dressed in a gray serge suit with vest. Perfectly tailored."

"Ha! Old Bendon looked like Icabod Crane — tall, gangling, skinny, and he wore nothing but the academic uniform: khaki pants three inches too short, dirty and un-ironed, showing sagging mismatched socks, a wrinkled button-down dingy white shirt, and a cheap blue sport coat with an ill-fitting collar, a loose twisted tie, and a layer of dandruff."

"Oh, my God, who is this waiting for me?"

"I don't know, but I know you don't want him."

"Well, I'm calling because I'm suspicious. I've never heard of a heart surgeon named Bendon and certainly we know all of the big ones now by face and name. He claims he called and got the information about the transplant from Northwest Heart."

"No way. We've discussed this with no one. Don't get in his limousine."

"I won't, but I've got to move fast before he comes looking for me."

"Where are you now?"

"United, behind baggage claim. I came down the back stairs to a pay phone out of sight of the exit."

"Are you near the arrival exit?"

"Yes."

"Good. Now listen. Back up, stay out of his sight, go down the narrow hallway away from the phones and around the corner. This will lead you into the back door to the United

Baggage Claim. Get the first person you meet to lead you out to the police parking area. I'll call them."

"Oh, thank you so much."

"Be careful. We have begun to think somebody is playing dirty in this business."

"See you in a few minutes, I hope."

The police cruiser, its sirens wailing, sped past United arrival gates. Dr. Bendon stood with one hand on the handle of the open limousine door at the curb. He raised his other hand and signaled up the street. The two men moved from the parking sign and ambled toward the limousine. She sank as low as possible into the seat, but none of the three men looked toward the police car.

After delivering the heart Joan returned to Norfolk, went to bed, and slept until five o'clock the next morning. She took a cab to the hospital at seven and found Mann surrounded as usual by a host of people needing something from him. In their midst he remained calm and polite. He resembled the cloistered: straight black hair going gray, very white skin, medium height, just shy of stoutness, and already in his late thirties going to physical softness from lack of exercise, the mark of too deep a dedication. She felt a profound respect and an urge to protect him. He spotted her. She raised an eyebrow, turned, and began walking away. He followed.

In a small cubbyhole behind a closed door, Joan described the events of the past thirty-six hours. Mann said, "Well, this is all too plausible, but it's hard to believe anyone could mean harm to a person like you on an errand of mercy."

"I know. Nevertheless, what went on with me is very real and frightening. Why would they want the heart I was carrying to Chicago?"

"For somebody besides Adams Simpson, obviously," said Mann.

"Logically, yes. And I wonder how many recipients were on the waiting list for this particular heart."

"Twenty in the United States, as I remember, none of them sicker than Simpson."

"But Simpson was next on the waiting list."

"He had been declared the sickest under the new regulations from the federal Department of Health and Human Services."

"Do you recall the blood type and body habitus?"

"Let me see now. Oh yes, Type B blood, and tall."

The statement caught her off guard for a moment and she hesitated. "The same as my type ... I'm type B and ... and ..." her voice becoming very quiet, "... and tall!" She finished the statement all in a rush, blanched, and sank back in her chair. "Oh my God, Marcus. Do you suppose they wanted both hearts, to kill two birds with one stone? Did they have the names of everybody waiting for a heart with my qualifications?"

"I don't like to speculate. But I can no longer hope you are over reacting."

"You are right. How did they find my blood type and my flight plans to O'Hare? Someone had to be right at the center of things to know ... everything happened so quickly — the brain death, the organ salvage, all took place in less than an hour. And how did they really know the name of the recipient? The man, whatever his name, did not learn the facts from the Passavant operating room and heart team. The Northwestern Hospital complex did not leak it. No one there had all of this information. Are our phone lines tapped? Have they planted listening devices in our offices, in our homes? And is there someone here in the operating rooms betraying us?"

"We can have all possibilities checked, if we need to. In the meantime, have you seen any evidence of anyone following you here?"

"No, but I didn't want to risk phoning you at home last

night or at your office this morning or from my house. My car is still right where I left it three nights ago."

"We can swing by there on the way to the office."

"I suspect it may be under surveillance."

"All right. Let's go to the office."

"Good idea, but I don't think we should tell anybody anything at the moment. Let's slip in the back way."

"Why?"

"Because I have my own ideas about who might be leaking information. I want to surprise her. If she is guilty, she probably thinks I'm dead by now."

"Agreed. And are you going to tell me who?"

"Not now, not until I know more. The accusation is too serious."

"Yes. Oh yes, indeed!"

Gladys Gleason sat slumped over a keyboard and a pile of papers. Joan glided across the room and whispered, "Good morning Gladys." Gladys jumped and turned, her mouth dropped open, her unkempt face paled, and she gasped, recovered quickly, and said, "Oh! You startled me, Joan."

"Sorry, just speaking."

"How was your trip to Chicago? You came and went mighty quick."

"Not a hitch. I came right back and I imagine they had the new heart in Adams Simpson before I was halfway home. What's on the schedule today?"

"Right now? A kidney and a gut to Detroit, but Kenny took them. We don't know where the other one will go yet. They can use it at Sentara if no priority makes claims."

"An injury?"

"Another motorcycle."

"Pity."

"Yes. Oh, I just remembered, could you run a batch of freeze-dried bone grafts over to Sentara? They will be needed tomorrow in both orthopedics and neurosurgery."

"Sure. Will lunch time be okay?"

"Yes, and there may be something else by then."

Joan went down the hallway to Mann's office. She closed the door, pulled a chair near his elbow, and began talking just above a whisper. Marcus, we need a tape recorder locked in one of your desk drawers, and attached to the trunk line. This would record all incoming and outgoing calls."

"Why?"

"I am convinced we have a spy."

"Still not going to tell me who?"

"I want to hear her in action myself first, and so should you."

"Where does one get such apparatus?"

"Any electronics store. There is one just a block away."

"I'll go myself. I don't want you walking the street alone."

Marcus returned within the hour, locked his door, and with Joan's help installed the recorder in a bottom drawer of his desk. She had just settled down to her computer when the phone rang. Gladys Gleason said, "Joan, the other kidney goes to New York at once. Kenny has already left for Detroit; Betty has called in sick. You are the only one left. You would be back by late afternoon."

"Are the bone grafts ready to go?"

"Yes."

"Okay, I'll drop them off at the Sentara operating rooms and pick up the kidney. Do you have ground transportation?"

"Yes."

At La Guardia, Frank and Joan found their limousine and delivered the kidney to New York Hospital. On the return, weather delayed clearance for takeoff, and they arrived in Norfolk at four-thirty. Fog and misty rain had closed in. Frank gave her a ride to a delicatessen near Sentara hospital and her apartment.

She had been at the fruit bin a few minutes when she sensed a presence. She glanced up and her heart almost stopped. At first she thought Dr. James Bendon stood next to her. The man had the same build, and wore almost identical well-cut gray serge clothes, vest included, and a gray fedora. But not quite — he had a duller, younger face, and an even less benign countenance. He spoke casually, "Lovely fruit and vegetables. We are blessed indeed to have such abundance. I live on practically nothing else, my wife and I."

We are blessed sounded ecclesiastic, the secular made sacred by intonation. Sacred fruit. Sacred vegetables. Almost surely a phony, but she said, "Indeed we are. Everyone would fare so much better if they ate more of this and less of fat."

"Oh yes," he said. Joan eyed his girth. She suspected he ate anything but a high fruit high vegetable diet. Then he tipped his hat and said, "Let me introduce myself. I am Judge Walter Edwards, of the Federal Courts."

"Well, how do you do, Judge Edwards." She did not give him her name and wondered if he already knew. He did not push the introduction further. She moved away and gathered a small bag of fruit, a few more odds and ends, and a carton of skim milk.

Joan hesitated on the sidewalk for a moment, looking both directions, and Judge Walter Edwards appeared at her side. "Are you walking? I could give you a ride. You will get wet in this rain."

"Thanks, no." She turned to go. *How the hell does he know I don't have my car?* She thought for a moment he had gone his own way, but then she heard footsteps catching up. She turned her head and saw the black BMW. Three men wearing hats and dressed exactly like Judge Walter Edwards sat stolidly, their faces turned toward her, the car parked at the curb, headed in the other direction. The motor started, the tires squealed, and the car lurched into a U-turn, reckless in the midst of busy traffic.

The judge closed in and grabbed her elbow. She broke into a run, and he ran too, holding on. She leapt forward, broke loose from his grip, landed on her left foot, pirouetted and swung the bag of groceries in an arch, and threw it crashing into the man's face. The milk carton ruptured and spilled down his front. She leapt to her right foot, then forward on the left, and in a powerful lunge, drop-kicked him square in the crotch. She stepped to the side as he grabbed his testicles, and brought a quick chop blow to the back of his neck. He went down, crumbled to the sidewalk.

The car reached the curb as a rear door began to open and a foot, then a leg aimed toward the sidewalk. She turned, ran along the brick wall, gained momentum, leapt to grab the top, and slung herself over the wall into the St. Christopher Cemetery. She ran among the gravestones, and scaled the opposite wall onto the next street. Tires squealed at the corner below, and the car headed toward her street. She went back over the wall and glided beneath the shelter of overhanging limbs. Behind the foliage, she peeked as the BMW raced by, the passengers scanning both sides of the street. She felt like an animal trapped in a maze: the cemetery full of old molding stones, the ancient brick church, the wet trees above, the heavy traffic moving on the four surrounding streets. The BMW stopped at the distant corner. The doors opened and three men got out and walked in divergent directions. One went into the church. In a matter of seconds he very likely would exit a side door into the cemetery and begin a minute search. She went over the back wall and crossed the street, weaving between honking cars, into the woods, and began running, ducking beneath the foliage to the other side and to the next street.

In a moment, with tires screeching, they came down Olney Road in her direction. She folded herself on the ground behind a garbage can. The BMW raced by, sped through the open blocks, and made a reckless sliding turn to the right. She stepped onto the sidewalk and raced in the same direction, to reach a side street with foliage and houses before they returned to search Olney Road again. She made it, still running with all of her strength, to the line of sycamores. She began to tire, and rapidly lost strength. A siren wailed, and she turned to look. In the distance and coming her direction, the square orange box of an ambulance appeared, its rotating lights flickering. She leapt forward, and tires squealed again, and a car dared the ambulance and oncoming traffic and moved over to her curb, its tires singing softly on the rain-wet street. She glanced around while exerting every remaining bit of strength. Out of a young, handsome, rugged face, big intense black eyes looked at her, entreating. Half turned in his seat, the man offered an open rear door. And in her confusion and panic she recognized the startling head of curly red hair. She bounded over the grass strip and through the door, and fell on the floor panting desperately for air, her chest about to burst, her heart fluttering and pounding wildly. She had found Eric.

And now she lay snug in his bed nearly a day later. But they would hunt her down and the safety of his home would be only temporary. She would have to defend herself eventually, but right now she wanted to rest and think and stay hidden until she had a plan.

CHAPTER 8

The towering walls of green granite, the mirror-like surfaces of polished stone, the vast expanses of sparkling glass, the extreme cleanliness, the Spartan neatness, surprised Ivan on his second visit to Xanadu. Nowhere did he see disorder — no clutter, no loose stacks of unfinished paperwork, no disorganized housekeeping, no noise, no loitering, no joking and loud laughter, no dust, no cobwebs, no lint, no flies.

Kahan explained all the specialty rooms; then they toured the private pavilions, the laboratories, and the vast rooms set aside for tissue banking. The most modern equipment available awaited installation.

"Where are your storage refrigerators?" Ivan asked.

Kahan laughed. "Oh, I almost forgot." He opened a door and they stepped out into vast darkened caverns deeper in the mountain and he switched on an outdoor floodlight. They crossed a large stone-paved space, entered a glass-enclosed elevator, and at express speed ascended one hundred and fifty stories of rock bluffs within the caverns. Heavy steel scaffolding zipped by the transparent elevator walls. The doors opened onto a floor resting on girders strung across from bluff to bluff. A huge cave of shiny ice towered out of sight above great stocks of frozen supplies on the floor of steel scaffolding.

"We are above eighteen thousand feet here and the ice never melts at this level. Most of our refrigeration for storage is natural. The temperature stays the same at each level always. We don't really have seasons at this altitude and this latitude," explained Kahan. "We simply store in insulated cartons. The temperature ranges from five degrees below zero Fahrenheit here at this level, to forty above at the foot of the elevator shaft. We store at all levels according to the need. The freight elevators are computerized, and we can call down supplies with the keyboard. Robots load at the various levels.

Thus we could keep freeze-dried bone at this elevation, and blood and other fluids at the lowest level. Of course, you realize our elevator is pressurized and has a rich oxygen supply."

"How astonishing and convenient. But I am curious as to who does the surgery."

"Unbelievably easy, and we have the very best. It's the American system and the European system combined; that is, we get them from the finest places in the world: Baltimore, New York, Chicago, Boston, San Francisco, Cleveland, Paris, London, Stockholm, Zurich, Los Angeles, and others, all eager to come here."

"How fortunate for them and you."

"Indeed. And I am grateful to you for giving Bryant to us. He has done a most commendable job."

"An able and dedicated man."

"And his family is happy and thriving in this setting."

"He has lived up to my expectations?"

"Exceeded them, perhaps."

"Maybe ... and his children?"

"They are a great boon to the spirit of Xanadu. Everyone, my dear Prescott, should have children. Only when you clasp your own to your bosom do you become a complete man."

"It has to happen. You can't push it."

They descended in the elevator and returned to Kahan's conference room where he continued, "We need a heart for Moha's wife."

"I don't know how I could even begin to help."

"His doctor says Moha's wife will die in one of her attacks one day, and he has recommended a new heart. You will meet her tonight at dinner. Later during your visit, we will discuss ways to accomplish the things we must do, among them, finding desperately needed hearts."

"Who is your heart surgeon?"

"With Moha's financial help, I sent an exceptionally able

young surgeon, Dr. Adrian Gambela, to Boston for three years of training in heart surgery. He returned here in March to begin our program, and now we await the right donor."

"Will Moha's wife be all right in the meantime?"

"Apparently so if she avoids becoming too excited."

"Why not take her to a center in Europe or the United States?"

"Because they might go there and never be able to obtain a heart. And if they did, who could rely upon it being the right type and pure?"

Ivan sensed something bordering on the fanatical, or mired deep in misunderstanding, so he refrained from further questions.

Kahan continued, "The uproar has not died down in the United States about foreign patients who paid enormous fees to receive American donor organs, while the American patients died awaiting their turn. The word leaked out and the discovery created a backlash. The Saudis had been given preference over Americans, some of whom had been waiting more than three years for kidney transplants. The American press got wind of it and had a field day with the facts — *Americans dying while American hearts and kidneys were being given to foreigners.* A series of Pulitzer Prize reports effectively killed the chances of a foreigner getting an American heart. It's a problem we cannot overcome under the present concepts now being honored, or avoided, one way or another."

"I'm well aware of the picture."

"This problem most of all I wish to discuss with you. Dinner will be served in one hour. Moha and his wife will be our guests. You are not married, even yet, I understand."

"Correct."

"Then you will have a charming companion for the evening."

"Thank you."

Ivan went to his room. A black tie outfit had been laid out across the bed. He bathed and dressed, then stood at the window looking over a dense growth of enormous trees. A gentle knock at the door interrupted his thoughts. He turned as the door opened. A woman entered the room and came toward him. "Ivan, I'm Teresa, your companion for the evening."

"How pleasant, indeed." He took her hand, cupped it in both of his, lingering a second longer than necessary. Kahan had picked a woman of great appeal, a perfect match — tall, almost six feet, up to his chin, large black sloe eyes, rich black curly hair, voluptuous lips and a capacious mouth — a slender, bright, vivacious Tatar of exceptional beauty. And, he thought, very intelligent.

"You were enjoying the view."

"The ambience. Altogether captivating."

"Yes. Once well acquainted with Xanadu, you never want to leave."

"True, I'm afraid, to the point of concern."

She studied him for a moment and then said, "Oh no, this is not the land of the Lotus, not the land of dreamy forgetfulness."

"Good."

"I have been instructed to bring you down to dinner."

"I suspect this will be a feast of much more than mere food and wine."

"Yes. Kahan has great intellectual range without conventional strictures."

"Wonderful."

"Perhaps so, if you can cast aside impedimenta."

"A compelling challenge. We shall see."

The head of the table remained unoccupied as Kahan took a less formal seat beside his wife, Sofya. He wore a rich, luxuriant black beard growing in swirls, reflecting bronze and gold highlights in the glow of candles. His hair, as rich in color, curled down onto his collar. He looked both fierce and benign, both rugged and handsome, both controlled and lascivious, both noble and satanic. She too had the Tatar look, a certain exotic beauty.

After the meal, the group moved from the dining area to Kahan's library. There, over cordials, the conversation at first went from polite amenity to more personal exploration. Kahan said to Ivan, "I understand you have two degrees from Yale."

"Three. I went to undergraduate school there, too."

"Ahh, yes, the fundamentals before one goes on to more concentrated pursuits."

"The fun years. And you?" asked Ivan.

"Oxford. And you did both philosophy and religion?"

"Started in philosophy and got a master's degree first, then branched off into religion — one led to the other — and a Ph.D."

"I've heard rumors of your doctoral thesis."

"Yes, it created a stir. In fact, the furor has not died down yet. And your degree … Economics I would guess?"

"Oh, no. The same as yours, religion, or religions, all of them."

"And you did not pursue it," Ivan said.

"But I did, especially in the true meaning of the word: *a binding*, from the Latin *religare*. The science of our endeavors certainly binds us together, those of us involved. "

"Yes, an age-old tale, now with the modern twist of science, but we are all descendants of the shaman, who knew no schism between medicine and magic," said Ivan.

"Well, certainly, and they both were one and the same in the beginning. And to this day, religion has no science, and medicine has plenty of the inexact."

"I agree entirely. Medicine, despite having acquired commendable scientific foundations with time, nevertheless goes to a great extent on faith and belief."

"Both medicine and religion try to answer mankind's biggest and most haunting question, and belief serves only to close the mind to evolving possibilities," said Kahan.

"And in searching moments of human intelligence, people at every level of knowledge experience the striving toward the God within themselves, the evangelist when he abandons all reason in a frenzy of shouting resembling the witchcraft of a shaking dancing shaman, you and I when we bring together the means of extending lives, the surgeon when he starts the implanted heart to beating again, the physician who births a new life — a brief fulfillment from the power everywhere around us, the accomplishment of a fleeting and divine moment."

Sofya spoke. "What was your thesis, Ivan?"

"Something more or less forced upon me during my second reading of the Old Testament. Although the astonishment had been there initially, I had to have a second go at it to bolster my first impressions. I titled the thesis *Mathematical Summations in the Old Testament* — excesses, in other words."

"Benign enough, and esoteric to the point of being harmless," said Sofya.

"Not when one adds up the total consequences of the acts executed under the command of Moses."

"Oh?"

"But the subject is a bit rank for polite conversation."

"Oh, come now. Let's hear it," said Sofya.

"Well, I'm not so sure."

"Oh, I insist."

Ivan hesitated, the room became very still, and Sofya studied him with a bemused expression. Finally he said, "All right. Here goes. One of the more glaring sums, or exuberances, has to do with sacrifices. In one place, over six hundred thousand people were forced to bring one or two animals each to be sacrificed before the altar. The priest would sprinkle blood from each on the horns of the altar and on the altar itself and the surrounding ground, then burn all of the organs, along with the fat, on this one altar; then cook the meat on this same altar — all of this going on in one tent with the people, the livestock, the weather, and the swarming flies. Surely this created one of the biggest messes, and one of the worst of public health hazards. Can you imagine the muck on a rainy day — blood, mud, and manure? The altar measured seven feet in each direction, far smaller than your average meat-market counter, and dedicated to the slaughter and blood ceremonies from thousands of cattle, goats, sheep, pigeons, doves, partridges. It had to be virtually buried in blood and gore."

Sofya said, "Well, I see what you mean. Are there other examples?"

"Oh, indeed! To take another astounding example, in the time beginning with the exodus from Egypt and continuing until final settlement in the promised land, how many nations did Moses invade and conquer and possess and in the process kill all the children and all the men of each country, and all the women except the young girls who were saved for the soldiers? All of this genocide came easy for Moses' subjects as a reward for their conversion to monotheism. And furthermore, how many of his own people did he put to death for not believing as he believed, for not obeying the edicts to the letter? Add all of it up; the sum by even the nebulous historical facts is astounding. Perhaps no subsequent debacle, even to this day, has created more hapless victims. And another mathematical peak — none of these people died an easy, quick death; none died by the sudden oblivion of chemicals or explosives. They were all, including the babies, put to the sword, or the rope, or fire, or worse."

"There are others?"

"Numerous others, but these illustrate the gist of the thesis."

Kahan spoke. "And you pursued quite a different career after you left Yale."

"Not altogether. Could we not say this modern practice of

retrieving human organs and tissue is a new wrinkle in the old, old sacraments of human sacrifice — the modern Eucharist? Has not the offering of a human life to Omnipotence been a ceremony costing a life to buy life or to save lives through one channel or another? Spilled blood appeased the gods, who then favored the survivors. Sacrifice bought life from the gods, in those beliefs," said Ivan.

"The meaning of sacrifice, indeed."

"Be it so, yes, I pursue a religion."

"But you are still in shallow water."

"I know."

"What do you mean?" asked Sofya.

"The essence of the sacrifice has always been the beating heart, and the spilling blood, not the motionless organs or just static body parts taken after death."

"And what we have left of it besides the tale in modern times, the wine and the wafer, continues to shape both politics and history."

"The bread, the wafer, the flesh, you mean, is really the heart?" asked Sofya.

"In its deepest meaning, yes, the beating heart. When we talk about transplants, we really are talking about the heart. Everything else pales by comparison: the heart hauled out while still beating as in the ancient sacrifices, as in the brain- dead donor, as in certain cannibalistic rites."

"Indeed!" said Kahan.

"We have trampled on philanthropic toes, but we have brought life and comfort to hundreds of people, so far, by supplying human parts unavailable otherwise," said Ivan.

"And think of the good you could do by supplying living organs for those in worse trouble yet, the people who suffer perhaps a great deal more than those needing supplies from only the tissue bank," said Kahan.

"Of course, but here our supply remains limited to the victims of tragedy, those in a state of hovering death from injury or a sudden catastrophic stroke of disease, like a spontaneous brain hemorrhage. From this so called *donor pool,* only so many living organs can be recovered. Literally thousands of people will die while awaiting organs."

Kahan said, "Yes, yes indeed, but let us look at the limited supply. Does its existence not surprise you? Where does it really come from? What had to happen to make the very first living organ available for transplantation? From only one source, yes, only one: the perfidy of man."

"Perfidy?" said Sofya.

"Yes, and a rather intrepid perfidy. Though he does not realize it yet, he has broken the bonds on the tethered monster, euthanasia," said Kahan

"Oh?"

"Oh, yes. Mankind changed the definition of death, a definition he had so carefully guarded down through the ages — life is driven by the heart, and life continues until the heart stops. Then, as a matter of expediency, he came up with the phrase *brain death,* and called it legal death. All of a sudden the big change — life no longer lies in the heart. Life is a matter of awareness, and death a state of *no consciousness,* as we understand it in words, a state of oblivion in a person who cannot breathe unless helped. So we think. God knows what this person could tell you if the impossible happened: recovery from real death.

"This alteration in definition and in law will prove to be the break in the dam. Although the changes were made for the sole reason of procuring donors, the purpose, nevertheless, is euthanasian in effect, though not by intent. At present, the definition holds the flood back, but the definition can be changed to include the next parameter of brain dysfunction, those people who are unconscious but are able to breathe without help. Great political pressure is being brought to bear on lawmaking bodies in both Europe and the United States to initiate this change. After this escalation, what next?"

"Hurrying the final exodus for a purpose," said Ivan.

"And the purpose is undergoing changes too, an evolution of purpose," said Kahan. "I hear our more dedicated physicians speaking of it in great frustration. Organ procurement has changed the tone of the practice of medicine. Emergency room and intensive care physicians, and especially the nursing personnel, are quick to declare brain death, and the moment they think it they tend to slack off on treatment; in fact, the treatment may never become aggressive as it would have in days before this era. They become organ gatherers instead of doctors or nurses. They become judges — not dedicated doctors humbled in the presence of such tragedy — who play at being God, and they judge instead of practicing medicine. This adds a frightening tone, and I do not trust the atmosphere it creates. The word *harvest* incites these dedicated physicians to rage."

"Yes, to be sure," said Ivan.

"I think mankind, without knowing it, has entered an entirely new realm of death. Ancient nomadic peoples practiced exposure on the hobbling burdens they could not carry along in the migratory quest for food and shelter, among them the deformed newborn who had no chance of survival in a useful self-supporting state, and the aged when they became too decrepit to continue the seasonal treks. But nobody changed the definition of death."

"Are you speaking against the concept of donors?" asked Ivan

"Quite the contrary. I speak only against deception. A person with a beating heart is not dead. Call the state in which he exists between life and death what you will, but to name it for advantageous reasons is to take a cynical and arbitrary attitude toward the significance of death itself: It betrays a lack of full seriousness, *another arrogance of man at his worst.* Every sensible person understands this situation, and most people want the organs to be used to help someone else, so the correct name should be applied to the potential donor's condition. As it stands now, confusion reigns. Advocates want to declare the donor brain dead and then tell the family the patient has died. When a family later comes to know and feel the truth – the heart still beating while they were being informed of death, and still beating when the orderlies wheeled the patient into the operating room, and still beating when the surgeons hauled it out — all hell breaks loose, as it certainly should."

"Yes," said Ivan. "Confusion reigns all right, but the human psyche will not tolerate this deception. Throughout nature one sequence of life follows another as day follows night. After death the inevitable putrefaction creates a stink intolerable to the human nose, hence the custom of burial, or cremation, or the buzzard roost. Post mortem rot is not a sequel of brain death."

"Well, that distinction should clarify muddled thinking," said Kahan.

"Yes. God created death; man contrived brain-death."

After a moment of silence Kahan said, "What is the real difference between these machinations of the transplant industry and the rituals of an Aztec sacrifice to a sun god?" Then he answered his own question. "Mainly, the difference in the donor's route to this sacrificial destiny, in each case the treacherous hand of caprice."

Ivan said, "Yes, we are in the era of cannibalizing body parts from a few of the almost dead."

"Ahhhhh!" said Kahan. "Now you have struck a blow. Cannibalism, indeed! Think about it! While a new heart or kidney or whatever does not go in through the mouth and the stomach, it *does* go in. The recipient consumes it, and a certain assimilation occurs here, too, some of its cells migrating always to live in remote areas of the adoptive body as do digested parts from the victim of a cannibalistic ritual. We do indeed cannibalize from people whose lives have been sacrificed one way or another."

"Only one of the many ways people everywhere consume other people."

"But I am leading up to something."

"I have guessed as much."

Sofya stood and asked to be excused. The women left the room. Kahan continued, "We have specially equipped helicopters and small jets bringing nearby donors, the victims of violence, to us on respiratory support. From greater distances, we bring them in an ambulance plane at supersonic speed. Upon arrival the donors all go directly to our brain ICU for evaluation. We use most of them; we pull the plug on the others when they prove to be useless and at the same time hopelessly irretrievable."

"I should have guessed as much."

"But there is need for more organs, and for more controlled timing, and there is also need in this world for a certain justice."

"The other source, I suppose," said Ivan.

"Yes. And we probably would have more than enough if we chose only from those who live above the law and slip out of the clutches of justice repeatedly to continue being a menace to civilized society."

"But how?"

"They would simply disappear quietly, with no violence and no trace, no evidence."

"Who?"

"People who do the most harm, usually from a trusted position ... the white collar criminals, the stock market raiders, the hidden crooks, gang leaders of all types, the priests who rape little boys, the preachers who seduce their own church members, and a host of other miscreants. These categories provide an almost unlimited supply, not to speak of the useless, the dead-beats."

"Justice, indeed!"

"And the wife beaters, the child abusers, the husband killers, bad surgeons, dumb lazy internists, psychopathic nurses, smartassed cops — as much as they deserve it, we would not need to bother," said Kahan.

"There would have to be a place, an almost unreachable one."

"I've been considering the problem. Would you like to help us set up laboratories in a fully equipped ship, of the latest design and large capacity, and capable of spending most or even all of its time in international waters?"

"Quality control only?"

"Yes."

"Hmm."

"The ship would go to many ports in many countries, carrying freight."

"Among other cargo, I take it?"

"Yes."

"Tissue banking, and live organs?"

"Both."

"The personnel and the operation?"

"Leave the details entirely to us."

"The supply?" asked Ivan.

"From every country in the world, but you would have nothing to do with procurement."

"The United States also?"

"Don't you need justice there, too?" asked Kahan.

"Ahh, yes."

"Would you want to supply living organs for hospitals in the States?" asked Kahan.

"I am against having anything to do with live organs in the United States," said Ivan.

"Probably wise. But why?"

"A very nasty political situation is developing there, in the name of fair competition, medical politics — actually transplant politics — at its worst. The victims and their families, often their deprived dependents, are asked, even legislated, to supply the means free of charge. It can't last, it's a lopsided situation, it's grossly unfair to the victims, it's exorbitantly costly to the recipient, it's ridiculously lucrative to the hospital, it brings fame and wealth to the surgeon.

"And in non-living tissue it brings unimaginable riches to the supply charlatans."

"Irrelevant to us, I hope," said Kahan.

"At the moment, yes. And what would be my responsibilities?"

"Quality control in all aspects of both the tissue bank and the live organ supply aboard ship, and here in Xanadu Hospital, as well," said Kahan.

"We can honor your request."

"We have, as you may know, our own network, called SamuelS, with a well-trained corps of people to bring in donor candidates. Each will go to the ship as a happy tourist on his way to worldly adventures, and I promise you no one will ever be used unless his or her removal improves society by the removal."

"The beginning?"

"The ship, the ABATE, lies at anchor in the Norfolk waters, now taking on supplies and perhaps donors too."

"I would never go aboard."

"You could designate and train someone to carry out your instructions for the hospital and the ship. They would be the same, I assume."

"Yes ... but you pick the person, I train him in the proper techniques to be used in a conventional laboratory dedicated to tissue banking. Then he can practice what I teach him wherever he chooses to find employment. I will outline a protocol for hospital techniques and these could be used anywhere, including aboard ship," said Ivan.

"Good."

"You will have to get a live-organ technician elsewhere."

"Yes. As a matter of fact we have one already. Top flight."

"Good. Now, I'm curious about something you just mentioned."

"What?"

"How will you get them to go willingly?"

"Oh, well, through the most extraordinary events we have been lucky to obtain the services of one of the greats in pharmacology, Dr. John Marion, who also happens to be a most accomplished anesthesiologist. A truck driver wiped out Marion's entire family on the highway last summer, and got off on technicalities in court, although this was not the first manslaughter charge against him. Dr. Marion will provide us with drug mixtures for special effects, and Dr. Marion's reward will be the truck driver, our first American target.

"Dr. Marion is a master at creating mind-altering drug combinations. We use his minor potions on lesser targets, say those who present no problem. We then go to greater exotic effects in the more wary and ferocious. He also will help direct drug research here in the hospital laboratories," said Kahan.

"This is certainly a departure on new paths. I would not trust this justice in other hands," said Ivan.

"Justice ... real justice, a just justice, does not endure anywhere."

"I know only too well."

"We will double and triple check the evidence, I can assure you."

"I have no doubts. Another question — where is your point of departure in the Norfolk area to the ship at anchor?" asked Ivan.

"We have an old dry dock with its attached buildings near Ocean View. We keep a number of speedboats hidden inside, very remote to Mercury headquarters."

"Good."

"Okay. Now we need to discuss Legation in Norfolk."

"Yes," said Ivan.

"Its reputation there?"

"Shady."

"Well, I'm afraid The Reverend hasn't reached his zenith yet ... not yet. His delusions of grandeur and his greed continue to grow. And he recently purchased a crematorium," said Kahan.

"Spreading his business empire, I suppose."

"No! He can burn anything hidden in a box, maybe a big dog from the pound or the street, and return its deceiving ashes to the waiting and bereaved relatives. In the meantime their beloved dead is worth about two hundred and fifty thousand dollars retrieved in all its usable parts. And the paupers without curious relatives could reap him a rich harvest leaving not the slightest trace of evidence," said Kahan.

"My God! Sooner or later he will have to be eliminated."

"Another very disturbing development ... My agent in charge stateside, Herman Hodder, says a LifeChain spy sold the name of a person with the right credentials for Moha's wife to The Reverend himself, and the person's name is Joan Pully."

"What are you doing about the situation?"

"I have given orders for SamuelS to guard her with every resource necessary."

"Good."

"Now, Moha still must have the proper heart," said Kahan.

Ivan perceived the taint of fanaticism again and did not comment. They continued the negotiations.

Kahan said, "I really want you here at Xanadu. We need your expertise and supervision. If you accept we could establish satellite companies, or branches of Mercury, for distribution of tissue-bank material to reputable hospitals in Europe and other countries. You could return to the States as often as you desired, using one of our planes."

"I will be watching your development, and help in every

way possible from the States, and I must return there tomorrow."

"Teresa is going with you."

"Oh!"

"Yes, I give her to you. She gives herself. She truly wants to go."

"You are too generous."

"You should know, though, she will always be a SamuelS, always loyal to the goals of SamuelS."

"Yes," said Ivan. "Yes, indeed."

They finished the brandy, and parted for the night. Teresa, dressed in chiffon, greeted Ivan at the door. When he left for home the next day she went with him, without a word of explanation.

After their first night together he knew Kahan's meaning when he spoke of children. But Teresa belonged to the SamuelS organization and the Xanadu hospital. Teresa had been given to him for a purpose.

CHAPTER 9

Joe and Willy sat in the black BMW parked outside Tony's and surveyed the street. After a few minutes, a young woman came out of the shadows and moved toward the bar. "There she is," said Barney.

"Yeah, Jenny James. Not bad." They waited.

Jenny James walked toward Tony's, musing to herself. She liked the sound of her name, its light alliteration a happy jingle to the ear. She had a new friend who listened and laughed with her, a great outlet for the long tedious evenings. And in her slender, lanky body she had a deep pelvic hunger, too, craving with passionate longing for penetration pinning her to the bed, driving her on her back, while she reached for the ceiling with extended legs seeking the zenith absent from her being. And this one, Ralph, had not moved in on her like the others, the one-night-stands who had arrived and gone one after another. He had shown her kindness and consideration, listening to her talk.

Tonight she anticipated his advances, and her own surrender. She drifted dreamily in a lightsome insight and she did not care to look too far beneath the surface presented by any acquaintance. She felt a power, but not the vibes emanating from Ralph. Something about his presence aroused a desire in her to be fucked hard, violently. His naked cue ball head, his pugnacious look, aroused a surrendering weakness, because she would not have a chance to defend herself once he started, even if she wanted to.

Tony, behind the bar, watched her go to a table near the back of the room. He had a drink ready and took it to her immediately. "Hello, Jenny."

"Hi, Tony. What are you bringing me?"

"Your usual. A real sweet Manhattan."

"Oh great! Just what I'm hankering for — you had it ready and waiting?"

"I saw you coming down the street." He placed the drinkon the table and helped with her raincoat, and laid it over the back of a chair. "Enjoy."

Ralph came from the back of the building, with the appearance of having gone to the men's room. In feigned self-consciousness, he checked his fly with a swift hand movement. Jenny watched as he approached. His tight crotch-hugging pants outlined heavy equipment. Her eyes lingered below his belt and she felt another wave of excitement. Butterflies fluttered in her belly.

"Hello, Jenny."

"Hi, Ralph. I didn't know you were here. I was watching the front door."

He sat down at the small table, facing her. "I got here a little early and went back to the men's room."

She laughed, and eyed appraisingly his round shaved head. Already she had slipped off a shoe and her foot progressed above his knee. He glanced toward the bar and Tony nodded. She held her drink up, sipping through a straw, looking seductively over the rim at Ralph.

"Say, baby, I like what you're doing," he whispered, leaning forward. "How would you like to go to my place for drinks and a late dinner? I haven't told you, but I used to be the chef at Laqsuees."

"Oh Ralph, how very nice. I would love it. Why haven't you asked me sooner?"

"I bide my time for great things."

"You are so sweet, and sexy." She gazed steadily at him, her eyes wide with excitement.

On the back seat she draped herself against Ralph, put a naked arm around his neck and reached for his crotch with the other hand. A surge of alarm and excitement and fear possessed him, but she began to go limp, her exploring hand stopped, and she slumped against his body. Tall, with just the right ampleness of breasts and hips, *built like a fuckin' cello,* a thin woman, and hot, hotter than a goddamn fox, ready and rearin' to go — women like this bite and claw and scream, and love it when he hurts them. They all fall in love instantly, and sulk when they don't gain control. But he can't wait to get rid of this one because he feels a strange excitement, and excitement could be dangerous to his equanimity and performance. He had begun to wonder if Tony had given her the wrong drink.

Ralph despised Legation headquarters. The place gave him the creeps. He never knew whether or not he would come out alive once he went beyond its forbidding walls. He aroused Jenny, and helped her out of the taxi. The driver actuated the overhead door, backed out, and waited.

Ralph supported and half dragged Jenny as they went into a distant room. Within a minute, Jenny slept soundly on a wooden table in the middle of a well-lit room. She now belonged to Chiron. This one Ralph did not want to see.

En route to another bar he thought of Chiron. In the bars and nighttime world, Ralph had met Chiron and learned about his lurid medical history. Chiron, due to his exceptional manual dexterity, had been called *The Wizard* during his career in general surgery, but advanced emphysema, a failing heart, and a damaged liver had disabled him. In the end stages of the three diseases he received a combined heart-lung-liver transplant. Something happened during the operation. Blood in the bypass pump sludged and sent showers of tiny clots to the brain circulation, and The Wizard awoke from his surgery another man, changed forever by myriads of little strokes, his brain damaged, his intelligence gone, but his surgical ability had been left intact. He could operate as fast and as skillfully as ever, cutting and sewing automatically. Ralph, familiar with a certain arrogance, giggled at the thought of this being some form of divine commentary if not justice.

Chiron's vocabulary had been reduced to a few words: usually, "I want to operate." Ralph had informed The Reverend of the deranged surgeon with the strange brainless skill. The Reverend immediately sent Smets to bring Chiron from a local bar. The sight shocked and repulsed The Reverend, but he recognized the unmistakable talent, and Chiron proved to be perfect for the job, as long as a technician stood by and guided him. Ralph received a handsome finder's fee and the further reward of watching Chiron operate, and he stayed frequently to witness another sacrifice.

He feels a peculiar thrill when the beating heart is delivered from the donor's body, and cannot decide whether Chiron thinks he really is operating on a patient at the moment, or realizes he is just taking organs. To begin, Chiron approaches the somnolent donor on the wooden table. An assistant passes a large cannula and points to a femoral pulse in the groin. Chiron takes the cannula, punctures the artery, connects a tube, and empties the patient's blood into a bucket. When blood flow slows to a trickle, and the donor slips unconscious into deep shock, Chiron receives a kitchen knife and proceeds with the operation. He splits the patient from neck to pubes, opens the sternum with a power saw, and flares the chest open with ratcheted bone-breaking carpenter's clamps. Then he cuts all the moorings at the neck level: the trachea, the esophagus, the blood vessels, and peels out the lungs, heart, liver, and digestive tract in one bundle and delivers it into a waiting receptacle, the heart still feebly beating. He goes back and gets the kidneys. No more than five minutes elapse from start to finish.

After Chiron separates the organs as they are to be sold, he sits on a stool, waiting, staring blankly into space, startled and puzzled as though he has not quite heard something. Occasionally he says, "I want to operate."

Ralph has watched some of his own clients being taken

apart on Chiron's old wooden table. Of the others, most were docile and submissive, too. But he also has witnessed the more violent ones who came unwillingly in the hands of other recruiters and were hanged immediately by a noose kept waiting just inside and above the third door. When brain dead from partial strangulation, they were lowered to the wooden table for Chiron. Ralph, surprised by the crude equipment, asked why Chiron has not been given real surgical instruments. Because The Reverend wanted no such evidence around should the place be raided, Smets explained.

When his workday ended, Chiron wandered about downtown. Ralph followed, until he discovered The Reverend's men on the same trail. After The Reverend hired him, Chiron wore a beeper like a tagged bear so he could be found when needed. Sometimes The Reverend or Smets had him flown to other cities for special jobs. He had truly unmatched skill at stripping many bodies rapidly without damaging the organs.

Chiron's appearance amazed and fascinated Ralph, as it changed progressively. After the initial multiple organ transplant, the effects of time and large doses of cyclosporin finished off his already diseased kidneys, and he received a new kidney. Then he wore a heart, lung, liver, and kidney belonging to other people. Over many months he became very hairy in spots, large fluffy tufts appearing on his forearms and the backs of his hands, and just below the angles of his jawbones. Big potato-sized tumors, lymphomas, grew under his scalp, raising peculiar mounds of shiny skin covered in sparse hair. He looked lopsided, fragile, and ill.

Ralph loved to watch The Reverend squirm, especially in the presence of Chiron's infrequent and peculiar flashes of insight from the dull plateaus of his mute impairment. "I am a Chimera," he announced one morning. "I am the living parts of several people." Then he laughed. "But I've got the heart of a convict." He looked at The Reverend with lightless, bland eyes staring at something beyond, and laughed again, showing wide-spaced, broken-off, discolored teeth. The Reverend shuddered.

Like a child, Chiron heard things not meant for his ears. He surprised Ralph in the presence of The Reverend and Smets with, "I want to operate on Joan Pully." God, they didn't know he even heard ordinary conversations. And like a child he became persistent. "I want to operate on Joan Pully." He repeated this statement at intervals, at odd times, with an air of chilling and stubborn determination.

The Reverend had Chiron followed for fear of losing him to an accident or foul play. Within sight, and usually closer, one of Smet's more benign detectives would protect Chiron, who sometimes wandered downtown to the Sentara General Hospital and loitered about the doctors' parking ramp, looking for his old parking space and his car. He no longer qualified for a license to drive. Lost in confusion, he often wandered into the hospital and ascended three flights of stairs to the operating rooms. On these meanderings he followed a familiar trail through the automatic doors to the receptionist's desk, where he announced his arrival. "I want to operate." The Legation man waited discretely out in the hallway.

When Chiron appeared, the receptionist secretively touched a call button on her desk, and John, the head orderly, came immediately to the vestibule. John resembled the enormous presence of a bronzed Buddha, three hundred pounds. Strong, and kind and gentle, he took Chiron by an arm each time and led him down to the orderlies' lounge, served coffee, and talked to him. John had held him in great respect as a surgeon, and now nursed him through these confused crises when he returned to the operating rooms. Chiron scared the daylights out of everyone except John, who saw in the wide vacuous grin and the empty eyes the remnants of a once exceptional talent, the remnants of *the Wizard*. After each visit, John guided Chiron out to the sidewalk, where Chiron always said, in parting, "I want to operate." The Reverend's man, there waiting, followed Chiron on his nightly rounds, then later reported his wanderings and his hospital visits to The Reverend or Smets, often in Ralph Green's presence. These thoughts made Ralph shudder. He would never dare go to sleep in Chiron's presence.

Ralph's taxi arrived at yet another bar. He found donors in other places besides Tony's. With any luck he would begin tonight cultivating the next candidate for Chiron's knife. But he had something far more important on his mind. He had heard the talk about the woman, Joan Pully, with a bounty of ten million dollars on her head. The name for some reason seemed familiar, and Chiron's senseless talk had given it credence. With Ralph's contacts and his subtle stalking techniques, he would find her and collect the money. Then he could quit this revolting business in bars. But he needed to find the contact.

Gladys Gleason, he had heard, worked just up the street at LifeChain, and he had heard she stopped off here in Maxim's in the early morning hours several times a week for a nightcap. For three successive evenings he had awaited her appearance, and tonight now looked hopeless, too. He had never seen her. Not too swift he had heard, but sharp and slippery, and watch your step with her or you just might end up a donor yourself. He shuddered. In light of her rumored tastes and proclivities, he dreaded what he needed to do in order to accomplish his ends. But do it he would.

As he motioned for his tab, the door swung open and a short, slightly dumpy woman walked in. Just his luck — this would have to be Gladys. He fought down revulsion. She appeared well into her thirties at least, maybe approaching forty, and she needed to be washed-up, scrubbed clean: sweaty oily skin, damp dark-brown hair matted in strings — a soiled appearance. She hesitated, her sharp little blue eyes swept the room, then she aggressively walked over and sat on a barstool to his right, and plopped a ten-dollar bill on the counter. “Draft, in a frozen mug,” she said. “And run a tab.”

Ralph sat alone at the bar, ten empty stools to her right and eight to his left. She had made the first move, let her make the next.

With both elbows resting atop the bar, she cupped the frozen mug in both hands, and began to drink. Droplets of melting ice ran down her left wrist into a sleeve while she stared over the rim into the stacked bottles behind the bartender. Ralph held his breath. The slob! One droplet, two droplets, three droplets disappeared into the soiled lip of discolored cloth. Suddenly, as though awakening to the presence of a crawling insect, she flipped her left wrist and beer sloshed onto Ralph’s right hand and into his snifter of brandy. “Oh, my goodness!” she exclaimed, and plopped down the beer, and began wiping at his hand and wrist with a paper napkin. “I’m so sorry. How clumsy of me.”

“No problem,” said Ralph, fighting for self-control.

She said to the bartender, “Bring the gentleman another brandy, please. I’ve ruined this one.” She turned to Ralph and said, “I’m Gladys Gleason.”

He said, “Ralph Green.” And they shook hands – oily and damp. He shuddered again.

She already knew. The Reverend’s donor-pimp — but thought the charade necessary. She could furnish him with very useful information, for a price. She placed a hand on his arm and said, “I’m really sorry for the mishap, but I’m so tired. I’ve been on duty eighteen hours without a break.”

“Oh, really. And what work demands such dedication?”

“I work for LifeChain.”

“And what is LifeChain?”

“Oh, you know, I’m sure you’ve heard of it. We procure tissue and live organs for transplants.”

“Oh, yes. And *you* do what exactly?”

"For all practical purposes, I run the place."

"I have only the vaguest idea."

"I dispatch all organ and tissue deliveries."

"Day and night?"

"Yes. Not much happens between one and eight a.m., but I have a way of monitoring those hours also."

"Well, yours is a very sensitive and responsible job, I assume."

"Indeed it is."

"Many lives are in your hands."

"Yes."

"And many trusted secrets."

"Without a doubt. And what do you do, if I may ask?"

"Me? I have a Ph.D. in physical therapy, but I run the training program for the Athletic Club. Name any muscle you want to strengthen, and I will show you how to do it." He mentioned nothing of his nighttime activities.

She eyed his big head, his bull neck and bulging chest and muscular arms, his short stature, and shaved scalp. He wore a tight-fitting short-sleeved jersey, and crotch squeezing pants. His milky blue, wide-set eyes bulged in a flat broad face, a pugnacious terrier look. A cold chill settled between her shoulder blades. He leaned toward her, his mouth coming close to her ear and said, almost in a whisper, "Tell me, Gladys, do you believe in donor cards?"

His conspiratorial manner sent a thrill through her belly, and after a moment she replied, "Indeed, I do. They give us much needed information, but the same information can be had from other sources, such as hospital records and military records, for instance. Getting such information is no problem for the resourceful. The pledge cards do, however, give us the right to proceed in emergency room situations when relatives are not available."

Then in a low murmur, he asked, "Do you have access to donor card files?"

"Access, yes, of course, but not everybody does. Why?"

"Does the donor not take a risk in signing the pledge, the card?"

"What do you mean?"

"Well, suppose a donor with a specific set of qualifications is needed, but does not become available. The family of the dying patient who needs a heart or liver or kidney or whatever is desperate ... they will pay anything for the right donor. You have access to such cards, you can find a name with the right qualifications, and the address is on the card, the phone number, and the like. Kidnappers, with this information, could take the person, produce a state of brain death, deliver the donor to the right hospital, and collect a handsome profit."

"My goodness," said Gladys. "How naughty!" She looked directly into the gaze of Ralph's wicked eyes, and knew he saw a gleam of mischief in her own.

"Now, is it possible?"

"Yes," she said.

"Then the pledge is risky."

"But very generous, don't you think?" she asked.

"The supreme sacrifice by whatever path."

Gladys became very quiet for a moment, slouched on the barstool, then she straightened up and said, "Hey! You know what? Come to think of it, you are right. It is a sacrifice, certainly if fate has taken a deliberate turn."

"Like an Aztec ritual meddling with the inevitable forces of nature?" he asked.

"Or the almighty righteousness of medicine with its burgeoning technology manipulating the end stages of life."

They both laughed and he said, "Yours is a cynical world of reality."

"I see nothing wrong with cannibalizing dead bodies. After all, I have not killed a one of them and never shall."

"Hey, right on, man! You know it is cannibalism, by a certain path."

"Which is only another form of sacrifice."

"So it is," he said.

"We might as well take advantage of it from a pedestal of neutrality, don't you think?"

After a moment of silence, he said, "Speaking of deliberate..."

But she cut him off. She placed a hand on his knee and slinked it upward as she murmured, "We should talk about this elsewhere. Let's go to my place." Ralph paid and they left.

While serving brandy in her living room, she returned to the subject at hand. "You have an interest in donor cards?"

He burned his queasiness with a deep swallow of brandy. "Yes, and you say you have access?"

"Yes. But the donor card concept is a bit naive. As I've already said, all the information you need is available elsewhere, and you don't need consent."

"More than the local supply?"

"I can pull up certain information in our files, in all eyebank files over the nation, and in the files of the division of motor vehicles in most states."

"The last one is illegal."

"Only to most people. I have a way."

"And it pays off in a wealth of information?"

"Quite. Then there is an interesting file with the qualifications of people who have pledged their organs to LifeChain and similar endeavors throughout the country."

"A growing collection, I imagine."

"Right."

After the first sip she placed her glass on the coffee table and said, "Will you excuse me a few moments? I must bathe after the long hours at work."

"Oh, by all means," he said, relieved. She disappeared down

a hallway. He sat in the semi-darkness, watching the evolving snow leap at him across a monitor screen. So, she keeps a computer running continuously at home, no doubt programmed into LifeChain, in touch twenty-four hours a day, probably.

To his relief she returned clean, shampooed, and blow-dried, in a semitransparent nightgown and a cloud of perfume. She sat on the couch against him, reached for her brandy with one hand while the fingertips of the other idly drifted onto his thigh, and with delicate touch moved upward. In the half-light her mouth found his. She tasted of toothpaste and brandy. At least he whiffed no bad odors, and his complete disdain for her aroused a free and capricious sadistic streak, with no inhibitions. He would give her what she wanted, already hot and wet and grabbing at him. He took her with an erection hard to the point of subliminal pain, there on the couch, and he slammed harder, with a vengeance, until she screamed and clawed at his face. He held her two wrists in one powerful grip to protect his own eyes, and rodding viciously to the barriers of her depths, took her again and again while she squealed and struggled. Then he pulled her up on her knees and took her from behind, then pulled her up on her feet and bent her forward, aiming her face toward the bedroom and, walking behind, took her again. Before they reached the bed, he took her three more times. Then they climbed the mattress. Mounted astride her, both feet planted flat on the sheet, with all the power of his thighs driving down, and with images of the delightful and lustful Jenny James firing his imagination, he rode her supine and flexed body in a frenzy to his own emptying.

"God-damn!" she said, as they lay languid and spent. And she talked. She skipped all the preliminaries. Surely he knew already, and would not make an issue of it. "I can get you all the donor information you want. I get fifty percent of the profits."

"Not with more of what you just got."

"God. Twenty-five percent?"

"Ten."

"And more of you each time?"

"Upon occasion."

"A deal. Just let me know what you need, and I can always find it somewhere, usually not out of town."

"Good." With such information he would not have to snoop around while looking for a particular type of donor. But tonight's work had another purpose. She stroked his thigh, working her way up until she took his penis in hand and began fingering the corona, then crawled down and eased it into her mouth. He said, "Would you like to have more of the man there than you can handle?"

She freed her mouth, and turned her face toward his. *There isn't more of this than I can handle.* But in the depths of the steady gaze, bottomless beyond the wide pupils, she saw a calculation, readable and deadly, and in the world he straddled, in the depravity of his persuasion, there would be no controlling this one. Nor did she wish to be introduced to the breadth and the depth of his jaded repertoire. So she said, "Yes, I would like to have more of the man here than I can handle," and she put the arousing purple head back in her mouth. When she finished he said, "Then give me Joan Pully."

"Nobody gives Joan Pully to anybody. I can tell you where she is, some of the time, but the rest is up to you. And I will have my two and a half million regardless of who takes her."

"Fair enough, provided the person who takes her gets the ten million."

"Someone will. The request put to LifeChain was serious and the search intense."

"Search for what?"

"A young woman about six feet tall, type-B blood, and pure at heart."

"What does pure at heart mean?"

"We would be wasting your time discussing that."

He hesitated, quelling a retort, then chose to ignore this impertinent estimation of his decadence and said, "Then, who?"

"Moha, the richest of the Saudis."

"Where?"

"At Kahan's, the new enterprise, the world's largest and most modern hospital, in Xanadu, where anyone can get a transplant if his doctors agree."

"How does he want the donor?"

"He is expecting a brain-dead patient, the victim of injury or a fatal stroke, delivered to one of Kahan's waiting planes to be flown to Xanadu hospital on life support, with the heart still beating."

"A variation on the conventional route."

"Moha intended nothing more, nor would Kahan tolerate it."

"Kahan won't know the difference."

"Ohhh, yes he will. Have you ever heard of SamuelS?"

"No. Who is SamuelS?"

"Kahan's organization has spread worldwide. His agents gather information and conduct procurement of organs and banked tissue for transplantation at Xanadu. They know what goes on. The CIA and FBI together couldn't outdo them."

"So?"

"Don't cross them. You would be called to make the supreme sacrifice yourself, to disappear into the chimeric world of transplanted organs and body parts, the most private and inaccessible of all hidden graves."

"God, the very idea gives me the creeps."

"Only reality again."

"How do you come to know all these facts about SamuelS?"

"Ivan Prescott, a Yale Ph.D. in Comparative Religion and the owner of Mercury, attends the LifeChain board meetings, where he lends his political and scientific expertise to helping run our lumbering organization. He has visited Xanadu and

Kahan many times, and brings back the facts and passes them on to the powers in the conference room."

"How do you manage to hear it?"

"Oh, I have my ways."

Sneaky bitch, I'll bet she does. "Is Joan Pully a deal?" he asked.

"Under my terms, yes."

"Fair enough."

"After she is finished I shall retire, and have nothing more to do with these desperate endeavors."

"And so shall I. Now, where is she?"

"She disappeared yesterday while men from Legation were trying to catch her for The Reverend."

"No clues?"

"None, but I will let you know. We will find her."

CHAPTER 10

At the scrub sink, the chief of heart surgery, Foster Kemp said, "I need to ask you a question, Eric. We've been hearing tales of your prowess."

"Okay," said Eric.

"Did you in fact open a chest in the emergency room one night last week?"

"Yes, a stab wound just below the left nipple, one puncture, stiletto, and almost dead from cardiac tamponade. We would have lost her if we had tried for the operating room, or if I had risked waiting for help to get there."

"Heart compressed badly?"

"Oh yes. The sac tense as a balloon, and a big clot erupted when I opened it, and the heart beat picked up at once."

"You sewed up the heart right there?"

"Only one hole, a small one, but squirting blood with every systole."

"How is the patient?"

"Fortunately, all right."

"Well, well, well, heart surgery in the emergency room."

Eric wondered if Foster Kemp meant to condemn him for doing something rash, or did he approve of the daring. But no one could argue with the results; he had saved a life, nothing more, nothing less.

The moment to begin surgery approached. But Foster Kemp surprised everyone by taking an observer's stance at the head of the table. He turned and said, "Eric, do this operation." Then Eric, the intern, performed a triple coronary artery bypass from start to finish.

In the late afternoon Foster Kemp sent for him. The chief politely stood and shook hands when he arrived, then began. "Eric, tell me how you came to this point in your life."

"The hard way. The back steps, so to speak."

"So I hear ... worked your way up."

"Yes."

"What about the special skills?"

"You mean the cards and the amateur magician's tricks."

"I was speaking of your manual dexterity. But what about the cards and magic?"

"Sleight of hand techniques, I thought, would improve surgical skills, so I took lessons from an expert in both card tricks and magic."

"Who?"

"A master of sleight of hand and a genius in esoteric mathematics, at present a statistician on the faculty at Stanford. He ranks among the best worldwide in close-up magic. He performs shuffles and riffle shuffles perfectly time after time without fail. My notion to apply magic techniques to the performance of surgery interested him, and he accepted me as a student."

"You went to California?"

"Several summers. Hitchhiked both ways."

"Okay. And where did you learn the surgery?"

"Started sewing techniques at twelve years, using chicken skins and pork skins and cloth and bone, and practiced clamping old discarded hemostats onto the edges of cloth and dead animal flesh, learning how to do this with each hand or both hands in coordination. Then from the age of fifteen I worked as a surgical assistant at a large charity hospital in the operating rooms and in the animal labs. There was plenty of clamping, sewing, and cutting there."

"Why so young?"

"Musicians start early, very early, like three or five, but surgeons are held back until they finish medical school before ever touching the instruments, an age more like twenty-five on the average. I don't think skills acquired in adulthood could ever reach the innate second nature dexterity coming naturally from earlier training."

"Had you ever done a bypass operation before today?"

"Yes sir."

"Where and when?"

"In the labs of other hospitals several years ago, then night before last in the laboratories here."

"Transplants, too, I assume."

"A couple, yes."

"Extraordinary, I must say."

"Thank you, sir."

Eight years had passed since the day of his first major operation. And now as his period of training drew to a close with no time to spare he had to remain true to the people who trained him, yet he had to squelch the impulse to bolt and go to Joan.

Marcus Mann, gowned and capped, came through the operating room doors carrying a cardiac container. In passing, Eric said to Marcus, "I will be back in a moment. I have something of great interest to tell you."

"I'll wait right here after I deliver this heart."

When Eric returned, neither of them paid any attention to the bystanders in the hallway-the nurses, the orderlies, the technicians, the loiterers. Eric led the way to an empty room, shut the door, and drew up two stainless steel stools. They sat facing each other in the unlit room. He said, "Joan Pully."

Marcus said, "Do you know her whereabouts?"

"Yes, I do."

"Is she safe?"

"I'll wager she's never been safer."

"Dr. Stuart, for God's sake don't play games."

"I'm not playing games." He described the rescue, then said, "She is convinced she is in danger, and she suspects her pursuers are getting information from an insider in LifeChain."

"Can I see her?"

"Not safe under the circumstances. If she is correct about her fears, you are being watched constantly, too, and your movements would lead them to her."

"We need her."

"Sending her on another mission would surely expose her sooner or later to being abducted."

"This is hard for me to comprehend."

"Marcus, I saw them several times myself, three well-dressed thugs in a black BMW M5 combing the streets at high speed, and later parked and watching her apartment house, dangerous, frustrated, and I would guess mad as hell. I've got to go now and help with this transplant."

"Dr. Stuart, how do I know?"

"Don't even think about it. She trusted me in the moment it took to rescue her, and she now is alive and safe. You are in the same boat."

CHAPTER 11

After the death of his family, John Marion endured through the summer and fall days grieving behind the drapes during the long hours of heart surgery, seething for justice.

A new voice had entered the surgical arena nearly three years past. The accent of Dr. Adrian Gambela carried something of the Greek, something of the Turk, something different defying definition. Gambela had exceptional ability and intelligence. He had been sent to Boston for training and would return to pioneer heart surgery at a very special hospital in a far reach of the world. He said little and studied people with a heady brown-eyed gaze. His formidable presence resembled a statue from antiquity, Homer-like. One day, a week following his tragedy, Marion caught Gambela gazing at him after a long operation. Marion became aware of his own eyes, burning from weeping. Not a word passed between them, but he realized Dr. Gambela knew and understood. Could Gambela read his mind, his heart, and feel his grief and his anger?

Then he came to know. In mid December nearly six months after the tragedy, Gambela, now near completion of training in the heart program, approached Marion and invited him to Xanadu for Christmas, and to meet the great Kahan. Marion had dreaded the coming holidays without his family, and accepted. They flew on Christmas Eve day to a non-Christmas country. The setting astounded Marion. Kahan and his family offered such hospitality, such respect and courtesy.

And Kahan led him across the barriers to another mind, the one now driving him anew, a realm of ultimate justice upon this earth, during this life. A stillness and isolation within himself came to blunt the acuteness of his grief. This breaking of the shackles released him from the servitude to conventions and unfettered his life.

Dr. Gambela had done his work well. Kahan knew all the details before they arrived at Xanadu for the holidays. Marion, the supreme master of drugs, knew how to alter consciousness, how to produce states of twilight sleep, states of walking sleep, periods of hypnotic transcendent transportation into another consciousness, beatific states susceptible to the slightest suggestion and obedient to any command, profound states of prolonged unconsciousness without threat to safe breathing, states of protracted hibernation, attacks of wild drunken dangerous behavior, and maniacal homicidal rampages. And Kahan needed him. "We know everything about the truck driver, all of his habits, all of his movements, his continued reckless driving, his threat to other innocent defenseless people, his nasty arrogance, his bragging about wiping out little cars full of little people. He matches several of our people waiting for transplants, and we will use him as soon as Dr. Gambela returns and opens the new Cardiac Suite in March. We promise you the trucker if you come to work for us."

Momentarily, Marion had not quite known, yet he did. He felt no resistance to the all-powerful seduction of revenge, the righting of a terrible wrong. He sensed something of extraordinary exotic ramifications, a strange tantalizing excitement. Emotion leapt up and his mind played with possibilities. Could it be he would no longer have to live with and tolerate helpless rage at injustice, at terrible wrongs never righted in this life? Should he flee this bastion of extraordinary power? Or should he stay for a gratification rewarded to few people in a lifetime?

With Kahan he walked the grounds at Xanadu in the balmy December days and talked. Kahan took his time, introducing him to the concepts of nature honored in his domain. "We take from an abundant and unending supply, and elevate it to greater advantage. We choose our targets to fit the pattern of overdue justice. Thus, we have personal gratification, too. We serve more than one great purpose. No violence, no pain ever, no bloodshed on the streets — we do it all with love and charm and seduction and the kindest sleep. And the other and more abundant source — we take from the lives wasted by war and other violence and give longer and better life to the ruined and the dying. This is our revelation to mankind, the resolution of our religious instincts, a satisfaction of divine craving. Are you willing? Can you cross into this other existence, never to turn back, never have to work again, never to do endless hours of pedestrian servitude — never be bound again by ordinary conventions, by ordinary concepts of right and wrong, of sin and redemption, of guilt and innocence, or by ordinary emotions? Can you? Are you ready to breathe the new freedom, to emancipate from earthbound grief, to join the liberated?"

"But what of *right,* what of doing unto others?"

"My dear little American friend, perpetual victim of a terrible superstition, show me one thing upon this earth not invented by God Himself. If you can, then I can show you something perhaps wrong, perhaps sinful, or dirty."

"But ours is a democratic country."

"Yours is a country of make-believe, blind to the realities of its motorized mayhem, its bodies in the streets, its oppression from the lower strata up. Who rules your streets ... your almighty fatherly and ever-protective government, or the riff-raff rabble running amuck beyond the reach of the law? Who rules your highways, the state patrol or the truckers speeding recklessly outside the law?"

"Well you are right, I'm afraid."

"Indeed! Now, if you could retire at this moment, where would you want to live?"

Marion thought of an old dream. "In snow country, probably Vail."

"Good! Now let us show you our *caverns measureless to man.*"

They passed by the water flowing down toward the sea and through the shades of towering virgin forests, and left the grounds and entered through heavy thick iron-grill doors, a palace as bright as ice. "These are the laboratories where we make things and search for things to prolong the life of man: the vaccines, the antibiotics, the drugs devised to alter the brain's behavior, the pain killers, the cancer cures — everything." Kahan explained the building of molecular crystals into materials with the most unusual physical properties. Here they make a protein and sugar structure hard as a needle, something akin to hair and no bigger, and to porcupine quills and to hard candy, and porous enough to carry doses of drugs. In the body fluids it becomes instantly unstable and rapidly melts, dissimulates and releases whatever is built into its matrix.

"We can shoot these like a dart to deliver antibiotics, vaccines and other drugs, and thus we can bring peace, or sleep, or a tranquil state, and many alterations of the mind, and many cures of deadly diseases. You will be asked to prescribe the loading for the effect we want, the dosage calculations for all of the drugs."

They moved on to another room and Kahan said, "And here isolated in this separate room we have exciting developments. We are employing structural genomics for the rational design of new drugs, the protein structures teased into crystals. We have some on hand already, one of them a very useful topical anesthetic with quicker action than pontocaine dropped on a naked nerve ... very useful on targets. They retain no lasting impression of having been shot. We have named it *Bliss*. You could help us with the effects we are looking for."

"Of course, but I won't deal with outright death."

"You will not be asked to. We want only subtleties."

In the science laboratories, he watched the materials build, the bright tiny sharp needles taking shape. They melted quickly in mild salt solutions, they disappeared almost instantly in a few drops of blood, and others blended within a few seconds into the fibers of a steak, and another into the meat of a chicken leg. And in the mechanical department, the gas and spring-loaded guns were mounted into fountain pens, walking sticks, crutches, ski poles, pocketknives, lunch pails, briefcases, and hard-backed purses.

Then Marion and Kahan took the guns and each shot them into dartboard targets, and marveled at their accuracy, how straight the tiny missiles went even in the wind. They watched as technicians shot the needles into rabbits. Most of the animals hardly flinched and kept on nibbling at food in the cages until the drug, whatever it might be, took effect, always within seconds. All the little guns hurled the missiles with no sound perceptible among the everyday ordinary noises of the street or of people in motion: perfect for subtle action in crowded places. You could hand a person your fountain pen, swing your walking stick high in sprightly stride, carry your ski poles in one hand at mid-shank while skiing down beside or behind the target. And the entire mechanism comes out in one piece leaving the container intact for its other everyday purpose.

"Very effective," said Marion.

"Indeed."

"So who will use these weapons?" asked Marion.

"Many agents within my organization, SamuelS. But we have one expert marksman of exceptional ability for the very special and difficult targets. His name is Tim. We want you to help train him in the effects of drugs, and direct him toward certain anatomical landmarks."

During the remaining days of this first visit, Marion began the task of drug loading the missiles. Into each he introduced a micro-tip of the drug *Bliss* to diminish the sting of penetration and to obliterate later pain. And he loaded the remainder of the shaft with anesthetics or antibiotics or different strength sedatives or hallucinogens or whatever he needed for special purposes. Coagulants at the end of the shaft prevented bleeding in the wound entry.

Marion slept in a room trimmed with ornate gold scrolling and rococo filigree molding, on a deep firm pallet atop layers of plush Persian rugs redolent of patchouli, and other haunting aromas and incense, too. In the remaining nights before they left to return to Boston and after his allegiance crossed over to Kahan and his ways, a woman almost his age came to attend him. She undressed him and bathed him and dressed him and slept with him. And he knew physical release for the first time since grief overwhelmed him.

Kahan had said, "We know your income. Save it, and pay your taxes on it alone. Retire within six weeks. A house will be waiting in Vail. Everything will be supplied for you. Deal only in cash. We will call you when we need you and talk cryptically, but you will understand. You will always be given the complete facts on each target, which you will have the right to turn down. Your authority will be even more final than The Judge's decision."

"The Judge? Who is The Judge?"

"He has another name, of course. Congressional liberals and inverted racists crucified him with false testimony before nationwide and worldwide television audiences, and denied his nomination to the Supreme Court. Lying scoundrels who live above the law tainted his impeccable reputation as a legal scholar without peer. In other words, they Bjorked him. Then he lost a wife who died while awaiting a heart transplant. He readily accepted my offer."

"Oh."

"Judge Taylor takes all the information collected by SamuelS on any potential donor, then with a chosen council decides whether or not this person meets our rigid criteria."

"Your criteria?"

"The lawless who continue to be a menace to society and are usable donors."

"Will there be a court of appeals?"

"Yes. I was going to approach the subject with you. We will need a drug combination to make any man bare his soul in a state of religious fervor."

"You need a shaman."

"Exactly, but the shaman will need your expertise for controlled dosage."

"You have one?"

"Yes."

When they left in daylight after the five-day visit, the helicopter lifted Dr. Marion and Dr. Gambela over the towering ancient forests, above the waterfalls, above the mountain full of caverns. The hospital and castle were one gigantic building sloping down out of the rock face, rising up and roofed by the mountain itself. Low-rise wings spread in each direction from its base, housing many private dwellings.

Looking down on the compound, Dr. Gambela said, "The fence walls, the solid brick walls, go five miles one way from the wings, and turn five miles the other, turn again and come back to the castle, and the river runs a winding course five miles across the grounds then below the caves before plunging on toward the ocean." Turrets topped the walls along the way and marked the corners, and sentries in splendid gold and red garb paced back and forth. "His land, he dreamed it into reality, Kahan, and he dreams it more and more into being. He will have his way to the benefit of all patients who come here."

"Is this treasure not vulnerable to evil forces?"

"As are all values, yes, but let me show you." Gambela leaned forward and spoke to the pilot. "We have plenty of time, and it's a clear day. Would you show us the mountain?"

The helicopter veered away and upward until the mountain profile came into full view, tall, peaked, snow capped, surrounded by a sea of green. Then they flew its circumference a mile high from the top, and Gambela pulled two pairs of binoculars out of a storage bag and handed one to Marion, then pointed to the mountain periphery. "There you see in the foliage the camouflage, the guns, the soldiers, the tents, and huts."

"Ahh, yes," said Marion.

"These are troops from all the nations who contribute to Xanadu, and they are here to guard its portals. Each has its own encampment. They ring the entire mountain, a united nations like none other, guarding the Mecca they might themselves need someday."

Marion said, "This is heartening, indeed, amidst the chaos of the modern world. A sanctuary for the desperate and frightened who have no other place to turn."

"Yes, but unfortunately they have to guard it against another menace — the hordes of people who have heard of its magic and come as pilgrims seeking solace for diseases not treated at Xanadu."

"Pitiful," said Marion.

"Oh yes, a real Mecca is needed for those people too."

"Will there be one?"

"It's in the plans, I understand, but only after Xanadu has been developed."

The helicopter completed its tour, came down to the base, and landed near a sleek jet plane standing rakish and dynamic, glinting in the morning sun. "I've never seen such a plane," said Marion.

"It's the newest addition to the Xanadu fleet, a supersonic ambulance built by the makers of the Concorde."

"Does one have to be sick to be a passenger?"

"Its specific purpose is to transport the brain dead on life support from any place in the world to Xanadu. But Kahan wanted you to ride to Boston in it."

"Why?"

"It will be at your disposal when you move here and become a true citizen of the world."

"Oh, I don't know."

"Oh, you will, eventually."

"You seem so sure."

"Kahan has his ways."

After the Christmas visit to Xanadu, Marion came back to his old life only briefly, the emotions changed forever. He worked one more day and quit clean. The hospital administrator confronted him. "But Dr. Marion, you can't quit without proper notice. You have to give us time to find a replacement."

"If I died, if I dropped in my tracks, you would walk over me and not miss a step. A few people with scant schedules would come to the funeral, the surgical schedule would go on while the preacher intoned over my sealed box, and not a one of you would visit the cemetery ever after. I have seen too many doctors drop in their tracks not to know better. I have been to too many of these funerals. So I quit clean today."

And he moved to Vail, where he stepped into a scene of unexpected beauty. The house looked down on Gore Creek and around a curve at a chute of murmuring rapids. The sound of running water rose constantly to his bedroom through the closed windows. Kahan had chosen the house well, supplied it with an enviable generic library, an unmatched pharmacology collection, and a little laboratory and shop for loading the unique guns and for target practice.

But one more thing — the woman, his companion at Xanadu, greeted him at the door when he arrived at Vail. She took charge of his clothes, his cooking, his groceries, his mail, his bookkeeping. She had preceded him from Xanadu and relieved him of all trivia. She bathed him and shaved him, and slept with him. She turned the house into a perfumed oasis, a little piece of Kahan's pleasure dome. And in an exercise room she worked out with him daily before his bath. But she carried the aura of an automaton, silent and efficient.

She gave him keys to the car supplied with the house. In the garage he found a Mercedes 600, a V-12. Its dynamic lines gave it the stance of speeding while standing still. The enormity of the situation then sank in: The circumstances he had fallen into, sooner or later, would require great speed on the road. His mood became somber. But the ensuing weeks had passed quietly, while he skied every day and worked on the drug formulations.

And the woman — he lay beside her, spent after love. But the physical release could not assuage a taunting absence. He longed for family. Her favors were as over-rich as pure sugar, emotionally barren as pornography, vacuous like mindless surrender to lust, but accepted because it brought exhaustion and sleep; he counted her a blessing but not a fulfillment. He tried to break through the barrier, and she answered all attempts at conversation, all of his attempts to reach her, with submissive single words of agreement or complete silence, creating the impression of non-comprehension. So he asked himself, why? Had she been placed there to spy, and like the warrior cultures, to infiltrate and ultimately deliver a death-blow? Or did she actually live far removed from felicitous emotions? The dark eyes, the dark hair, the olive skin were not sparked by animation; he thought *stoical*, not obtunded, but in rigid control of herself. This would not change.

CHAPTER 12

When Eric Stuart returned home at six in the evening, nearly forty hours after leaving for work, new and pleasant aromas filled his house: cleanliness, cooking, and perfume, a new homey ambience. Joan greeted him with two glasses of chilled white wine, and a blue-eyed gaze of adoration. His emotions rushed; he knew the sense of family he had been without so long, but caution kept him from speaking of it yet. If right, it would not only wait but would grow, too.

"Welcome home."

"Thank you. Welcome home has not been said to me in many a year."

"Nor have I had anyone to say it to."

"Well, something new for both of us." He lifted his glass to hers, "To your health."

"And to yours."

After sitting quietly, relaxing, sipping, he said, "You will be relieved to know I had a quiet and very private talk with Marcus Mann today."

"Oh, good. I hope he was relieved."

"Perhaps, but I do not think he entirely believes or trusts me."

"He has to."

"Precisely what I told him."

"He worries me. He is such a good person, so determined to do the right thing."

"I have cautioned him not to be seen talking to me. Someone alert to possibilities has only to pass on my name, then they would know where to look for you."

"I hang in the balance, but I feel secure tonight. Do you want your shower and massage before dinner or afterward?"

Eric hesitated. Mann had passed on some new and disturbing news, but it could wait. He said, "I'm not hungry."

"Good. I'll finish making the salad while you shower."

She went to the kitchen.

Eric lay prone on an exercise platform. Joan approached, placed her hands on her hips a moment, looked down at his lean, muscular back, then reached out and grasped the top band of his shorts with both hands, and said, "Raise up a little." He lifted his hips and she shucked him bare. She slapped him playfully on a buttock and said, "Thanks for the respect."

He turned his head, smiled at her, and said, "You're welcome, and there's lots of it."

"Have you ever had a massage by a woman, Eric?"

"I have never had a massage by anybody, man or woman."

"You're kidding."

"I am not kidding. Why would I need a massage, before tonight, that is?"

"Ha! Why would you need one tonight?"

"I'm overdue."

She laughed. "You're funny."

"You're gorgeous, and precious."

She began on his back.

He said, "Are you sure?"

"Oh Eric, you promised me, and I am so ready. Now I am the one overdue."

He sat up, hung his legs over the table edge, and stood. His rigid penis protruded straight out. She stood before him, stark naked, mesmerized. He stooped, gathered her in his arms, and carried her to the bedroom, and lay upon the bed with her. There, he took a long time, a slow approach, quiet talk, kisses, caresses, and murmurs of adoration, and more talk, and gentleness, a slow touch, no hurry. Honey-toned skin down the bow of concave belly, erect nipples, the alert mischievous eyes intent and riveted, locked on his own gaze, searching — he teased her to a gradual opening like a budding flower responding to sunshine. She relaxed, surrendered, stimulated to a peak of readiness, and he moved carefully, slowly, every motion protracted, sustained. Quiet and receptive, she waited, anticipating. He rested and kissed her lips and nipples, and moved gently, slowly, and stopped to caress and kiss, then moved gently, over and over, until her body coiled upward in a spasm and she rewarded him with a final cry ... "Eric, Oh, God! Eric!"

Then she lay entwined in his arms and they slept briefly. She aroused and ran an idle finger around his lips and onto the tip of his nose, and stuck a finger into his mouth. She said, "It was so wonderful, and didn't hurt like I have been led to believe it would."

"Not at all?"

"Oh yes, but not so bad."

"I tried to be gentle."

She placed both hands on his cheeks and lovingly caressed his face. "You were ever so gentle. Are you hungry now?"

"Ravenous."

"Dinner's done, so let's eat."

He flung back the covers, jumped up naked, then stretched and smiled down at her. He turned his back and bent forward to remove a clean leisure suit from a bureau drawer. She bounded out of bed, jumped on her left foot, and kicked him squarely with her right, a loud smack on the naked buttocks. He jerked up in total surprise. "What the hell?"

"For knowing how to so well, lover." And she grabbed him, wrapped her arms and one leg around him, hugged tightly and said, "God, am I lucky!"

At dinner, she said, "I made stew from a little of everything I could find in the refrigerator and freezer. We need a trip to the grocery store."

He tasted. "Delicious. What's the flavor?"

"Herbs, including the last of your saffron."

"Ahh. I will sleep tonight."

"Do you have to go in so early tomorrow?"

"The same time."

"Then it's your bedtime already."

"No. The grocery first."

"I'll go with you."

"Absolutely not; you might be found by your pursuers. Besides, I do it very quickly."

"Well I'm sorry."

"I would go anyway even if you were not here. This is my shopping night."

"I've made a list of the things you need, just the basics, besides whatever you want."

"Okay, but before leaving there is something I've got to tell you."

"What?"

"Do you know a courier named Williams?"

"Why, yes. Chester Williams."

"Well, the news is not good. Mann told me today. Williams disappeared en route to Memphis with a heart. Memphis never got the heart, and they lost a man, too. The van driver who went to meet Williams at the airport disappeared without a trace. Not a clue has been found."

"Oh, Eric, then Williams is the first person we've lost from our own region, the first to disappear from number eleven of UNOS. The boy was a new recruit, eager, ambitious, naive, gullible, in awe of his job ... not at all equipped for the savage irony of this world."

"Well, now they've closed the circle."

"And no doubt will start another cycle of their evil."

Eric finished his meal and left with the list. When he returned within the hour, the kitchen had been cleaned; he put the groceries away and found her in bed half asleep. She snuggled drowsily to him when he slid under the covers.

CHAPTER 13

Late the next afternoon, just as Eric's team prepared to remove a living heart from a brain-dead patient, Marcus Mann entered the surgical suite, doing courier work to pinch-hit for Joan. Eric went down the hallway to a vacant operating room and Marcus followed. They stood just inside the unlit room and talked. In his concentration, Eric heard but gave no heed to the distant subliminal frying noise of the overhead speakers. An emotion tugged at him. He should be doing, or noticing something, but nothing came to mind when he paused for thought, and he moved on without listening to the little voice of warning.

"Marcus, she is safe, but she worries because she thinks you might try to find her and blow the cover."

"Eric, Dr. Stuart, I have inquired about you, and as a result I trust whatever it is you are doing."

"Well, I hope you asked the right person."

"I think so."

"And not by phone, I hope."

"Only from my home."

Eric blanched and his stomach sank. "Oh God. I would think if someone has tapped your office phone, he has tapped your home phone too."

"I wouldn't think so. Besides, I used the children's phone."

"Well, okay. I've got to go help with this job now. Too bad the heart has to go to Pittsburgh. We could use it here. Three people are waiting for type-A with this particular body build."

"I know, but I can't change the system, and I'm sure it's going to get worse instead of better."

"Why?"

"I think the courts will rule against us, and more organs will be taken out of our area for use in the Richmond area and the Virginia suburbs of Washington."

"The rule is not fair to local people."

"You're damn right it's not. And too often the organs will go to a non-teaching hospital, where the surgeon's ambition and his ego exceed his ability and his experience. But it's the system in this state. The tidewater area is the stepchild of the politicians in control."

"What's to be done?"

"I don't know. I can't defy them alone. Anyway, Smith will be back from a kidney run by the time you get through and I am sending him with the heart. We booked him on a nine p.m. direct flight. Our plane is in Seattle. You will have to hurry if we are going to make the flight."

Eric entered the operating room from the scrub sink as they rolled the brain-dead donor through the doors.

An idle pump technician sauntered to a pay phone in a hallway outside the surgical suite. He dialed a number at LifeChain. Gladys Gleason answered, "Hello."

"Identity here," he said.

"Status here."

"I might have something interesting. We need to meet."

"Tell me."

"Oh, no. We have to negotiate this one."

"Are you off duty?"

"Yes."

"All right. Thirty minutes."

"Same spot."

"The same ... seafood or steak?"

"Seafood."

Fifteen miles away and twenty minutes later they sat in a back booth and ordered beer and steamed shrimp. They ate casually and talked low, their heads together.

"Now tell me."

"First, type A ... medium and muscular," he said.

"Anticipated it."

"Do you know who runs the heart tonight? "

"Not yet."

"I do," he said.

"Oh, who?"

"Smith. And the Legation crowd plays rough. He could get hurt. We don't want any..."

"Stop right there and listen. At twenty-five apiece, don't ask questions," she said.

"Twenty...!"

"Thousand. They need this one and several more desperately."

"Have you heard from Joan Pully?" he asked.

"No. Gone four days now. What's the interesting news?"

"Probably something very hot."

"Do you know where she is?"

"Not for certain, but I know where to look."

"Where?"

"Just a minute now. The rewards for this one are really big, and I want three to one if she is there."

"We have an agreement. We share fifty-fifty."

"Only on passing routine donor information. This one is detective work. If I don't tell, you won't find."

"Seventy-five percent for you and twenty-five for me?"

"Maybe they will pay more if we wait a few days."

"I am not going to start anything of the kind with these people. They will eliminate me, and I think they would eliminate you anyway if they found out," she said.

"You agree to the deal?"

"You don't leave me any choice."

"All right. There is a cardiac fellow named Eric Stuart, a tall, rugged, redheaded guy, smart as hell, really gifted with his hands. Foster Kemp let him do a bypass while he was still an intern eight years ago, by himself. Unheard of ... an intern is just cutting his surgical teeth, so to speak, on tonsils, hernias, appendices, warts and bumps, while undergoing an everlasting humbling from slave labor and scut work. And I've never seen anything like it. The guy even then was better than most seasoned surgeons who completed their training years before. But he has had his nose close to Marcus Mann. The two of them went into a vacant operating room yesterday and talked for fifteen minutes. I hid in the adjacent scrub room, and I could hear just enough to know I was onto something. They did it again today and I managed to switch on the intercom ahead of them and heard the entire conversation."

"What did they say?"

"Plenty. I have already told you about Smith."

"Okay. Now where is Joan Pully?"

"I believe she is holed up in Dr. Stuart's home."

"And where does he live?"

"How would I know? It should be easy enough to find."

"Right. It's Legation's problem, not ours. I've got to get back and notify The Reverend."

They finished their meal and went out into the parking lot. As they prepared to separate, he said, "I don't like Legation. Their gangster tactics could get us into serious trouble."

"Not unless you talk too much," she said.

"I don't talk."

"So be it. Good night."

"Good night."

As Gladys drove toward Norfolk and LifeChain headquarters, she giggled to herself. Stanley Steinfelt had no idea she would make two and a half million with the capture of Joan Pully. She would pay him something to make him think he had received seventy-five percent of a fee she already had negotiated with Legation.

Smith slept most of the way to Pittsburgh. The heart can strapped in the middle seat did not worry him. But he had been cautioned. Chester Williams had disappeared without a trace, and the mystery remained unsolved. And the cycle had started again in Region One with the total disappearance of an ambulance crew carrying a heart in the middle of downtown Boston. But organs had to be delivered. Smith slept with his hand resting on the container. Few people were on the flight, and the ones he saw aroused no suspicion. He felt all right about everything. He thought about his wife and his two little children just before he went to sleep.

He awoke when the wheels bumped the runway. He went through the terminal swinging the bucket by its handle, out to the lobby, and down stairs to the arrival gates. The white van with a Pittsburgh General logo on its side panel stood at the curb. Smith went to the passenger side and got in the front seat. No one spoke and the van left the curb. The driver turned the siren on when they hit the interstate and pushed his speed up to ninety, then a hundred, and they went screaming into Pittsburgh. Smith watched the skyscrapers approaching rapidly in the night. Then they were in the streets, moving toward the riverfront, the van tires screeching, the siren wail diminishing.

The van suddenly cut sharp and dived down a ramp toward a rapidly rising door, and out of sight in dark caverns. The driver and the man riding behind him got out. Smith followed with the cannister in his grip. A man came to each side and escorted him further inside, and a white door closed behind them with a peculiar clank. "Wait here," said the driver as both men went through the next door. It too closed with an odd finality. Smith heard a low-pitched hissing sound, and looked up. Something spewed through the latticework of the exhaust shield in the ceiling. He went to the first door then the second. Both were locked. Banging on the panels brought no response. He felt dizzy, and terrified and short of breath. He inhaled deeply, trying to get air, and lost consciousness in his own terror.

Smith came to, freezing, and a violent pain gripped his right flank. As he opened his eyes he saw trash, a garbage can close to his nose, broken tree limbs, scattered filthy paper, empty tin cans, and broken bottles. He moved and found himself lying on cold wet ground under a dim streetlight, a few feet from the curb. Cars whizzed by in both directions of a throughway. He tried to get up and the pain knocked him back to the ground. He tried several times again and finally got to his knees, reached the metal garbage can, braced himself on its top, and rose to his feet. He felt woozy, nauseated, and watery weak. He bent forward against the can, and knocked the top off. He braced himself on the open rim and rolled it toward the street. Broken glass rattled in its depths. Painfully, slowly, he made the street, and wobbled on the curb. The garbage can slipped out of his hands and rolled onto the pavement, and he fell face first into the dirt beside the curb, an arm and a leg flopping into the gutter. The can continued to roll. Smith heard it rattle into the opposite lane and a tinny boom when a car struck it, the screech of brakes, another hollow rattle as a second car crashed the can, and a third, then the boom of two cars crashing together, and metal crunching as a third one plowed into the wreckage, then the repeated noise of a chain pileup. Traffic stopped in both directions.

When Smith regained consciousness again sirens wailed at the curb, police cars and fire engines and ambulances were arriving, blue and red lights flashed on both sides of the street. Then a policeman bent over him. "Sir, sir, which car were you riding in?"

"I wasn't riding in a car."

"Then how did you get here?"

"The garbage can."

"Another smart assed drunk." And the policeman, with his foot, rocked one of Smith's drawn-up knees.

A violent pain seared through his side and Smith screamed. A crowd began to gather. Another policeman arrived. Smith said, lifting a beseeching hand, "Please help me officer, help me, please. Somebody has done something terrible to me and dumped me here in the trash. My side, my right side has had something awful done to it."

A woman stepped forward, bent over and lifted Smith's jacket, then his shirttail. She screamed, dropped the clothes, and backed up looking at the blood dripping from her hand. Then she said to the first officer, "You stupid bastards are certainly a bunch of heroes. I saw you kick this man who was begging for help, you dumb son-of-a-bitch," and she drew her purse back by the strap and hit him in the face.

He stepped toward her as the second policeman bent over and opened Smith's clothes. He straightened up, looking at his bloody hand, shaking it. "My God. Something has ripped a huge gash in this guy and his gut sac is hanging out. He's bleeding badly. Get the rescue squad over here." The first officer stopped in his tracks and the crowd drew closer, threatening. Smith passed out again.

When he came to, he felt the warmth of indoors. His eyes traveled up to the flourescent lights overhead, then to the bag of blood hanging on a pole above the table, and traced a red tube down to a vein in his outstretched and bound arm. Blood! *My God, they are giving me blood.* A doctor appeared, a young friendly one. "Mr. Smith, do you remember what happened to you?"

"It's coming back, all kind of hazy, but I believe somebody kidnaped me. I was on my way to Pittsburgh General with a heart to be transplanted tonight or last night, whenever it was. The van went underground somewhere near the hospital and I was gassed in a locked room. Then I woke up freezing on a pile of trash with this horrible pain in my side. I was trying to get help in the street when the garbage can I was leaning on slipped out of my hands and got away."

"Boy, you got attention all right. The cops are still laughing about the pile-up the garbage can caused."

"Doctor, what's wrong with me?"

"Well, the good news first. You will be okay. You are alive, not crippled, your brain and spinal cord are not damaged."

"Okay, okay, you're building up to something. Now what's the bad news?"

"The bad news is not so bad, everything considered. They took just one of your kidneys."

"I never heard of such a thing, have you?"

"Yes, I'm afraid we have. But sometimes they take both, and they have let more than one bleed to death. It's becoming more and more common."

"Why, the dirty devils!"

"I certainly agree. Now to more immediate things — we have to take you to the operating room, clean the depths of the wound they made, and sew you up. We will need to use a general anesthetic. Who shall we call for permission."?

"I give you permission myself. Don't call my wife. Call my boss, Marcus Mann, President of LifeChain. He will break the news gently to my wife. She will panic if you phone. His number is in my wallet."

"Are you a LifeChain courier?"

"Yes, I was delivering a heart."

"Well, we didn't understand at first, in all of the excitement … Jesus, what a crime. Done to the people who do the most to try to help others. We will get you straightened out pronto, my friend."

———

Smith awakened after daylight to find Marcus Mann leaning on a side rail of his bed.

"Hello, Tom."

"Hi, Marcus."

"How do you feel?"

He moved about. "Ohhh, sore as hell."

"I guess so, but you are going to be all right."

"I suppose, if I can live with one kidney."

"You can without question."

"What happened to the heart? Have you heard?"

"Well, it never got to Pittsburgh General. We think it went to Mexico."

"Who was in the Pittsburgh van?"

"We don't know. The real driver was waylaid at gunpoint while stopped at a intersection, and left standing in the cold."

"I'm sorry I lost the heart."

"Not to worry. We are just so relieved. Do you want to go home? Every doctor in town is eager to help take care of you."

"Oh Lord, yes, and I don't ever want to leave it again."

"We have the jet here, and permission to move you if you want."

"Man, let's go."

After Gladys notified The Reverend about Joan's hiding place, she found Ralph Green at home asleep at three in the afternoon. He stayed up almost all night every night stalking donors and other seductions in bars and nightclubs. "We have news," she said.

"Oh, so soon."

"Just now."

"Usable, I hope."

"Depends entirely, I suspect, upon your ingenuity."

"Try me."

"She is being hidden by a young heart surgeon in his home near the hospital."

"The address?"

"I don't know exactly, but it should be easy to find. His name is Eric Stuart."

"I'll find him... and, oh yes, I was going to call you ... I need a Type-A tall, two-hundred pounds or thereabouts."

"Give me ten minutes on the computer and I'll call you."

"I'll be right here."

Six minutes later she phoned with a name, Frank Tibbins, and his address.

"Great," he said.

"Don't you need more?"

"What do you mean?"

"Like his driver's license, his social security number, his job, his age."

"You have the information?"

"Oh, yes."

"How?"

"I have my ways. Here ...let's see ... Oh, yes. He's a plumber, owns his own business, listed in the yellow pages, age thirty-two"

"Thanks. You've saved me a lot of trouble."

"Ten percent, and I know what The Reverend pays."

"Ten percent of my share?"

"Right. And a visit from you."

"Of course."

"When?"

"At payoff time."

Ralph turned to plumbers in the yellow pages. This one would be too easy. Tibbins himself answered the phone in the late afternoon. Mr. Green felt so distressed and exasperated with his overflowing commode, the third time and two unsuccessful plumbers already, and something must be done about it right away. And he had heard so much about Tibbins Plumbing. He wanted Tibbins himself, regardless of cost. The overflow had created such a mess. Could he come over right away? There would be a hundred dollar tip in cash regardless of the bill. Tibbins on his way home would stop by. It would take only a minute or two for such a simple problem. But he might have to use a rooter. Great! Mr. Green expressed his gratitude. He would have a drink waiting. Does Tibbins like scotch or bourbon? Tibbins didn't care much for either, but bourbon would be nice.

Ralph crammed an old towel down the commode, flushed it until water ran over onto the floor, then removed the towel and threw it in the washing machine. He went to his bar and prepared bourbon mixed with a double dose of drugs he knew and used often. The concoction worked every time. And while waiting he found Eric Stuart's address in the cross-reference directory.

Tibbins, hot and tired and impatient, grudgingly accepted the proffered cold glass, drank it dry in one gulp, and went to work on the commode. The rooter had progressed three feet down the drain when Tibbins slumped forward, bruising his nose on the wet tile floor, and lay quite still. Ten minutes later, a van backed into Ralph Green's garage and the door came down. Two men ascended to the living quarters and carried a man-sized form in a giant green leaf bag down the stairs, placed it in the van, and drove away. The third man took the plumber's keys and drove the Tibbins Plumbing van to a garage. Ralph never had to worry about evidence. All vehicles belonging to donors were disassembled within fifteen minutes of arrival in the spare parts business operated by hidden ownership within The Reverend's empire. All paint, all signs, all serial numbers were burned or brazed off immediately. Ralph did not always know the destiny of the organs his endeavors produced, but this one he knew to be important. The heart, lungs, liver, pancreas, and the intestinal tract were being flown to Mexico City by private plane. Somebody with big money lay dying for the need of a heart. The Reverend would get a million dollars, Ralph half of it, and ten percent of his half to Gladys, fifty thousand. By getting her down from twenty five percent, he had saved himself seventy-five thousand. Not bad. He could roll in the hay with worse than Gladys for seventy-five thousand.

Ralph drove to Eric's house. He walked around the sides and back, trying to peek through windows, but only the nightlights faintly glowed behind the closed blinds, with no sign of life. Joan Pully. The name still seemed somehow familiar. On a hunch, he went to the Athletic Club and pulled up the roster of all people enrolled in his training program. And there he found her picture. Ahhh yes, he did know her — quite a good karate student, in fact competent to the point of being dangerous. Interesting, and exciting too ... this one he could court. She stirred up none of the queasiness he felt in the presence of most women. But it would take time, and perhaps he would begin with her next lesson.

CHAPTER 14

After dinner, Joan said, "Eric, I have something disturbing to tell you."

"I'm a big boy."

"I know, but I still hate to bring it up."

"What?"

"Your house is under surveillance."

"By whom?"

"The men in the black BMW."

"Are you sure?"

"Absolutely."

"What were they doing?"

"Parked at the curb across the street, and looking straight ahead, then cruising slowly up and down the street, the well-dressed men in gray serge, like the one who had his hands on me. Then they got out and walked by on the sidewalk."

"Have they seen you?"

"No. I have stayed hidden. I just peeked out through one slat of the Venetian blinds. But Eric, I wonder how they know to look at this house."

"There can be only one explanation. We have been betrayed, and the betrayal had to occur in the operating rooms at Sentara."

"How?"

"Somehow, someone has overheard me talking to Marcus Mann."

"Oh God."

"Well, stay hidden and don't answer the phone."

"Do you think the line has been tapped?"

"Very likely, if all their other activities are as serious as they seem to be. Have you used the phone at all?"

"Not once."

"Good. Then they are not sure you are here. Do you want to go to the police?"

"No. They would have to come live with me, or put me in jail for protection."

"Perhaps I should take you to your father's place."

"Another form of prison, and he would be beside himself with anger. I would go to him only as a last resort."

She slept the night entwined in Eric's arms again, and aroused only when he left the next morning shortly after four a.m. She chained the door as he went out and locked the deadbolt, then checked the latches on the rear door and went back to bed.

During breakfast the doorbell rang. She tiptoed to the door and looked through the peep glass. Her heart almost stopped. Three men dressed in gray serge stood at the entranceway. One pressed the doorbell button; the others stood back against the front wall so they would not be seen at once by anyone opening the door. They looked distorted and bottle shaped through the lens. The blurred and delicate greens of June leaves colored the landscape across the street.

She backed away from the door and stood against the wall. The ringing persisted for ten minutes. Then after a moment of silence, a secretive scraping sound started and the end of a card appeared and traveled along the crack between the door and the facing. It struck the deadbolt then the chain, and withdrew. She peeked through the lens again. The men descended the front steps and went to the BMW across the street.

She checked the rear door latches, then sat at the breakfast bar sipping coffee, and ate from a bowl of fresh fruit. She thought of calling the hospital and having Eric paged, but decided against it; a tapped line would give away her actual presence, and she thought Eric had too many responsibilities to be fighting this battle. Anyway, how well could he hold his own in a fight with thugs, and what would be his ability in combat? He might get hurt or killed. She should have asked him. She sipped her coffee and began planning her own defense.

Near noon, Joan, curious about the street beyond the front door, went to a blind and peered out. She gasped as she recognized the man sitting in a black coupe at the opposite curb, the brutal trainer who had put her through the ropes of Karate three times a week at the Athletic Club, Ralph Green. He watched the house while she watched him. He waited a few minutes, then got out, turned to lift something off the opposite front seat, and crossed the street. He mounted the steps to Eric's front door, and rang the bell. A bouquet lay across the crook of his left arm, a large bundle of red roses half hidden in gossamer green ferns. The bell responded in prolonged and uproarious clamor. Ralph finally gave up and retreated, leaving the roses against the door. Ralph, with his pugnacious visage, his bare-skin head, his powerful body build, and the perversity oozing from his every pore, had always aroused her caution and her defenses. Could he be after her, too? And if so, he would be especially difficult to deal with.

Joe said, "We gonna' ditch this BMW tonight and use the old van with the plumber's sign on it."

"Why?" asked Barney.

"Cause we been seen in the car too much. And we're going to change clothes, to look like plumbers."

"Geez, I hate the damned old trap, but I'll sure be glad to get out of these stiff duds. I don't like the color gray anyhow, and this damned collar has about sawed off my neck. Anyway, how the hell you expect us to get into Stuart's garage?"

"With a remote for opening any garage door."

"I ain't crazy about this, and a lot of other things going on, like where is Willie?" said Barney.

"Gone out of town. The Reverend sent him to pick up a target in Atlanta."

"Yeah, well, Roger ain't come back yet, either, after three months."

"You can ask. I won't."

"No. I ain't askin' nobody nothin'. So let's take this dame one way or another."

"You know the instructions, take your time, be careful, don't start no fuss, draw no attention, but take 'em, except this one has to be alive and well."

"And little Ned?"

"Hurt. He ain't come back to work yet."

"Where is he?"

"Do you know where he is?"

"No, or I wouldn' of been askin'."

"Then I don't either."

"So just the two of us are left," said Barney.

"Yeah, yeah. But she's only a skinny woman. We can handle her. It's gonna' be an easy ten million."

"Well, I ain't forgot what she done to Little Ned."

"Little Ned lost his cool and chased her."

"We ain't gonna' lose our cool?"

"No, we're going to fix her plumbing, if she's there. Personally, I don't think anybody's in the house after the Doc leaves every other morning. We ain't heard a sound, and no lights have been turned on at night when he ain't there, just the old night light burning all the time anyway."

"I ain't lookin' forward to going into a dark house, just the two of us."

"Look, Barney, when the door opens and his car ain't there, in you go. Then just stay in the van and be ready to go when I get her. Understand? "

"Yeah, okay, but I don't like it none. What are we going to do with her if we catch her?"

"Gladys will tell us where to take her and how to collect the ten million dollars, then we skip the country."

"But Smets knows we're goin' to the Doc's house and what for."

"I know, but we ain't goin' back to headquarters after we

take her," said Joe.

"Whooah, I don't know as I like this, not one bit."

"You are in it already, so just shut up."

Joan guessed they would not return in the daytime, nor try the front door again. So they somehow would have to get to the back door into the kitchen inside the house at the head of stairs leading up from the garage. Waiting in the falling dusk, she made her decisions and wrote a note for Eric to find later.

Every drop of cooking oil in the house simmered in water just below the boiling point in a large stew pot on the stove, a three-gallon mixture altogether. Several short, coiled segments of rope lay on the kitchen counter beside two cans of lighter fluid from the medicine cabinet, Eric's brand of cleaning fluid she guessed. The back door to the kitchen stood open. As darkness gathered, the silence on the street deepened.

Barney stick shifted the old van and cruised the streets slowly. He grumbled, "Ain't nobody ever goin' to believe we're plumbers, poking along like this. They all drive like maniacs hurrying to get to another rip off."

"Well, it's nearly dark enough already," said Joe.

"We done been by twice and there ain't no sign of life in there. I'm spooked, I'm tellin' ya. I think we ought to call this whole thing off."

"Ten million dollars says take her, so we take her."

"No takin', see, no takin'. You talk about seduction and you talk about takin'. Big difference."

"Like I keep tellin' ya', Barney, we gonna ... I'm gonna' fix her plumbin. You stay under the wheel, ready to go."

"What da' ya' mean, ready to go? I can't keep the fuckin' engine running with the garage door closed. We'd all die of exhaust."

"Don't keep the engine running. Just be ready to start it

fast, and open the door with the remote."

Joan sat at the window in the dusk, and watched the street through the parted blind. The van had cruised by twice already. On the third pass it turned into Eric's driveway, and she thought for a minute the driver intended to turn around and go the other direction. Then the grinding noise started and the opening garage door shook the floor. The van eased forward.

She went to the kitchen, pocketed a can of lighter fluid, and carried the boiling pot from the stove to the balcony rail above the garage. The automatic light on the electric door lifter came on. The van eased in, the motor shut off, and the garage door began to descend. The panel door on the passenger side of the van slid open, and a short fat man with bushy black hair took a toolbox out, sidled behind the rear bumper, and turned toward the stairs. He stopped at the driver's door, directly beneath her. She recognized the faces, sans the gray serge. The driver whispered, "I tell ya there ain't nobody here."

As though this stimulated the first man to look, he turned his head and peered up. Joan dumped the fluid. It hit him on the face and neck, and she dropped the pot on his head. A large splash flew through the van window into the driver's face. She whirled back into the kitchen and threw the main power switch. The door lifter light and the nightlights went out and the house became completely dark. The van motor started, its lights came on, but the garage door would not open, and the driver yelled, "Shit! Oh, shit! Oh, shit! God dammit, shit! I'm blind! I can't see nothin'." He backed the van into the door, and revved up the motor. The wheels spun, sending up clouds of dust and black smoke, but the door held.

She went down the steps, opened the driver's door, and grabbed him by the collar. Almost blind, he groped wildly. Avoiding his flailing arms, she pulled him out of the van, swung his body forward, and kneed him in the crotch. He doubled over; she grabbed an arm, twisted it behind his back, and brought the wrist almost up to the shoulder, yanking upward. With the other hand she reached into the van, cut off the motor, and removed the keys. The driver screamed with this new pain, and she pushed him up the stairs, yanking the arm upward on each step. He went desperately, screaming, holding his crotch with his other hand. She pushed him through the door and threw the main switch, and the door motor light and the night lights returned to life. "You want a karate chop like I gave your buddy the other day?"

"No ma'am!" He vomited and collapsed on the kitchen floor. She kept his arm up almost to the fracture point, and doused his face with lighter fluid. While he coughed and gasped, she reached the rope on the kitchen counter, found his other arm, and bound his wrists behind his back. On his belly, with his arms bound behind, he reminded her of a trussed-up hog. She bound his ankles. Then she said, "Now lets talk."

"I don't know nothin' about nothin' ... I just do the errands."

She went behind the kitchen counter and returned with a butcher knife. She stooped and put the blade flat against his nose. "Feel the butcher knife? Now what do you want? You can talk and get off in good health or I can give you the neck chop then cut off your balls. Which do you want?"

"Talk!" he said.

"Well, talk and talk fast. What's your name and who do you work for?"

"Barney, I'm Barney and we work for Legation, but I ain't supposed to know it."

"Who runs Legation?"

"The Boss."

She slapped the side of the butcher knife blade against the floor and said, "Don't waste any more of my time."

"They say his name is The Reverend, but I ain't ever seen him."

"And what do you do for him?"

"We're supposed to get whoever he sends us for, with gentle sweet ways, no rough stuff, no blood, no evidence."

"How do you get your information from LifeChain?"

"LifeChain. Oh, dat place. Oh, uh, from Willy's girlfriend."

"And what is her name?"

"Gladys something. Oh yeah, Gleason. Looks like a rat woman."

"And where is Willy now?"

"We hear the boss sent him to Atlanta to get somebody."

"And who is the man down stairs?"

"Joe."

"Who was after me in the grocery store?"

"Little Ned, and he ain't recovered yet."

"And who was the smooth talking character who called himself Dr. Bendon?"

"Smooth talking?"

"On the flight with me to Chicago."

"Oh, dat guy. A lawyer named Wilson."

"Where is he now?"

"Honest, I don't know. The boss uses him and his two cronies to smooth talk women mostly."

"Where are your headquarters?"

"I don't know. We just go to an old warehouse on the waterfront. It's a funeral home and a blood bank up front."

"Funeral home! What else goes on in there?"

"Plenty."

"I'll bet. Now, one more question … who leaks information from Sentara operating rooms to Gladys Gleason?"

"I don't know his name, but he's dat little mean lookin' guy, gettin' kind'a old now."

She went down the steps into the garage. Joe had managed to get to his feet. He groped blindly about, flinging his arms wildly, shouting, "I'm blind, I can't see ... my face, Oh, my God, my face!" and he lunged, stepped in the puddle of fluid, and his feet slipped. He fell on his back. He flipped over and crawled about blindly, smearing oil into the concrete floor. He finally got to his feet again, and began to strike out. His fist hit the side of the van and he yelled with a new pain. Joan stepped over the wet area, ducked below the flailing arms and chopped him on the back of the neck with her hand. He crumbled. She grasped his collar, dragged him beneath the rear bumper to the other side of the van and slid him, like a sack of potatoes, through the open side door.

She ascended the stairs, brought the lighter fluid near Barney's nose again, and sat on the floor two feet away. "Now we are going to talk again, Barney, otherwise more of this, and I will light a match to it this time."

"Oh, no ma'am, I'll tell you anything I know."

"Why were you chasing me?"

"To get the ten million dollars."

"What ten million dollars?"

"The great Moha offered it."

"For what?"

"A donor for his wife, age twenty-three, tall and healthy, type-B, and a virgin. She needs a new heart."

"How do you know this?"

"Gladys told Willie."

"How did she know?"

"Moha called The Reverend in his looking. The Reverend can get a organ for anybody anytime. And The Reverend called LifeChain and Gladys took the call, then she sold your qualities to him. She thought you would be the perfect donor."

"And Moha wanted me kidnaped and delivered to him alive and whole."

"No ma'am ... He wanted a brain-dead patient, cause of a accident or stroke, flown to him on one of them breathing machines. He ain't said nothin' about hurting nobody. But The Reverend was going to accommodate him and make you brain-dead before delivery."

"And what were you and Joe up to?"

"Smets sent us."

"Who is Smets?"

"The Reverend's top dog."

"And you were going to take me to him?"

"We were going to bypass him and collect the money ourselves."

"And who is Moha?"

"Some super rich Saudi."

"And where would the heart be used?"

"At Kahan's."

"And who is Kahan?"

"Another rich giant running a hospital in Africa."

Joan grasped Barney's ankle rope, and pulled him feet first down the stairs. He thumped from step to step, yelling. She hauled him into the van next to Joe, and shut the door. A touch on the wall switch and the garage door opened. She pulled the shift lever to neutral and placed the keys on the seat. She got a two-by-four out of a corner, and using it as a pry-pole under the front bumper, started the van rolling backward. She hit the wall switch again as the van cleared the house. The door closed. The van rolled backward across the street and came to rest with its rear wheels against the opposite curb.

Then she went upstairs, washed her hands, finished the note to Eric, and stuffed her belongings in her pants and jacket pockets.

She crawled through the back window of the storage room. Out in the woods on foot she moved behind shrubs and brick walls to the next street and stopped a taxi. At an electronics store, while the cab waited, she purchased a listening device resembling a stethoscope. This instrument, placed on a phone body would transmit sound with the receiver in place. She went to LifeChain offices.

Ralph Green arrived for another look and found the van

crosswise of the street. He approached on foot and peered in. God, she had made a mess of these two klutzes. But then he himself had taught her perhaps too well. In karate still her master, he would take her sooner or later, but by persuasion if possible. Ralph went home thinking about the tall thin body of the elegant Joan Pully, feeling desire, an emotion women almost never aroused in him.

Smets, with several employees at Legation headquarters listened to the bugs transmit from the van. His face flushed and he sputtered with anger. "Listen to those two toads. Barney, stupid bloke, dragging his heels — this is his last job." Then Smets grew quiet, his jaws clenched, his face ashen as they listened. Joe's screaming, and Barney's surprised gasp brought Smets into action. He leapt up, and yelled, "Tommy, get over to Doc Stuart's house quick and see what the hell is happening. Somebody is in plenty of trouble. Get to em' and get em' out of there and back here before the police arrive. That slob Barney will sing like a bird if they catch him."

———

Smets seldom came down to the room with the wooden table unless trouble brewed. He came this time fed up with treachery and incompetence, and he took action. Under his direction, Willie, through Chiron, already had joined the chimerical world where he now lived as parts of several other people. Little Ned had followed him the same day. In his present anger he sent Barney and Joe to the wooden table. Chiron spent not more than five minutes on each man, humming while Smets stood by.

The Reverend Lotte called a meeting, and raged at Smets. "Where the hell is Joan Pully?"

"Disappeared from Dr. Stuart's house."

"Get her!" he yelled, "and bring her to me."

"Dead or alive?"

"Alive, of course. Dead she is worth chicken feed. Alive, ten million dollars."

"Dead would be easy. Alive has been impossible."

"Do it anyway."

"What about Ralph Green? Can't he take her?"

"She's too smart to fall for his blarney. Anyway, I don't trust him. He might try to collect the ten million himself. Smets, don't let Green in on this."

CHAPTER 15

While waiting in mid-June for his first target, Dr. John Marion wrote drug directions for SamuelS and Xanadu, and for use aboard the ABATE. He summoned Ivan to help and to be his guest at Vail. Neither man had seen the ship, and neither intended to, ever. The ABATE'S captain checked into The Lodge At Vail and appeared at Marion's house each morning for a meeting, beginning before breakfast and continuing with little interruption into the night. Ivan Prescott set the protocols for tissue retrieval. The handling of live organs would be in the hands of organ technicians.

The captain presented plans of the ABATE'S structure, along with pictures, and a thorough description of the vessel's accommodations and its daily operations. The top deck and the freight hold carry loaded containers destined for various ports. The ship makes runs from Norfolk and New York through the waters along the west and east coasts of Africa, the east coast of India, Saudi Arabia, the Suez Canal, and the Mediterranean Sea. It loads and unloads containers at numerous ports and takes on passengers from countries of Africa, the Middle East, and India. All will walk up the gangplank willingly, even happily. Others will board in New York and Norfolk. Passengers from more distant lands will agreeably take a plane ride to Nairobi, Johannesburg, Harare, Addis Ababa, San'a, or another of the surrounding cities and islands, then be lifted by helicopter to the big landing pad on the ABATE's foredeck. Each person will be contented or submissive under the influence of Dr. Marion's drugs, some even excited by the travel. Passenger quarters on the ABATE are elegant.

Once established in routine, the Captain explained, the ship will stay in international waters most of the time. The lower hold beneath the bridge and three decks down from the passenger quarters, contains medical facilities for care of the passengers and the crew, and laboratories equipped to study each passenger for transmissible diseases, to perform blood typing and cross matching, and to evaluate their useable organs.

Two surgical technicians remove the donor organs. They know the technical aspects and the anatomy the way a farmer knows his fields and the surrounding landscape, but they could not describe the procedures in writing. Each has lost unjustly a relative or someone very close. The loss has changed his life permanently and brought grief crying out for retribution. Each has been rewarded with justice done to the offender in the very room where they work. The same is true of every employee in the medical quarters of the ship, and the Captain himself who still grieves for his murdered baby daughter, though the rapist's home-coming from prison got a reception the captain had awaited fifteen years, reaching its culmination in the ABATE operating rooms.

The captain outlined his operational plans. The ship, in the waters off the east coast of mid-Africa, will continue to take hearts on demand, as well as other organs, for the Xanadu operating rooms, to be delivered by helicopter. The abundant bank tissue will go out on second flights. Marion and Prescott confined their instructions to improving the operating room equipment and the refrigeration. The handling of donors, of tissue, of live organs, the delivery systems, and the use of drugs would have to be in the hands of trained people who would be sent aboard. Kahan would have to recruit them for the training.

All of this accomplished, the ABATE's captain, with documents in hand, went to his ship. Ivan lingered another day before returning to Norfolk, so they had time for talk. Ivan said, "John, tell me about the court of appeals."

"You are concerned about justice?"

"Always. Too often, the wrong person has been put to death, even in the most ponderous of judicial systems."

"Confession. Regardless of the evidence, nobody can be

absolutely sure until the culprit admits his guilt. The drugs produce an exalted state of mind without restraints or caution, and the subject tells everything, with all the details."

"How and when?"

"Judge Taylor's court first passes sentence on the basis of evidence gathered by SamuelS. Then, once the person has been taken under the influence of drugs in his state of permissiveness, we offer him a sort of communion of which he partakes willingly. Along with the little wafers of peyotl, as in the pagan ceremony so resembling the Eucharist with its own wafer symbolizing the beating heart, we substitute for the usual wine a red liquid of ayahuasca or caapi, known to the Indians of Brazil, Colombia, and Ecuador as *vine of the soul.* Aldous Huxley described the effects of pure mescaline, one of the components of peyotl, as *the miracle, moment by moment, of naked existence ... a sacramental vision of reality.* Adding the caapi in small amounts proved, indeed, to be a stroke of luck. It pushes the subject into baring his soul, and he spills his guilt to the gods in an hallucinatory state of divination, then collapses into calm exhaustion."

"You have believable controls?"

"Tested on many volunteers. The controls were all guilty of many foibles, which they had forgotten, and admitted when they later heard their own recorded confessions, but none were guilty of any truly damaging antisocial behavior."

"Do you administer these drugs yourself?"

"Oh no. I never touch a donor."

"Who does it, if I may ask?"

"Kahan has a shaman."

"A shaman!"

"Yes, a man from the bush."

"Is the shaman's the final test?"

"No. At the last moment a technician injects into each potential donor the isolated chemicals, the psychotropic alkaloids, from both peyotl and caapi. The silent operating room listens to the confession again. If the results match the first test, then the operation is carried out."

After a moment of reflection, Ivan said, "We moderns lose our perspective, if we ever acquired a real one. In light of the past, this is the most insignificant of departures from an arid ecclesiastical morality."

"To what are you referring?"

"History of mankind ... its realities."

"Specifically."

"For instance, Charlemagne beheaded forty-five hundred Saxon rebels in one morning for refusing Christian baptism."

"Your point?"

"Millions upon millions of people have died uselessly and vainly in the name of beliefs, one kind or another. True freedom has never been a reality anywhere," said Ivan.

"The truth is amazing. And I suppose this is a justice?"

"More like compromise, the soul of diplomacy, one of the stronger foundations of civilization. At the moment, in regard to this very minor harvest, this weeding out of undesirables, we must adopt a sensible viewpoint. Compare it to the grim toll of wars and persecutions and crime. If we do not support the endeavors of these men who strive for perfection, then lesser men will fill the void and flourish in murderous mediocrity and flagrant charlatanism," said Ivan.

"But something is missing. Surely the prodigious Kahan has a greater reserve."

"Ahh yes, Dr. Marion, very astute. Indeed. Kahan thinks the world is just entering an era of global disorder not to end until the human race awakens to reason, if it ever does. So Kahan intends to make the most of it by retrieving spare parts to extend the lives of those not involved in the conflict. And for this reason he moved quickly. Now, Xanadu hospital receives donors from areas of killing the world over, some thirty to forty wars currently raging around the globe.

"But most of the hearts and organs come from the nations

of Africa, and the neighboring countries. Constant fighting between the tribes and small nations, and the civil wars creates a steady supply of gunshot wounds of the head. Soldiers, mercenaries, and others are paid to bring victims to relay stations. First-aid squads then relay them to Xanadu.

"And now the victims of terrorists and the retaliation against terrorists add to the abundance."

"So others may live better lives, the soul of sacrifice."

"Yes."

Later in the afternoon, Marion said goodbye to Prescott. Within a few hours, a call came from Kahan. Would Marion come to Xanadu at once to begin the training of Timothy, the marksman? Of course. Ruth drove him to Eagle-Vail airport the next morning for the first leg of his flight to Africa.

Timothy, a slight and quick little man, could keep a tin can rolling in the air until he emptied a .45 revolver, drawn from its holster after the target had been launched. Marion taught him, with charts and models, the anatomical targets necessary for special results. In the laboratory, Tim used the fountain pen, the ski pole, the walking stick, and the other enclosures to shoot rabbits, squirrels, sheep, and calves. None were carried down to death. In place of humans they used a cadaver.

Within five days Marion knew Timothy had mastered the various anatomical approaches they would use. Kahan listened as Marion reported Tim's progress and expressed his gratitude. Then he said, "Before you leave I must mention two grave problems." Then he talked about the betrayal of Joan Pully by a spy in LifeChain, and about the war on UNOS. The next day, Marion returned to Vail.

CHAPTER 16

In the early predawn hour, Dr. Marion lay awake listening to the musical babble of Gore Creek beneath his bedroom window. A gentle knock sounded at the door and Ruth entered with a fax message: *write the trucker.* Marion arose, showered, and dressed. A few minutes later the phone rang with the cryptic first call: *The eagle will receive a bird at dawn.* Ruth drove him to the Eagle-Vail airport in the early morning darkness.

At the small airport in Jonestown, Marion deplaned and transferred to an automobile on the tarmac. They drove to Interstate 64, and headed east. Marion sat on the back seat with a SamuelS man who said nothing until the roar of an approaching truck filled the silence, speeding in the slow lane, overtaking them, bearing down almost on their rear bumper. Then the man said, "Don't look back."

The truck veered sharply to the left, partially in both lanes. The enormous silver cab roared past, spouting two coiling stacks of black smoke from its upright diesel exhausts. It whipped back into the slow lane, throwing a cloud of rocks and grit. The violent winds of the speeding truck rocked their car. Marion's driver flicked a dashboard switch and said across to the back seat, "Ninety-two."

His back seat companion said to Marion, "Buck Chambers," pointing toward the disappearing truck. Marion's driver kept in sight of it, mile after mile. They reached hill country, and the truck went down grades in excess of one hundred miles an hour in short bursts of uncontrolled momentum and slowed uphill. But the truck stayed in the fast lane. Blocked automobile traffic piled up for miles behind. Downhill the truck outran traffic and soon overtook a station wagon in the fast lane passing a slower car. The truck showered down on the smaller vehicle, driven by a harassed woman and occupied by too many children, three on a seat facing the rear, their knees against the back door. As the front bumper of the roaring truck came up to the rear bumper of the wagon, the driver leaned on the horn, blasting the countryside with a foghorn bleat. The woman jumped and lost control. The station wagon veered to the left, the front wheel hit the gravel shoulder and then the grass, and the vehicle went off the shallow embankment and out into the weedy strip between lanes, bouncing and careening in a cloud of flying dust and debris. It veered and lurched side to side, skidded sideways, teetered up on two wheels, righted itself, fell back on all wheels and came to a halt after skidding around a hundred and eighty degrees in a cloud of drifting dust. The truck sped on. Marion's driver slowed, the man on the back seat said not to stop.

Marion got to his knees on the back seat, and watched the careening wagon receding in the distance. When it stopped without overturning, he sat down, and the man said to the driver, "Get out of here, keep the truck in sight." And to Marion, "Don't take chances."

"The son of a bitch ... God what I wouldn't like to do to him."

"We have had him in sight now for days. He does this all the way to the end of his cross-country run."

They moved along at the pace set by the truck. The countryside opened up, the truck gathered speed on the straightaway. A red Porsche zipped out of the lineup into the slow lane, accelerating to get around. The truck whipped sharply and cut him off. The Porsche braked frantically, dipping on its nose, leaving four sharp black rows of tire marks on the pavement.

Marion said, "Damn!"

The frying two-way radio came to life with a nasty cackle and two truckers began an exchange: "Hot damn ... Got me one poke ass and one smart ass."

"Hayeeee, good buddy ... Smoky's two miles ahead past

exit sign 179. He's giving a little old man a ticket for going 66 miles an hour, one over the limit."

"Busy brave man ... a real hero."

"Protector of the public."

"Where you headin'?"

"Norfolk."

"Unloadin' and moving out?"

"Naw man. I'm takin' me a little vacation. Flyin' out to Mexico City for a week."

"Mexico City! What's there?"

"At's whir Mable wants it."

"Who's Mable?"

"Oh man, what a Momma! Met her last week in L.A."

"How? At a bar?"

"Naw man, like all the rest of 'em ... she's heard about me and come lookin'."

"Ahh, what's yo ole lady thinka that?"

"What she don't know ain't gonna kill 'er."

"Flyin' together?"

"Meetin' me there."

"Be careful."

"Ten forty, good buddy, but right now I gotta scare me tha crap outta another poke ass in the fast lane."

Marion and his companions watched again as the truck lunged at a small sedan working its way past a slower car. But this one did not panic. The driver ignored the truck, and the trucker had to hit the brakes, and he rode his horn again, blaring noise loud as a ship. The little car slowed down, its driver aroused to stubbornness and defiance. The truck whipped into the slow lane to pass, and crowded a line of cars; the drivers had to brake hard to avoid collisions.

Marion said, "Is he lying about the woman?"

His companion gave him a meaningful look and said, carefully, his voice modulated so the driver could not hear, "The boss knows what he is doing."

This information gave Marion new insight into the extent of Kahan's operation. He said, "How much longer does this go on?"

"As long as he is on the road and no cops are in sight."

"How far to Norfolk?"

"Two hundred miles, but he will stop at a rest station fifty miles from here and spend a while in the men's room."

"How do you know?"

"He always does. He never stops anywhere he has not stopped before, and he has been on the road since breakfast. He has an amazing bladder capacity. A man of habits, all bad."

"Plans?"

"I take it you have decided to do this one?"

"I can't wait."

"Good. At the truck yard in Virginia Beach, he will shower and dress in the trucker's quarters, then take a taxi to the airport at seven-thirty for a ten o'clock Delta flight with connections in Dallas. After checking his luggage he will go to the restaurant for a big meal. As Chambers finishes eating, Tim will tranquilize him so he will follow us obediently."

"Then?"

"Would you like to hear Chamber's confession?"

"Indeed."

At the airport, Marion and his backseat companion took a table near the rear of the restaurant by a window looking out toward the sunset. An unidentified man and Tim joined them.

At seven o'clock Buck Chambers arrived freshly shaven and resplendent in a white silk cowboy outfit, his hair wet and slicked up into a pompadour. His gut hung over a wide leather belt with a round silver buckle the size of a saucer. The waitress seated him at a round table alone in the middle of the dining area. He called her honey, and baby, and ordered a double martini, and ravenously and rudely ate a large bloody-rare sirloin steak. He bragged about his three days and two nights on the road without sleep while he drove all the way cross-country, his use of amphetamines to stay awake, and his trip to Mexico. "Baby, am ah gonna sleep on the plane ... Always go first class ... Ahm a big man, need room to stretch out."

"Coffee, and dessert sir?" said the waitress.

"Man yeah. Honey, gimmy thuh biggest vanilla ice cream sundae yew can whip up and a cup of yo best black coffee."

Tim weaved among the tables, the pen concealed in his right palm, with the writing end pointed outward. His hand, in the normal motions of walking, swung near Chamber's shoulder, and he pressed the pocket-clip trigger. He walked out of the terminal into the parking lot and disappeared.

Before he finished his dessert, Chambers motions slowed and became plastic; he slumped a bit, his loud talk modulated, and he half turned in his chair to survey the room, his head weaving, like a man dizzy with his own importance. He could pass for a drunk beginning to get too much under his belt.

Marion's companions got up and disappeared into the lobby. The waitress brought Chambers' bill, "Will there be anything else, sir?"

"Naw honey, jis let me givya my credit card."

She returned with the paperwork; he signed and rose to leave. He teetered, and took unsteady steps. Marion's companions came to meet Chambers, greeting him as though he had been expected. They shook hands, and one said, "Let's go have a drink in the Tea Garden ... it's two hours 'til plane time."

"All right good buddy, ten forty."

By the time the car reached SamuelS's headquarters, Chambers had gone deeper into a state of silly and benign compliance. Three men appeared from the depths of the boathouse and took Chambers inside, removed his wallet, his passport, his jewelry, his plane tickets, and his money. They sacked him into a sleeping bag, and sat him up against a wall. A door opened at the head of stairs leading down to the water level, and the shaman entered the room.

Marion had not expected the shaman's style. The features and tan skin suggested something Indian and Spaniard. He wore a pin-stripped suit. He opened a little black medical bag, laid out two white pills, and from a pint bottle poured a medicine glass full of a clear red liquid, then offered them to the trucker. Chambers swallowed the wafers and slugged down the fluid. Within half an hour, SamuelS had recorded the trucker's gleeful confession of the damage he had done on the highways.

"What of the little helpless people you have killed?" asked the shaman.

"Trash ... in my way."

"Don't you think it sad?"

"Knocked 'em over like kingpins."

"Why?"

"I'm king of the highways, goin' somewhere important with important loads. They're loitering, nowhere to go and nothin' to do."

"Do you remember the doctor's family last year?"

"Station wagon poke assin' in the rain."

"Five little children and their mother killed. Do you have regrets, do you feel remorse?"

"I am the strong, they are the weak. Piss ants die under the feet of elephants, pygmies under the feet of giants, gnats in the swipe of a busy hand."

Then they took Buck Chambers down in the elevator to a water slip inside the building, and in the shadows boarded a thirty-three foot Cigarette, and strapped him on a bunk. The shaman drew up a deck chair and sat guard. Two of the men returned to the elevator, and the third locked the cabin and stood a few minutes at the wheel, listening to the night: the slapping of water against the bulkhead and boat hull, the far-off bluff of tugboat whistles, the threat of foghorns in the harbor.

After a few minutes, the man released the tie lines, leaned against a piling, and pushed the boat backward out of its slip. It began to drift with the outgoing tide, moving down the coast beneath the shadows of overhanging trees. Twenty minutes later, and a half-mile from the dock and out in deep water, he started the engines, turned on the running lights, and moved out into the channel. Orders were explicit: no direct route, no speeding, no hijinks, no impulsive behavior, nothing to get attention. The boat went out into Hampton Roads, in the calm warm night, and circled among the anchored freighters in the mouth of the James River until it reached the silhouette of the ABATE, and eased beneath its dangling cables. The pilot reversed the propellers, killed the engines, and hooked to the bow and stern rings. Men above on the ABATE leaned over the rail, watching. The running lights went off: the signal. The boat lifted out of the water and up until hands pulled it over the rails and it sank to the deck. The shaman jumped out and accompanied the drowsy Chambers down to passenger quarters.

CHAPTER 17

The puddle in Eric's garage and oily footprints on the steps sent a weird sensation diving through the pit of his stomach. He ascended the stairs, flipped on the lights, and found Joan's note. Walking toward the smell of oil and lighter fluid and the sweat of excitement, he called into the silence of the house, his own voice echoing against emptiness.

The note told him how she subdued the men who got in the house and about Ralph Green. One of the thugs verified the name of the LifeChain leak, Gladys Gleason, and confirmed the presence of an inside source in Sentara.

Eric opened the front door and found the wilted bouquet of roses. He threw them in the garbage, left the house, and returned to the hospital. A heart and other organs were to be removed from a brain-dead woman at nine p.m., the victim of a spontaneous cerebral hemorrhage. Marcus Mann would be there to oversee dispatching one or more couriers. Eric wondered how anyone had managed to overhear his secret conversation with Marcus.

Then he knew. Stupid! How could he have been so careless? Anybody sitting at the control center of the operating suite could turn on the intercom and the television monitor and see and hear everything going on in any particular room. But this station stood out in the center of the entrance and everybody could monitor activities from there. The other station, in the operating room supervisor's office out of sight around a corner, stayed locked after hours.

In the operating suite, Marcus Mann, capped and gowned, stood with his arms folded, talking to a resident. People milled about, waiting to get started. Eric dressed and went down the hallway. Marcus followed. They entered room nine together and Eric said, "I'll be right back." He went out the opposite door into a parallel hallway, now in darkness, and approached the supervisor's office. Through the glass partition a greenish light and the number nine glowed on the small television screen. A figure sat at the desk in the dark and leaned forward toward the screen with an ear cocked to the speaker. A faint strain of whistling, the clanking of basins, the scraping of a steel stool across the tile floor all came through, and the image of Marcus blurred across the screen in color, his voice singing *Swing low Sweet chariot, Comin' for to carry me home.* Eric moved closer for a better look, and recognized the man hunched over the screen. He retraced his steps to room nine, entered by banging the door open, and said, "Sorry to keep you waiting."

"No problem. I have nothing to do. The organs are all being used here. Just a matter of good luck, the way the numbers came up."

"I'm delighted."

They exchanged a few more words about the donor. Then Mann said, "What are you doing here this late? Isn't this your night off?"

"Yes, but I'm just finishing, and the patient getting the heart asked me to see him through the start of his anesthesia."

"Then I guess we both should get down to the room."

"Yes."

They went out the door into the hallway and Eric picked up a progress note pad on a wall desk and wrote, *bad news, meet me in the lobby at the Athletic Club as soon as you can get away.* Marcus wrote, *ten o'clock.*

At the club Eric brought Marcus up to date on Joan. Then he said, "Now I know the hospital spy."

"Who is he?"

"One of the pump technicians. The one with the new thirty-six foot cruiser. He was among the group standing in the entrance when I guided you down to room nine the first time we talked there. He watched us, I suppose, until he knew which room, then hightailed it to the supervisor's office and tuned in. This means he has a master key to her office and perhaps to everything including the drug lockers in anesthesia, and if he does I suspect he steals and sells drugs also."

"We need to find Joan."

"She is taking care of herself somewhere it seems. She will find us. Can she really defend herself?"

"I would guess so. She not only is resourceful, but she also has a black belt in karate."

"She never mentioned the karate."

"And I forgot modesty. She would never tell you about her accomplishments, but she would not hide behind a facade of spurious humility either."

"So, what can we do about her?"

"I hope she will just hide until things blow over."

"No. I don't think so, Marcus. This situation is much too serious. It will not blow over because it is only the beginning of human ways of filling a great need. Joan believes the pursuers want to eliminate her because she knows Gladys Gleason supplies information about donors and donor organs."

"I guess you're right. I just keep hoping it will go away. So, what next?"

"I will watch the technician."

"And I will try to see what Gladys Gleason is doing."

"Should we inform the hospital administrator?"

"Let's not blow our cover, nor stir up anymore legal trouble now. The pending court action against us is enough for the moment."

"What's to come of it?"

"We will be out-voted, I'm sure, and there's nothing I can do about it. Pioneering has earned us no consideration."

"I'm sorry, and I wish I could help. But, Marcus, I am more concerned about you for other reasons."

"Why? What do you mean?"

"Maybe you are not really mean enough to handle this situation alone."

"I don't understand."

"Your job with the spy requires a determined deviousness, one to outmatch hers."

"Why?"

"Because, she will continue to betray the couriers she dispatches to various cities with organs."

"Eric, give me a chance. I have as much deviousness waiting beneath the surface as the next man, so let me use it on these two thieves. We will set them up."

"Well, thank God."

"On the surface, however, discretion, I suppose, will continue to be necessary. I think we should meet here until the situation changes. I will simply give you a time on the phone and say nothing else."

"Agreed."

"And the situation is getting worse. Another courier disappeared last night in Region Two of UNOS in downtown Philadelphia. An ambulance racing with a heart for a waiting team just disappeared. It simply vanished, like it had been sucked underground, leaving not a trace of the vehicle or the crew riding in it. We are facing a well-organized operation, wickedly motivated. I don't know why the news media is not having a field day."

"I guess the public is not as taken with the transplant dilemma as they are with basketball or football."

"Yeah, you're right. It's not really a serious problem to most people."

CHAPTER 18

Kahan picked the next target and sent for Marion. Herman Hodder came to Marion's suite in the Waldorf for an eleven o'clock brunch. Herman described the target and their plans for taking him. This one, Carl Varner, nicknamed *The Wolf*, a financial wizard of the keenest ability but unscrupulous principles, got richer and richer by raiding and destroying companies. SamuelS had collected the evidence. Marion would get to hear the details in Judge Taylor's court.

Socially, Varner entertained lavishly, saw the Broadway plays, and among other places went to concerts at Carnegie Hall and Lincoln Center. His young, beautiful, and charming wife smoothed the way, entertaining people who would never have honored him with their presence had she not been there. And he had bizarre habits to match his wicked genius. At least three times a week, after a night out, he took the limousine downtown to his office on Wall Street. He told his wife he did his most astute work in the early morning hours when world markets in the Far East were opening.

Actually, he dismissed the chauffeur, walked through the lobby and out a side door. Then he went around the block, and took a cab to his girlfriend's apartment, his apartment rather, one he had bought for her. On these nights he entered the apartment building and appeared again only at eleven a.m. the next day. SamuelS would be watching the entrance as he strode out and took a cab to his office.

After the meal, Herman inserted a tape in the VCR and they watched a summary of Varner's destruction of numerous small companies. Herman explained the main offense — his raider techniques and the milking of newly purchased companies, the lowering of quality and safety standards on drugs and foods, and the deaths caused by these hidden changes. "His trial will be held tomorrow at eleven a.m. We would like to offer you the opportunity to be present,"

Herman said, "Where?"

"At the United Nations, in a private conference room on the same floor with the International Court of Justice, the World Court."

"A United Nations function?"

"No. Not an official function of *the* United Nations, but certainly a united function of all nations involved in Xanadu."

"Yes. This I must see."

The Judge, too, did not dress in the raiment of his profession. He wore an old blue blazer, a white shirt with button-down collar, and striped tie.

Jury selection proceeded. Each candidate faced the Judge alone, the others waiting in seclusion. Three would be chosen. The first candidate, passed without question, a Frenchman from Lyon, whose grandchild had become ill and died within a day. The virulent infection failed to respond to the appropriate antibiotic. The drug had been diluted to save money for the new owner, who had acquired the company in a hostile takeover.

The judge selected the second juror, a woman from Italy whose husband had been killed when the steering mechanism failed on his new car. Raiders had taken over the steering-gear factory and lowered the standards for quick profit.

The judge selected a third juror, a black woman from Cape Town, whose child died of botulism from contaminated canned beef. A hostile raider lowered standards for greater profit. Several hundred people lost their lives from the epidemic of food poisoning.

The jury then assembled in the judge's presence, and SamuelS agents presented the evidence against Carl Varner. Company after company had been ruined by his avarice. After a vicious takeover, the raider drained each company until the quality, nurtured by the founders, went by the wayside for quick profit.

In doing this to the companies, he did worse things to people, the trusting customers. Baby foods, altered to increase profits, deprived the babies of needed nutrients. The omission of expensive lifesaving ingredients from drug combinations proved fatal, but the prices went higher. Inert filler replaced the lost bulk from lowered dosage levels. The sacrifice of quality control led to quicker and greater profits. Canning companies of impeccable reputation, a trust earned over the decades, began cheating their customers with contaminated and diluted foods. The list of infractions went on and on.

Varner's removal would have a domino effect on a vast empire. The jury returned a verdict of guilty on all charges. None of them knew the identity of the offender, or the proposed disposition of Varner.

Marion's car sped downtown and the driver parked across the street from Varner's office building. Within a few minutes, another limousine appeared. Varner hopped out and entered the building. Tim stepped to the curb, gripping a small black briefcase under his right arm, handle up, snaps pointed out, and moved forward. The side door around the corner flew open and Varner came out striding, swinging his walking stick, affecting a jubilant dandy. His black cape, flying in the force of his gait, flared open, revealing its red inner lining. Tim increased his pace, came within three feet of Varner's back, placed his finger on a tiny button on the back of the case, and pressed. The shot produced the tiniest click and a weak recoil. He slackened his pace. Varner maintained his forceful strut for a few seconds.

Tim disappeared. Varner slowed and his knees seemed to sag, the twirling cane popped point down against the pavement. Herman, with another SamuelS, rushed to his side and took him by the elbows. The driver moved the limousine up to the curb. Herman drew Varner into the back seat next to

Marion.

Varner sank into profound and docile drowsiness, and slept soundly. Marion had calculated his dosage carefully — just enough to render him powerless for a few minutes and a secondary drug to make him sleepy and docile for several hours. The limousine disappeared into an old warehouse and Herman and his helper removed Varner from the back seat, and guided him into an anteroom.

In the center of the room, Varner, a large man given to early obesity, sat in a straight-backed chair. His head wobbled in a state of drugged submissiveness as he surveyed his surroundings, his luxuriant face sagging, his lush black hair disheveled, the large, luminous, hazel eyes inflamed, long curled eyelashes wet, heavy moist lips pouting, the large ears flushed. Marion and Herman took seats against the wall. SamuelS agents ringed the room.

In a few minutes the Cigarette drifted into the slip within the shed. The shaman stepped off onto the dock. This time he wore the ordinary clothes of a dockhand. Later, Marion realized the shaman had created this appearance to provoke the arrogance of Varner. The shaman poured a tumbler half-full of a red liquid. He handed two little snow-white wafers to Varner and offered the glass. Varner regarded him with an insolent, intolerant look, but in his drugged state, swallowed the wafers and gulped the red fluid.

The shaman waited fifteen minutes. Stillness and silence enveloped the room. Distant and muted water licked at the sides of the floating dock. Varner aroused from his stupor, looked down his nose at the shaman, and began to pace the room. The shaman said, "Speak to God."

Varner whirled, "I am God! I am richer than God, who gave me the power to accumulate vast fortunes to build great empires and great cathedrals, and to raise myself above the ordinary masses who are no better than swine in their stupidity, like you, the ordinary inconsequential who gobble and squander the earth's resources for no purpose whatsoever except to propagate the same line of worthless rabble. I have succeeded; my money will build memorials to my name. My name will live on when the ordinary have been forgotten."

"What of those who have suffered at your hands, Mr. Varner?"

"Of no consequence. They were worthless and ordinary. The most powerful of men have always sacrificed the stupid and the willing for the sake of great accomplishment. Look at Napoleon, Alexander the Great, Joseph Stalin, Genghis Kahn."

"Are you proud, Mr. Varner?"

"Proud? Of course I'm proud. I've done what I set out to do."

"Did you know your methods would kill people, and starve others?"

"Of course I knew. Did Napoleon know soldiers would die in battle? Did Hitler know worthless civilians would die under his bombs?"

"*Did* they know?"

"Of course they knew, and it is of no consequence, just as little stupid people are of no consequence to me."

"What has this gained you?"

"I live at the top of the heap. People bow and scrape in my presence. I am powerful."

"And what are your plans for the future, your intentions?"

"I shall own everything. I shall continue until I am all powerful." Varner lay down on the floor and went to sleep.

The shaman stepped before Herman, bowed deeply from the waist forward, straightened up and marched out of the room. The SamuelS men, at a signal from Herman, sacked Varner into a sleeping bag, and took him down an elevator to the Cigarette. Herman and Marion went to the limousine. Another man entered the boat dock, turned out the lights, boarded the boat, and sat under the wheel listening. Then he actuated the electronic controls of the door facing the water and in pitch darkness let the Cigarette drift out into the harbor. He started the engines. A half hour later he eased the boat alongside the ABATE out in the New York harbor, and hooked the lift cables to the bow and stern.

Marion went to his hotel room and changed clothes. Three hours later, Ruth met him at the Eagle-Vail airport.

CHAPTER 19

Joan Pully went through the back entrance of LifeChain's main building after midnight and entered Marcus Mann's office. With the door locked, the lights off, and the blinds drawn, she switched on the computer. On the national scene a new message appeared. A heart went out from Charlotte to Pittsburgh more than two hours ago in the hands of a courier named Stevens. She unlocked the lower desk drawer and ran the tape on the recorder back to ten p.m. She listened to the sounds of someone punching out a number, then the voice of Gladys Gleason: "Hello, Legation. Savior here."

"Bless you my child, the Reverend Lotte speaking."

"Does one have need to be born again?"

"Always somewhere in the world. Yes, one does. Can you help a lost soul see the light?"

Then she sold him a courier en route from Charlotte to Pittsburgh with a heart. "Ahh, yes, a double jeopardy. You have our gratitude," The Reverend said.

"I shall."

"Indeed, and may the Lord's blessings come to you."

"And just how blessed will I be, Reverend?"

"Would thirty thousand soothe your soul?"

"So long as just the two of us know about it."

"Your cohort will be kept in the dark."

Gladys hung up. Now Joan had proof. Gladys Gleason sells inside information to people who make a profit from human organs, and betrays not just the local system, but the entire network as well.

Double jeopardy — they steal the heart in the bucket and take God knows what from the courier, probably all of his organs, too. At this very moment, Stevens probably already had been disassembled in the merciless hands of Legation somewhere in Pittsburgh, and the heart he carried in a bucket, as well as his own, delivered to unknown destinations.

Joan turned off the computer and sat in the dark, waiting until Gladys Gleason left LifeChain headquarters. Then she started to think about the situation she had fallen into. The inevitable had happened. The power of money and the will of people to fill their immediate needs regardless of the consequences, sooner or later, had to create a thriving black market in human organs. The pitiful inadequacies of the donor pool, supplied only by the victims of a bleeding stroke, or trauma, could not be tolerated indefinitely while the waiting recipients faced certain death or unbearable lives without the needed organs. Now it had happened. Legation would murder in the most cryptic and brutal way and would kill from ambush.

Then she made her decision. She would run no more. The organ thieves would continue to pursue her. Let them. And for the sheer sport of it, she would hunt them in turn, and if she died she would die enjoying the fight. In the meantime, nothing would deprive her of the pleasures of living, and to live to the fullest now she wanted Eric.

As she reached for the phone to call his house, the wiretaps be damned, headlights cut the darkness of the lot again and went off. The car parked. A door slammed, and footsteps crossed the lot. She tried the desk drawers for a gun or knife, and found no weapons. A key rattled in the back door, footsteps came down the hallway, the key went into Marcus Mann's door, the door opened, and a person stepped in and flicked on the overhead lights. Marcus Mann stopped still in his tracks, his mouth dropped open in astonishment.

"Good evening to you, Mr. Mann."

"Jesus Christ, Joan, what are you doing here?"

"Spying. Turn off the lights and sit down. We have some talking to do."

He pulled up a chair next to her, and she turned off the lamp. She said, "Why are you here this time of night?"

"On my way home, and stopped off to pick up a laptop for homework over the weekend. I have just left Eric Stuart. We met at the Athletic Club, and talked about this situation. Then I went home with him and we cleaned up the oil in his garage and kitchen. What did you do, have a good old fashioned massacre in there?"

"More or less, so to speak."

Marcus chuckled, and continued, "Tonight Eric caught one of the pump technicians listening to us through the intercom system in Sentara operating rooms."

"God! Who?"

"They call him Stiney. His name is Stanley Steinfelt."

"The nerve of the damned little creep; he's been after me for months to go out on his new boat. I wondered where he got the money, wife and three neglected children at home, the sonofabitch. Does he know anything?"

"Yes, Eric and I think the two spies are working together, and we plan to set them up."

Then Joan told Marcus about the betrayal she had just heard on the tape.

"If Stevens is missing we will know by tomorrow," said Marcus.

"Obviously, someone is trying to destroy the voluntary system, but why?"

"To make the way safe for selfish enterprise in organ procurement."

"Who would wage such a war?"

"Well ... who does Gladys Gleason sell to?" asked Marcus.

"The Reverend is the only one I've heard dealing with her."

"Then he may be the culprit behind the war. If so, she is in deep."

"Gleason is a dilemma, indeed. Why don't you just fire her?" asked Joan.

"I can't without bringing formal charges, which would create a terrible public clamor. Besides, I have a better plan," said Marcus.

"Good. This situation will stop all organ distribution if it continues."

"We need to keep her on duty and to monitor all of her phone conversations, and take preventive action accordingly."

"The police?"

"Involving the police would tip our hand to Gladys. No. Let's do it our way now. We will deceive her or cancel delivery if necessary to save a courier."

"Okay, but I will not stop. I will deliver any organ anywhere it needs to go."

"Now Joan, I can't let you take the risk."

"Don't try to stop me."

"But I am responsible for you and all other couriers."

"Marcus, do me a favor, will you?"

"I suppose."

"Let's get out of here, get in your car, and say nothing. Then deliver me to Eric's door, ring the bell, and when he answers, leave."

"Yes, indeed I will. What a relief. At least you will be safe with him for the night."

"Glad to be rid of me?"

"You said it. I didn't. But, yes I am. I was worrying all along about what to do with you for the night."

"I appreciate your concern."

Eric, in his pajamas, peeked through the eyepiece at the face of Marcus Mann out in the night. He undid the latch, unlocked the deadbolt, and opened the door as Marcus descended the front steps. Joan came from behind the pilaster, pushed the door further open and sidled in. She took Eric in her arms, hugged and kissed him, and snuggled against his chest. Eric, sleepy and surprised, grasped her by the shoulders, held her away at arms length, looked her over carefully and said, "Are you all right?"

"Yes, but I've had an interesting day."

"Are you hungry? Have you had dinner?"

"Not hungry."

"Well come on to bed. You need rest."

"You go back to sleep. I will soak in the tub first. I'm covered in the sweat of high excitement."

"A drink?"

"Brandy."

He brought the brandies to the bathroom as she undressed. "Here I am again, still wearing the same jumpsuit, sans another rag."

"But whole and healthy."

She stepped into the filling tub. "Yes, so far. Marcus has brought me up to date on Steinfelt and Brown. She sat in the rising water, bubbles reaching the tub rim.

"I am sure whoever has been chasing you found your whereabouts through Steinfelt, who listened through the intercom to me talk to Marcus about you," said Eric.

"I expect you are right, the little rat. Gladys had no way of knowing unless someone told her."

"The two work together."

"Yes, and they've been up to this for awhile now. I think her betrayal accounts for the men in gray following me to Chicago."

"So what now?"

"Eric, I'm going to come and go as I please. I do not intend to run again. But I am through with passive techniques. I intend to hunt them."

"This puts me at a distinct disadvantage. I do not want you to go unprotected, but at the same time my commitment is to the sick people at the hospital and I cannot get away."

"No. I am not your responsibility. At least you do not owe me protection. If you knew more of my history you might expect protection from me."

"I know a little of it. You have a black belt in karate, and you are very smart, among other things."

"You've been talking to Marcus."

"Yes."

"He didn't tell you everything, because he does not know it all."

"Oh?"

"I can shoot a pistol."

"Helpless little thing, aren't you."

"Don't make fun."

"With your array of defenses, I wish to remain your obedient servant, madam."

"Eric, I am getting out of the tub in a moment, I am coming to bed, I am going to make passionate love to you, you are going to work tomorrow, and I am leaving again. You will hear from me sporadically and you will not know where to find me in the meantime, so don't try."

"Like it or not, I have no choice."

"Precisely, and I have no intention of letting you get killed or injured when you have your mind on the ill and are devoting your energies to them."

"Well, you know where to find me, always."

"I do, and I will be back, believe me, to collect you someday."

"I hope so."

"And you have to get up a little early in the morning so you can walk to work."

"Why?"

"Because I will need your car. I'm going to take a little ride down in the country."

Eric started to ask *where* and stopped himself. She sensed the unasked question, but she did not want to tell him the truth. She had heard rumors of a heart going to Atlanta within the next forty-eight hours and she wanted to arm herself for a fight if the occasion arose. She said, "I need to pay a visit to the Pully Farm." She stopped talking and moved into his arms.

Eric awoke in the darkness of four a.m. and reached for Joan. He found an empty space with the covers folded up, and he sensed a strange emptiness and silence in the house. He leapt out of bed, called her, and received no answer. He searched the bathroom, the kitchen, and other areas. Then he realized she had dressed and disappeared into the early morning darkness. He went onto the balcony beyond the kitchen, peered down, and found the garage empty. A profound loneliness came over him, then a great apprehension and a worry. And at the same time a practical thought of reasonableness — he could only accept events as they unfolded and go about his business.

CHAPTER 20

At Kahan's request, Herman Hodder brought Marion to Africa again. At the crowded Xanadu airport a Concorde ambulance and another Gulfstream V stood on the tarmac, along with a dozen or more military jets from different countries, and a monstrous camouflaged helicopter. "What goes on here?" Marion asked.

"The airplanes ... the Concorde and the Gulfstream belong to Xanadu, the others to the various countries guarding the mountain. The helicopter is a Soviet Mi-17 armed transport ship used for support of the mercenaries in Angola and Sierra Leone, as well as other countries."

"What's it doing here?"

"The mercenaries are only too glad to accept a further profit from their victims. They get a hundred dollars for each brain-dead soldier, or disease-free brain-dead civilian they bring here, and sometimes there are twenty or more brain-dead patients on life support aboard one flight."

"My God," said Marion. "He uses so many?"

"Well, it's not an everyday thing, and he has begun to ship live organs to major medical centers in need."

"Oh, really. Like where?"

"Berlin, Moscow, London, Paris ... others, but only when he has something not needed here."

"Aren't those places too far away?"

"Not on the Concorde ambulance, especially when he sends the brain-dead donor on life support."

A Range Rover took Marion up miles of winding road, climbing through virgin forest and constantly changing ground cover and foliage before they eased between hidden gates in the dense growth and entered the compound. The driveway wound among gardens to the compound of buildings rising out of the mountain. The driver led him to the library, where

Kahan stood and said, "Dr. Marion, I trust you had a pleasant journey."

"Indeed."

"Please take a chair." Kahan placed himself at Marion's side in an informal manner. And he came to the point at once.

"Excellent work, and I am very pleased. So, let me review with you our accomplishments." Then he explained how the drug concoctions had helped take out ten targets in the United States alone. They had removed three sadistic wife beaters, a serial murderer who got off free three times, three punk gang leaders who had murdered several people and terrorized their neighborhoods, a mafia Don, a woman who had poisoned three husbands without being caught, and an arrogant, wizened Midwestern federal judge, Richard Wyndall Blanton, known for his cruel and unusual sentences, and nicknamed by his legal peers, *Little Hanging Dick*. This judge had never attended law school, his appointment purely political with no relation to ability. His heart proved to be worthless.

"The drugs are working well for your men, I take it," said Marion.

"Oh, indeed yes. And we are into another source of organs now, which I hope will do much to improve the world in which we live."

"An entirely new one?" asked Marion.

"Not exactly ... more like part of what we are already doing. The Global Mafia."

"I read bad things about them."

"No borders, evil, vicious, lawless, and with their high tech capabilities, a threat to all mankind. They have had their hands, at least temporarily, on nuclear warheads," said Kahan.

"Have you taken...?"

"Yes, SamuelS agents have taken three of the leaders to date with the help of your drugs."

"How?"

"Sooner or later when the target has to go home, somewhere—a house, an apartment, a hotel room we will be nearby watching and waiting, and one marksman or another at the opportune moment gets off a shot containing the drugs of permissiveness," said Kahan.

"And the victim never knows he has been injected?"

"Never. Then later, at home, he receives a phone call telling him where to go. Always a taxi waits at the curb. He gets in, and the cab moves off. After this one-way trip, we change the license plates and the logo. A cab with a particular appearance and a particular driver never appears on the streets again. Three excellent donors so far, and three nasty racketeers removed from the streets of Moscow. We are moving into other areas of their activities."

"I'm delighted the drugs work so well."

"They make a man very obedient to suggestion."

"Good."

"Has the Mafia retaliated?"

"They are puzzled and confused. No force has been used, no clues left, and the donors have totally disappeared without a trace."

"I trust your good luck will continue."

"Not a matter of luck. In a crowd, the fountain pen makes no sound, and causes no pain, no violence, no bloodshed, and no disturbance. Then the person responds to a guiding touch on the elbow, or a word whispered into his ear or the instructions of a phone call, and without a word to anyone, goes as though summoned to follow some mysterious force, like a lemming, or the dupes of the Pied Piper."

"Good."

"And we are now into the scene of international terrorism, also. The confessions brought about with your drugs lead us to an ever-growing number of the indoctrinated awaiting orders for suicidal attacks. We are happy to anticipate and accommodate their wishes and thankful for the rich supply of healthy young organs. Unfortunately, we have to do this secretly, and we could never afford to let your government and news media know about our activities."

"I am honored to expedite this method of elimination."

"But on to other matters ... we must stop Legation."

"You have a plan?"

"Legation now has four regional managers who have become very effective in brutal kidnaping techniques, and they operate from the eastern seaboard to the west coast of the United States. They have developed teams further north and south, and eventually will spread into the international arena. The leader, The Reverend Lotte, has no scruples. He refuses to respect the germ theory, the facts of blood and tissue typing, or anything to with immunology. As far as he is concerned, diseases such as AIDS, hepatitis, cancer, syphilis, tuberculosis, and Creutzfeldt-Jacob are not transmitted in transplanted organs and tissue.

Legation must be stopped, and my advisors in SamuelS think the best way is simple elimination of the existing leaders."

Marion relaxed in his chair, leaned his head back, and studied the gold rococo filigree on the ceiling. A surge of resistance had rushed him the moment Kahan began revealing his intentions. Now his resistance faded. He sat up and said, "I'm beginning to understand the need."

"Then this should be very exciting. But the regional managers must be taken one at a time leaving no evidence. And no one should ever suspect elimination by human hands, yet the shock of coincidence should sober even the most stupid culprit. If it would ease your conscience, you can help us take each manager while he is attacking a victim. Timothy would continue in his present capacity."

Kahan paused for thought, then said, "And another problem, Moha's wife."

"I've heard something of the situation,"

"She loses consciousness and stops living. Her doctor says

she has a fifty percent chance of dying suddenly any time now."

"Her doctor?"

"Yes, their most trusted friend. The family doctor now into the third generation, more than fifty years."

"He must be about eighty."

"Almost ninety, but a very wise, very sage man. He says she needs a new heart."

"How old is she?"

"Twenty-four."

Marion suspected Moha, and subsequently Kahan, might be the victims of bad advice. "He is having this done as soon as he obtains the right heart?"

"Yes," said Kahan. Then he became apprehensive. "Dr. Marion, he has no choice. What is he to do?"

"Are you actually *asking* me what to do?"

"Yes, I would appreciate your opinion."

"I think Moha needs to be sure about the condition of his wife's heart."

"But his most trusted physician has seen her many times and I have told you what he says."

"With all due respect to Moha's personal physician, I would want other opinions for so grim a prognosis, even if the first one came from the world's greatest cardiologist. Anyone can be wrong, and everyone *is* sooner or later."

"But this would hurt the old man's pride, and he is a very proud man."

"All right. Are you willing to risk a patient's life to save face for a ninety year old physician?"

Kahan hesitated, then surprised Marion with another question. "Who would we get for Moha's wife?"

"Take her to the cardiologists in Boston where Dr. Gambela trained in heart surgery, the Mecca, so to speak."

"But the circumstances of her attacks are a source of great embarrassment, and a matter of the utmost privacy to Moha."

"Would I be privy to the secret?"

"Since you are involved already, yes. The attacks occur only during lovemaking. Her excitement knows no bounds until she loses consciousness."

Marion thought, *Well, congratulations to Moha,* but suppressed the facetious impulse and said, "After a lot of very fast and very heavy breathing?"

"Yes, but how did you know?"

"And she is a tall, thin woman?"

"Yes. What does this lead to?"

"The possibility of a less serious problem — she may have mitral valve prolapse, a condition seen more frequently in young women of slender body build. Also very fast breathing during excitement can cause a form of fainting. The two conditions together certainly could lead to these episodes. And they, I can tell you in no uncertain terms, do not create the need for a heart transplant."

"Do you think it could really be so simple?"

"I would take odds against what you have been told."

"Can you arrange it?"

"Dr. Gambela can."

"Would you go with her?"

"Yes, but I won't get off the plane."

"I will ask Dr. Gambela to go, too," said Kahan.

"When?"

"At the end of your visit, two days from now. And from there my pilots will take you on to Denver."

"Okay, and what about Legation?"

"You will do it?"

"Has this been reported to the police, or the FDA, or to any other official watchdog?"

"Ha! You Americans! You are so naive about justice. Of course it has. But the process moves too slowly and through such devious paths. No one, or all of these organizations combined, could stop this mischief. Besides, your people do not look for injustice; they look for someone disobeying or ignoring a law, as it exists. This, contrary to the other cause, carries less risk and less work for law enforcement officers than going after the dangerous ones."

"How often I have seen it happening!"

"I take your reticence to be an unspoken agreement."

"Yes."

"Then we have a few more preliminaries. Now it's time to enjoy your visit. I have chosen a very special hostess. If you like her, she will return to Vail with you."

"Ruth does a very commendable job."

"Ruth?"

"Yes, the woman at Vail now."

"We don't know her as Ruth. But no, she was not meant to be with you permanently, and she has another assignment. I will see you with your new companion at dinner this evening. She will be here momentarily."

Kahan bowed and left the room. Insight gripped Marion and a cold chill ran down his back. Now he knew. Ruth had been given to him for a special reason and she had served her purpose. He had been tested and approved. Had he not proven reliable, something could have happened to him, an unexplained and unexplainable exodus.

A side door opened and a woman of medium height, petite with at the same time a restrained voluptuousness, large burning black eyes and short black bobbed hair, moved into the room with grace and poise. The keen and beautiful visage, the smoldering intensity, the sensuous aura delighted and frightened him at the same time. The fear turned to caution, and when she smiled and spoke, the caution went, too. He relaxed. She extended a hand, and came toward him. "Dr. Marion, I am Sarah." She wore a riding habit.

Astonished, and for the moment speechless, Marion took her hand, his mind clamoring with possibilities. Had Kahan sent him a nemesis? And if so, what lay in store? He need not question. He sensed the answer: a future sparked with great change, and in the distant reaches of his inborn wisdom he knew in an instant Kahan now had control. He responded, "Hello Sarah. I'm in your hands, I believe."

"Kahan has asked me to show you the grounds. Do you ride horseback?"

"Not since boyhood."

"We should ride."

"All right."

He changed to riding clothes and they went over streams and through virgin forests and picnicked beside the river. Sitting on the blanket within noontime shade, Marion said, "And what is the odor in the forest? I smell it stronger out here than back in the palace."

"The incense trees. The pungent pleasant aroma clears your lungs. And something else mingles with it now, have you noticed?"

"Yes, something haunting."

"A tiny musk deer, imported from western China. They live hidden in the forest in the rhododendron thickets."

"Does Kahan hunt the animals for their musk?"

"Oh no, he won't allow them to be touched. He loves the fragrance."

"Where on earth are we?"

"Dreamland, the land without reality."

"And all the little streams meander about, and the river twists back and forth, winding."

"And flows into the caverns, disappears underground, then races out in rapids to the sea."

"How far have we come?"

"Almost five miles west. The back wall lies just beyond the next trees."

"The land lies five miles in the other direction, north. We will go there now if you like."

"I'm ready. But what's beyond the walls?"

"The hill forest, and further down, the rain forest. And in both are the animals and the birds of Africa. The walls keep the big cats, the predators, outside."

They cantered back to the stables at dusk after having ridden fifteen miles.

The six sat at a round table, Sofya on Kahan's left, Sarah across the table, and Marion next to her. Moha and Adela completed the circle, a small and intimate party.

Marion sipped sparingly of the wines, and ate only a few bites from each course. Kahan's appetite befitted his great size. Moha, the largest man in the room, though less refined and elegant, sat next to his tall, blonde, thin wife, Adela, who contrasted sharply to the larger darker people.

The conversation at first ran to wine and food, to music and literature. Then Kahan began reciting sketchy lines of poetry. After playing with clever rhymes and a bit of outlandish doggerel, he paused for a silent moment, then looked at Marion, his black eyes intense, and said, *The force that through the green fuse drives the flower/Drives my green age; ... The force that drives the water through the rocks /Drives my red blood...* Marion almost gasped with astonishment — the commonality of all things, in the words of Dylan Thomas, and he knew then the essence of Kahan. And when he heard Coleridge: *In Xanadu did Kubla Kahn/A stately pleasure dome decree/ Where Alph the sacred river ran/Through caverns measureless to man/Down to a sunless sea,* he, in an overwhelming wave of emotion and insight, knew where they were.

At the end of the evening, with the very essence of his being awash in a sea of sentiment, he followed Sarah to their quarters. His excitement ran at too high a pitch for sleep. They sat on the balcony. The musk now pervaded the cool night, tantalizing and disturbing.

A full moon lit the landscape and outlined the nearby forest in a diffused translucent glow. A bass and alto chorus of frog voices vibrated through the forest with rising and falling song, and birds strange to him called and warbled out toward the horizon. Beyond the walls, the remote and muted roar of lions and the howls of jackals in the risky distance sobered the pastoral darkness.

In a turret above them and to the near right the lighted windows grew dim. As if answering his unasked question, Sarah said, "Guest's quarters. Kahan on the top level lives an existence filled with sensitivity and insight."

"Yes, I am beginning to gain some understanding." Marion paused a moment, then completed the Dylan Thomas stanza Kahan had begun, "Ahh yes... *And I am dumb to tell the crooked rose/My youth is bent by the same wintry fever."*

"Oh my, why didn't you join in at dinner?"

"I was afraid he might stop."

"Perhaps, and I think he deliberately revealed himself."

Something disturbed the tranquil sounds of the night, interrupted the flow and pulse of the moon-shadowed landscape. After a brief pause, it sounded again, a low moan, and a muffled outcry, and Marion completed the Coleridge stanza, *"A savage place! As holy and enchanted/As e'er beneath a waning moon was haunted/By woman wailing for her demon-lover!"*

"Unfair to hide from him," Sarah scolded, but a greater noise interrupted ... A scream erupted from the windows above, then a hysterical succession of panting, rushing, passionate outpourings; Ohhhhs succeeding each other rapid fire, the sound of fast, frantic breathing becoming desperate, the sound of strangling, gurgling, the shouts of Moha, "Allah!" then no sounds except Moha, "Help, somebody help!"

Sarah jumped from her chair, grabbed Marion by the wrist, and said, "Come on, something different has happened this time."

Adela lay sprawled supine across the bed, her limbs flailed out helplessly, her skin starkly pallid. Moha had drawn a sheet over her pelvis, wrapping the other end around his own waist. Marion rushed to her and placed a finger over her carotid region and felt no pulse for two seconds. Her face began to take on the deepening, profound, and resigned neutrality of the newly dead. Then the faintest thrust returned, thready, and nothing more for two absent beats, and again faint and distant. She had not breathed. Marion pulled her mouth open, grasped her tongue, and pulled the tip out past her lips, signaled Sarah to grasp and hold it, then proceeded to pump Adela's chest. After three or four strokes he paused and lifted his hands, waiting. She took a slow, sighing inhalation, and Marion said, "Ahh." And she breathed again, and picked up the rhythm. At his signal Sarah released the tongue. Adela swallowed, turned her head, and begin to blink. Sarah went to the bath, washed her hands, then to a closet and brought Moha a robe and helped him into it.

"Thank God you were here, Dr. Marion. I can never repay you for saving her."

"I didn't save her. She would have come around."

"For all I could tell she was gone."

"Frightening, I know."

"What are we to do?"

"Take her to Boston as planned."

"And in the meantime?"

"And in the meantime, separate apartments, doctor's orders. And have an attendant sit with her tonight."

"I will sit with her myself."

"No. A neutral party, please."

Sarah came to the bed with two glasses of amber fluid, and handed one to him. Both sipped. He recognized the rarest of brandies. "Wide awake and excited aren't you?" she said.

"Oh, yes. Sleep seems impossible."

She slipped out of her robe, slid under the covers, and turned on her stomach. “Two sensitive men, tonight,” she said. “My facade is in shambles.”

“Enchanted.”

“Yes. It’s like you said earlier today, dreamland, the land without reality.”

“Kahan dreamed it and he built it to a realness greater than reality. Moha’s behavior has cast a pall over the enchantment. If Adela died it would be a real blow to the spirit of the new hospital.”

“I don’t think she will die, not from the attacks she has now, but we must get her into the right hands.”

Moon shining through the open balcony doors and windows lit the room in dreamy shadows, and a shaft of moon fell across the bed, bright on her face and eyes. She studied his face, touched it with her fingertips, and said, “I think it is time to take you down to sleep.” She placed a palm on his face, her warm fingertips touching an ear, her lips to his in the exotic African night, the taste of warm mouth opening, the sweet breath.

The next day she led him into the hospital and the surgical suites, then into a large ward with the characteristics of a neurosurgical ICU. A respirator breathed for each of more than two-dozen patients, the chorus of hissing noises all too familiar to the memory of his days of anesthesiology. He studied the rows of gauze-swaddled heads. “What have we here?” he asked.

“Brain-dead patients who will become donors for live hearts within the next few days.”

“And they came from where?”

“Mostly from nearby countries, Rwanda, Uganda, Zaire, and others — battlefields and scenes of genocide. But we are getting them from the world over now.”

"The relatives ... What do the relatives have to say about this?"

"The relatives are refugees, fleeing for their lives, and no one would know where to find them if anyone cared."

"So you proceed."

"Yes, it's either use them or let the donors go to waste. Every brain dead victim brought here by mercenaries and other soldiers — and they are all paid to do so — has been stripped of identity."

"Are they carefully evaluated?"

"Each one is unconscious from a wound of the brain, and each is respirator dependent. As a practical matter these criteria are enough for a decision. Transmissible disease is carefully screened."

"Practical, yes."

After a moment she said, "Come, and I will show you the storage area for frozen material."

"The frozen material?" he asked.

"On the floor of the ice cap ... come." They left the vehicle and went to the glass-enclosed elevator. They zoomed up the hundred and fifty stories to the steel platform and the frozen storage areas. Sarah left the elevator and preceded Marion along a catwalk bordering the icy cliff. Electric lines snaked along the walls of ice to huge deep freezers. She lifted the top of one of the freezers, and dense fog swirled upward. The freezer contained hundreds of frost-encrusted plastic bags. Sarah explained, "Body bags, each from a different person. These are the parts retrieved for banked tissue: corneas, tendons, heart valves, and the like."

"Where did they come from?"

"Every country in the world."

"How long can such material be kept in this state for later use?" Marion asked.

"Indefinitely. For instance, the fibroblasts in heart valves frozen under liquid nitrogen would be viable after ten thousand years or longer. Popular imagination calls this state suspended animation in cryogenics."

"Fascinating," said Marion.

"Yes, but the method has very limited practical application. A whole heart cannot be frozen and used later because it could not be thawed uniformly, and the idea of a whole person having his life suspended in this manner won't work."

"Yes, I know,"

In the rarified atmosphere of a Boston hospital, world famous for its excellence, the cardiologist said Moha's wife did not have a heart problem requiring any type of surgery. He explained the physiological sequence leading to syncope, fainting, in a state of extreme excitement, and the simple treatment used to alleviate the reaction. As expected, Moha did not believe him. Gambela interceded and a loud harangue in their native language ensued. Dr. Gambela would not perform heart surgery on Moha's wife. Neither would any other reputable heart surgeon anywhere in the world.

Then Moha said, "You work for a hospital to which I have given enormous financial support. I am in a position to tell you what to do."

And Gambela said, "I do not work for you, and I will never work for you. I will work for God and patients in the Xanadu Hospital, but you will not tell me when or how to do heart surgery."

Moha stared at Gambela, at the intense black eyes, like his own, blacker yet in angry defiance, and calmed down, his self-possession returned. Then comprehension of the real meaning dawned on him, and the Arabian giant buried his beard in his hands and wept tears of relief.

CHAPTER 21

Kahan summoned Marion to New York. At brunch in Marion's hotel suite Herman Hodder revealed the next target, a man named Fergerson, one of the four regional Legation managers. Herman brought a list of Fergerson's victims, those who concerned LifeChain and Mercury. The cruelty appalled Marion. Fergerson, the regional manager closest to The Reverend Lotte, had come to New York to continue organizing the operation where the supply should be the most plentiful, just one more of his frequent trips there for the same purpose. SamuelS agents, under Herman's direction, had watched his methods and knew his habits. Judge Taylor and his jury already had studied all the evidence and condemned Fergerson to death, complete death. *Sans the Chimera, Sans the Shaman,* the warrant read. He would not have the honor of being a donor, no part of him to continue living. Only those offenders of society who will become donors are allowed the chemical appeal.

"Then there is no doubt," Marion said.

"Yes, SamuelS has absolute proof."

"And the method for this one?"

"Through one of his foibles."

Marion readily agreed.

Fergerson liked bars and nightclubs, but he had to hire his women. He would make the rounds, but he always ended his evenings at his favorite, The Roof, before going to his hotel with his companion. But Fergerson did not know when to quit drinking. The alcohol flushed his kidneys, and as the evening progressed he had to go to the men's room at ever more frequent intervals.

At midnight, Marion, in the disguise of an old man, arrived at The Roof with Sarah. They took a table in a rear corner of the darkened room. Herman sat at the bar in direct view of Marion.

They waited until Fergerson had been there for more than an hour, up front toward the bar, where a redheaded companion plied him with charm and drink until he had become loud and careless. When Fergerson began his third trip to the men's room, Marion stood up, and mimicking the shuffling gait of senility, limped on the cane in the same direction. Timothy followed. Sarah paid in cash, and went out the front entrance of the restaurant.

In the lavatory, Marion leaned his cane against the wall and stepped up to a urinal. Timothy entered the room, picked up Marion's cane, and walked down the row of walled-off urinals, past Marion, and found Fergerson's back filling the fifth compartment. Timothy raised the walking stick, aimed it at the center of the neck just where the skull ends at the upper edge of the collar, and pressed the tiny hidden release. He stood the cane where he had found it, and disappeared.

Fergerson staggered and righted himself, Then he crumpled onto the tile floor, his pants still unzipped, his penis shrunken and dangling and dribbling on his fly.

Marion knew the drug in the tiny missile had dissolved into the fluid of the big spinal fluid cistern where the brain ends, and spread to paralyze the control centers for breathing and for heart action. Fergerson died within a minute. Marion picked up his cane, and left the restaurant to join Sarah in a waiting cab.

Herman and his companions watched the front door. The ambulance arrived; two men carried out a loaded stretcher. Fergerson's redheaded companion rushed into the street and caught a cab. Herman followed the ambulance to its destination. A few minutes later, from a pay phone, he posed as the police department calling. Fergerson had been pronounced dead on arrival and declared a coroner's case, and an autopsy had been scheduled at eight a.m. Herman then went to his suite at the hotel.

SamuelS held its own private inquest the following afternoon. Marion predicted the results. At autopsy, everything else being normal, the doctors opened the head last. This approach hid the tiny missile entry site into the spinal cavity. The tiny puncture wound through the coverings of the brain stem, just where it joined the spinal cord, went unnoticed. The tiny missile had been absorbed long before the autopsy. Marion had expected the autopsy to reveal no cause of death and would be called negative.

"So what has happened?" he asked Herman.

"The autopsy was completed earlier this morning."

"Revealing what, if anything?"

"Negative for heart disease and injury."

"I trust a proper disposition has been made."

"Oh yes, I went to the police at noon posing as a bereaved relative, presented proof and claimed the body. I turned it over to an undertaker, paid him cash for the cheapest cremation available, and proclaimed myself to be a Unitarian. I read two pastoral poems to the upturned profile of the dead Fergerson, and disappeared."

"The drug screen?"

"Incomplete as yet, but whatever it shows can make no difference now."

Kahan expressed his pleasure with the way Marion had prepared the drugs used on Fergerson. "Three more district managers to go," he said, "but we must be careful. Fergerson was the ringleader, but not the most vicious nor the most expert killer." Then he asked, "What is the situation, Herman?"

"Dr. Marion awaits our instructions in a New York hotel. He will prepare the drugs for the strike when we are ready, and of course our action depends on the opportunity presenting itself. We intend to go as fast as possible without revealing ourselves."

"Good. But we do not have time to waste."

"Yes. Unless stopped, they will bring the entire legitimate network to a standstill. It will be too dangerous for a courier to travel with an organ, and they will be too frightened to do so."

"It then would become a matter for the federal authorities in the States."

"And the FBI, the CIA, the FDA, and maybe the IRS, one and maybe all, would subject the entire system, worldwide, to damaging interference."

"And probably fight with each other, interminably entangling and paralyzing our efforts. Waste no time."

CHAPTER 22

Ralph Green pushed the accelerator pedal to the floor and the speedometer needle on the Plymouth crept above ninety-five, the top number. Headlights moved ahead at extraordinary speed ninety degrees to his right as he rounded a curve. An exit popped up and he took it, and followed in the direction the lights had turned.

Joan drove on toward the Pully compound in North Carolina, past the familiar fields of sprouting June plantings. An hour later and within a mile of the compound, she stopped for breakfast in a roadside café, the gathering place of hunters, fishermen, and farmers. Several men she had known while growing up on the Pully Farm greeted her as she entered the room. She lingered over the country sausage and eggs, and steaming black coffee, laughing and talking at a table with old friends. She let time pass so she would not arrive at the farm too early.

Ralph spotted the car. He slammed on his brakes, entered the grounds, and parked among pickup trucks and four-wheelers. Damn! In there among hicks and red necks, he would stand out in ridiculous exposure — no place to try his charm. Every eye in the room would be on him in a sudden complete and derisive silence. This would undo the enchantment he expected to lavish on her. He walked to the door and looked in through the glass panel. She sat at a table, surrounded by men of every age in heavy boots and field gear. Yokels! He returned to his car and sat behind the wheel, waiting and thinking. Another car entered the parking area and pulled up alongside his convertible. Ralph knew this vehicle, a big, black Ford sedan. SamuelS had bought several with the bigger supercharged engines made specifically for the highway patrol. Four men sat in the car; none made a move to get out. They all watched him, with steady gaze, saying nothing to each other. Few things made Ralph Green nervous, but this did. No amount of prowess stood a chance against honesty of purpose backed up by knives, blackjacks, iron knuckles, and automatic weapons. He eased his car back and turned toward town.

Just after daylight Joan entered the Pully Farms through a back gate and proceeded to the machine shop. There she found old Lyman, as she had expected to do this time of day. Lyman, a German immigrant trained in machining techniques in the old country, had worked for the Pullys thirty years and never wanted to leave. He could make anything — the best gun barrels, the finest swords, the inner workings of a grandfather's clock. She had spent a lot of time lingering around his shop watching him work as she grew up, with him in the bosom of the family. He made the sword she had used so successfully in fencing competitions, and the dagger she used in unnerving close-up combat. He had come to watch her compete and had wept tears of pride when she won first place. He would do anything in the world for her.

When she entered the shop he greeted her like his own prodigal child. After she hugged him and went through the usual small talk, he said, "You must be here for a reason. Did you come to hunt ducks with me again, or to target practice with pistol on the beach?"

"Oh, Lyman, I would love to, and it would be so much fun, but it will have to wait. I need a favor in a hurry."

"Okay."

"Another sword and another dagger."

"More competition?"

"Of a different sort. I need a real sword this time, stiffer than the one you made for dueling, a blade too strong to bend or break under great stress, and with exceedingly sharp edges."

"And the dagger?"

"Make it fit into the handle of the sword, so the sword can be used without first removing the dagger, and so the dagger can be used by removing it from the sword. Together they will look like one weapon only, a sword."

"Hmmm."

"And Lyman, make the case for the sword to look like and function like a walking cane, and line the cane with a lead shield so neither the sword nor the dagger can be seen in the fluoroscope machines in airports."

"Well, are you goin' to hijack an airplane?"

"No, Lyman, nothing dishonorable. Do you have all the materials you need?"

"Oh, yes. Plenty of everything here, even the sheets of lead, and the blades and handles already made, leftovers from other jobs."

"How long will it take?"

"Are you in a hurry?"

"Very much so."

"I can have it ready same time tomorrow."

"Lyman, you are a savior."

"You deserve anything you want."

"Lyman, I don't want Pop to know about the sword and dagger, and I don't want him to know I've been here."

"Why?"

"You know Pop. You can't trust his temper when evil is afoot."

"You be careful, girl."

"See you early in the morning."

"I go to work right now."

SamuelS had watched the Stuart house all night. They recognized Ralph when he parked at the curb, and watched his amateurish efforts to tail Joan. At one hundred thirty the Ford still had plenty of reserve to overtake either car. They easily followed him to the restaurant. After silently intimidating Ralph into giving up for the day, they waited until Joan left the café, then entered and had breakfast at a table by the window where they could watch the road. After breakfast they went toward the farm to intercept her return. With good timing the Ford entered the main gates and stopped between the pillars as her car came slowly down the field road. She had to stop. Only one SamuelS agent left their car and approached her window. His appearance puzzled her: the dark skin, black hair cut short, brown eyes, sports clothes with no hat. Someone lost and wanting directions? Secret police? Or worse? She braced to speed through the adjacent rail fence or to defend herself, waiting, tense, ready to move.

As he came to her window, he stooped and spoke. "Miss Pully, we are friends, and guardians." He spoke in the clipped tonguing of Arabic language. She waited. "We want to warn you. You were being followed this morning by a Ralph Green."

"Yes, I know Ralph Green. He is a trainer in the Athletic Club in town, and an instructor in martial arts," she said.

"He also collects organ donors for The Reverend Lotte."

"When and how?"

"At night, in bars and nightclubs, and perhaps other places."

"Why me?"

"You would be not only an ideal donor, but also a very valuable one, for The Reverend Lotte."

"What does this mean?"

"We can only warn you."

"Who sent you; who are you?"

"We are SamuelS, and Kahan and Xanadu are in our domain. We have been assigned to protect you."

"Do your men dress in gray suits and gray hats?"

"Ours don't. Legation's do."

"Then I have not seen you before."

"We try to be very discreet, but today revealed ourselves because danger grows for you."

"I thank you."

The man had stood in a bent position leaning toward her window while he talked, his big brown eyes luminous and concerned. He appeared to be genuine. Now he stood straight, backed away, and said, "We will always be watching until the danger has passed." Then he turned and strode to the black Ford. The driver backed into the public road and backed opposite to the route toward town and waited. Joan moved forward and began her return. The Ford followed at a discreet distance. She would never be able to lose it. And she really didn't want to. Ralph Greene! She had always sensed something evil about him and now she knew. He betrayed people to murder and donor-ship.

Lyman had made the most beautiful black walking cane she had ever seen. It balanced perfectly despite the expected extra weight. Lyman had altered a handle left over from her foils, and it looked like neither sword handle nor walking cane head, a perfect disguise. She tinkered with a knurled ring, and the dagger slid out revealing its long, sharp, tapered blade. The turn of the other knurled ring unsheathed the entire sword. She touched the top of Lyman's anvil with the side of the blade and it rang like a bell. "Oh Lyman, it is perfect, and beautiful too."

"Well, thank you."

"I wonder if the blades are truly hidden by the lead."

When she said this while sheathing the sword, Lyman handed her an x-ray picture of the walking cane. It looked like a cane with a solid metal core. No hint of blade could be seen. "Lyman, how did you get the x-ray picture?"

"My granddaughter, Villma. She is x-ray technician and works at the Resort Hospital. She x-rayed it this morning at four o'clock."

"Will you thank her for me?"

"She knows. Now let me show you something." He took the cane and showed her how to lock the knurled rings with secret detents. A prying inspector would not be able to release the weapons.

"What do I owe you, Lyman?"

"Your own safety. Go away now before Pully finds you and makes trouble for me ... and be safe."

She hugged him, kissed him on the cheek, and left him with tears in his eyes.

As she lowered Eric's garage door an hour and a half later, the black Ford moved slowly up the street. She locked up the house and slept until late afternoon.

Eric Stuart and Marcus Mann met the next day in a small office in the hospital administrative suite.

"What's happening now?" asked Eric.

"Atlanta tonight."

"Joan?"

"Yes."

"Commercial?"

"Delta."

"Will you send someone with her?"

"No. We have a plan worked out, and it must be kept secret. But you can be assured I will be supporting her in every way possible."

"Are you going with her?"

"Literally, no."

"Have you been watching Gladys?"

"Oh, yes. She hangs around 'til well after midnight, hovering over the files and the computer system like a mother hen. Nothing gets past her. But we have had no organs going out since the Charlotte incident," said Marcus.

"Any new developments?"

"Yes. Additional zones continue to lose couriers to an apparent second sweep across country. So far we have been spared. But we expect the worst. And the usual sporadic strikes continue ... the Charlotte courier, Stevens, and the hospital driver are still missing. I'm sure both men have been used for live organs and spare parts."

"Could Stevens have absconded with the heart and sold it for enormous profit, as the news media has speculated?" asked Eric.

"The idea was planted by a very resourceful hospital administrator to take the heat off until this crisis passes."

"Why?"

"It tempers or delays a public outcry," said Marcus.

"But it harms the boy's reputation."

"I'm not taking sides, but expediency under the circumstances may save the day. Chances are he will never return to protest his innocence."

"Tragically, you are probably right. Is something being done?"

"The police in several states and the FBI are looking for Stevens, but he totally disappeared, just as Williams did," said Marcus. "And the same is true of the recent ambulance disappearances in regions one, two, three, four, five, and just last night, a sixth, in region six, in downtown Seattle."

"I suspect the victims went into the shallowest of graves."

"Where they cannot be unearthed. So be it. In the meantime, what has Stanley Steinfelt been up to?" asked Marcus.

"He watches me very carefully. From the hallway, I have seen him in the drug room on two occasions in the last two days. This increases my suspicions. I think he is stealing and selling drugs, and Lord knows what else. I have thought we ought to bait him," said Eric.

"Yes, I agree. We will when we are ready to spring a trap. Shall we meet here again in forty-eight hours?"

"Yes."

"By the way, what has happened with the suit against us for organ distribution?"

"A pretrial ruling giving the new non-teaching services the organs they want."

"Damn!" said Stuart.

"Damn is right."

"This means every damned jack-leg in every small town hospital in the country will have a go at transplanting hearts, where they will do maybe one a month. Imagine your playing ability if you golfed only once a month."

"Well, I don't golf, but I know what you mean."

CHAPTER 23

In the Atlanta airport, a man in gray clothes walked, businesslike close behind, not looking directly at Joan. She began running, dodging among slower passengers, and dashed out on the sidewalk. A hospital van stood at the curb, clearly marked. She had not expected this, and continued toward the row of waiting taxis. The driver got out of the van, ran to catch up, and called, "Miss Pully!"

She stopped and turned. He appeared presentable enough, thirty something, wearing a surgical scrub suit and a long white hospital coat. "We are here from the hospital to pick you up."

"Oh, I was not expecting you. Let's get out of here quick, someone is chasing me."

They took the interstate and turned off finally onto a road she had never traveled on previous deliveries. The driver turned to her and said, "Have you been to Piedmont Hospital before?"

Suspicious, she answered, "No, this is my first trip to Atlanta."

"Oh, really."

"Yes, just one of those great things I've missed in life so far," she said, looking down on her hands holding the container. The driver took a turn to the right, a direction she knew to be the wrong way. She glanced over her shoulder into the rear of the van. The usual cabinets and paraphernalia could be hiding another person.

The road ran toward a brick wall and a Seven Eleven in the distance. She said, "I'm sorry to be a bother, but I've got to go to the bathroom, if you could stop for just a minute at that Seven Eleven."

"We are almost at the hospital. Can't you wait a minute or two more?"

"Something I ate on the plane is making me sick."

"We are almost there."

As they approached the store she said, "Listen, stop this damned thing, I'm about to shit in my pants!" She crossed her legs and groaned and opened the door of the moving vehicle. The driver glanced at her as though beautiful young women were above such earthy needs. The desperate look on her face sobered him, and he swerved the van toward the rear of the store, jamming his brakes. She leapt out, carrying the bucket, and limped on her cane toward the outside entrance to the ladies' room, and disappeared.

She waited a few minutes, then sauntered casually out past the van and up the street, across an intersection and continued alongside the brick wall. The driver regained his senses, and shouted. A commotion arose from the rear of the van and two men broke out running toward her. She turned a corner and ducked under bushes. She set the bucket on top of the wall, leapt over, and brought the bucket down with her. She stood almost at the next corner, a few feet from an iron gate with high spikes. Vines of ivy climbed throughout its interstices, hiding the street. Heavy traffic sped in both directions, and running feet went by, the two men shouting to each other, completely around the block and back again, and stopped on the sidewalk across the wall from her hiding place. The driver said to the other, "You go back the way we came, and I'll circle the other direction, but run. If she gets away from us, the boss will have our asses."

"Jesus, let me catch my breath," the other man said. They stood panting for a moment, the moment she needed. She ran to the gate, released the detent on her cane handle, opened the lower knurled ring, pulled out the sword, and waited. Running steps started in the opposite direction and faded away, then steps started in her direction; they turned the corner and came slapping down the pavement outside the wall toward the gate. She guessed at the timing and thrusted the sword, flat side down, through the grill of the gate, edge toward the runner, and braced her self behind its handle resting against a vertical rail. Something hit the blade with tremendous force, and a gargled cry erupted. She retracted the blade. It dripped blood. She pulled the ivy aside and peeked through. A head rolled over the curb.

She lifted herself atop the wall, swung the bucket up, and snapped off its lid. As the second man ran beneath her, she dumped the full bucket straight down on his head. It fit like an enormous hat; out of it came cavernous sounds, a deep gasp, and strangling breath. The bucket had contained nothing but pure formaldehyde. The man screamed muffled noises, "My eyes, I can't see!" gurgling and gasping, and he staggered into traffic. She hesitated, crouched atop the wall, hidden by overhanging limbs. A speeding delivery truck, without ever braking, hit him and he crashed, bucket first, into a large oak tree across the street.

The motor still idled in the empty van. She drove to Piedmont Hospital, and found Marcus Mann sitting in the lobby, waiting. Without a word he rose to meet her. They took a cab to the Lear.

"Do they have the heart?" she asked as they left the ground.

"Putting it in already."

"Good. No hitch getting here?"

"None. You were the perfect foil. We had a tailwind and got here before you took off."

"The trick worked perfectly."

"Yes. Stanley believed the conversation Eric and I carelessly let him overhear, and he fed it to Gladys. I'll bet she catches holy hell from somebody for this."

"She may get what she deserves."

"Not yet. She's too valuable to them. God, would I like to be home in bed, but we have a slow return against headwinds."

"Oh let's climb to forty thousand and forget the headwinds."

"Good idea," said Marcus. "How did you make out?"

"You would not believe it if I told you. Maybe it will be in the papers."

"I guess I have to wait."

"Yeah. I'm very modest, you know."

"Yes, I know. Incidentally, why are you walking with a cane?"

"Oh, I sprained my ankle yesterday afternoon on the stairs."

"Hope it heals soon."

"Thanks, Marcus. You are a dear man."

Marcus Mann drove from the Piedmont airport, and delivered Joan to Eric's house at three a.m. When Eric opened the door, Marcus retreated down the steps.

From across the park in front of the house, Ralph Green lowered his infrared glasses and said, "Dammit! She's either nowhere, or she's with people." He needed to get at her in privacy. In frustration he went home. At this hour he would make no progress in the bars, but a plan began to form in his imagination. Stuart is gone two whole days and a night at each stretch. Perfect. If he could just get to her and casually and sweetly offer to come to the house to give her karate lessons. He would bring his own floor mat. Then, after he won her confidence, the conquest would be easy.

Eric Stuart said, "Damn, am I glad to see you!" His tone startled Joan, and his pale and haggard appearance sobered her.

"Why, Eric. What's wrong?"

"Worried about you ... a lure in danger."

" I had such fun."

"What do you mean, fun?"

"Fooling them."

"Decoys as well as ducks get shot up."

"I know, but I stayed out of range."

"I'll just bet."

"Well, I'm here without a scratch."

"And cool as a morning breeze, a lot cooler than the hospital atmosphere."

"Meaning what, Eric?"

"The rumors are flying thick and fast."

"About what?"

"The organ couriers. Word is out about the missing ones, and others who have been robbed of kidneys and corneas."

"So what will happen?"

"Trouble is brewing."

SamuelS operatives stayed in Atlanta to access the results of the night's work, and they reported to Herman Hodder. Atlanta made the morning national news. Already a city known for its high crime rate and particular savagery, it added two to the number of violent deaths, two to the variety of brutality. The peculiar double death on a busy street near the fringes of town puzzled the police. One man in operating room garb had been cleanly decapitated, and the other strangled and drowned and blinded in formaldehyde — the solution par excellence for preserving dead flesh — and finished off when he staggered into traffic while struggling for breath. The ruptured white five-gallon plastic pail stayed in place over the second victim's head. The police found the top on the ground inside the brick wall. They could not identify the bodies. The victims' papers were false; the names were there, but no relative could be found and the addresses proved to be spurious also. Cause for the violence remained unknown. Both men had wallets and hundreds of dollars in their pockets. The money led police to guess drugs as the cause of violence, but why the unusual methods?

Marcus Mann, listening to the early morning news while shaving, paid scant attention until the commentator began talking about the white plastic bucket. Then he understood, and chuckled.

At Legation, The Reverend Lotte heard the names and recognized the monikers and began to curse. He called a meeting. Three men dead in four days — what the hell was going on? This had to be Mercury. "Smets, how do you explain this?"

"Reverend, we have seen nobody. These guys, these two in Atlanta, had worked for us several years. They stole a hospital van from the parking pool at Piedmont Hospital to meet the courier and they end up dead and we don't know what happened to the heart or the courier. Police found the van in the patient parking lot, unharmed."

"Who was the courier?"

"Some kid, Gladys said, a boy named Weston."

"We had a man on the Delta flight."

"He says he followed the courier to the hospital van at the airport, a sissy looking boy he thought, but he couldn't be sure."

"They got some kind of giant courier who can wipe out grown men like swatting flies?"

"We ain't seen nothin' that looked dangerous."

"Mercury's behind this. I want you to get them dressed-up dudes."

"We ain't seen them either. They've disappeared, completely. We don't even see the car no more, the big black Cadillac they drive."

"Smets, we need to have a meeting of all regional directors ... get Jones, Butler, and Carlson flown into here today ... we have a conference tonight."

"I'll call them right away. Tomorrow morning would be better. Jones and Carlson can't get here today from out west in time for a meeting."

"All right, tomorrow."

Herman Hodder arrived for another conference in Marion's New York hotel room at two p.m. "Jones will be sitting in a window seat, 34A, in the tail of the airplane directly in front of a row of seats reserved for SamuelS. Legation has called an emergency meeting and no first-class seats are available. He will have had to change planes in Chicago and will be angry, silent, and sullen all the time.

"Judge Taylor and his court have passed sentence, and again, no shaman and no chimera. Jones is the lieutenant in charge of the entire northwest area, and the most prolific and vicious murderer of the lot, and the strongest advocate of organ pirating. His favorite cruelty is to take both corneas and leave the victim staggering about the street in blind and terrible agony. Kahan hates this one above all of the other four devils. Timothy has the window seat in your row."

"Well and good," said Marion. "But you don't need me to witness this one. Tim is fully qualified and reliable. He knows what to do, and when and how. His fountain pen will be loaded with the right drug at the right dosage."

"Okay, if you so wish."

"That's my judgment."

"What if Jones changes seats, or takes another flight?"

"Tim is not only a marksman, he is a wily hunter as well, and in that case we would only be in his way."

"On the run or in a crowd, the neck shot would be difficult."

"Tim carries two or three pens in his pocket. Two shots in muscle elsewhere are as good as one in the neck."

"Okay."

"You have him booked?"

"Yes."

"Good. Let him do this one solo."

Legation met with the two remaining regional managers, Butler and Carlson, but delays had pushed the hour to late afternoon the next day. The Reverend Lotte raged again, in total frustration. Jones' aid had appeared at a Norfolk emergency room in the ambulance with dead Jones. Four Legation men had been killed in four days, two of his managers, one of them the ringleader.

CHAPTER 24

SamuelS listened to Legation, and the word went to Kahan, who sent Marion to reconnoiter the facts, and to inform Eric and Joan. At Sentara, Marion phoned Eric on his second day of lecturing and teaching. More to the fact, he avoided finding him on the first day; visiting professors of international acclaim usually do not seek out doctors at the fellowship level. Marion refused other invitations from faculty members. He asked Eric to take him to dinner tomorrow night, and added, *bring your friend Joan.*

"I don't know where she is."

"Delivering another heart in New Orleans, and she will be back today. Dr. Stuart, you know that long dagger she carries in the head of her walking cane … well four of Legation's thugs kidnapped her and the heart she was carrying to the Oschner Clinic. They drove her to an old warehouse on the riverfront. Upon arrival she slipped the dagger into one of them on the back seat next to her, and when another opened her door she shoved the dead one out, leapt to her feet and slashed his throat. The remaining two, the driver and the second backseat companion, rushed her with drawn guns and a SamualS agent shot them dead."

"What walking cane?"

"Oh. The one hiding the sword she used so effectively in Atlanta."

Eric said, "Holy God!"

Marion enchanted Joan. *She* intrigued Marion. Toward the end of the evening Marion had learned enough about Joan and Eric to make his decision, and he confided in them the nature of his mission, describing in detail the operations of Legation and SamuelS. Then he revealed the real reason for coming to her — Mercury and SamuelS had overheard the directives given by The Reverend Lotte to have her and Eric killed. The Reverend had turned violent about the damage he thought she had done to him in Atlanta and New Orleans. SamuelS would continue to be there wherever she went and would intervene only if it became necessary.

SamuelS would trail and protect Eric, too, whenever he left the hospital. But they believed Legation did not know Eric by sight, not yet, and had learned of his existence only through the betrayals by Gladys and Stiney. The only Legation people who had seen Joan were now dead.

Joan said, "I know something of this. An agent of SamuelS stopped me on a country road recently. He said Ralph Green was following me."

"I have not been told about Ralph Green," said Marion.

"The SamuelS agent identified him as a collector of donors for The Reverend Lotte. I know him as a trainer and karate teacher at The Athletic Club."

Then Eric asked about the supply of organs and tissue going to Xanadu. Marion described in detail the sources from worldwide violence and the other supply from undesirables.

"You mean to say certain living, healthy people will be taken and used in this manner?"

"As peaches from a tree, or lambs from a flock, or trees from a forest. And the mortality rate will be diminutive compared to the murder rate in this country alone, in this time of terror and violence. In fact, with the removal of certain offenders, the murder rate may diminish."

"This will not be condoned by..."

"Certain moralistic attitudes. But as a person with a high order of intelligence, you understand the purpose of moralistic principles."

"Realistically yes, but you will have to deal with the vast majority who think otherwise."

"God, the Omnipotent, put everything known to man on this earth before man got here. Sin is a manmade concept.

Mankind at his worst cannot begin to contrive the cruelties or the wickedness of nature. His nastiest murder pales beside the countless daily deaths by the cycles of life running spontaneously."

"Well, indeed. You are, of course, absolutely right, but way ahead of your time."

"In a way yes, and in a way, no. Human sacrifice is an old, old practice. But its purpose has always been one and the same: to give up one person to improve the lot of others. The Aztecs, for instance, thought to appease the gods with the blood and the beating heart of a virgin maiden, expecting better crops in return and, therefore, a better life for the entire tribe."

"A concept totally outmoded."

"Is it, now? Millions still practice the sacrifice of the Mass, the Eucharist, one of the sacraments in Christian churches, the modern evolutionary product of the original blood sacrifice of a living human victim. In fact, they eat the symbolic flesh and drink the symbolic blood of the imaginary person who they have been led to believe to be the sacrificed immaculately conceived Son of God, to atone for the contrived notion of sin. This ceremony keeps alive the practice of symbolic human sacrifice, and symbolic cannibalism. And does not a donor, too, become the sacrificed? A donor's fate becomes acceptable only because of the tragic, spontaneous, unplanned, uncontrollable event leading to donor death. In both situations the heart must be removed while still beating, while the victim is still alive ... thus the little sacramental wafer is nothing less than the symbolic beating heart."

"My God," said Eric, "How blind we can be in the rawness of everyday reality."

"And transplanting a living heart into another person whose life is temporarily suspended is the essence of the notion of transplantation. All other transplant endeavors pale by comparison. But time has caught up with us. Demand will fill the need."

"Can we afford to be so frank?"

"We no longer can afford to continue the pretense."

"How do you or how does Kahan justify the taking of organs from what he considers to be the unjust?"

"He saw the pattern a long time ago, and now he simply takes the developing trend a few steps ahead of the evolving changes."

"I don't think I follow you exactly."

"Society the world over is changing. The concepts imbued by Western civilization are fading; anarchy will get worse before it gets better. The terrorists on both sides, those who turn loaded passenger planes into suicidal and homicidal bombs, and those who respond with a rain of conventional bombs render an increasing carnage, and an abundance of the near dead. SamuelS and Xanadu stand ready to take advantage of the growing resources from violence, wherever it occurs."

"Commendable, indeed."

"All peoples will begin to seek a global refuge. Now a person desperate for an organ transplant has to choose between the haphazard luck of the American and the European systems, or the absolute chaos of less advanced countries. Since justice may be just as archaic and obtunded by due process, Xanadu will become a haven of relief to both problems."

"Perhaps."

"In the advance toward a global society, medicine of this sort will become available in the Mecca of all Meccas, and many an organ will be salvaged in the chaos of war and civilian violence. Otherwise, this priceless material would go to waste. And the other source removes the tyrant, who would escape, from the society he harms ... such sporting good fun to take the scoundrels who are getting away with it."

"Well and good."

"And, of course, this society would never touch the prisons full of useless people, especially those carrying lifetime sentences? On the contrary, look at what the Chinese are doing."

"What are they doing?"

"The recent use of prisoners as organ donors, after execution."

"Oh, yes. It was in the news."

"And a friend of mine, a professor of Ophthalmology at a renowned medical school on the east coast went to Beijing to teach cornea transplantation techniques. He was offered fresh corneas from living prisoners. He declined."

"I had not heard," said Eric.

"Kahan has elected to move into a supply of people society could profit by losing. Once you remove the mental impedimenta, it differs from no other harvest."

"Would your God approve?"

"If you want to apply the name, God, to nature with all of its unseen forces, then remember these forces also spawn tuberculosis, cancer, yellow fever, bubonic plague, syphilis, AIDS, injury, hepatitis, mental retardation, cerebral palsy, insanity, serial murderers, perverts of every kind, suicide, pain, depression, grief, unhappiness ... all of human experience including birth, and death itself, and take untold millions down to a premature end for what immediate purpose but to feed the worm and the vulture — a relentless, haphazard harvest serving only to make room for other people at best. Our harvest, on the other hand, serves the purpose of prolonging and improving useful lives, at the same time weeding out those who harm the state of any society. But to ask the question seems to me to underestimate the power of God. Does he approve? Does he approve of his own inventions? Being all-powerful, he certainly could stop it if he disapproved."

"It all is a matter of attitude."

"It was to the cannibals, to the conquistadors, to all the religions practicing human sacrifice at one time or another to appease imagined gods, to the fathers of the sweat shops, to the owners of coal mines, to Moses and then Joshua on the trek to the Promised Land, to the slave traders, and the religious leaders who murdered and tortured those who chose not to believe the same as they themselves did. Read Leviticus and Numbers, and the dismaying historical records of Cardinal de Richelieu, for instance."

"And it is here to stay?"

"Yes, but far removed from your professional realm. The only reason to inform you of this organization and its operation is to follow Kahan's orders to protect Joan, and now you. And I might warn you, Eric, once Legation learns of your real significance, they will come after you with greater determination for knowing as much as Joan knows about their operation."

Joan said, "Oh Eric, I got you into this."

"I got myself in by stopping to pick you up, and I have no regrets."

Marion said, "The important thing now is to protect yourselves. It would be much better if you went into hiding, Joan, until this war ends. And it will end in the annihilation of Legation one way or another."

"I do not intend to hide. This has become my fight, too. And I intend to continue. In fact, I am enjoying it immensely. You know by nature I am a pacifist, almost a vegetarian, and I weep for the fallen sparrow, but I love to undo tyrants. Right now my job is to deliver live organs to those who need them, and I shall continue to do this to fulfill my own personal duties and to take the place of those who risk too much on a mission."

"Well, we will always be there watching."

"Don't get in my way."

Marion chuckled. "I know better already."

"So be it." She kissed him on the cheek.

Eric returned to work, frustrated. Out of habit he practiced diligence in beholden duties first, then among all things. In athletic routines, his Jujitsu instructor had begun to approach his student with nervous caution. In money, Eric in high school accumulated over a million dollars from the right penny stock investment, and in college over a hundred million in computer software investments. And he still worked for whatever he set out to accomplish. But now Joan eluded his industry, and went her own self-sufficient, daredevil way. Over this one hope he had no control.

CHAPTER 25

SamuelS went along and reported later to Herman. Timothy had been coached by Marion to do this job using long needles and the topical anesthetic, *Bliss*, along with a drug combination for deeper injection. He would work through the cloth at the junction of the back and the bottom of Butler's airplane seat.

He sat in 8A directly behind Butler. After takeoff, Butler abruptly tilted his seat back as far as it would go, almost into Timothy's lap. Tim braced his knees against the seat back, and covered himself with a blanket. He grasped his walking cane, brought it under the blanket, and went to work.

When the plane landed an hour and a half later, Butler sat slumped in his seat. After the plane had emptied, the stewardesses went down the aisle to awaken the reluctant sleeping passenger in 7A. She unfastened his seat belt and he slid forward, his knees against the seat in front. She called for help. Butler drew an occasional breath, and had a slow, thready pulse. All of this quit in the ambulance en route to the nearest emergency room, where the attending doctor, after all resuscitation measures failed, pronounced Butler dead. The tentative diagnosis became *heart attack.* The coroner did a cursory autopsy but he went nowhere near the needle mark in a fat buttock. No physical abnormalities could be found. No marks were noted on the usual inspection and photography of the body.

The results of the routine drug screen arrived 48 hours later, showing an elevated blood stream level of several drugs difficult to identify, except a trace of cocaine. Marion had put it there as a red herring to draw attention away from his own effective combinations. He knew this death initially would be called heart attack and the examination would be careless and cursory. But Kahan and Herman would leave nothing to chance. A SamuelS man claimed Butler as a relative. Quick cremation destroyed all remaining evidence before the drug screen had been reported. Drug abuse would be the final conclusion of the coroner.

The Reverend Lotte sat before the remnants of his staff in the early evening. Smets had returned on a late afternoon flight from New Orleans with negative news. The autopsy did not explain the death of Butler — it revealed no cause.

"Smets, where is that girl? Smets, I want her found and dispatched, now."

"I've been in New Orleans, where you sent me. I have not had time to look for her."

"Well, find her. Where does she live? Where does she stay? Shoot, do anything to get rid of her."

"We don't know. Nobody has seen her recently and lived to tell about it, if she is the one doing this."

"The whole system is coming apart. Our men in every city are refusing to lay a hand on a courier. They're all gettin' the creeps. We're losing this war. LifeChain is getting stronger instead of weaker, and we're getting killed."

"I'm getting the creeps myself. Three of the four regional managers dead already of no cause at all. So, who's next? Me?
You? After they get Carlson here."

"What do you mean, get Carlson?" shouted Carlson.

"The pattern looks to me like it's been set, three of the four top managers gone already ... seems obvious who's next. They are destroying Legation one at a time, and after you it's me and finally, The Reverend."

"I want my shot at that dame."

"I'm not so sure I want you killed right now. So just go back to Denver and leave her to us. And take every organ and all the other parts you possibly can. Our funds will start getting low if this killing keeps up." Then he said to Smets, "And speaking of money, how are we doing with our customers who go to the fire?"

"On a good one we clear more than two hundred grand. And we're salvaging as many or more from other funeral homes, the referrals, as from our own. It was a great idea, Reverend, buying the biggest and best crematorium in town."

"Yeah, I know, and I want you to start buying them up in every city."

"All right. We can't go wrong this way."

"So, what are you using?"

"Cardboard boxes, mostly."

"And for those who insist on polished wood, or shining metal?"

"Oh, we take them out at the last minute, after the relatives can get no closer to the flames. Cleaned, the boxes look like new and we sell them again."

"What for ashes?"

"Carcasses of pigs, and half carcasses of hogs, from the slaughter house, garbage from the kitchen."

The Reverend thought for a moment, staring at the floor. "I tell you what. The winos who come to sell blood — put them to work. After you bleed them, give each one a free bottle of wine when he delivers a dog to you from the pound, any kind that weighs more than fifty pounds."

"And how will we get the dogs to cooperate?"

"Chloroform, Smets, chloroform. Marvelous dispatcher. I keep some around the house myself."

"And where will we keep a supply of willing dogs?"

"In the deep freeze, Smets. They will be most cooperative."

"Okay, if you say so."

"Yeah, well do it. And now, tell me this ... where is Tashkent, Uzbekistan?

"Don't know. Why?"

"I've got another idea."

"I'm listenin'."

"I want you to buy a travel agency, a big one with international offices."

"What for?"

"One way travel, Smets. The road to destiny, the road to heaven."

"Where did you get such an idea?"

"The associated press, World Report."

"Yeah?"

"Yeah. This couple, a doctor and his professor wife in remote Bukhara ...seems they sold cheap trips and hard-to-get Western visas, only their clients went on trips a organ at a time. But they got careless and the police got wise and found leftovers and lots of cash. Of course, we won't do anything dumb like that, will we, Smets?"

"Naw, but we got all we can handle right now, boss."

"We can always handle more cash, and it's always a delight to watch narrow avarice leading the horde to destiny, the Lord meting out justice for another of the deadly sins."

"Yeah, well, I got a itchy feel like destiny might be nibbling at my ass, too. We need to get rid of these devils who are after us."

"Okay. Now, who can do this job on Pully? Who is the meanest, deadliest, cleanest you know?"

"It would cost you at least a hundred grand."

"It's worth it. Who?"

"Harry Snider."

"The suspender?"

"Yes."

"Find him while I find Gladys."

SamuelS agents listened to the Legation conversations, and Herman chuckled. He phoned Ivan at Mercury and asked, "Are you listening?"

"To Legation? God, yes."

"Should we let Gladys talk?"

"Yes," Ivan said. "Let her talk. The more they come out in the open the more they get themselves killed. Suspension. Do you know him?"

"I know about him ... lots of notches on his gun and he has never been caught, not yet," said Herman.

"Should we warn Joan?"

"Where would you find her?"

"I guess you're right. What about Kahan?"

"He always knows more than we do."

Joan Pully slipped out the back window of Eric's house, cut through the woods to a taxi stand, and arrived at the LifeChain building after nine p.m. She entered Marcus Mann's office, turned on no lights, switched on the computer, and pulled the phone to the desk edge. The computer screen blinked on and the national chain showed slow activity. The local area remained quiet. She opened her purse and removed the tiny listening device. A half hour went by; the building remained silent as though deserted. Then without warning, the phone console lit up, line one began to flash, and Joan listened without lifting the receiver as Gladys answered the call from Legation. The Reverend Lotte demanded to know how to find Joan Pully.

"Why would I know?" asked Gladys.

"Because you do know."

"I did not agree to give you that type of information. Our deal confines itself to the source of organs."

"Listen, Gladys, you are in enough trouble with us already, and we want cooperation and we want it now."

"It will cost you another ten."

"And ten for your Stiney creep too?"

"No, just me. We won't let him know about this one."

"Okay, now where is she?"

"She has holed up, I think, with Eric Stuart, who is a fellow in heart surgery at Sentara."

"And where does he live?"

"I don't know, but I'm sure you can find it. Anyway, why do you want to know?"

"You want her to stay around?"

"I think she knows something. I don't like the way she hangs out here."

"You don't? Then where does Eric Stuart live?"

"What are you doing this time? I have been surprised more than once to see her back here."

"Your worries would be at an end. This one goes to *Suspension*, and we can use him on you too, if the need arises."

Gladys gasped. "Oh my God, Harry Snider. New York."

"Yes, my dear, and he will be here no later than morning. I'm sure he would welcome more than one job while he's at it."

Then Gladys gave Eric's address to The Reverend. Joan sat in stunned silence, her heart racing. She had heard rumors of Harry Snider, but she really knew nothing about him. She must warn Eric. It would take awhile for Snider to get to Norfolk from New York, yet he could drive it in six hours or negotiate the airports and a flight in little more than three. She would be waiting. She went to the nearest pay phone to call a taxi.

CHAPTER 26

Eric had gone to bed and slept soundly. Joan went to the kitchen, ate a light snack, then sat in a living room chair to plan for the arrival of Harry Snider. At the moment she could not recall the specifics except his peculiar aura, something extraordinarily ugly, and dangerous. Most likely nothing would happen tonight, but she would be on guard anyway. She waited up, rocking, thinking, dreading the danger of so sinister and deadly an enemy hidden and stalking her in the coming days. But she would not awaken Eric.

The night sounds came to her, muted by the closed windows. Traffic along the street out front diminished, and after midnight only an occasional car went by. She dozed, then awoke at three a.m., and thought of going to bed. But she drowsed again, and somewhere distant in her perception a dampened, remote, almost subliminal sound failed to complete its course. The momentum of the night stagnated in a lacuna of waiting. She stopped rocking, and remained stone still, drowsing in a somnolent vigil, and her mind began to listen, then her mind came to know an acute presence — the whispering rolling of a slowing wheel coming to rest near a curb, perhaps one cracked acorn, or a slung pebble gives it away to a distant ear, and an unsuspected awareness begins to monitor the sequence of night sounds. She stood, crossed the room, and opened the back door over the garage. She found and placed a meat cleaver and a copper pot on the kitchen counter and returned to her chair.

Harry Snider approached the assigned house. In every action he copied cat motion, never making a sound, never leaving a trace of evidence. And he never moved against any hit except in the somnolent shadows after midnight, to strangle, to stab, almost never to use the little hidden .25 tucked in his armpit holster beneath a tight sweater, its silencer in another pocket. Legation had found and hired him in New York at eight p.m. No surprise. He had done jobs for them before. No one bothered him when he cruised at 100 mph on the Jersey Turnpike, and the usual goons in Delaware and Maryland had gone to bed. A girl. How could she be harming a preacher, he wondered? This one would be easy, nothing but a woman. He would be back in New York before lunch, a hundred thousand dollars richer, and in cash.

He had slowly coursed by Eric's house several times, getting an idea of the layout, evaluating the front steps leading up to the living area on the second floor, and the rear window on the ground level. He parked a block away, and walked on grass to avoid the sound of feet.

In the silence Joan sensed something monstrous and very quiet building to a climax. In imagination she went down the back stairs from the living area, and through the storage room behind a wall in front of the parking spaces to the window at ground level in the rear of the house, the only break in the wall of the ground floor except the garage door.

At Eric's rear window, Snider moved the sash up and slithered over the sill. In the darkness he tested each area of the floor with his toes before trusting his weight to it as he crept across the storage area and found the stairs beside Eric's parked car. He ascended on all fours, crawling a creakless, slow, sustained progression toward the short balcony down to the kitchen entrance.

Joan, waiting above, heard nothing. But the awareness of silence seemed to come to the back of the house. She knew the ground floor window now stood open; the breeze crossed the storeroom, ascended the stairs, came down the hallway, and brushed her face. She blipped a passing thought ... even so expert a burglar can grow careless, and not take the time to close a window. Then with chilling insight she realized this had not been carelessness, it had a purpose other than escape, but she had no time to change tactics now.

She climbed atop the kitchen counter above the entrance door and peeked down the hallway. He crawled like a slinking cat over the top step, rose to his feet on the balcony and moved toward the kitchen entrance with incredible speed and agility. She raised the copper pot at arms length, and slammed it down over the top of his head as he came through the entrance. She leapt to the floor, grabbed the meat cleaver off the counter and struck the pot rim a crimping blow with the back of the blade. The room exploded in reverberating ringing metallic echoes. Snider went down, but his instinctive and reflexive defenses reacted with astounding strength. He grabbed one of her legs while falling, and sent her skidding across the floor, crashing into the opposite baseboard. Two other shadows came through the kitchen door.

Overhead blinding bright lights exploded the darkness. Eric, pajama clad, stood in the bedroom doorway a split instant before he erupted into action. Snider, on his back across the room from her, wrestled with the copper pot. He rolled over on his belly, got up on his knees tugging at the rim with both hands, rose, staggered, then vomited inside the pot, and slime ran down his front. She had accomplished what she intended to do: virtually destroyed his hearing apparatus with the noise, and with the same blow crimped the pot tight on his head and neck. His disturbed vestibular apparatus now led him retching in lurching circles of vertigo. The cleaver lay in the middle of the room. Both accomplices drew automatics at the same time. In a wave of panic and fear for Eric's safety Joan leapt up to go to his rescue. The muzzle of a gun came up toward her but Eric hit both intruders with surprising violence and speed. One thing she had neglected in her accomplishments, the Ninjitsu hidden hand techniques. She had never seen such a lightening hammer fist blow, at the back of the head where it meets the neck, twice with split-second rapidity, and the two intruders lay twitching and gasping, each spinal cord shocked at the base of the skull.

She reached the meat cleaver. Eric raised his palm. She stopped and he put a finger to his lips, and motioned her to back away. Snider now lurched in violent circles about the room, striking out, totally disoriented in space. Eric got a pair of shears out of a drawer. He tiptoed to Snider, delivered a backhand chop to his belly. Snider slumped forward. Eric slit his clothes down the back and shucked him out. He cut a shoulder strap and found the .25 automatic encased in its contrived cloth sheath, and removed a dagger from the split pants. Snider now wore nothing but the copper pot and his black shoes and white socks.

Eric backed across the room and waited. Snider stood again and began to lurch in circles, striking out wildly. Eric watched, then retrieved a broom. Snider vomited beneath the pot again. The room reeked, a sour nauseating stench. Eric calculated for a moment then went to Snider's other side. He reached out with the broom and touched a flailing hand. Snider leapt toward the broom. Eric moved aside, then glided to the kitchen door, reached with the broom and tickled Snider again. Snider lunged forward, and Eric backed through the door. He reached forward with the broom again and touched Snider's hand. Snider lurched blindly through the doorway slamming his fists against wood and went half way down the balcony toward the stairs. Eric descended a couple of steps and started to reach with the broom again and saw Joan come through the door with the meat cleaver raised. Snider lunged forward again. Eric turned and skipped down the stairs to the garage floor. Joan brought the cleaver down flat side onto the pot. The house filled again with reverberating ringing noise. Snider pitched forward, and tumbled downstairs. He hit the floor head first on the back half of a somersault. Bone popped. The pot flew off and rolled into the opposite wall. Joan at the head of the stairs, and Eric on the garage floor, watched Snider twitch then stop breathing. Eric checked the heart and pulse, straightened up, and said, "Dead ... Broke his neck, I guess."

Joan said, "Oh God, Eric, what are we going to do with three dead men in the house?"

Four SamuelS men arrived at Eric's house late. They thought Snider would be hours yet en route. He had told Smets he intended driving down. He surely would not have had time to get ready for the trip then drive all the way from New York. To their surprise, they found the lights glaring through Eric's living room windows, and the car with the New York license plates parked down the street. They suspected the worst, circled the house, and found the open rear window. One approached and listened. He heard Joan Pully saying, "Eric, where did you learn that maneuver?"

"My instructor."

The man stuck his head through the window and whispered loudly, "Dr. Stuart." Both Eric and Joan started, and turned toward the open storeroom door. "SamuelS," the voice said. "Are you all right?"

"You are a bit late," said Joan.

"We guessed the timing wrong. We thought we were ahead of him."

"We are all right," said Eric.

"Do you need help?"

"We have a minor problem, here."

"May we help?"

"How many of you?"

"Four."

"Come in through the window and shut it."

The four men gathered at the foot of the stairwell and looked down at the dead form of Harry Snider. "Do you know this man?" asked Eric.

"Harry Snider, one of the worst. What happened?"

"Well, he fell, more or less, but best you look upstairs also." They filed up the steps ahead of Joan who walked with her arms folded across each other, the cleaver sticking up in her right hand. Eric followed. The men surrounded the two forms on the living room floor. "Do you know them?"

"Yeah, we know them. They are almost as bad as Snider, or were. They worked together on the tougher assignments. I can't believe this. Three dead, not a drop of blood anywhere, and not a scratch on either of you. How did you do it?"

"We wrestled," said Eric, "But now, what to do with them?"

"We would be glad to take them off your hands."

"Well, I suppose we really should call the police."

"Oh, please don't, Dr. Stuart. It would cause all sorts of trouble and do no good either. For one thing, Legation would get off the hook completely."

"Then what do you propose."

"We will stack them across Legation's front door."

Eric laughed, "Okay," he said, "How?"

"Turn out all lights and let us back into your garage."

After they left, Eric drove his car back in and closed the garage door. He picked up a mop and scrubbed the garage floor, then progressed up the stairs swabbing each step. When he reached the landing, Joan knelt on the floor cleaning up Snider's mess with a rag. Eric swiped his way down the balcony and into the kitchen with the mop. The house had turned cold and silent. He stooped, took the rag from Joan's hand, and lifted her up. She stood, tremulous, vulnerable, spent. He whispered, "I will finish this ... you go to bed." Without a word, she left the room and in a moment the sound of the shower murmured through the house.

Ralph Green followed Joan from LifeChain headquarters. After she entered Eric's house, he parked and waited, aware of something ominous and peculiar about the night. Hours later, when Snider crept behind the house, Ralph, sensed movements in the shadows, and crouched lower in his seat. Then the living room lights flashed on, and the SamuelS vehicle cruised by and made a panic stop. Three men jumped out and rounded the house. Through infrared field glasses Ralph watched the garage door open, the moving automobiles, then Eric and Joan and three strange men and something vague bulging on the floor in the darkened garage before the car left. He went home, again frustrated. But he would pursue her until his luck changed.

Joan stepped out of the bath, dried off, and slipped into the bed. She picked up a book and began reading. Eric showered and joined her. She put the book down but left the light on. "I was not dirty, I just felt dirty," she whispered, as he crawled in bed, and she moved over to him. They lay facing each other, almost nose to nose.

"I felt the same. Did you know they were coming?" He whispered, too.

"I had reason to expect it."

"Why didn't you tell me?"

"You were asleep and dead tired."

"And you came damned close to getting yourself killed."

"I did not expect the other two until I realized he had left the window open."

"The unexpected is the worst of all treacheries."

"Eric, are you scolding me?"

"Yes," he said, still whispering.

"I'm so sorry."

"I'm not. I'm just damned glad you are here to be scolded."

They lay facing each other in the light, her eyes focused on his in a steady gaze, and she touched his face with gentle fingertips. "Eric why are we whispering ... still whispering?"

"Fear, I guess, of the unknown."

"Of what might still lurk in this house ... the hovering spirits of three evil men, newly dead? Could they still be here?"

"Who could know the answer?"

"They could not harm us?"

He reached a hand behind her back, and felt the helpless trembling, and he drew her to his belly, encircling in a hovering embrace. "Joan I could not stand to lose you. It would be unbearable."

"You are not going to lose me."

"We came within a split second tonight."

Eric brushed her mouth gently with his, and lingered, and her lips parted. The warm moisture, the tactile tongue, drew to his center, but in the whirling periphery of awareness dark ominous shadows of reality hovered. And at once, and beyond volition his emotions escaped, the fear and anger and fright turned primal. She touched with a hand and clasped with a womb of warm fingers and guided him.

He folded gently down onto her body and in the serene languor gathered her up in his arms and cradled her, and nuzzled up her neck and said into her ear, "I love you, Oh God ... how I love you."

They talked.

"I love you too, Eric," she whispered, "And I am just beginning to understand the word."

"Yes, and I know for the first time I am no longer alone in the world."

"Nor I, and I knew it the first night," she said.

"You had the courage to tell me then. I'm so lucky."

"*We* are so lucky."

"I know, to have this depth," he said.

"And there is something else. Something magical and beyond logic has just happened in this room. I can't quite define it."

"I know."

"What?"

"I have just given you a son."

"You can't know for sure."

"No, but I feel it."

"Imagine!"

"I do imagine it and I have every day now for a long time."

"It's what you want?"

"To clasp him to my heart will be another completion."

"Suppose it's a girl?"

"With all the wiles of a woman inherent in her newborn body moving against my chest in the bosom of my hand ... what could be more charming and endearing?"

"Could it be, Eric, could his spirit already exists here now with us?"

"The spirit of the yet unborn here and the spirits of those who would have taken our lives — are they out in the vast unknown ... or are they all in this room now?"

"I do wonder."

"And what of all the others?"

"Who?"

"Well, since we are speaking of the ethereal, if you are just pregnant with our son, then some two hundred million of his brothers and sisters are at this moment perishing in the primeval sanctuary of woman."

"Oh Eric, that makes my tunnel of love a living tomb."

"One of God's mysterious inventions."

At five-fifteen in the morning, SamuelS, in a van parked across the street, watched its own men arrive in a black Ford sedan, unload Snider and his cohorts from the trunk, and place them across the third garage door of Legation headquarters. One rang the bell, and they left. The door lifted and Fred appeared. In astonishment he stared down at the three bodies stacked on each other, the top one naked except his socks and shoes, his cut up clothing draped across his bare back.

For help and support, Fred turned toward the interior of

Legation quarters and called out to The Reverend. He would just be arriving in his usual mysterious way. No one, no employee, nor anyone else, had ever seen him enter or leave the building; he simply appeared there early in the morning. And the employees dared not ask for an explanation, because holiness moved and defended The Reverend. No one answered Fred's shouts. He recovered and dragged the bodies inside and closed the door.

The Reverend heard the panic in Fred's shouts and ascended the stairs from his office in the basement, and peeked from his hiding place down on the bodies. He recognized the dead men, and for the first time a shock of fear surged through his belly. His enemies had answered his most deadly assault in the same manner as his other attempts — his men stone dead without a clue. He contained his emotions and spoke to Fred over the intercom. "Wake up Chiron."

In his boardroom later, The Reverend faced Smets. Carlson had already returned to Denver. "Smets, who did this?"

"The possibilities, you must realize, are quite limited. Either the girl turned the tables on them, or SamuelS was there waiting."

"Is the girl still alive?"

"I think so. Dr. Stuart is at work in the hospital today and he spent last night at his home."

"Then who brought Snider and his cronies here? Stuart?"

"Stuart, I venture, does not know we exist, and if he did he would not know our location, nor would he risk getting caught with three dead bodies."

"That leaves Mercury, or the girl. I would not put it past her. I think she would haul three dead bodies."

"I don't. Give the girl credit. All of her dispatches so far, if she is the person responsible, have been done with wit and finesse. She would not haul a body. That's too crude for her."

"Then it was Mercury."

"Mercury is innocent. They don't know nothin', and they ain't got the 'quipment or the guts to do anything."

"We got to do something big to prove ourselves, to frighten off whoever is doing this."

Then he outlined his plan to Smets. Smets turned pale and said, "Hey, I don't know about that, Reverend." And The Reverend phoned Gladys. Ivan Prescott and Walter Exum at Mercury headquarters listened in astonishment. The vicious daring surprised even the SamuelS men.

CHAPTER 27

Joan entered the back door of LifeChain after hours. She let herself into Marcus Mann's office, flipped on the computer, and took the small listening device out of her purse. Startling news appeared on the screen. A donor in Bristol, Virginia, could supply a heart, a liver, lungs, kidneys, and the digestive system. Blood type, body size, age, and tissue typing matched patients at the Sentara center. Eric had talked about the likelihood of a situation like this — only a matter of time until it happens — in which they would either have to fly the donor in, with all of the support equipment running and take the organs after arrival, or the surgical team would fly to the donor, take the organs and fly back, then spend the rest of the day or night doing the transplants.

A phone light came on. Joan listened while Gladys Gleason betrayed the Sentara team to Legation. She negotiated a fee of fifty thousand dollars, and agreed to supply all information. The Reverend Lotte wanted the blood type, weight, and height on every person on the trip.

"I don't know who will be chosen, but I can give you the information on everybody who works in the heart room at Sentara. But why do you want it, Reverend? You don't believe in it," said Gladys.

"For sale purposes only, my dear," said The Reverend.

"Just a moment, while I pull up the screen." The computer keys rattled, then Gladys read off the statistics to The Reverend. Joan held her breath.

They would take not only the donor but also the chief of cardiac surgery, his nursing team, part of his house staff, and his technicians … everybody on the trip. Oh, my God! Eric might be on the plane, too. The Reverend wanted details. Gladys said she would call back.

Joan stayed in the office waiting, busy at the computer. Finally Gladys phoned The Reverend with details of the plans.

The LifeChain jet will take off the day after tomorrow afternoon at four o'clock from Piedmont Aviation in Norfolk with the heart team aboard, land at Bristol within two hours, and return with organs retrieved by the team. Then Gladys gave The Reverend a list of the people scheduled to go, Eric and Marcus Mann among them.

Joan left LifeChain headquarters and drove to the Pully farm in Eric's car. Her sudden unannounced visit and the request for a favor surprised her father. This proud daughter seldom asked for anything.

"Now, Daddy, you have got to hold your temper until I get through telling you. Promise?"

"Promise."

"Good." Then she told him about Eric rescuing her, about Legation, about Marcus Mann and LifeChain, about the betrayals, the disappearance of couriers, organ pirating, the extraordinary dedication of the medical teams pioneering organ transplantation, the urgency of their trips when they try to outrun the limited ischemic times, and about the recent open warfare on UNOS.

She described the scheduled trip to retrieve multiple organs, and Legation's brazen plan to rob the live organs and to kidnap and destroy the entire transplant team.

"What would you have me do?"

"Well, we will say nothing to the people involved. The team will fly down to Bristol on the LifeChain plane, and proceed to the hospital and retrieve the organs. Before they leave the Piedmont runways in Norfolk I will be picked up by a plane at Langley Air Force Base, and flown to Bristol Airport."

"How will you get to Langley?"

"A Pully farmhand will drive me in a muddy farm pickup truck. In Bristol the Air Force plane will stand by and wait for my return. Air Force personnel will escort me to the hospital.

When the transplant team leaves the hospital I will grab Eric and take the entire team and the organs to the waiting escort and on to the waiting Air Force plane."

"Who is Eric?"

"Daddy, he is the cardiac fellow at Sentara who rescued me."

"Ahh, indeed." His eyes twinkled teasingly.

"Now, Daddy, stop kidding."

"Sorry, go ahead."

"I will return with the team to Langley, a waiting Air Force helicopter will fly me and the team to Sentara, and later I will drive to Piedmont to meet the LifeChain plane."

"What will you drive?"

"Eric's car."

"Okay. And nobody but the crew will be on the LifeChain plane returning from Bristol?"

"Oh, no. We send a fake team and fake organ canisters aboard. Legation will try to take them either at Bristol, or at Piedmont after the plane lands."

"Why do you want to meet them?"

"Oh, I wouldn't miss all the fun for anything."

"How do you know they will try something there instead of Bristol?"

"My guess. I don't think they want the plane and the crew."

"Probably right. So, what can I do?"

"Get the Air Force involved for me."

"Any commanding officer should be glad of the opportunity to help with something so noble."

"No. No they are not. Marcus Mann, president of LifeChain, has tried to get the Air Force to fly organs at supersonic speeds when the ischemic time was very critical. They refused."

"What's ischemic time?"

"The time an organ can live without its own blood supply, the time lapsing from removal of the organ to the time of transplanting it into another person."

"Why wouldn't the military planes fly them?"

"Their supersonic planes carry only one or two people, and besides, they have their own transplant programs and this is competition."

"Damn. Who goes back to military duty after an organ transplant?"

"Nobody."

"Then why do they do it?"

"All the services build their own hierarchies in medicine."

"What a waste of money."

"I hear our doctors say it's the costliest medical care in the country, and the lowest in quality."

"Now, how can we get you an Air Force plane tomorrow night?"

"Pull strings, Daddy, pull strings. Senator Thurston owes you his career and he is on the Armed Services Committee. Call him and tell him what you want, and don't forget the escorts."

"I'll make you a deal."

"What?"

"I bring the fake heart team aboard the LifeChain plane in Bristol for the return trip."

"Who?"

"Veterans of two wars, hand-to-hand combat experts, Navy Frogmen, ex-spies, all of them tough."

"Hankering for blood, are you?"

"It's been a long time."

"Exceedingly dangerous, and you have to be prepared for the action to start at either Bristol or Norfolk."

"The doubt only adds spice. Like you, I am guessing Norfolk, but we will be ready in any event."

"I would know better than to refuse. Anyway, how do you plan to get to Bristol?"

"Don't worry. We will be in the hospital lobby waiting

when you arrive."

"Good. I will need to have a conference with two or three of your Navy frogmen before the trip."

"It can be arranged."

"I feel a vast relief."

"Which hospital?"

"Oh, I almost forgot ... Bristol General, out on the edge of town."

"Consider it done. Now spend the night with us and have dinner. We haven't seen you in months. And I can have the frogmen here early tomorrow."

She thought a moment about the safety of home and said, "Well, I think I will, thank you."

After breakfast the next morning, Joan met with the two frogmen and talked for half an hour describing her plans. They were gleefull over the mischief she plotted and assured her it could be done. She explained the plans to her father and drove back to Eric's home.

Marcus Mann stood just inside the operating room door at Bristol General. Joan peeked in, and his jaw dropped. She crooked a come-hither finger at him.

"Joan! What on earth?" he exclaimed.

She motioned him to be quiet and walked ahead to the end of the hallway. Then she told him the plan.

When the team came out of the operating room, Joan led them to the waiting Air Force helicopter and they were lifted with canisters of organs to the waiting plane. A little more than an hour after takeoff, they landed at Langley. A helicopter lifted Joan and the team over the water to Norfolk and Sentara. Joan went to Eric's car and drove to Piedmont airfield.

During the return flight, Pully talked with his men, his neighbors, men of his substance, equally incensed by the kidnap plot of the organ pirates. All had seen active combat, and all were armed with .45 automatics, brass knuckles, and blackjacks. In bags they carried enough rags to gag a dozen men, a big coil of rope, hatchets, and other tools. The former frogmen were experts in underwater explosives and demolition.

At Piedmont, the plane taxied to the open tarmac. Joan had parked in a shadow a few minutes before the hospital van arrived, presumably for the heart team. This could not be the hospital crew because she had canceled the arrangement with ground transportation at the hospital. Two or three Legation bandits would be waiting inside, and others would be ready at another destination, probably the Norfolk headquarters.

Joseph Pully's team filed down the steps, four of them carrying a canister each. Pully himself looked the part of the senior surgeon. Joan did not recognize the driver of the van who appeared to be alone. He politely opened the side door of the van and the group entered. Pully went to the front seat beside the driver.

Underway, the driver said to Pully, "I understand, Dr. Kemp, that you need to get to the operating room as quick as possible to save the organs."

"Yes," said Pully. "Yes we do."

"Then you don't mind if I take a shortcut, do you?"

"Of course not. Anything you can do to help will be appreciated." Pully played the game. The van sped down the Norfolk Virginia Beach expressway, its siren wailing. In downtown Norfolk, the van took numerous tire-squealing turns along a series of narrow streets, then dived through the opened doors of a large building.

Joan followed at a distance, taking the curves much better in Eric's car. She deviated through the shadows and other parked cars and stopped at the shed wall as the van entered. She slithered under the closing door like a limbo dancer, into a warehouse full of shadows.

The team unloaded from the van, and the driver said, "Now gentlemen, if you will just go through the big white door in the rear, you will find a shortcut to the operating rooms."

Pully, acting his role, said, "Well I'll be damned. In all my years here I never knew about this entrance to the hospital or the operating rooms." The driver could not know Pully himself, as a major fund-raiser, had helped plan the hospital and approved the blueprints before construction began.

"Oh, yes," said the driver. "We drivers have to know a lot of shortcuts."

"Good for you," said Pully. "I guess we don't really show our appreciation as we should."

The ex-frogmen carrying the canisters held onto them dearly as the team went toward the distant white door. The door flew open and three men in white gowns surrounded the team, and escorted them into a brightly lit room. Joan stifled a gasp when she spotted the noose hanging high above. The gowned men snatched the pails. One of the three, Smets, stepped forward and addressed Pully. "Well, Dr. Kemp, we have a little job for you to do. I want you to take the organs apart, you and your team. I want separate heart, lungs, kidneys, liver, pancreas, and we don't have any time to waste."

Pully said, "All right, if your men will open the canisters and pour the contents out on the table while we scrub up, we will proceed."

"You don't need to scrub, just put on gloves."

"Better if we scrubbed at the sink over there."

"Make it brief. Which one of you is Eric Stuart?"

Pully answered, "Stuart? Oh, Stuart stayed behind in Bristol to help remove bone and corneas and other things that could wait a little longer."

Smets grabbed one bucket and turned to the men with

him and said, "Open the buckets on the tables as Dr. Kemp requests."

Smets and the other three men lifted the four canisters, one on each end of the two wooden tables. Pully and his crew crossed to the sinks, rolling up their sleeves. Pully turned on the one faucet and stuck his hands under the water and began to wash. The others crowded in and imitated him, faking familiarity. Knowing what to expect next, they turned their backs to the room and hunched over the running water.

A pair of hands pulled the top off each canister. The simultaneous explosion of four buckets filled the room with a sharp boom. Bucket fragments hit Smets and his men in the face, and a shower of flying fluid drenched them. The nonflammable fluid, acetic acid, would not corrode through plastic or kill a pilot if an accidental explosion occurred during flight. But it would put eyes out of commission on direct contact, and on clothes it fumed and choked the wearer.

The acid disabled Smets and his crew. The veterans at the sink returned to combat with enthusiasm. They grabbed Smets, strung him up on the overhead noose, and turned him loose, kicking. One man ran to the ambulance and returned with a black bag. He opened it and began to unwind rope. They cut the rope in long segments, wound hangman's knots, and slung the other ends over the beams above. They strung up the remaining three as fast as they could get the ropes ready. Joan watched in the distance.

A back door eased open and a crouching form carrying a pistol in one hand came through, and slunk among the shadows toward her and the unaware group in the middle of the brightly lit room. She squatted behind a cabinet lateral to his path. He went past and she edged forward. She stepped out and chopped him at the base of his skull. He pitched forward into the pool of light and his pistol skidded out of reach. They hanged him next.

Chiron came home from his night's revelry, entered Legation headquarters, and climbed to his bunk. He looked at the hanged men and said, "I want to operate. I want to operate on Joan Pully." He smiled, turned on his side, and went to sleep.

At 5 a.m., The Reverend went upstairs to check on a strange smell. In the warehouse, Smets and four others dangled dead from ropes attached to overhead beams. The Reverend noted an odd and unnerving coincidence: Smets had been treated to the soiled slick noose his men had used to claim so many donors by partial strangulation. The rear entry door of the abandoned stolen hospital ambulance stood open … five bodies and a stolen ambulance to dispose of by himself.

The Reverend waited for his secretaries to arrive. He spoke to them over the intercom system, telling them to take the day off with pay. Then The Reverend himself went to U-haul and rented a one-ton refrigerated truck, returned to the warehouse, cut the bodies down, stacked them in the truck, locked its doors, and plugged in the auxiliary refrigerator line to the house current. As he finished this task, haggard and wet with sweat, something stirred in the bunk along the wall above. Chiron raised his head and grinned down at The Reverend. God! Lotte had forgotten about him. Chiron climbed down, walked up to Lotte and said, "I want to operate." The Reverend turned his back and went to his office. He would dispose of Chiron in a minute, but Chiron struck fear to his solar plexus. Too nasty to touch, he thought. Had Chiron seen Lotte moving the bodies? Did he understand? Would he talk?

Two men arrived from Richmond two and a half hours after The Reverend's first call for help. They drove the loaded truck to Legation headquarters in Richmond. At night the new help from Baltimore took the Sentara ambulance to the beachfront and abandoned it.

The Reverend had no one to call to a meeting. Carlson in

Denver, and now in charge of all four territories working frantically to supplant the missing three — Fergerson, Butler, and Jones — had no time to spare. Only The Reverend himself remained at main headquarters. Desperate beyond anger, he began scheming again.

CHAPTER 28

Pleased with Dr. Gambela's great surgical success in the two months since his return to Xanadu, Kahan called for a conference. Perhaps Gambela could offer needed advice about the future of the hospital. Did Gambela know of Eric Stuart, a young surgeon of extraordinary talent near the completion of his training in cardiac surgery at Norfolk?

Yes, he did. Stuart already had made a name for himself in the world of cardiac surgery, already recognized as a master surgeon while still in training. And he had proven his intellectual abilities by publishing a dozen papers describing techniques to improve the everyday practice of heart surgery, and had made important contributions from the research laboratories.

"You will need a second man soon, Dr. Gambela, without doubt. There is already too much for one to do."

"Yes." Gambela had grown to appreciate the sensible ways of Kahan.

"And you must get away frequently to visit other clinics and to attend conferences and meetings."

"Yes, I should."

"As a matter of fact, I have already received several requests from the better places for you to come as visiting professor, to teach the latest techniques."

"Well, for the time being they will have to come here and join the visitors we see every day."

"Yes, until we get help. And speaking of help, what do you think might induce Dr. Stuart to join our staff?" asked Kahan.

"The strongest factor in our favor is the disenchantment caused by increasing faults in the American system."

"And they are?"

"The limited supply of organs, the vicious donor politics, the political fighting over the limited donor pool, senseless crime in the streets threatening the safety of every American family, and finally, the death knell of American leadership in medicine — the Managed Care system. It is destroying specialty control and putting the least able of all physicians in charge. And these clowns are being paid to keep patients out of the hands of the specialists who should be treating them, and who are responsible, almost without exception, for scientific advances in medicine."

"Pity," said Kahan.

"Can you imagine an insurance industry calling the shots in the practice of medicine?"

"I cannot imagine it tolerably."

"Can you imagine a typing clerk in charge of computer science?"

"An apt analogy."

"Yes, and it's too bad. The Americans pioneered the science of organ transplantation; now the system is stymied by circumstances."

"No doubt the leadership is threatened," said Kahan, "while we are fortunate to be growing."

"We will need many heart surgeons as the demand grows."

"I know, and I intend to offer Dr. Stuart every temptation to join us, with your approval, of course."

"Indeed." Gambela returned to his work, pleased with the prospect of getting competent help.

Herman Hodder once again came to Xanadu at Kahan's request. Kahan, in an agitated state, paced back and forth. "As you know, Herman, The Reverend Lotte has stepped up the pressure on UNOS again. Three more couriers have disappeared in the past week and three prominent businessmen, who made the mistake of drinking in bars, have been sent home blind, sans corneas, and in the most horrible pain. And three more couriers have been found bleeding and their kidneys gone. Calls have come from Ivan Prescott, in acute agitation, on behalf of himself and Marcus Mann at LifeChain. The news has broken, and investigative reporters are moving in with a vengeance, accusing the hospitals of a cover up."

"Yes, we do know."

"This will stop!" Then he gave instructions: SamuelS should take out Carlson and leave no evidence of willful elimination. Take him now before he has time to organize his forces in the west and in the rest of the United States. And guard Joan Pully.

"Joan Pully is not easy to guard. We never know what she will do next."

Kahan laughed. "I like that girl. When this is over we will bring her here as our guest, along with Eric Stuart."

"You are not likely to get her here anyway except willingly."

"I hope she remains forever true to her principles."

"No doubt about Stuart and the girl. One would follow the other here."

"We need him."

"And who else?"

"Well, there is Ivan Prescott, who would lend a scholarly, erudite air and provide the highest standards in the laboratories."

"In the States now, and forever hooked on Teresa," said Herman.

"Perhaps," said Kahan, looking Herman in the eye.

"And?" said Herman.

Kahan seemed lost for a second, and said, "Oh, well, Dr. Marion's period of grief is slowly resolving and he ought to be ready soon to pursue his great talents in our laboratories."

"And Sarah will see to it, no doubt."

"I believe a very deep devotion is in full bloom."

"Aren't you afraid of losing both Teresa and Sarah to Cupid's persuasion?" asked Herman.

"No, they are sworn SamuelSs, and SamuelSs may die,

but they never desert. They are allowed to marry and stay, but not to leave."

"Indeed."

"Yes," said Kahan. "Things are shaping up, but we must move on. Use Dr. Marion to the utmost advantage, take Carlson first; then we will have only The Reverend Lotte to worry about."

"As you wish, but have you thought about what will remain after destruction of Legation headquarters and loss of leadership?"

"Yes."

"We will have no way to monitor the remaining activities."

"The entire organization will be splintered and will become a series of small-time operations with little power. Should any one become big enough to be a threat we can take the necessary steps then. After The Reverend's regional managers are gone, I plan to report Legation systematically to law enforcement agencies. The remnants of Legation will be harassed if not disabled by the law, cumbersome though it be. Then we will target the United States only for removal of undesirables."

"If you say so, but there is such a rich abundance of weeding to be done in the fat country."

"We must never let unbridled emotion dictate our moves."

"What's to come of the voluntary system in the United States in the future?"

"Obviously it's inefficient. By count, fifty percent of donors are lost to prejudice and superstition and ignorance, and just plain resentment of the politics involved. Perhaps we can change the situation," said Kahan.

"What do you have in mind?"

"Money, my dear friend. Money. It does so much to clarify thinking."

"How?"

Establish a donor fund. Every family gets paid, and the system reimburses itself. I will start it with an immense contribution."

"I suspect you are on the right track."

"Of course. Why should the most priceless of commodities be given away? As an example, I have never understood the philosophy of free blood transfusions, and the confusion and inefficiency created by this failed attempt at altruism."

"Well, and I certainly think the donor's family should have some say-so about who gets the organ," said Hermann.

"How about the highest bidder?"

"Now *that* would stimulate the salvaging of organs, the kindest of all generosity."

"We shall see."

"And the Reverend Lotte?"

"Ah yes, something unusual for him. We need someone who has very special ability in this approach to justice, to plot something ironic and filled with historical retribution. I have a source in mind."

"How about Chiron himself? He could be turned against Lotte."

"Demon enough, but we need something more appropriate to the Reverend's ways."

CHAPTER 29

Joan found Marcus in his office. "Do you know the LifeChain director at Cincinnati?" she asked.

"Sure I know him. He's a friend of mine. We've survived at least two near crashes together delivering organs."

"Legation has bought the entire clockworks on a Cincinnati donor, to be flown to Denver by private jet tonight. I want to take the place of one of the two couriers, or just go along with both."

"Joan, I hesitate to expose you to any more danger."

"Do you want to help me or do you want me to do this one all alone?"

"After the Bristol experience we owe you something, so whatever you want."

"Then please call your friend and arrange for me to be on the plane tonight. I will meet them at the airport in Cincinnati. But please don't tell him why. He might do something to spook everybody or call in the wrong people to try to help."

"As you say, be careful."

The two couriers, hugging their canisters, sat alone in the rear passenger compartment. Joan dropped into deep sleep before the takeoff. She awoke when the plane touched down gently at the old Stapleton airport. It taxied onto the abandoned tarmac and drew up close to a helicopter pad.

Joan's unexpected trip to Denver with the supply of live donor organs changed Herman Hodder's plans for the attack on Carlson. Marion had been alerted a few minutes after he checked into the Brown Palace. Now he sat to the left of Sarah in the back seat of the Mercedes 600 hidden in night shadows near the helicopter pad. Tim sat on her right. Herman in the front seat stared out into the darkness, his bulky shoulders rigidly straight.

The helicopter descended after Marion's car parked. Watching its spidery and stressful wobbling in the air, he wondered who might be piloting the contraption. Spread legs, and protruding controls came into view through the glass bulb as it settled to the pavement: impersonal, foreboding because nothing about it carried real identity. The pilot could be anybody. The chopper squatted down and sprang up and settled, its arms coasted to a halt and no one got out. In the distance, a night guard beside an open gate in the chain-link fence around the abandoned field never moved.

The sound of a motorcycle entered the darkness. Subdued, slow, and muffled, it moved without lights into the shadows just outside the well-lit helicopter landing pad and stopped somewhere out of sight. The helicopter pilot did not look in the direction of the sound. Marion remained silent, thinking of the foreboding statement the motorcycle sound had just made in the darkness, a presentiment of waiting danger, and the mood settled into the car like an enveloping fog. Tim stared out the window.

The plane arrived, the door opened, and steps folded down. The helicopter engines started then dropped to idle; the doors swung open and the pilot and another man jumped to the pavement and moved toward the plane. Another noise erupted from the sky and an ambulance helicopter hovered toward pavement. A red cross shone against a round white circle on the fuselage.

The two couriers carrying the containers had descended halfway down the steps, Joan with her walking cane behind them, when a large sedan moved regally onto the tarmac. In it sat four men she knew to be SamuelS agents, all dressed in identical sport clothes. Two of the men got out of the car and advanced toward the plane.

Joan looked skyward at the descending helicopter. She propped on her cane and pole vaulted out of the steps onto the tarmac and sprinted back under the jet into the darkness and came in a circle beneath the first helicopter. She snapped open the door to the battery compartment, and grabbed a handful of wires. The dagger came out of the handle of her cane and she severed the wires from the electrodes. Sparks flew and blinking lights atop the rotors went out. The engines died. She crawled under the fuselage and punctured the fuel tanks with the tip of the dagger. Without missing a step, she circled back and grabbed each courier by an arm and ran to the second helicopter as it settled to the pavement. She recognized the pilot and pushed the couriers aboard, and followed. They lifted off toward the hospital.

The two men from the first helicopter broke and ran to their machine. Frantic efforts to start the engines failed. SamuelS's guns had been drawn. One SamuelS rapped on the glass bulb, and ordered the occupants out onto the pavement. Both were frisked and relieved of their pistols. One SamuelS went aboard and returned with two machine pistols. A SamuelS ordered both men back into the helicopter, and locked the doors shut.

A motorcycle roared in the darkness of the parking area, and a bright cyclops beam swept across the area as the bike turned at fast speed. Marion's driver followed.

One of the SamuelS's let the air out of the helicopter tires while the another stood by with his gun aimed at the occupants.

The man on the bike wore black tight-fitting clothes and a black helmet. Herman turned toward the back seat and said to Marion, "Carlson rides the motorcycle."

"Carlson?"

"He will do anything to escape. I think he expected to be aboard the other helicopter by now with his victims."

"Where to?"

"He will try to reach I-70 east, I guess, then make a fast run toward Limon."

"Okay, he will have to slow or stop for a turn up the ramp."

Ahead, a pre-fab house in tow blocked the funnel shaped ramp entry. The motorcycle stopped behind it to avoid the unpaved shoulder. The car came alongside, straddling over into the weedy gravel embankment. Marion passed his cane across to Tim. The motorcycle uproar diminished as the engine dropped to idle. The rider astride the bike with his toes touching the pavement stared ahead while bracing to start again. Tim lowered his window, reached out with the cane, and tapped a handlebar on the bike. Carlson looked toward him, and Tim, being boyish, smiled and said, "Nice bike you got there, fella. I bet it will do a hundred and fifty."

Carlson flipped open the visor of his black helmet and raised a gloved right hand making a circle with his thumb and middle finger. Smiling and looking at him, Tim brought the cane down, the end sweeping past the tightly clad thigh. The sound of the shot went unnoticed in the noise and confusion.

Traffic moved up the ramp, the motorcycle roared, and at the highway entrance dashed out of line and accelerated east toward Limon and tore away with the throttles wide open. Marion's driver kept up ... Marion counted the seconds for the shot to take effect, a mixture of paralyzing drugs with more prolonged action than pure succinylcholine. The driver spoke, "Already up to one hundred ten."

Carlson began to sag. The motorcycle moved ahead as the front wheel turned out of control and the long skid began. It flipped on its side, pitching Carlson down the highway. His head struck the pavement, the black helmet shattered into flying fragments and a red geyser spurted up from the concrete as the top of his head disappeared. The motorcycle bounced, leapt, twisted, and bent into a tangled mass slinging bolts and parts and smoke and fire, then exploded into flames. Carlson flipped and bounced down the highway, tatters of clothes and pieces of flesh flying away. Herman directed the driver again, they took an off ramp, turned, and came back on I-70 west, and sped toward the hospital.

At the Denver General landing pad, they watched as Joan came out the emergency entrance with the two couriers and boarded the waiting helicopter. Marion's car returned to Stapleton, arriving after Joan and the couriers had taken off aboard the jet. Marion sat with the people in his car, hidden in the shadows again, and watched the proceedings. Silence surrounded them. The guard still paced in a pool of light at the distant gate. Gasoline from the punctured tanks of the disabled Legation helicopter seeped across the pavement, and the two cowed and angry Legation hoods sat inside the bulb. A rope had been triple looped over the body of the chopper, encircling and securing the doors. The two SamuelS men guarding the helicopter went to their car. They sat for a moment, watching and waiting. The man on the left side of the rear seat rolled his window down, lit a cigarette, gazed through the smoke at the prisoners in the glass bulb, then pitched the burning butt into the trail of gasoline. As the fuel flared up, the car sped away and rounded the corner of the building toward the gates. The flame roared under the helicopter and the explosion rocked the building and the retreating car, and blew bits of helicopter through the fence into the highway.

CHAPTER 30

Joan peeked through the front blinds of Eric's home. A black Ford sedan stood at the opposite curb and she recognized the olive skinned man, with black hair and black eyebrows who had spoken to her in the gates of the Pulley farm.

She eased through the back window on the ground floor and went across the woods behind the house to the street beyond. She spotted a SamuelS automobile on the back street, too. She stayed hidden and moved through undergrowth along unused paths toward her apartment seven blocks away.

There she cleaned away a coating of dust in the living room, bedroom, and kitchen, then packed a bag with several outfits, all of them leisure suits of one sort or another. She emptied the refrigerator of spoiling perishables, then put out the garbage and walked to the supermarket.

The cloudless sky, the June leaves now nearly grown, the morning air balmy, the sun warm on her face — she had been cloistered far too long. She thought of The Reverend Lotte. She suspected him of subtleties and frank deceptions of the most devious sort.

The new sounds on The Reverend's receivers in his Legation office got his immediate attention. He played with the switches and his pulse raced. He could hardly believe it — from the bug in Joan Pully's apartment. It had remained silent so long. On impulse he almost yelled for the dead Smets. But he yelled for Fred and they ran to his car. After he had driven past Joan's building several times, coursing through the neighborhood, The Reverend saw her walking toward the shopping center. Tall, elegant, and beautiful — this had to be Joan Pully. He had never seen her before. If not Joan, he wanted to meet the woman anyway. You never know. This could turn into something great. He congratulated himself on being ready, and followed at a distance, creeping along in his car. She crossed the parking lot and entered the grocery store. He parked in the no-parking area along the curb, in the fire lane, in front of Super Grocer across her path of entry and her likely path of exit. He would try first to take her with subtlety and deception. He entered the store, obtained a large cart, and proceeded to shop.

Imitating an old man, bent over, and crippled by arthritis, feeble in all his motions, he followed her at a distance in the store. When she went to checkout he passed through the express lane. He stood behind a pillar outside the store entrance, fumbling with car keys until she completed her purchase. As she came through the exit he moved into her line of vision and shambled toward his car, walking shuffling, mincing steps. Holding his bags in one hand he fumbled, trying to manage the groceries and open the car door. A bag in the crook of an arm began to sag and slip out of his clutches. His hands shook with old age and palsy.

He guessed right about her inclinations. She came to help. She took the key out of his hand, unlocked the door, took his grocery bags, and bent forward to place them on the back floor, all the time holding onto her own bag with the other hand. The feeble old man crouched forward hiding her bent form. Then he shoved her into the rear seat, slid in himself and closed the door.

Joan pitched head first over the groceries onto the floor, face down into an amorphous mass of junk and blankets. Something hidden beneath the blankets took her mouth in an iron grip, and struck her on the back of the neck. She lost consciousness.

She awoke with her hands cuffed behind her back, her mouth taped shut, and her ankles tied together. The car smelled of bruised fruit and vegetables. A large red-faced man wearing a big black hat sat in the back seat above her. A sharp pain in her neck and head, nausea, and the urgency of impending heaves drove her to near panic. The sky in motion blurred past the opposite window. Waving green limbs of trees overhanging the streets appeared and passed, shadows and spots of shade crawling in undulant patterns over the seats and floor of the moving car and over her supine body. She shut her eyes to obliterate the motion.

Nausea continued and she willfully quelled the urge to vomit, and the terror of choking on the acid vileness. The car went along the winding streets, around corners too fast, and she rolled along the floor to and fro against the seats. Finally the car slowed and entered a building and stopped.

The Reverend Lotte, dizzy with triumph, and anything but old and feeble now, stomped about and danced a jig on the warehouse pavement and laughed and slapped his thigh like Hitler's frenzied jubilation in newsreels at the fall of France. The man in the back seat got out, turned and reached into the car, pulled Joan out, threw her belly down over his shoulder, and went through the back door of the garage into the inner building. He carried her into a distant room and laid her on a bunk, flipped her over, and removed the tape from her mouth. He untied the rope around her ankles, and unsnapped the handcuffs. She sat up.

Two large men stood, one on either side of the only door into the cell, each with his arms folded across his chest. The man who had overpowered her stood beside the bed. She eyed him, rubbed the back of her neck, every muscle taut and alert, ready to spring. She felt through her clothes, her pockets; house keys, money, and purse were gone, and by now the captors would know her identity without doubt.

Iron bars crisscrossed two windows near the ceiling. A heavy iron-grated door swung open inside the room. She had become a helpless prisoner in a cell waiting to be closed.

The man spoke again. "I am Fred, at your service, madam." And waving a hand toward the two guards, he continued, "These two able gentlemen are my assistants. Their job is to guarantee you an uneventful stay with us. You will find a bath through the little door there," — he turned and pointed — "your food will be brought to you, and a maid will do your laundry. When I leave, these two men will stand guard outside your door to obey your every wish. I trust you have a pleasant stay." He bowed, removed his big black hat in an elaborate and spurious gesture of gallantry, revealing a big round completely naked head, and large flap-like ears. He turned, replaced his hat, and left. The guards shut the iron door behind themselves, then the wooden door, and the room became devoid of sound. Joan sat in astonished anger, seething at the sarcastic politeness of Fred. This would be a final minor score to settle.

Fred made no bones about his apprehensions and fears. He wanted to feed her through the system immediately. He had already seen the burning hatred in her eyes, and it struck fear to his very core. Give her to Chiron, now! But The Reverend had greater aspirations. He sensed a personal triumph, a great victory, and he wanted an immense profit. He would try to go directly to the person who had offered ten million dollars for a donor with credentials the same as those of Joan Pully. He owed Gladys Gleason, but he would not let his promise bother his conscience.

The Reverend Lotte awoke Moha at three a.m. with glad news. He had found an ideal donor. Moha no longer needed a donor, and almost said so, but caught himself in time. His fear of Kahan's wrath made him doubly cautious, and he resorted to subterfuge. "You do? Is it Joan Pully by any chance?"

The Reverend controlled his astonishment, and answered smoothly, "Yes, it is."

"Is she in good health?"

"Yes, she is here safe with me."

"Well, keep her in the best of health. Someone will call you with further instructions."

"It's ten million, you know."

"Yes, I know. Rest assured you will get it, but only if she remains unharmed."

Moha called Kahan, and Kahan called Herman Hodder.

"We are relieved to have your instructions," said Herman.

"Good. And Herman, what did The Reverend promise Gladys?"

"A fourth. Two-and-a-half million."

"See that she knows The Reverend got his ten million."

Herman called The Reverend. "You have a tall type-B woman in her twenties and in good health?"

"For whom do you call?"

"One in need to be born again."

"Where?"

"An extradition."

"Ah, yes. It is available."

"Your terms?"

"His terms. Ten."

"How?"

"The bills themselves, one thousand each."

"Delivered when and where?"

"An exchange at the time."

"You will deliver to us?"

"Yes. You name the place," said The Reverend.

"At Piedmont field, a Gulfstream V belonging to the American company *Explorations Limited,* its logo and name on the tail upright — and how will we know you?"

"Funeral flags will fly on the front fenders of the vehicle making the delivery," said The Reverend.

"Ten thousand bills weigh a lot. Are you prepared?"

"My delivery will be quite heavy, too. Pack the money in a pine casket of the cheapest sort."

"When will you be ready?"

"Approximately mid-afternoon tomorrow."

"Good. We will be there."

Joan sat on her bed most of the time, waiting and angry. No one had unlocked the iron-latticed door from the time she entered. She exercised and read and at first refused the food trays passed through a slot. Then she sniffed and tasted carefully and became more confident. On the third day she ate a generous lunch. Within the hour she became too sleepy to sit up.

She remembered nothing until Herman Hodder removed the lid from the pine casket and untied her blindfold. He had already rescued her once, if not twice before. She glared angrily at him, and he started back at the fury. He gave her a sly sign, his thumb and middle finger making a zero. She glimpsed the overhead and realized she had been brought aboard an airplane.

Under the suspicious eyes of Legation, two men lifted another casket out of a bunk, brought it forward, and opened the lid, revealing the contents to Fred. The casket, chock full of new one thousand dollar bills, satisfied him. Herman closed the lid, and The Reverend's men placed it in the hearse, and drove away, blue flags flying with the white word *Funeral,* one on each front fender.

When the plane came out of its steep climb over the Atlantic, Herman Hodder gently raised Joan's shoulders and then lifted her entire body onto a bunk. He tenderly removed the tape from her mouth, opened and removed the handcuffs, untied the rope around her ankles, and unsnapped the strait jacket. She sat up and rubbed her face. She studied Herman and he did not know what to expect next — a karate kick, a karate chop, a foot in his stomach, or something more intelligent. She said, "It will be a long damned time before I try to help another feeble old man with his groceries."

"You meant well."

From the tiny airport Joan rode in the rear seat with the nurse, and a SamuelS guard in front with the driver of the Range Rover as they wound up through the twisting mountain roads above the airstrip. The jungle heat diminished as they climbed. When they went through the hidden gates at the end of the road and entered the grounds Joan felt the dissipation of somberness. The weight of concern with danger and death all lifted and she knew she had been brought to an unusual destination, to a freedom existing nowhere else in otherworldly strictures.

She met Kahan with Sofya at dinner, and Gambela and his wife. In the ambience of this setting — the music, the splendor — she knew both men had been at work all day, Kahan managing the hospital with such sure control as could only be imagined in an American hospital, and Gambela transplanting several hearts in one day without the impediment of inept or careless help.

The meal soon ended and the guests returned toward their quarters. Joan went to bed in her own apartment. But she stayed awake, worrying about Eric. What lay in store? He would leave training and step into the competitive and entrepreneurial world of American medicine, now sullied by intrusion of the insurance industry. His life would no longer be his own. Great hope and enthusiasm of youth would gradually be ground out of him as the years vanished in a whirlwind of action, much of it given to futile attempts against inertia of the system. She liked Xanadu, each physician an endowed artist with no impedimenta and no trivia to defeat his energies, but she would say only so much to Eric. He should see for himself and make up his mind without coercion.

CHAPTER 31

Pully and his crew set up a watch on activities around Legation headquarters. A light came on at four-thirty a.m. in an upstairs window of the house next door, then the light at five o'clock in the Legation basement window. Pully, a history buff, turned to his memory of the city's past, and went to his books. The house next door to Legation headquarters had been a prison during the Revolutionary War. Underground tunnels were known to exist in those days, and he wondered if one might have been opened and waterproofed and put back into use. This must be the answer, and now he had a plan for attack.

After midnight, his first crew silenced the alarm system and surrounded the warehouse building. A second crew arrived by boat, and entered through a door just off the water, ascended the stairs in the darkness, and overpowered two guards asleep in their chairs. The crew took the casket full of money, the file cabinets, and all of The Reverend's computers to the boat within minutes. They cast off and drifted out into the bay, while another boatload of men slipped beneath the overhang of the building. Pully took command of this group. The old Navy frogs leapt over the side. Some, wearing scuba outfits, went beneath the water, and others infiltrated the building. They placed incendiary demolition charges in critical locations to implode and burn the building. They distributed large blocks of pure sodium on all floors, then hooked the series of charges to a radio detonator and left in the darkness. The boat drifted toward the house along the shore beneath overhanging tree limbs, and an anchor slipped into the water. From there they watched the dark windows. At four-thirty a.m., a light came on upstairs in the house. At five a.m. the below ground-level window of Legation lit up. Pully, with his finger on the radio button, waited fifteen seconds for The Reverend to get well inside the building then activated the charges. The building coughed, trembled, and collapsed inward, rumbling deep within itself. The Legation light vanished and those in the house quivered and returned to normal. The anchor came out of the water, and the boat drifted far down the coast before the engine started.

Flames leapt high above the glowing debris, a blue core of intense heat destroying and burning everything caught under its weight. The men hidden in the foliage around the building met two blocks away in the early dawn and drove away in a van.

Chiron wandered in a drunken stupor toward home and in the dawn light came upon the flaming ruins. He turned away, and an hour later entered Sentara General hospital and wandered into the surgical suite. No one attended the receptionist's desk so early in the morning. He got by and went into the doctor's lounge and fell asleep on a couch.

The next night, Herman Hodder arrived with the armored truck, the driver, and two guards. Pully, already familiar with rumors of Herman's commanding presence, sensed his identity before Herman had a chance to introduce himself, "Mr. Pully, I came to face you myself ... I am..."

Pully interrupted. "Don't tell me. If you are who I think you are, I do not want to know your name. I do not want the responsibility. We have carried out our part of the bargain and the records and the money are here for you. I do not want the money, because I have no use for any of the dangers, be it counterfeit, marked for identity, or genuinely free of all encumbrances. Under no circumstances do we want to be accused of money laundering. I also do not want to know the identity of any Legation operations in other cities. We have not opened the files, and I prefer you open them off my premises. We want no part in the gathering of organs except to help LifeChain."

"We were hoping you would be willing to help eliminate..."

"No, no, no. We have lived up to our commitment and we will not go out of our own bailiwick."

"Kahan has given us directions to respect your every wish. Therefore, we will make no further attempts to embroil you in the necessary warfare. And Kahan wishes me to assure you your daughter Joan Pully is safe with him and his family and she will be returned as soon as her pursuers have been eliminated."

"I thank you. Now may we help you load these containers?"

"No. The two guards can handle the file cabinets and computer equipment. The coffin with its contents remains here."

"We don't want it. We don't need it."

"LifeChain does, and Kahan insists. So whether you want it or not, Mr. Pully, it is yours to pay for the demolition job you did, and the remainder goes to LifeChain. We will not take it."

The two guards loaded the file cabinets and the computers into the armored truck. As the engine started, Herman turned, his powerful body filling the doorway. He studied the roomful of men for a fleeting bemused second from the mound of his burly serenity, bowed formally, and turned to the walkway. Pully stared at the vacant doorway as the truck receded down the drive, mesmerized by the rare encounter with an equal.

CHAPTER 32

Dr. Marion received a summons to Norfolk at midnight. After the plane took off, Herman Hodder informed him of the latest developments. Marion said, "Well?"

"Kahan wants you to bring Dr. Eric Stuart to him, in Xanadu."

"What the hell! Does he expect me to kidnap him? The man is a house officer, that is to say a house slave dedicated to the care of the sick and dying. He can't just up and leave."

"It has been arranged."

"Does Eric Stuart know this?"

"No. Kahan expects you to tell him."

"So, how was it arranged?"

"Through diplomatic channels. Kahan contributes heavily to United Nations funds. The United States government contributes heavily to the hospital building funds and the research grants. Kahan has let it be known he needs the very special expertise of Dr. Eric Stuart, and he will have no one else."

"This must set the other physicians on staff into a frenzy of curiosity, if not jealousy."

"None of them know it except Eric's boss, who has been sworn to secrecy. Each fellow gets a two-week vacation anyway, and it was just a matter of switching schedules around a bit."

"And Stuart?"

"Kahan thinks he is not safe either, until the last vestige of organized Legation has been wiped out."

"There is more to it, I'll wager," said Marion.

"Like what?"

"Dr. Gambela already needs help. Stuart finishes his three years of cardiac fellowship on July first, and he is one of the hottest young talents anywhere. And Kahan wants him. He told me so on my last visit to Xanadu."

"Kahan thinks ahead."

"Does Joseph Mixter Pully know of his daughter's whereabouts?"

"He does indeed."

"And The Reverend himself?"

"They are reasonably sure they got him. The chances are they did, but The Reverend is mighty smart in his own way, and mighty slick."

"Hmmmmm."

Herman then finished giving Marion the details.

Dr. Marion called the hospital operator from a pay phone in the lobby, posed as a referring physician, and had Dr. Stuart paged. Stuart answered almost at once. Marion asked him to come down to the lobby, and there informed Eric of Joan's whereabouts, and how she got there.

Eric remained silent for a moment, then said, "I have been worried and waiting, but I never expected this."

"She is safe."

"What am I to do?"

"Kahan has asked me to bring you to him in his country."

"Oh, my God! You know I can't ..."

"Eric, it has been arranged. Your chief knows about Kahan's request, and your visit has been approved at every level."

"I know nothing about it."

"Highly secret ... best not to let anyone know of your destination and reasons except your boss. And he does not and will not know the real reasons. This is your night off duty?"

"Yes."

"He will call you and tell you before five o'clock. Your vacation time has been rearranged."

"I don't really want to go. I plan to spend the two weeks in the laboratory practicing some new implant techniques I have in mind."

"We know."

"You know! How did you know?"

"Joan told him, and Kahan has reserved a section of his laboratories for you with plenty of help, such as you would never get here."

"You leave me no excuse."

"For numerous reasons, you will never regret going."

"When are we leaving?"

"As soon as you get off duty tonight."

The operator began paging Eric. He answered on his mobile phone, spoke briefly, and said to Marion, "This is it, I suppose. The chief wants me in his office at once."

"We will wait beside your car in the parking ramp."

The chairman of surgery stopped dictating when Eric entered his office. Dr. Foster Kemp, in his erudite urbanity, would never in pretentious busyness keep an underling waiting while he finished a sentence or a paragraph. He rose to his feet, reached across his desk to shake hands and said, "Well Eric, news of your talents has spread far and wide. Someone in a faraway and nebulous place has caused an upheaval in diplomatic circles to get you to his country. Your vacation has been rearranged, and you may leave now."

"But Dr. Kemp, the patient I operated on today..."

"Eric, she is my patient, remember, and I promise you, I will be the cardiac fellow on her case myself in your absence."

"I appreciate your generosity, Dr. Kemp. And I want you to know I had nothing whatsoever to do with planning this, and I do not really want to go."

"But you don't have a choice. The president of the United States knows about it, the secretary general of the United Nations arranged it, and your senator, through whom it was done, is wild with envy and curiosity. To refuse to go would be letting everyone down. Besides, I am looking forward with the keenest curiosity to meeting Joan Pully when you bring her back. I have grown to suspect she saved all our lives and salvaged our surgery the night we flew to Bristol. Right?"

"Actually, we have not had an opportunity to discuss it fully."

"But she did, didn't she?"

"Yes, she did, but I am not privy to the details."

"Remarkable. You are lucky."

"Thank you."

Aboard the flight, Eric slept until the attendant awoke him in broad daylight. He sat up, momentarily disoriented. "Time to get ready for breakfast. We land in an hour."

Eric and Marion and Sarah rode the Range Rover up the mountain, past elephants and giraffes among the trees, lions in the grass, dozens of variations on deer and elk, monkeys in the limbs overhead, and exotic birds of many varieties. Hawks and eagles floated and dived through the sky among drifting vultures. The jungle gradually gave way to the mountainside foliage of a cooler climate.

At Xanadu, a houseman led Eric through the castle, out along the courtyard to Joan. When he entered the living room, she rose from the couch.

At dinner the conversation eventually turned to the cardiac operating room and Dr. Gambela. After a long dinner, and many wines and cordials, they retired to quarters. Joan and Eric occupied a house built into the wall surrounding the compound. Its parapets along the inside wall extended to the water's edge. The master bedroom on the top floor overlooked the land beyond on one side, and the singing stream on the other. The night breezes stirred through open windows, subduing the sounds of Africa: the whisper of wind in the forests, the music of running water, the distant calls of birds, the roar of a hidden lion, the chorus of lesser beings. Eric said, "How could Kahan know I love the sounds of water and the open country?"

"He knows, and I am sure because he chose this house for us."

"Why did he put the two of us in a four bedroom house?"

She giggled. "Oh, Eric he's very discreet. This way, no one can really know where we slept."

"Well, if you want to fool him, best you wreck a second bed after we get up tomorrow."

"Oh, I will ... the one farthest from ours. And Kahan has another reason, I'm sure."

"What?"

"I think he is offering you a permanent house."

The next morning, Marion and Sarah led the way through the hospital in the caverns, showing Eric the works. In the afternoon Eric went to the cardiac rooms and watched Gambela transplant a heart. Then Gambela invited him to scrub on the next operation. Immediately they began working in concert as though already a team. They kept three rooms busy.

On the following day, Eric went to work in the animal laboratory, transplanting hearts, livers, then multiple organs: heart and lung combinations, liver pancreas and intestine combinations. Kahan had at his disposal every drug of any type ever manufactured. Kahan came to the laboratories to visit and to watch the proceedings. He displayed an extraordinary interest for a person not trained in medicine, and stood for hours watching Eric trim and sew, looking through the observer limb of the microscope. He remained calm, never became obtrusive, never jarred or shook an instrument, and observed strict operating room protocol.

Eric worked with the finest laboratory equipment obtainable, the quarter of a million dollar surgical microscope better than the one used in the operating room for patients back in the States. Real nurses and trained surgical assistants were assigned to help, sparing Eric all the preliminaries, the preparations, and the drudgery. Eric suspected this attention and these privileges would lead to something Kahan had on his mind. But Kahan remained circumspect. Eric remained cautious.

Then it all came out at dinner on the last night of Eric's visit. They discussed his age: just thirty, in his eighth year of post-graduate training. Kahan wondered, "Is all this necessary?"

"It is the system, the period of apprenticeship, under the masters."

"You could do the surgery here and now."

"And get away with it, yes, here in this remoteness, but never with the acceptance and the approval of the real masters in other parts of the world. I'm too near the end to cut it short."

Marion studied Eric solemnly across the table, raised an eyebrow, and almost imperceptibly bowed to him.

Kahan continued, "I respect your decision, and I suppose your answer pleases me more than if you had accepted. But consider us when you finish training. Dr. Gambela needs help already, with more work waiting than one person can do."

"I thank you, and the time is short, less than a month away. If you still want me here then, I will come for another visit."

"Good. And we don't want you to leave now."

"It's a temptation to stay forever, but I have to get back to the hospital where I'm needed."

"We will send you back tomorrow, but you must be very careful. The remnants of Legation are still dangerous. I think you should sleep in the hospital until you hear from us. The people who are out to kill Joan are after you, too. And don't use your car until we clear it. We have had it watched since the night you left, but it had been parked there forty-eight hours before we began our surveillance. It may be loaded with a bomb."

"Do you really think so?"

"These are deadly, evil people. And Joan, almost single-handed has brought their organization to the verge of ruin. They are of a righteous mentality, bent on revenge and retribution. Joan, by the way, stays here with Dr. Marion and Sarah and the rest of the household until she can return in complete safety," said Kahan.

"I have come to appreciate what you are doing."

"Now, to another problem."

"Yes."

"We must do something to assure greater retrieval of organs from the brain dead in the States."

"I agree. Perhaps a blitz of information would prove persuasive," said Eric.

"Perhaps, yes, but I suspect with tepid results, and also it might stir up a perverse resistance."

"That, I suppose, is the nature of man."

"Well then, how about a persuasion that transcends even the strongest convictions."

"You mean like money?"

"Exactly."

"Do you have a method in mind?"

"Yes. Perhaps. Why don't we give it a try?"

"I'm willing."

"Okay. The next time a unique retrieval has been refused on religious or emotional grounds, let's try the money persuasion."

"How?"

"Offer as much as fifty thousand dollars for all the organs and tissue bank material."

"The sale of organs and tissue is illegal in the States."

"Don't buy. The family simply gets the money from a third party for their generosity."

"Should I contact you?"

"Ivan Prescott at Mercury. He is wily enough after his

experiences with his highly successful tissue bank. We have been talking about this problem now for months, he and I, and we have developed a plan. Simply call him and payment will be available."

"Who will pay the bill, ultimately?"

"We have formed a benevolent fund into which desperate families, even the insurance carriers and others, will gladly pay once they see the wisdom of our ways. Otherwise, the highest bidder will become the only alternative."

"Well, the very next time, I will try this tactic."

"Dr. Stuart, I'll wager you it will never fail with the right figure."

"I would not want to bet against you."

Marion, in the arms of Sarah said, "You have brought a new life, an awakening, a return to survival, and I want a family."

"So do I, but I am sworn to the death, and you can be my blood husband only by becoming a SamuelS. Would you?"

"I would, yes, but I have concerns."

"Let me try to answer the questions, the doubts bothering you, as well they should. You would be then a SamuelS, and with your new freedom even more a Renaissance man, and both of us citizens of the world. The children would be SamuelSs for life and citizens of the world, too. Our home, our base, would be here, our children protected by the might of the entire Arabian and middle east cartel and the wealth and power of Europe, and other countries as well. Asian countries including Japan are joining Xanadu daily now, believe it or not. This most effective of all efforts to unite nations of the world for medical purposes has established a ring of fiercely ready defenses around the mountain. Kahan wants you here and will not relent and I cannot desert the cause. I am in the greatest seriousness sworn to it."

"What would it be like between us then?"

"Exactly as it is now. Under those circumstances I would belong entirely to you, and you to me and our family of children, and I always will be as you have come to know me."

"You have treated me with the utmost diplomacy."

"And you have respected me as a fellow human being in this life, this world, as an equal in every way possible between man and woman."

"With this said, could we be married?" he asked.

"Yes, in a pagan ceremony, a natural mating for life, totally free of any words born of superstitious ritual, as our lives have been and will always be free of such cant, both in speech and actions."

"You speak of religion?"

"Yes. God is everywhere invisible and everywhere manifest. No honest man has ever seen his face or heard his name. I am near this power every waking moment as I have come to know you are, and I do not want it sullied by the peculiar and deadly politics of cultism, whether it be a worldwide movement or just a rift in everyday existence."

"I think we would do well as husband and wife."

CHAPTER 33

The hospital confinement became wearing and Eric considered taking a common-sense approach: simply go to his car and return home. When about to give in to this urge, he received a page from the receptionist at the front desk in the main lobby of the hospital: "Dr. Stuart, there is a gentlemen sitting down here who insists I ask you to come down to see him. He has waited all morning while you were in surgery."

"Where is he?"

"Sitting across the lobby from me."

"Can he hear you?"

"No."

"What's his name?"

"A funny one ... John Quicksilver, he says."

Mercury! "What does he look like?"

"Medium sized, well dressed..."

"I'll be right down."

The man, well tailored in a gray suit, stood when Eric entered the lobby, folded the newspaper he had been reading, and walked toward the exit. He went through the revolving door and out onto the sidewalk. Eric, without glancing toward the receptionist, followed. The man rounded a corner and went out of sight. Eric caught up. The man continued to walk, and talked without turning his head. "Dr. Stuart, Kahan asked Mercury to tell you to use cabs if you need transportation. Do not go near your car, and do not go home under any circumstances."

"Yes?"

"Legation headquarters has been destroyed, burned to the ground."

"I did not know."

"They are out of business, sixty centers across the nation were closed down and all management in other cities has been arrested."

"So...?"

"Kahan senses something wrong."

"What do you mean?"

"Well, Kahan is very psychic. He mutters. He has not heard the last echo ... the concert cannot end without the final chord?"

"Well...?"

"He thinks something is afoot, something still lurks."

"Hmmm."

"Nice talking to you, Dr. Stuart. Take care of yourself. Kahan with SamuelS is doing his best to protect you, and we at Mercury are doing our best to help." They had reached a corner of the sidewalk. The man turned and strode off toward the city. *Quicksilver!* Eric went back to work.

The hospital scene now palled since his return from Xanadu, where the equipment and the backup help amounted to a surgeon's dream of perfection. And seeing Joan again had reconfirmed the knowledge in his heart. He wanted her for wife and family, and no one else. In only a few days he could claim her, but his intuition warned him of unseen dangers. Queasy fear stirred in his gut. Would he after all be deprived of the dream so near to reality?

The patients dying in the Cardiac ICU while awaiting for donors to happen, and the disorder and inefficiency in the operating rooms and the hospital in general, now discouraged him more than ever. His experience in Xanadu had confirmed his suspicions: A hospital could be run as efficiently as a five-star hotel if the employees worked under the right leadership. Compared to Xanadu, all American hospitals, even the best, appeared trashy, disorderly, and not always entirely clean. Controlled by the inertia of indolent hands, and the grip of cost accounting, they all operate more or less the same. Kahan's offers sorely tempted him.

Foster Kemp paged Eric and said, "Can you meet me in the emergency room? Something very strange is happening down there, two pregnant women named Lewis wanting their babies taken and used to transplant kidneys and brain to their Parkinsonian father who is on dialysis. They have been using the term LRD, referring to living related donor, I suppose.

The director of nurses met them at the door. The ob-gyn nurses and residents, accustomed to the most bizarre of the bizarre, were beside themselves. Lewis and his daughters had been there for more than an hour. Pregnancy tests were positive on both women. The old man sat on a metal stool, his feet planted apart on the floor, his torso bent forward in a rigid plastic posture, his face frozen in wooden inanimateness and aimed toward the distant wall, his jaw hanging, his mouth open with saliva drooling from one corner, his rigid arms postured in flexion and the right hand shaking in perpetual pill-rolling motion. He smelled uremic, the stink of old piss.

The two women sat side by side on an examining table. Both appeared to be in their late thirties. They confronted the world with the defiant and facetious mien of old maid desperation, bold and insolent enough to surpass obstructing conventions.

The older of the two spoke. "We want our babies taken and used to cure Poppa. He is their daddy, too, so they are even closer kin to him than we are, and the kidneys and brain ought to take all right. We each got him drunk on wine and made him do it, just like the real Lot in Genesis, and he claims he don't remember it."

Foster Kemp, with the most commanding dignity, stood with his arms folded, listening. Gray, tanned, tall and large, he seemed to tower beside the examining table, on his face the most humbled look of compassion, gazing at them out of sharp blue eyes. Then he unfolded his arms and spoke, "Ladies, girls, you have done a very brave thing for your father. But certain problems hold us back. First, the tiny kidneys would make the surgery extremely difficult, and perhaps impossible. If we wait for them to grow to usable size, we cannot then take the lives of the babies. As to the brain, fetal tissue from the brain and from one gland in particular, the adrenal, is used experimentally now, but it is simply placed in the existing brain. It seems to be promising in some cases, but no one is quite sure yet. The whole brain cannot be transplanted."

"You mean to say you won't do it for us and that pore sufferin' thing setting there shaking?"

"We will get the brain surgeons to talk to you."

"Lot's daughters slept with their father and bore him two sons who fathered two whole new nations. Moab started the Moabites, and Benammi started the Ammonites, but I guess this jist ain't biblical times no more."

"Well, I'll tell you what we will do. I will turn this whole situation over to the ethics committee of the hospital and let them advise both you and me. And we will leave the decision about terminating the pregnancies to you and the doctors who do those operations. But I would advise you not to have an abortion solely for the purpose of donating fetal tissue, because legally and technically we might not be able to do any useful transplant right now."

"Thank you, doctor."

Kemp and Eric came from behind the curtains and out into the hallway. Kemp turned to Eric and said, "Boy! Now aren't they pitiful. And this is only the beginning. Just you wait. As the transplant business really gets rolling, we are going to see some astonishing new wrinkles in human endeavor."

"Apparently."

"Human behavior always deviates to fill a need. Then ingenuity and perversity can know no limit ... and speaking of that, what's new in the courier problem?"

"Another one missing, in the third region of UNOS this time. An ambulance and its crew disappeared in Miami while racing from the airport to the hospital."

"A heart?"

"Yes. Flown by private jet from Atlanta."

"Eric, what the hell is going on?"

"Open war on the volunteer system, and this looks like the second time around the eleven regions. The fourth might be next, Texas or Oklahoma."

"God, I wish there could be a supply with no drawbacks." They parted ways in the hall, and Eric left thinking of Xanadu and all it had to offer in the mountains of Africa.

After the last scheduled surgery each day, Eric went with Foster Kemp's entourage to make rounds in the cardiac wards. In the Intensive Care Unit, relatives sat by each bed, waiting, expectant, with hope in their eyes, but when they realized no hearts were available at the moment, their expressions changed, the light died from their faces once again. The supply of hearts and other organs would never catch up with the growing demand as the technology improved.

As always, Eric felt diminished and depressed by the hopeless gloom in these wards. But before the night ended he would watch a reversal of these emotions. Despondency and bitterness would give to avarice, the worst kind: the wish for another's death. The joy and hope would spring up at the news of another person brain-dead in an accident, hope tied to macabre misfortune, lighting the gleam in the family eye. One of the dying people might be given a chance by the happenstance of another person's foul luck and the family released from a prison of grief. The action became frantic; they would keep the heart at Sentara. Foster Kemp, busy with the families, then the preparation of the recipient says, "Eric would you explant the donor ... he's ready in the next room?"

Explant the donor. The face showing beneath the drapes on the table feminized by the death upon it, the lids shut, the nose and lips resigned in quietude, creating the appearance of innocence, a woman, in her thirties, the victim of a bleeding aneurysm — so it appears to be. A transplant general surgeon has split a furrow from the collar to pubes, a typical autopsy incision. The released organs have risen up, escaping above the wound margins. The surgeon has divided the liver by a vertical black gulch, the charred marks of the cautery used to control tedious liver bleeding. Half a liver will go to each of two recipients. While Eric watches, the gut crawls in the surgeon's hands, its blood supply tediously sought and found and the stumps saved. The respirator moves the lungs in and out, the heart thrusting out in the open, literally climbing out of the chest, twisting on its self wildly. ALIVE! Who could logically call this *death* with the heart beating in such desperate thrusts, the tip of its wringing cone pointing almost straight up? *Him*, someone said, fell from a scaffold, forty years old, five mouths to feed. Cycles, Eric thinks, to the innocence and angelic mien of woman, passive, totally passive, irretrievably surrendered to death's journey. It bothers him. Why? A twinge of concern for the temerity of taking live organs, but it makes sense; nothing else does. All the rest is pure emotion and the result either way is death for the donor, already in the down cycle to his ultimate parts again whether you step in or not and make a move to stop the beating heart before it stops itself forever, and save it to prolong its own and the life of another in a down cycle to eventual death, but with normal awareness, not really death, otherwise vultures, worms, and rot, the cycling atoms to try life again in another form perchance.

The general surgeon steps away, and Stuart begins. He must defy the fighting heart, subdue it, stop its frantic lurching to escape, its wringing muscle, its wild animal response to human help proffered, resisting interference with its mute intelligence. *I am not your enemy, I will give you longer life, trust me, otherwise you will be dead within minutes to remain dead, stay with me and you will come back to life in minutes, to live on,* he nods to the anesthesiologist who increases the flow of nutrients into a vein, carrying a cardioplegic, a drug to stop the heart beating. They deflate the lungs, let them down, bury the stunned heart in crushed ice, cross clamp the aorta, the main channel of blood leaving the heart, and the heart falls slack, and he recalls his first experience of this moment while still only a medical student observing at the head of the table, recognizing this moment for its profundity and finality, he said then, *and now this is the real moment of death* and the surgeon's violent, emotional reaction ... NO! NO! NO! He died yesterday; he has been dead since yesterday when we declared him. *With his heart still beating violently?* Stuart thought, but said nothing more, chastised by superiors. Now, in identical surgeon's shoes, but with the same student emotions embroiled inside, he proceeds, to cut all the connecting vessels until the heart falls out slack in his hands. He inspects it, a big one from a big man, the blood vessels and the valves all healthy and normal. The donor has given up the beating heart.

As Stuart prepares to leave the room with the heart immersed in a pan of ice, he glances into the sheeny cavity from where it came, the now empty chamber of the valiant heart, the scene of all its struggles, the haunt of the conscience, the field of all its inner battles, now bereft, the disquieting portals where the major vessels entered like the open tunnels of secret caves in a mysterious mountain. He thinks of the first man to know. Servetus said the heart sends the blood to the lungs for air and brings it back, and the Calvinists burned him to death at the stake for heresy in 1553 A.D., and he quells a terrible twinge at the sight of the excavated donor, now so utterly still. Joan ... Where is she at this moment ... lying on some hidden crude table, an empty shell, too, mined of her precious heart? But he has to move on and goes to the recipient and gives up the heart to Foster Kemp, patiently waiting, and the heart goes in and they both sew auricles to auricles, pulmonary artery to pulmonary artery, aorta to aorta, unclamp the aorta and flush the new and quivering heart full of blood, stop the cardioplegics, shock the heart with tiny electrodes, and the heart begins beating again, like miniature resurrection. Foster Kemp speaks reverently almost as if he is in prayer: *I never cease to be amazed at this moment.*

They remove the tubes directing blood into the pump. And now the new heart is on its own and nothing is left to do except close the wound on this patient, who has a new heart and a new life, the heart beating with no connection to the brain, now totally controlled by its own inner nerves and blood chemistry, the circulating catecholamines, the chemicals of automatic function below the level of awareness. His thoughts go to the other room, where the second team has taken the divided liver, the digestive tract, the pancreas, the kidneys, the lungs, and now a third team takes bone and cartilage and blood vessels and skin and other parts to be used non-alive, to be freeze-dried and used in numerous other people to restore function to joints and bones and surfaces. Then the remainder, the mined shell, will go the route of all flesh, where all of him would have gone unless they had saved parts for others, and he thinks all doors have been closed on this life, all doors opened on the others ... such a fatal and final exodus. Where is Joan? Has something like this happened to her while he blindly devotes his duty to the sick? A wave of frustration, of controlled agitation, sweeps over him. Eric left the room chastened, as always, following a heart transplant.

CHAPTER 34

When The Reverend Lotte opened the door at the Legation end of his tunnel a few seconds before the explosion, he sensed a change, but not quick enough to stay the hand reaching for the light switch. He whirled, leapt back, slammed the Legation door shut, and raced down the dank tunnel to the other end. As he twisted the knob and pushed the door, the explosion blew him face first on his belly into the basement of his house, and a sea of mud covered him in a violent wave. He came up gasping, grabbed the stairs as he slid by, and crawled up the steps in the slime. He stood in the doorway, looking down, watching the sea reclaim this below-sea-level space, filling it to the top of the staircase with sludge. Mud dripped off his head and clothes, plopping down on the kitchen linoleum.

He cracked a Venetian blind onto the bleary landscape, and watched Legation headquarters burn. Fire trucks arrived and hoses poured water into the inferno. When water hit the pure sodium in the blaze, the fire roared up with explosive force. Sparks and flame blew in violent geysers, and the firemen had to back off. Then they stayed around its periphery and just let it burn out.

At daylight, The Reverend rose from his kitchen chair, tracked mud into his bathroom, stripped, and bathed. He could afford to be untidy. His own defeated wife had left long ago, but one or another of several church wives, who secretly took care of his needs, would clean up this mess too, and keep quiet. Husbands, he had taught them, very likely do not find out one thing without coming to know it all.

The Reverend Lotte burned his black wig, destroyed the Benjamin Franklin glasses, and disappeared entirely and forever into the persona of The Reverend Plough, his real identity, and stayed hidden in his house beside the water until the furor died down. Then, as the bald Plough with half his face behind big horn-rimmed glasses, he continued his church activities. He would rebuild his empire at the right time. And by now Joan Pully should have become a donor in some foreign land, but he did not really believe so, and he harbored a seething rage for revenge against her. The Reverend Plough preached and waited.

Her lover, Willy, had told Gladys about Legation headquarters before he disappeared, and gave her the address of a place hidden behind a funeral home and a blood bank facade in an old waterfront warehouse. She decided to drive by and challenge The Reverend, if she could find him. She would like to know what he looked like anyway, and maybe she could get to know him better, something physical. Perhaps a little romance would give her the upper hand; she would get her money one way or another.

She found a burned-over square of ground stinking of char and ashes, and the wind blew an acrid stench of something chemical and deadly. Within the confines of this scorched area, water — black, ominous, bubbling up something foul — filled a large square pit brim full to the surface of the surrounding lawn, the remains of a basement or cellar, no doubt. The old house next door across the narrow inlet, isolated and bleak with its back to the water, stood two stories tall in an air of boardinghouse decrepitude, its brick besmirched with coat after coat of whitewash atop the old grime on it and on the tacky and slothful electric conduit, tangled wires, and pipes fastened to the walls.

Gladys shivered and turned her attention back to the pool of black water with black remnants of burned wood floating on its surface, charcoal and ash scum idly undulant in the cold breeze, twisted molten metal protruding from the pit edges. The tide rode high in the inlet; the water came to the same level in the burned-over cellar pit. As Gladys studied the ruins, she recalled the news. An old warehouse building on the waterfront had exploded and burned. This must be it. But, of course, the media had no knowledge of Legation.

She went to the city real estate office. There the maps revealed the plat and the ownership of the house, the First Degree Congregational Church Parsonage. The burned building next door had belonged to the business, the Savior Funeral Home, Inc. She looked for the name Lotte among property owners and found none.

Two hours later she returned to the Legation sight. The tide had turned and the water level in the inlet had dropped more than a foot. The water level in the cellar pit had dropped the same amount. Then Gladys knew. Something underground connected the bay to the cellar, and she wondered if a passage went to the parsonage also.

She found the First Degree Congregational Church fifteen miles out in the country. The bulletin board stood in a white, peeling wooden frame near the road. White chipped and corroding metal letters hung haphazardly into black felt ridges, spelling out the meeting times beneath the title *The Reverend Earl Plough, Minister.*

Gladys picked Friday night. She slipped into the back of the church after the seven p.m. services were well underway and the sermon had begun. A middle-aged man in galluses and with a belt around a ponderous belly, expounded from the pulpit, his bald head sweaty, his face half hidden behind enormous horn-rim glasses, his white shirt soaked through at the armpits. He preached about the power of love. Gladys slumped in the rearmost pew and listened. She heard the same pronunciations, the same inflections, and the same false sounding benignity she had heard on the phone many times. Within ten minutes she kneeled forward, crouched, and slipped out of the church, quite sure he had not seen her, and went to her car and waited.

She followed the preacher to the First Degree Congregational Parsonage in Norfolk. The naked bulb over the door of the side entrance went off as Gladys slinked up the steps. She knocked and waited, then knocked again, louder and insistent. The door cracked open and The Reverend Earl Plough peered out. "Yes?"

"May I come in Reverend? I need your counseling," she said. In the dark, he saw a young woman, who appeared to be coy and perhaps a bit brazen. He hesitated at first and then opened the door. She stepped in.

The Reverend had grown accustomed to women paying impromptu afternoon and night visits to his home, usually the middle-aged frumpy ones desperate for attention. This one appeared to be in her thirties, of medium height, with brown hair and blue eyes, and not bad at first glance, maybe interesting. "Come on in, make yourself at home. Can I get you a drink, coffee, tea, wine, anything?"

"Why yes, I think a glass of white wine would be mighty nice."

He went to the refrigerator and took out a bottle. He poured two glasses, and handed one to her. They clinked rims. "Cheers," he said. "Have a seat."

At the kitchen table, she propped her elbows on the top, both hands around her glass, revealing broken fingernail polish and traces of grime. Eyeing him above the rim of the glass, almost staring, she said, "You live here alone, Brother Plough?"

Something in the lilt of this question caught his attention. The cadence sounded familiar, in the intonation a hint of secular sarcasm mocking sacred endeavor. Where had he heard the inflection before? He had never seen her in his congregation. "Yes," he said, "I do."

"Big house. You must get lonesome."

"No. I never do. I work very hard all the time, caring for my flock, and have little time for being lonesome."

"But you have to sleep by yourself. Don't you need someone then?"

Coming to the point already. The little butterfly wing fluttered in The Reverend's solar plexus region and a lurch of permissiveness went down his belly, and a tingling sensation out to the head of his penis, stirring its dormant state. He looked at her. She wore a low-cut dress revealing an expanse of soggy, oily skin over the beginnings of her mounds. He wondered if he could coax her into taking a bath first. "Well yes," he said. "I do, I guess I have to admit, feel it then most of all. Perhaps someday I will get lucky and find the right one."

"Hmmm," she said, studying him with a steady gaze, "I'm kind of lonesome tonight myself."

"You have no one?"

"No. Single and live alone."

"You should have plenty of men after you. You are young and attractive."

"Brother Plough, I like older men."

"Ahhh. Why?"

"For one thing they have greater staying power."

"What are your wishes?"

"I was kind of hoping you would invite me to spend the night. I heard your sermon tonight about the warmth of love, and I got a feeling — it emanated back to me in the rear of the church. You have greater warmth and understanding than I have ever known."

"Bless you my child," he said. "I would be delighted to extend the hospitality of my home to you."

Gladys heard the accent, the syntax. There could be no doubt The Reverend Earl Plough and The Reverend Lotte were one and the same, each leading a double life. She would string him along and get him involved before she demanded the rest of her two-and-a-half million.

She yawned and stretched, "Oh my. I have had a long

day."

"Well my dear, my bath is just down the hallway, through the bedroom, plenty of towels and everything, even new toothbrushes." He hoped to God she'd brush her teeth. "Would you like more wine?"

"Sure, but I have my own toothbrush in my purse." She held up her glass as he poured, then said, while looking into his eyes, "And bring the bottle with you."

He went into another bathroom, showered, and came to the bedroom wearing only a terrycloth bathrobe, too small for his big belly, and got in bed. Gladys came out wearing one of his robes, drying her hair with a towel. She sat on the opposite side of the bed, her head bent forward while she continued drying. She had used her perfume generously. She dropped the towel on the floor, let the robe fall off, slid under the covers and over to The Reverend.

When he had finished his brief ministrations to the lonesome, to the accompaniment of her loud appreciative yelps, The Reverend rolled over on his back, fell into a deep sleep, snored loudly for ten minutes, then awakened. He got up. "Be right back," he said, but Gladys already slept and snored. He went into his bathroom and locked the door. While washing himself he saw Gladys's purse on the radiator, and found her driver's license in a small pocketbook. Gladys Gleason. *Ahh, indeed. No wonder the voice sounded familiar.* He opened the door and tiptoed into the room. Gladys slept soundly. He turned back into the bath, closed and locked the door again, opened the medicine cabinet, searching, and found his chloroform. He saturated a large bath towel, and returned to the bed. She slept with her head thrown back, her mouth open, snoring. Without hesitation, The Reverend brought the towel near her face so she inhaled the fumes without irritation, and when she did not resist, he brought it closer. She never aroused. Her breathing slowed, the snoring stopped, and after a couple of minutes she gasped deeply. Then he eased the cloth down on her face, raised the can and began a chloroform drip.

After Gladys stopped breathing, he left the towel over her face, went into the kitchen, secured the blinds, and opened the cellar door. He returned, removed the towel, lifted her naked form over his shoulder and carried her to the cellar steps. He brought her down into his arms, aimed her head forward and slid her out and down, and let her slip into the sea of mud. She went out of sight and a second later only bubbles rose from the void where she had gone under. He returned to the bedroom, gathered up the towel, the empty chloroform can, her clothes, and her purse. The chloroform on the towel burned furiously when he lit it in the fireplace, taking the purse, the clothes, and her other belongings up with it.

The next day he gathered all the ashes with metal remnants of the can and her belongings: the keys, the cosmetic kits, the metal frame of her purse, her fingernail file, placed them in a garbage bag, loaded the bag with brick bats, and sank it in the cellar mud. He secured the cellar door with the large hasp and an old fashioned heavy lock he had used for years. Nothing appeared to be different.

The Reverend Earl Plough kept his ministry going. No one would know his other identity, and anyone left in the Legation organization would assume him to be dead. Seething under the humiliation of having his organization destroyed, he drove by Eric's house several times each day and night, and never saw a sign of life. In his uneasiness, he wondered where Joan Pully might be.

CHAPTER 35

Stanley Steinfelt grew angrier day by day. He seethed with a rage he could neither control nor understand, and he could hardly bear the sorry sight of his wife's chronic black eye, bruised face, and hangdog depression on the constant verge of tears. A man of his talents deserved better than a cowed, weepy woman of no abilities, and a bunch of snot-nosed little brats with their lost helpless attitude, as dumb as their mother. Had he not been saddled with this burden, no telling how far he would have gone in this world.

The operating room supervisor, Jenny McCloud, came to work with a bruised swollen face and a rim of black and yellow stain around one eye. She had to work; no one could take her place. The astounded personnel held her in high esteem and hesitated to ask. She stayed in her office as much as possible with the door locked.

The chief of cardiac anesthesiology watched her silent grief and embarrassment for a day or two then decided he had had enough of being neutral. He knocked on the door of her office. She looked up at the little bald man with sharp blue eyes behind metal-rimmed spectacles, a person known by his peers to be candidly honest. She let him in.

He sat down beside her desk and waited. She sat with her head bowed, her petite but sensual figure slumped in despondency, her gray-green eyes averted in denial. He considered her to be a real lady, a good woman, an excellent nurse, and he knew she still grieved for her husband. Finally, he spoke, "Now Jenny McCloud, your many friends have waited silently while you have suffered, all of them afraid to ask, but enough is enough. I want to know what has happened to you."

She turned her swollen bruised face, looked him in the eye for a minute, fighting for self control, but tears welled up and her cheeks trembled. Her hands lifted, her fingers plowed into her graying luminous hair, and she buried her cheeks in her palms. Finally she regained her voice, looked up again, and said, "Oh, I can't tell you. I can't tell anyone. It's just too God awful."

"Well, you can tell me. Or you can come home with me and tell my wife, if you can't tell a man. But I know you are caught up in something foreign to you and something dangerous. Somebody is getting away with physical abuse."

She turned to him again. "Oh, Dr. Williams, what am I going to do? I'm so frightened. He is so evil."

"We can begin with the answer to one question."

"I fear for my safety, my job, my future if I tell anybody."

"One question. Who?"

"Dr. Williams, he would kill me if he found out I told anyone."

"You can come live with us until you're out of danger, if you need to."

"What are you going to do?"

"Put a stop to the abuse, every kind being used against you: physical, mental, intimidation, and I would guess now, from what you have said, blackmail."

"My God, Dr. Williams, how did you know? Does everybody know?"

"Of course not, my dear, I can only surmise from your appearance and what you have said. I have heard no gossip about you."

She studied him for a minute, as he sat waiting, then said one word, "Stiney."

Williams waited, his face calm and kind, as she picked absent mindedly at the hem of her uniform, tears rolling down her cheeks, then continued, "Dr. Williams, one night more than a year ago I was working late and he caught me in a dark corner of the back hallway. I swear I don't know why ... I would have died declaring I would never do such a thing. He pushed me into a corner, lifted my skirt, took off my pants, pulled up one of my legs, stuck himself in me and pounded until I was out of breath and weak as water. He was as hard as a rock, big as a horse, and as brutal as a rapist. I had more orgasms in five minutes than I had in the last ten years of my marriage. I put up no resistance. I was excited beyond even the slightest effort to control my emotions. It's like everything had been damned up, and I thought under control, since my husband's death, and he broke the dam and it all came out in a torrent. I have no idea how I could turn to this. He stank, and I imagined the odor of Pan himself. And after the first time I was hooked.

"He came to my apartment that night, and since then every night it pleases him to have his way with me. I have been helpless in his clutches."

"And he has a master key to everything up here."

Jenny hesitated, then said, "Yes, I think so. The day after the first encounter my key ring disappeared for a night. I thought I had lost it, searched frantically, and it was on my desk the next morning. I think he had all the keys, including the master, copied, but I have not dared confront him with the accusation."

"So, the physical abuse?"

"He has become more and more angry about something, and more and more cruel. He likes to humble, to degrade me physically. In bed, he rants and raves about the heart surgeons. He feels superior to all of them, but he is a coward in the presence of the most respected people like Dr. Kemp. And he hates the cardiac fellow who enjoys such a great reputation, Dr. Eric Stuart. I swear I am afraid he will try to do real harm to him. He has been especially vehement since the night of the multiple organ transplants when the team flew down to Bristol to get the organs and back here to do the surgery. I said something innocently to him the night he beat me. He turned on me in a rage and proceeded to pound me in the face, called me a whore, a slut, an old woman, then stalked out cursing and slamming doors, and has not returned since."

"Well, you have told me all I need to know. After we have dinner at my house tonight, my wife and I will take you home to pack, and you will live with us until we take care of Mr. Stanley Steinfelt."

Dr. Williams went to the physician's lounge and paged Eric Stuart. When Eric arrived, Dr. Williams led the way down to his own office. "Have a seat, Eric. I have a serious matter to discuss with you, and a very sensitive one."

"Before you start, be sure your intercom has been switched off."

Williams looked at Eric in surprise then tapped the speaker on his desk. It fried and sputtered. He snapped the switch off.

"Why?"

"We have a spy up here who listens in, at least when I am talking."

Then Williams began. "You, of course, know Stanley Steinfelt."

"Indeed."

"Do you mind telling me what I need to know about him?"

"I can tell you one hell of a lot. He apparently has access to every room up here including the head nurse's office at night. I caught him, myself, hunkered in the dark in Jenny McCloud's office long after hours, listening in on an operating room in which Marcus Mann and I were having a private conference, but I did not confront him. Marcus and I have reason to believe he has betrayed some of the couriers who have been organ pirated and some of those who are missing altogether. We suspect he works with the person who might be leaking information from LifeChain about organs en route from this operating room to those in other cities."

"Well, what had you intended doing about it, if anything?"

Eric caught the reprimand, but he did not want to tell Williams everything. He had told him about enough already. "We intended catching him when we had enough evidence to spring the trap."

"Anything else?"

"Yes, I think so, or at least I suspect so. Are you missing any drugs?"

"Yes. Emphatically, yes, but how did you know?"

"Well I don't know. But if he has a master key, and being who and what he is, I would lay odds ..."

"Excuse me for interrupting, Eric, but I have to tell you Stiney has come to me and he has accused you of stealing drugs out of the lockers and out of the stock rooms."

"Good! Let me make a suggestion."

"Yes."

"Remove all the drugs you and your staff will need for the next week, put them in your own personal locker, put your own lock on it and sprinkle all the remaining stock with fluorescein powder. We will then see who comes up with fluorescent hands."

"Let me say to you, Eric, not for one minute do I think you are guilty."

"Dr. Williams, I do not need money. You know, of course, I give my entire hospital salary to the nursing scholarship fund every month."

"No, Eric, I did not know, nor did I realize you come from a wealthy family."

"I don't. I made mine myself. I don't need to practice medicine for the sake of making money." Eric saw Dr. William's body go rigid a split second and knew he had hit home, and Williams would not try another reprimand. He fought down an impulse to allude to his substantial yearly income without touching the principle, but he did not want this information to be known by anyone. He continued, "If you will do the powder I will supply the proper lights to be used when least expected."

"I am not familiar with fluorescein. Where would I get it?"

"I have a supply in my locker. I was waiting to find an ally to help me catch the culprit. I have never been in the anesthesia supply room nor the stock room and I don't intend going to either one, ever."

At five minutes to six the next morning, Eric entered the cardiac surgery lounge with two men. The three helped themselves to coffee. Eric sat on a couch just inside the entrance door and beneath the wall light switch. The two men stationed themselves, one on the other side of the main entrance door, and the second near the door leading into the lavatories, the only escape routes. The room had no windows. Eric's two companions were armed detectives from the narcotics squad.

Eric knew Steinfelt had been in the hospital at least forty-five minutes. He always came into this lounge for coffee before going down to start the pump procedures. At six, Steinfelt entered the room, already dressed in a scrub suit. He carried a black medical bag. People in the hospital who did not know better mistook him for a doctor. He would never disappoint one of these people with the truth. In an air of haughty arrogance he spoke to no one, crossed the room, got a cup of coffee, and sat down in the middle of a couch along the wall opposite Eric. The door opened again and Dr. Williams stepped in. The first agent placed himself in front of the door. At the same moment, Eric reached back and shut off the light switch. The beam of Eric's light swept the darkness and lit up a pair of green hands. Steinfelt yelled, jumped up, spilling his coffee, and lunged toward the lavatories. Eric switched on the overhead lights as Steinfelt ran straight into the bulky form of the other narcotics agent, who handcuffed him so fast nobody saw it happen. Steinfelt began cursing and raving, "Goddam son-of-a-bitch, mother fucker, bastard, turn me the hell loose."

The agent said, "Mr. Steinfelt, you are under arrest for illegal possession of narcotics. If you use any more abusive language we will also charge you with resisting arrest. You have the right to remain silent. However, we have a search warrant for your person and for your equipment and for your locker and automobile. We will start right here with your little doctor's bag." The other agent picked up the bag and found it locked. "Where is the key, Steinfelt?"

"Pinned to the front of my shirt."

The agent opened the safety pin in Steinfelt's blouse and chose one of the keys and opened the bag. It had been stuffed full of Demerol vials, codeine, morphine and other narcotics. He did not touch the contents. "Dr. Stuart, would you shine your light on the contents of the bag?"

Eric turned off the room lights and shined his light into the bag. The contents lit up green. He hit the light switch again.

The agent then said to the anesthesiologist, "Dr. Williams, are the drugs in this bag necessary to Mr. Steinfelt's job, and if so were they issued to him through legal channels?"

"No to both. These drugs have been stolen from our stock sometime since late last evening, and this man would not be allowed to use them in the job he does in this hospital under any circumstances."

"Mr. Steinfelt, lead us to your locker."

Eric and Dr. Williams went with the agents and Steinfelt. Several dozen unopened vials lay hidden behind a stack of papers on the upper shelf, and an unopened carton of Demerol stood in the floor of the locker. "All right, Mr. Steinfelt, we will take you downtown and book you and lock you up."

"Please let me change into my street clothes and please don't disgrace me by marching me out through the hospital in handcuffs. I have worked hard here for twenty years."

The agent snapped the cuffs off and said, "Change."

At Steinfelt's car the detective said, "Where are the keys, Steinfelt?"

"In my pocket."

"Take them out and unlock the trunk."

The astonished agents stared at the opened trunk. It contained sealed cartons of half a dozen narcotics. Hundreds of single vials had been stuffed into every cranny among the cartons.

Steinfelt sat between the two agents on the rear seat. They rode across town and parked behind the police station and walked three abreast. Because of a full lot they had at least a block to go. Steinfelt could not believe the stupidity and the carelessness of these cops. They were letting him walk across the lot without handcuffs, and they had not thought to search his street clothes. Dummies. He bided his time, and he knew he could move quicker than these two thickheaded narcs built like gorillas. After all, he had hidden talents, better than even those of a heart surgeon, and with the immense unrecognized ability of his own hands he could do a better job than most, if not all of them. He had just never been given the chance.

His walk became jaunty, playful. He whistled a bit. He sensed they had relaxed their vigilance. And he had no intention of letting all of his life's work be ruined. After all, he had saved so many lives with his expertise at the pump. *Mr. Pump Man*, he liked to think of himself. From working with Gladys, he had saved over half a million dollars, enough to do for quite awhile. He would scare the hell out of these two stupid narcs, and while they were paralyzed with surprise, run for his boat and head south on the inland waterway.

In the shade of a tree, behind a parked car, he stopped, threw both hands out at waist level, palm down, raised them up and came down, sneezing hard toward the pavement and grappled at this back pocket as to get a handkerchief, but the attack hit again. He raised his hands and sneezed, and after a second of helpless waiting, sneezed a third time, and like a flash a hand went inside his coat as if groping for a tissue and whipped out holding a small automatic and he whirled on the men. Neither of them had been fooled. Before Steinfelt could point the gun, both agents began firing .45 magnums into his lurching body.

Jenny McCloud tiptoed into the cardiac room and whispered something to Dr. Williams under the drapes. He came out and addressed Dr. Kemp, who had already started the operation. "Dr. Kemp."

Kemp stopped operating and said, "Yes, Dr. Williams."

"The nurse just informed me Steinfelt pulled a gun on the narcotics agents and they shot him dead in the parking lot behind police headquarters."

Kemp, who had quietly abided Steinfelt for a long time, said, "Well, they come, and they go."

The pump technician jumped up and said, "You mean to say they shot Steiney plumb dead?"

"Yes," said Dr. Williams, "So Mrs. Mc Cloud tells me."

All activity in the room had come to a halt. Williams and Kemp and Stuart turned to the technician who just stared from behind his machinery with a stunned look. He had been working with Steinfelt for ten years now, and the doctors began to wonder if some grief had struck so hard he would not be able to continue the case. His eyes came back into focus, and he said, "Well thank God, at long last." He sat down and went back to tending the pump.

CHAPTER 36

SamuelS's men spent many discrete half-hearted hours sitting within sight of the black hole, watching the man enter and leave the parsonage, presumably Plough, not believing they were following a likely lead.

Then a few days after Gladys disappeared, The Reverend Plough made a different turn late one afternoon and slowly cruised by Eric Stuart's home. He went around the block, parked up the street, and watched the house for more than an hour. He did the same thing the next day. Herman realized he had been right all along. The Reverend Plough had more than one agenda.

A SamuelS crew tapped The Reverend's home phone while he conducted Sunday morning services at the First Degree Congregational Church. Another crew entered from the waterside, through a rear window, during the Sunday night services, and planted sound transmitters in the house. SamuelS headquarters began an around-the-clock vigil.

Then another watch appeared on the scene, in a way interfering with SamuelS's view. The big muscular man wore a black hat pulled far down on his forehead. He parked a block away and trained his field glasses on The Reverend's house and driveway. Every day he followed The Reverend's car, up close and reckless. Herman and his men dropped further behind. Now they had two people to watch. The newcomer appeared to be irritable and impatient. Herman could not identify him until he lifted his hat and mopped his brow. *FRED*! Herman recognized him from previous Legation surveillance.

Once convinced his suspicions were correct, Fred made a move. He phoned The Reverend Earl Plough early in the evening, disguised his voice, and posed as a representative of the United Community Fund. He wished to deliver a check. The Reverend avidly accepted donations, and invited him to come over at once. Fred parked a block away and walked to the house.

At the sound of feet crossing the front porch, The Reverend swung his door open and the man entered the living room without removing his hat. The Reverend closed the door and turned, "Welcome to the parsonage, friend."

Fred removed his hat. The Reverend turned pale. "Well, as I live and breathe," said Fred, "Reverend Plough and Reverend Lotte, one and the same."

"No, no," said Plough, "You are mistaken."

"Come, come, Reverend, I would know those two nasty little eyes and that big nose of yours anywhere. You must have worn a wig as The Reverend Lotte. I used to wonder how you could be at headquarters all the time. Tell me, how did you do it, go under ground some way or another from here to there, like a mole, or more like a worm, maybe?"

"Now Fred..."

"Ten million dollars went to your head, huh? And you burned the place down. Lucky for me I took the night off and got Jake to cover for me, but too bad for him, huh? *Bones burned to chalk,* as the newspapers said."

"Fred, I had nothing to do with the explosion and the fire."

"Explosion. What explosion?"

"The place blew up, or rather it blew in before it burned."

"Where's the ten million dollars?"

"Either stolen before the fire or burned up with the rest of the building. But more important, something else didn't burn, I have reason to believe."

"What didn't burn?"

"The files, identifying all Legation offices and employees."

"Geez! How stupid. And how do you know?"

"Every one of the Legation offices across the country has been raided by the police and most of the staffs arrested."

"Out of business, huh?"

"Yes, and as far as anyone else knows, you and I both are dead, and best we leave it that way."

"I want my back pay and I want a share of the ten million."

"I do not have either, Fred. All my funds were burned in the fire. The safe melted into a twisted mass, and I believe whoever destroyed the building took the money first."

"So, then tell me this. Where's Gladys?"

"Gladys who?"

"You know who. She got you practically everything you sold from down here. Gladys Gleason, that's who."

"Why should I know?"

"Because I think you do. She knew about the ten million. She found Joan Pully for you, and she was due her twenty-five percent. I think you welshed on her and she came here to collect."

"Why would you think that?"

"Don't be stupid. Or have you already been stupid, maybe real stupid? Because the police towed her abandoned car away, only four blocks from here, or did you know?"

"No, I didn't know."

"You got Gladys here?"

"No, but take a look around if you care to. What is she to you, anyway?"

"Gladys and me, we had a thing going, and it was real nice, real nice, real willing she was and she loved it, appreciated it. Sort of a neglected soul, and she liked anybody being kind to her. I think I *will* look around. She washed up real well, you know, or don't you know?

"Be my guest."

"I think it best I be satisfied." He then proceeded to look through the house, in all the closets, under the beds, and upstairs, the kitchen, the back hallway. As he turned and started back into the kitchen he saw the lock on the cellar door.

"What's this?"

"The cellar."

"What's down there?"

"Just a cellar."

"I need to see it."

The Reverend got his keys and removed the lock on the hasp. He swung the door open. Fred started toward the steps and stopped in astonishment, staring at the pool of mud. "What the hell!" he said.

"I would call it mud," said The Reverend.

"Just a cellar huh? Where did the mud come from?"

"It came in with the explosion."

"It blew your cellar wall in. Ain't you afraid your house will cave in?"

"It might," said The Reverend.

Fred turned and looked at him for a moment and a derisive expression crossed his face. He walked into the kitchen, picked up a heavy iron skillet from the stove, came back, and heaved it out into the cellar. A tulip-shaped geyser of mud splashed to the floor joists above, and the skillet sank at once. He turned to The Reverend and said, "You could hide anything in there, Reverend, even a body, couldn't you?"

"Fred," said The Reverend. "I think we both best let well enough alone, let things quiet down, and then we can start over."

"Reverend, excuse me, but starting over with you would be the last thing I want to do. Not you. I don't trust you anymore, never did. I'll bet you, Gladys lies at the bottom of that mud hole, and I'll bet the police would be only too glad to pump it dry to find out, *Your Innocence*!"

"Now Fred."

"Can the crap, I want my money!"

"Okay, okay. Just be patient; I will give you everything in my personal safe. Just wait." The Reverend went to a small safe in his bedroom. Then he went to a desk drawer, and returned counting a roll of bills. To his surprise Fred stood in the cellar doorway with his hands propped up on the jambs, staring down toward the mud, the stance of grief in his posture. The Reverend approached from the rear. He intended to give Fred the money if he had to, and he could not imagine why Fred did not turn to face him. He appeared to be lost in thought. But The Reverend had never been one to waste an opportunity. The sweep of his right hand went on into a follow through, the tip of the silencer popping against Fred's naked nape, the hand shoving while firing, propelling Fred forward into the cellar mud. He plunged beneath the surface. Bubbles erupted, and splashed mud began to drip off overhead joists. The Reverend shut the door and the hasp and replaced the lock. He burned Fred's big black hat in the fireplace.

The Reverend had in his fireproof wall safe, hidden in the chimney, three million dollars in cash, profits from the Legation operation, an adequate amount to allow an escape at the right time, and perhaps an early retirement, and a place at the southern tip of Florida, maybe in the Keys. Thank God for the mud hiding his most vulnerable secrets. The mud would slowly set up, dry, become hard and crusted so it would bear weight, and no one would think to look beneath its surface: perfect graves, indeed. He would remove the door and fill the opening and refinish the wall eventually.

But The Reverend worried. In his worst dreams he feared his uncanny deviousness had turned upon him. In nightmares and late-night ruminations, a morbid guilt told him he did not reckon realistically with the nature of water, the greatest of all dissectors, the most secret and pervasive of all invaders. In his semi-wakefulness, his mind followed devious rivulets winding down beneath shingles on molding leaky roofs. In his more sober insights of nature's power, relentless drips in mountain peaks destroyed granite and ironstone walls and brought crashing cave-ins after centuries of incessant and constant erosion. And water in bulk, given the power of tides and coastal storms, reshaped the land and uncovered old secrets and tragedies hidden for centuries. The Reverend knew no respite; his worries increased. He became harried, harassed by his own thoughts.

The Reverend Earl Plough received a letter addressed to Legation, with the correct address, but appearing in the parsonage mailbox. He opened the letter after only glancing at the address. The sender, Jacob Wirth, had escaped the arrests at Legation headquarters in Chicago, and wanted to reestablish business.

They must meet in person, and Wirth named the place and set the time: the Omni Hotel in downtown Norfolk, on the day after tomorrow. Plough knew the name, Jacob Wirth. He had assumed this person to be out of circulation, one of Legation's best men in Chicago, one likely to have been in headquarters when the arrests were made. Plough and Jacob Wirth had never seen each other, so it would not be necessary for Plough to disguise himself as Lotte.

In the living room of a small suite, a well-groomed man wearing a pinstriped suit and an almost formal gray tie shook hands and said, "Reverend Lotte, so good to meet you. We must reestablish our empire and keep the flow of organs going to those who so desperately need them."

"Thank you, Mr. Wirth. May the Lord help us to defeat our enemies," said Plough.

"Ah, yes indeed."

"What did you have in mind?"

"Well, with your permission we would like to begin by reestablishing the unit in Chicago. Three of us are left there, and we could recruit other people. Plenty are available and looking for work these days. The Savior Funeral Home of

Chicago is badly missed. With the Chicago operations under way, we could then begin to rebuild the main headquarters in Norfolk."

"I would be most anxious to proceed."

"We will need to be able to contact you by phone."

"No problem. I can supply you with an unlisted number," said Plough.

"And the matter of finances?"

"Right up front, I do not have any funds left. All of the money burned in the explosion and fire, or was stolen by the arsonists."

"Well now, we can't be expected to operate without funds," said Wirth.

"What happened to the funds at your headquarters?"

"Missing," Wirth said.

"Yes, I know the problem. I will have to look for resources ... Suppose I phone you when I see what arrangements can be made."

"Oh no, Reverend. We don't trust a permanent phone just yet. We will phone you from pay phones until we are once again safely established."

Plough wrote his unlisted number on Omni stationary and handed the paper to Wirth. "You can get me at this number after working hours."

Wirth looked at the note and pocketed it. "Good. I will phone in a few days. The more money you can raise, the more we can do at a faster pace."

"Give me a little time."

"All right. Now one other thing ... about Joan Pully."

"What about her?" asked Plough. He heard the betraying alarm in his own voice, and became cautious.

"Do you think Legation has a chance of recovery as long as she is alive?"

Plough waited for a moment. Surely Wirth knew nothing about the ransom money or Joan's real fate. So he gambled on an evasive answer: "Do you think she caused all of our trouble?"

"Oh, yes. We have reason to believe she started the entire war against us and was responsible for all the destruction."

With a sinking feeling, Plough understood. Wirth's words meant Joan Pully had escaped death once again, and Wirth had an uncomfortable edge on him with specific and secretive information. He controlled his emotions, and said, "Then she must be removed before we can have a safe chance to rebuild."

"We, in Chicago, have come to the same conclusion ourselves."

"I will see to this myself. No one else can be trusted."

"We were hoping you would make that decision. Do you need help?"

Plough stared at the floor, then, groping for information, said, "No. But she is nowhere to be found. I wonder where she might be." He hoped Joan Pully had become a donor as soon as she reached her destination after the day of the ransom payoff. But he had to play ignorant; Wirth just might know something about Joan's real whereabouts. He seemed to be hinting at an inside track.

Wirth said, "Well, things have quieted down and I suspect she will return soon."

This statement almost surely meant she posed a threat somewhere and Wirth knew the details, but The Reverend remained cautious. He said, "I will be watching."

"Don't relax your vigil."

"What do you mean?"

"As rumor has it, she now knows who you are and is planning to eliminate you next."

"Well now, how could one skinny little woman be such a threat?"

"I understand she has a new set of powerful friends in the Middle East. They are passionate and angry about the treatment she has received. And I also hear they are willing to help her, the mentality of the terrorists, Reverend."

Plough, now frightened, wanted to know her whereabouts, and how did Wirth know? But he said, "I trust in the Lord to protect me."

"She, too, may be trusting in the Lord to help her find you. I doubt that He chooses sides."

"I am the Lord's servant, and he walks beside me."

"Well, you may need him sooner than you think. Unless you eliminate her before she has a chance to enroll the help of the Arabic world and strike first ... Now, all that aside, would you care to have dinner? I can order room service, or do you know a place?"

"No. No thank you. I must return to those of my flock who need me and are waiting," said Plough. He suspected Wirth of knowing far more than he had revealed, maybe too much, and Plough wanted to nail him, but said no more for fear of revealing too much himself. Once he reestablished his empire, Wirth would pay dearly for this impertinence.

"Then we will call soon."

"Give me a week if you don't mind."

"We can wait, and we will appreciate your gracious help."

Plough retreated through the lobby and out into the night. Marion and Sarah got up from their chairs in the lobby and returned to suite 601. The SamuelS man who called himself Jacob Wirth awaited them. The other SamuelS men had gathered in the room. Wirth played back the video records made by a hidden camera. None of the people in the room had any doubt now about the true identity of The Reverend Earl Plough, and The Reverend Lotte.

Herman Hodder reported by phone to Kahan, who said, "Now, shall we proceed as planned?"

"Yes. Ralph Green, the seducer, will find the right person."

"What are his special skills?"

"He knows the whole subterranean nocturnal world of bars and dives, the places where lonely and desperate people go to relieve the tedium and boredom of empty lives. There, they easily become his prey ... men and women both."

"From your description it seems to me he qualifies for the ship."

"Oh, indeed, he does. But he is too valuable at the moment, because of his other talents."

"And we will be using one of his special talents?"

"Yes. Revenge and his concept of justice drive him like obsessions. And he knows where to find the most unique talents anywhere in this world of his."

"Talents for what?"

"For eliminating an injustice in the most imaginary and appropriate way by turning a victim's own foibles and self-deception to self-destruction."

"For The Reverend."

"For The Reverend, and his time has come."

"Proceed."

In a restaurant cubicle, Ralph listened to the details of Herman's requirements and his wishes for Plough. He replied, "I know The Reverend, whether it's Plough or Lotte, very well indeed. He lives in an imaginary world conceived for his own power and glory. Never for a moment has he ever touched on the reality of the claims he makes, either in the church or the tissue and organ world. I know just the man who deals in the most whimsical judgments."

"Then you understand."

"Yes, and I will need a day or so to make contacts." Then he asked, "Where is Joan Pully?"

"Your question is most appropriate. She is under guard in a foreign country."

"Oh, indeed."

"Yes, and she will never be safe if she returns while The Reverend is still here."

"So?"

"So, when The Reverend learns she is returning he will no doubt intensify his efforts to eliminate her."

"And just when will she return?"

"That is the crux of the situation. She will return at our discretion."

"Is The Reverend waiting?"

"Watching the house of Dr. Eric Stuart, expecting her to appear any minute."

"Ahhh, this opens a world of possibilities," said Ralph.

"I thought as much."

"The man I need from New York will be expensive."

"No restrictions."

This would be Ralph's personal revenge, too. And afterward perhaps he could capture Joan Pully even yet and collect the ten million dollar ransom for himself alone. The sooner they got rid of The Reverend, the sooner Joan Pully would return. Then he would take her himself.

SamuelS opened Eric's garage after midnight on each of the next two nights for an unmarked van loaded with supplies needed for Ralph Green's plan.

CHAPTER 37

Wirth left The Reverend no choice. He would have to strike first before Joan Pully brought the wrath of the Arabian world down on his head. He sat by the window of his kitchen, staring out at the burned-over area of Legation headquarters, thinking about the course his life had taken.

Without training, without finishing high school, he had simply begun to preach. Sin and damnation became his themes, salvation the answer he thrust upon people, redemption his promise. He ranted. From the first sermon he knew his power. He could reduce people to guilt, to submission, to worthlessness, and he could open their pockets. He unloaded. His anger and excitement and shouting reached a climax and he came away sweating, his shirt-sleeved armpits soaked, his brow dripping. He understood none of it. His mind produced it like a performance, a performance invariably leaving him wrung out, emptied as though he had had an epileptic seizure, and with an aftermath of something missing, a vague dissatisfaction.

Then the military draft caught up with him. Conscripted, he could not preach because he did not have the qualifications on paper. He became an infantryman, and his passion erupted in battle, in the liquid fire of gut-twisting fear, and the excitement of survival. The power of the rifle barrel, the justification of ripping open God's enemies, the devil's agents, with blazing trajectories, and the thrill of spilled blood fulfilled his evangelical fervor for the moment.

When the war ended he returned to preaching and settled on the Congregational denomination because they practiced Holy Communion. He felt such enormous control over his flocks when they docilely ate of the flesh and drank of the blood, and such penitence himself when he slipped the little wafer into his mouth, the heart of Christ still quivering in its last throes on The Cross, in this moment of fervor, the spilled blood of battle.

Then a peculiar thing happened to change the course of his ambition. A prosperous middle-aged farmer in his Jamestown congregation, Amos Beaver, suffered his third severe heart attack. The cardiologist down in Norfolk put him in the cardiac ICU and told the family Beaver's heart had worn out and he could survive only with a new heart. He would never go home without one.

The Reverend Plough stood by the bedside watching the man gasping for breath. How do you get a new heart? He had come to understand. You wait for somebody to die, somebody with your body build and with your blood type, and he has to die from brain injury — from ruined brain, either torn by violence or torn by severe spontaneous bleeding, and torn up so bad its owner will never recover, and so bad he cannot breathe without help, and so bad he has lost all awareness forever. The family had come to The Reverend, to leave nothing untried, for the laying on of hands. The Reverend Plough prayed for the miracle, loudly and clearly, with a palm down on the forehead of the balding farmer, proclaiming up toward the hospital ceiling, toward the heavens.

And he went looking and found some of the facts. The LifeChain network handles all of the hospital's organ distribution. A woman answered the phone. "LifeChain, Gladys speaking."

"What's your last name, Gladys?"

"Gleason. Gladys Gleason, may I help you?"

Then The Reverend Plough, from his repertoire of God's obedient servants, chose another name as he spoke. "Well, Gladys, this is The Reverend Lotte speaking. I have one of my flock here, one of my dearest Christians, in the Cardiac ICU at Sentara, and the doctors tell us a heart transplant is his only chance of living. And I understand you people know about such things and you obtain the heart and then determine where each should go for the next waiting patient dying for the need."

"Yes, you have heard right."

"We can't wait any longer."

Gladys laughed, "Well I'm afraid you have to."

"But this man is well-to-do. Can't he buy one somewhere?"

"You mean a heart ... buy a heart?"

"Yes. I mean buy a heart. Something practical. Something definite."

"Of course not, unless you want to go out and kill somebody. But if you do, just be sure to get the right blood type and the right body type, and you still might lose the heart to the next person in line. So if you go to the trouble, you best find your own hospital and your own heart surgeon willing to cooperate in that illegal endeavor."

"Well, tell me this, who determines who gets the next heart?"

"The computer, unless the surgeon changes the decision for one reason or another."

"Who knows what the computer shows or says, and who passes on the information?"

"Well, locally, I do."

"And who else?"

"Nobody, if I'm on duty. They just call for the information on waiting patients when a donor appears, and I pull it up on the screen and then pass it on."

"Who answers the phone at LifeChain?"

"I do."

"And are you there most of the time?"

"Nearly eighteen hours a day."

"Then you would be in a position to help someone in great need, some unfortunate but very worthy person to be born again into extended life."

Sensing his meaning, she said, "Help someone to be born again, Reverend?"

"Oh yes, yes indeed. Bless you, my daughter. May I call you again in my dedication to helping the sick and the suffering and the dying?"

"Indeed."

The Reverend lost no time. Beaver's desperate family approved any amount he needed. He promised to do his best, and went prowling the emergency rooms.

The patient had been picked up in the middle of the interstate. A search of his wallet revealed a donor card and a driver's license with his name, Steven Sims, and home address. The secretaries tried to phone. No phone could be found for the address or the name. The hospital authorities requested help from the police in the patient's town and they went to the address and found the house abandoned.

Another motorcycle — the entire top of the head had been burned and torn away by high-speed contact with highway concrete. Mere fragments of both hemispheres of the brain lay torn and bleeding in the remnant of the brainpan, as amorphous and gelatinous as lost glue. Both pupils of the eyes stood wide open and fixed.

They stopped compressing the bag, and waited. The patient made no attempt to breathe. An anesthesiologist then started a respirator. The patient obviously had all the criteria of fatal and irreversible brain damage and would not live much longer even with support. The senior neurosurgical resident, mumbling, *fuckin' donor-cycle, fool on a crotch-rocket,* removed the bandage and had a look for himself. He backed off and said, "Call the coroner, call a neurologist for a second opinion, call the hospital administrator's crew to get the hospital attorney for support, then declare him brain dead and proceed. His donor card gives us the legal right, but I think we need to be a little more humane to the family, if they can be found."

The Reverend approached the patient, bowed his head, shut his eyes, and began to pray in a low murmuring voice.

Opening his eyes and looking up toward the heavens to say *Amen*, he read the label and the patient's name on the hanging packet of blood. Steven Sims, type A, a perfect match for Amos Beaver.

Finishing his petitions to God, The Reverend rushed to a pay phone and called LifeChain. Gladys Gleason answered.

"Bless you, my child, The Reverend Lotte here."

"Yes," said Gladys.

"Do you have a Steven Sims in your computer?"

The keys clicked, then, "Yes, he just came on." Gladys waited, reading the screen.

"Ahh, good," said The Reverend. "Has he been assigned yet to a recipient?"

The keys clicked again, and Gladys said, "Yes."

"Does the heart by any chance go to Amos Beaver?"

Gladys studied the screen again. Amos Beaver, a patient in Sentara, stood next in line for a heart from a donor type A, size large. By a fortunate series of circumstances he would be the recipient. But Gladys sensed an opportunity and she said, "No, I'm afraid not ... it appears a man in Richmond has been waiting longer and seems to be sicker. The heart will be sent there."

"Gladys, at this moment does anyone besides you and me know this?"

"Ummm, well ... no."

"Then no one ever would know the difference if you assigned the heart to Beaver?"

"Risky business, I'm afraid."

"Please answer my question ... would anyone ever know?"

"Most likely not."

"Then I can make it well worth your while."

"Perhaps we should meet face to face to discuss this."

"Oh, no. That would not be necessary. Would twenty-five be enough?"

"Dollars?"

"Thousand."

She caught her breath, but she did not want him to hear her surprise nor her pleasure, so she said, "Is that all you can afford?"

"Fifty."

"Agreed. The surgery will be done this afternoon."

"Bless you, my child."

"Tis' a pleasure, Reverend."

Beaver's recovery enhanced The Reverend Plough's reputation. His congregation came to look upon him in the same light they would hold a successful faith healer. His fame spread. He became a miracle worker. After paying Gladys, he had nine hundred and fifty thousand dollars left from the million paid in cash by the Beaver family. Now he could start his television evangelism. But people began calling at once for live organs. He tried Gladys again and found her amenable. They did not meet. Neither would recognize the other on the street. She knew him as The Reverend Lotte, the name he had picked whimsically. The Reverend knew he had been chosen to deliver the good people from impending destruction in the wrath of the Lord. Sensing the possibilities, and the imminent dangers, he decided *Plough* would have to disappear from the transplant scene.

He chose a name, *Legation*, then a location. While looking at the abandoned warehouse across the inlet from the parsonage, he discovered an old sealed basement doorway, filled in with mismatching brick. Then he remembered a similar closed-off doorway in the parsonage cellar. Could this be a sealed tunnel leading from one building to the other? He thought so, and he gambled on it. He bought the warehouse. In secret he chiseled the brick from both doorways, confirming the tunnel, and slipped a framed door into each opening, re-plastered the scars, and painted over the evidence. Then

The Reverend Plough referred people who needed organs to Legation. The Reverend Plough could not in all consciousness pray for a donor, because he would at the same time be praying for the death of another person. He had to be fair to all of God's children. Members of his congregation thought this very magnanimous, and they turned to Legation without question.

And now The Reverend justified these activities, in his own thinking, to building the power and the glory of his following and his church. If the Omni meeting had produced nothing else, it did let him know about Joan Pully. He began watching Stuart's house again. He would get her the minute she returned before she had a chance to get him.

CHAPTER 38

Plough, spying from his parked car, watched a tall graceful woman, dressed in slacks and jacket, get out of a taxi at the curb and mount the steps of Eric's house. His heart raced. The cab driver followed with luggage. She fumbled in her purse, with head bent down; then unlocked the front door, and the driver set her bags inside and left. The door shut, the lights came on behind the blinds.

Now The Reverend had his first glimpse of Joan Pully since Fred placed her alive in the casket for delivery to Kahan's plane. God! What a leggy, gamy beauty with the saucy shamble of a fashion show mannequin parading on stage. Trembling in anticipation, he drove back to the parsonage to make his plans.

Later in the evening a man in a gray suit went to a pay phone in the hospital lobby, phoned the hospital, and said to the operator, "This is Dr. Gary Suttle ... page Dr. Eric Stuart for me, please."

In a moment Eric answered, "Dr. Stuart here."

"Quicksilver, Eric, by the pay phones in the lobby."

Eric appeared within five minutes, his hopes up. The man in the gray suit stepped forward and handed him a pamphlet. "Dr. Stuart, this is the information you requested from the drug company."

Surprised and puzzled, Eric took the pamphlet reflexively. He looked at the blank front of it and turned in astonishment, but the man had disappeared around a corner and out of sight. Eric opened the paper and read: *Kahan wishes to advise you to stay away from your house at all costs. The time is approaching. Do not go near your automobile.* Eric tore up the note, flushed the fragments down the nearest commode, and went back to work, disappointed, but obedient.

During the next two days and evenings, Plough drove by Eric's home many times, but saw no sign of action. On the third evening a Venetian blind had been raised and only a flimsy curtain hung over a well-lit front window. Joan sat in an easy chair beneath a bright reading lamp with a book open in her hands. She appeared dreamlike in the suffused light behind the single pane of glass and its gossamer covering.

Obviously she believed all of her enemies to be dead, especially the Legation people. The explosion and fire should have wiped them all out. Good! Let her think so. Her self-delusions, her complacency, now made things easier, and he would show her. She had not moved when he passed by the window again. An hour later he found the chair vacant. Fifteen minutes later all lights in the house went out.

The next evening she sat in the same chair near the window, smug and at ease. Indecision worried him. The target seemed perfect, but very dangerous. A shot from a car or from the woods across the street would make too much noise, even with a silencer, because the shattering glass from the large pane would crash down on the pavement. He waited, but sensed his opportunity being lost. Her carelessness would not last very long, and as usual she would be on her way. Desperation and anxiety forced his hand. He sought the Lord's will, and decided he had heard the commands: Stop the woman who would destroy the Lord's plans to save his sick and dying people. Stop her before she destroys one of the Lord's most important servants, you.

At nine-thirty the next night, camouflaged in his old combat clothes designed for night fighting, Plough insinuated himself in the woods across the street a half block away, and took up a vigil. He lay on his belly in a small thicket. After the street traffic died down, and bedtime fell on the neighborhood, Joan rose into the chair as though she had been lying on the floor waiting. The Reverend's pulse jumped. The glass between him and Joan posed the major hazard, but he could not let a mere glass panel stop him. He would escape through the bushes in the midst of the confusion the shot would cause.

He took the parts of the 30-30 rifle out of the compartments of his combat jacket and assembled the gun and its telescope in the darkness. He fastened on a long silencer and propped the barrel on a three-inch tripod standing on the ground, and sighted on the window. The light shone dimly through the crosshairs as he brought them onto Joan's head, held his breath, and slowly squeezed the trigger. The rifle emitted a muffled puff, kicked hard, and the window exploded, split into shards, and broken glass clattered and shattered on the driveway below. Joan's head lurched violently away and ruptured open, a geyser of red poured down the broken skull, down over the face. Plough disassembled the gun, hid it and the tripod in his clothes, and lay waiting. Nothing happened. Nobody came out of the adjacent building to investigate, nobody to report anything unusual. There seemed to be a silent ring of privacy and protection around him and the entire surrounding area. Then The Reverend Plough knew God protected him, His humble servant doing His will, surely a divine intervention.

Joan's body lay awry, slumped over to one side in the chair, while The Reverend took up his field glasses and watched. Then she righted herself, sat up, rose to her feet, turned on the spot and taking rigid mechanical steps, moved straight toward the window. The entire top of her head had been blown away, and gelatinous brain, pouring red, oozed down over the side of the destroyed skull and flowed over her face. She moved deliberately, slowly, almost majestically forward, entranced as a zombie, ready to go straight through the window. As she came face onto the broken glass, the lights went out. Plough, moaning in terror, began crawling backward out of the bushes, scrambled to his feet, and ran out of the woods toward his car.

At home, The Reverend, trembling and sweaty, tried to

calm himself with whiskey, then a hot shower. In his own guilty conscience he knew something had gone wrong; retribution waited in ominous secrecy. In bed, he tried to read, but could not concentrate. He turned out the light and listened to the night. A far off sound out in the swamp, hyena-like, bleated a peculiar macabre muted cachinnation in a hollow sepulchral wavering statement, and the phone rang. He snatched up the receiver and answered. A woman's sweet voice said, "Hello, Reverend Lotte, this is Joan Pully calling from Heaven ... I want to thank you so much for sending me here ... it is so warm, so beautiful, so comforting ... Reverend, wouldn't you like to join me ... I have an idea you will soon, anyway ... real soon."

The Reverend dropped the phone and, shaking with terror, reached for the light. He sat up all night and finished off his bottle of bourbon. In the morning the television and the radio news did not mention any type of disturbance on Eric's street, and nothing about it came on the evening news.

As night returned, he cruised by Eric's house. Joan Pully sat in the same chair reading by the same light behind an intact windowpane. Her head appeared to be normal. His terror deepened and he hurried home. In a panic he thought of shooting her again, but dropped the idea. He found an old bottle of sleeping pills, took three and went to bed. After midnight a loud noise in the street awoke him. As he sat up, a bright beam shot through a front window and lit up the living room, blipped the bedroom for an instant, and just as quickly went out. Plough went to another window and looked toward the street. A ghost of Joan Pully, draped in an airy, diaphanous shroud, stood at the curb in a pool of bright light, facing him. The open head oozed brain down over her bloodied cheek. Twenty-four hours had not clotted the fresh flowing blood nor aged the raw brain. The light went off, pitching the street into darkness, then a brighter beam shot through the room where he stood, and lit up his pajama-clad form framed in the window. The light switched back to the street and Joan had vanished. He recoiled, and fled to his bedroom and crawled into bed, his heart pounding. He did not believe in ghosts, but ghost or no ghost, someone knew too much. The phone rang and he snatched it off the hook, and yelled, "Hello!"

The same calm, deep, mellifluous voice as the night before, said, "Reverend Lotte. You are one day nearer to joining me here in Heaven ... Oh, it's sooooo lovely ... You are going to like it," She hung up just as The Reverend began to shout, "WHO ... WHO?"

He lay back in bed, listening to the darkness. The night grew very quiet, except the buzzing of nothingness in his ears. Then from out beyond the house, from the direction of the swamp, dreamlike but only too clearly, came the hyena laughing voice, laughing, "WHO ... WHO ... WHO ... WHOOOOEEEEE,"

Herman sat at the head of the conference table, Ralph Green on his right, and on his left a slender man of medium height, Steven Crain. Herman spoke. "The Reverend Plough now runs scared. He walks the floor all night and he has grown haggard and desperate. He can hardly conduct his services."

"So what next? asked Crain.

Turning to one of his men, Herman said, "See that Crain here has a conference with the good Dr. Marion."

"Would Dr. Marion be receptive to the idea?" asked Ralph.

"Dr. Marion cannot understand why we have waited so long. And I think he has a bevy of interesting possibilities waiting."

The Reverend Earl Plough felt better as soon as he swung into the heat of a sermon. He knew his power. Hellfire and damnation drove his fervor, and brought it to a bright glow in his passionate delivery, and with it he could whip a congregation into a frenzy of guilt and agitation, he could reduce them in contriteness to the meekness of lambs, he could lead them into weeping frenzied confessions of wickedness they didn't possess, and he could reduce them to stone silence in the profundity of their unworthiness.

Joan Pully chose this moment of The Reverend Plough's hysterical exultation to arrive late for the Sunday night services. With his right hand raised and pointing upward, head raised to the heavens, and shouting benedictions and damnations, Plough saw her only after she had progressed almost to the front of the aisle, and she just kept on coming toward him, walking the gait of a Parisian mannequin.

A cloud of tantalizing perfume followed and pervaded the church. She went to a front pew, sidled in, and took a seat down in front of the minister. She had changed the leggy slacks for an ultra svelte, ultra tight miniskirt split above mid-thigh, capping the radiant and exquisite sheen of stretched pantyhose. She crossed her legs, exposing a sleek thigh almost up to her crotch, and leveled her sincere gaze upon the pastor, smiling. Terror struck him mute. He stared stupidly in astonishment at her, and in the silence after his hushed voice, the soundless void filled with the fricative, insistent singing of insects out in the woods behind the church.

A change came over the congregation. Something of unimaginable significance existed between their preacher and the new visitor, who they saw as a beautiful provocative woman, unexpectedly there and out of place in the church. Their preacher and this woman had seen each other at another time and another place. The Reverend Plough's extended arm fell, his face turned ashen, sweat popped out on his forehead, and he leaned against the pulpit for support. Not a sound arose in the church, not the first titter. He seemed to be trying to suppress a compelling urge to turn and run, as he sought his own voice. "... Now let us hear another beautiful song from the choir."

The choirmaster approached, the choir stood, and he conducted them into song. Joan Pully swung her crossed leg, and watched Plough until the song came to an end. He avoided her gaze. In the moment of silence before the people stirred again, the sound came from somewhere out in the woods behind the church; it came muted but distinct, real beyond any doubt, hyena-like, a sardonic wild laughter, hooting this time, *Who ... who ... who ... whoooooeeee.* Joan kept her eyes on the minister, but he had to look even if he turned to a pillar of salt. He saw a steady, bemused, scornful reproach. He raised his arm again and shouted, "Brothers and sisters, I want you to all go home and pray to your God for forgiveness of your wickedness." But his words fell empty of power on the stirring heads of the restless congregation. They already had dismissed his reality.

Joan Pully sat on the front pew, coldly regarding The Reverend Plough, mercilessly bemused. The church emptied, and he alone remained, standing, leaning against the pulpit, trying to avoid her eyes. The last car left the churchyard, and she rose and began walking toward Plough, taking slow steps mimicking the rigid mechanical gait of the slaughtered Joan.

"Don't," he said. "Don't ... please don't come any nearer."

"But Brother Lotte, I find you so attractive, so charming ... I simply can't stay away from you any longer."

"No ... no, no, no ... stay away ... I meant you no harm ... I was only protecting God's empire that helps so many desperate people."

"But you don't understand. I have come to help you put it all together again."

"You destroyed it."

"I only defended the innocent."

"And deprived many desperate and dying of their only chance to live. No, no, no ... stay away ... stop! You have weakened God's church!"

"But my dear Brother Lotte..." She advanced; he broke and ran into the apse, dashed through a door into his office, and turned off the lights in the nave. She had prepared for this, and with a penlight found the door and entered The Reverend's office. She flipped on the lights. Plough sat at his desk, shaken, almost speechless. Joan crossed the room and sat in a chair opposite him. Plough said, "Who ... who are you?"

"Why Reverend. I am, of course, Joan Pully."

"But I thought ... I thought."

"You thought what, Reverend?"

"I thought you were dead."

"Ah! No. Here I am now, alive and very well, and ready to be with you."

"But I don't want..."

"Oh, come now Reverend, I know you better than that. I have heard how well you treat women, how good you are for the lonesome souls in your flock. Aren't you going to offer me a drink?"

"Well, I..."

"Ah! Yes, it's bourbon you like, isn't it? I was hoping you would have something special hidden away, like Wild Turkey. I do adore the twelve-year-old."

"In the bottom drawer of the cabinet."

She crossed the room. "May I?"

"Yes, help yourself."

She opened the cabinet, removed a bottle, and took two glasses from the shelves above. With her back turned, she opened her purse and retrieved a packet of powder. She tore off a corner and dumped the contents into the larger glass. She filled each half full with whiskey and came back to the desk. Plough slumped in his chair, a sweaty crumpled wreck. Joan handed his glass to him, extended her own, and said, "Here's to greater understanding and success." They touched rims. Joan sat on the edge of the desk and crossed her legs, revealing more thigh.

The Reverend Plough downed his whiskey in two gulps.

Joan slid off the desk, her skirt revealing a blip of buttock. She took Plough's empty glass back to the cupboard and mixed more drug and whiskey. She brought the drink along with the bottle back to Plough's desk. He drank half the liquor in one swallow. Joan reseated herself on the desk with her knees toward Plough's nose, and sipped once. He finished off his drink in another swallow, and held the glass in his hand. He stared at Joan's exposed thighs. She lifted the whiskey bottle and leaned forward, half filling the glass. Plough ogled the tunnel above her blouse. He took another sip. She watched for the first signs. Within ten minutes, a silly happiness came over his face.

She waited ten more minutes, then leaned forward and said, "Darling, why don't we turn off the lights."

Plough jumped up and went to the switch by the entrance. He returned, breathing heavily in the darkness, feeling his way along the desk. She stood up and whispered, "Here I am." Plough approached. She grasped his arm and drew him near. He embraced her roughly, and a hand went under the edge of the miniskirt and slid up a slick pantyhose buttock. "Oh! Earl, darling, you are in such a hurry, you big stud ... take your time, sweetheart, so I can really enjoy it too ... we have all night, and all the rest of your life if you like."

"Like, baby, like! Hell, I've never seen anything like you ever before," and he ground his pelvis forward into her front.

"Earl sweetheart, would you mind?"

"Mind what?"

"Mind if we go to my place, sweetheart? It would be so much more comfortable there, and I've got silk sheets on my bed."

"Oh yes, let's go."

"I will drive. Give me your keys."

Joan parked Plough's car in Eric's garage. In the kitchen, She took a bottle of Wild Turkey from a cabinet, poured two drinks, handed one to Plough, and said "Excuse me, I have to go to the bathroom." With drink in hand, she went down the hallway into Eric's bedroom and closed the door.

SamuelS men sat on and around the bed. One whistled in spurious awe. "Can that shit, you bastard," she said.

"Why darling Joan, you are not quite your sweet self to-night."

"Fuck you, smartass." She went into the bathroom, poured the drink down the drain and rinsed the glass. As she passed through the bedroom again, another person handed her a glass. "What's this?"

"For appearances, diluted apple juice, the same color as whiskey. What's The Reverend drinking?"

"The only Wild Turkey in the cabinet ... was it prepared?"

"Loaded. He ought to be ready for a bacchanalian frenzy before midnight."

"If I know The Reverend, he will be needing to take a piss before long, so you guys better get into your hiding places."

"Right. Keep him down there five more minutes."

"I'm staying here five more minutes ... give the stuff time to limber his Willy. I don't want anything to do with the business end of that creep."

"If he has started drinking, it won't be long."

Joan returned to the living room and found Plough in a state of euphoria, standing in a chair and peeing in the kitchen sink. Joan said, "Reverend darling, I don't think you are a real preacher."

He turned and jumped down on the floor, leaving his fly open. "I am not a real preacher? Not a real preacher? I have saved many a soul from eternal damnation. I have baptized more lost sinners than any..."

"Wait, wait, I know. But you have not been the real thing."

"I have been the real thing burning with the zeal of the born-again."

"Ah, yes, my darling man, but you have forgotten the Old

Testament."

"The Old Testament, the Old Testament, what do you mean, the Old Testament?"

"You have forgotten Moses and Aaron."

"Moses and Aaron, Moses and Aaron, Moses and Aaron!"

"Leviticus, Earl darling, Leviticus."

"Leviticus?"

"Yes, Leviticus. When is the last time you provided your poor sinful suffering flock with the only opportunity available in this evil world to absolve their wickedness, the way Moses did for Aaron and his sons and all of their people?"

"They come often to confess their sins."

"Confess ... something everybody knows. That won't do it."

"They cry."

"But not the real thing," said Joan.

"The real thing?"

"Yes, the real thing. Reverend. Have you ever seen sacrificial blood, the real thing, the blood of atonement?"

"The sacraments?"

"Ahh, yes, but no. The tepidness of Eucharist, of make believe – the best of wines is not real blood, and broken crusts are not real bones, and dry bread is dead. Reverend, have you witnessed the quivering heart?"

"Broken crusts are not real bones ... broken crusts are not real bones ... broken crusts are not real bones?" intoned The Reverend Plough.

"And above all, a little white wafer is not the fiery beating heart."

"... Not the fiery beating heart."

"Reverend, have you ever seen sacrificial blood?"

"No."

"Reverend, would you like to be the real thing, would you like to see sacrificial blood, Old Testament blood, the real thing? Reverend, would you like to become a real priest, the likes of Moses himself, the likes of the sons of Aaron, the most powerful of all leaders?"

"Yes, yesyesyesyesyes, oh, yes."

"Would you like to see the struggling, beating heart?"

"Yes, the struggling, beating heart."

"Then we have to sacrifice to the Lord."

"Yes."

"Reverend, would you like to sacrifice to the Lord?"

"Yes. Yes, yes!"

"Do you believe blood must be spilled to atone for sins?"

"For the wicked of the night, oh yes! For the wicked of the night."

"We would need an altar."

"Yes, an altar. We would need an altar."

"And a tabernacle for the altar."

"A tabernacle for the altar. And a tabernacle for the altar."

"In the forest, in the woods."

"In the forest, in the woods."

"We will go into the forest, into the woods."

"Go into the forest, into the woods."

"Then I will take you to a tabernacle in the woods, to an altar in the woods, to an ark in the woods."

"My church is in the woods."

"We have built you a tabernacle in the woods, an altar in the woods."

They entered the waiting car in the garage. Joan pulled on a pair of ultra thin kidskin gloves, then snuggled up to Plough in the back seat, put an arm around his neck, and whispered. Plough sat placidly, docile, subdued and very obedient, in a silly trance. He lifted one of her hands and sniffed, and mumbled, "Like scent of leather."

CHAPTER 39

The driver cut off the headlights when they went past the Jamestown church. The car left the macadam, turned down a gravel road, and entered the woods. Joan helped the preacher off the back seat, and they walked toward the trees. The car left. Joan and The Reverend Plough stood in the wood's edge, shadowed in darkness. A figure approached, carrying a burning torch and a bottle of wine and glasses. Joan poured and Plough drained his glass without pause, and hurled it into the bushes. The torch lit his face. Joan stood back in the edge of the flickering shadows and slyly poured her wine into the grass. The torchbearer wore a multicolored gown from neck to feet. He turned and led the way. Joan and Plough followed. They came to the edge of a structure. The torchbearer stopped and turned, holding the torch high.

Joan said, "We now come to your tabernacle, Reverend. Let us enter." Taking him by an elbow, she guided him into the entrance of a brush arbor. They went forward toward the center, and approached a fire burning within an altar looming up in shadows thrown by its own smoking flames. Its four curved horns, one mounted at each corner and pointing outward, cast ballooned and undulant shadows over the surrounding trees and undergrowth. The altar glowed inside like a furnace sending up sparks and smoke and heat. A goat tethered beneath an altar horn bleated passively and plaintively, in desultory response to nothing, chewing green leaves and weeds, stretching its rope, trying to find more food. Joan reached over one wall of the altar and took a garment off the floor. She lifted it by the shoulders and the skirt unfolded to the ground. Multicolored like the torchbearer's gown, but brighter, its purple and scarlet and blue and gold colors glowed richly in the dim light. "Your ephod, Reverend," said Joan. "Hold your arms out"

Plough raised his arms and she picked up the skirt, slipped

the gown over his head, his arms up the sleeves, then let it unfurl down to cover his shoes. She handed him the wine bottle, and he upended it to his mouth, drained the last drop, and flung it into the woods.

"Now, Reverend, place your hand on the head of the sacrifice."

Plough approached the goat and placed his left hand on its head. The goat became quite still as though waiting to be petted. Joan produced a stiletto from among her clothes, and holding the tip, extended it handle first to Plough. "Now ... cut its throat." Plough took the weapon in his right hand, and without hesitation pressed down on the head with his left hand and stooping, made a violent swipe across the throat with the stiletto. The trusting goat cried a surprised bleat. It gurgled and hung its head. Joan placed a bucket under the throat and the blood poured down, striking the bottom in two violent spouts sounding the shallow timbre of tin. The goat's head sank deeper and deeper as its heart emptied. Its knees buckled, and it came down front first, kneeling. It emanated an aura of waiting and of grief, hovering in suspense, then fell to its side.

Dr. Marion and Sarah, hidden in the woods' edge, continued to drug the bottles of wine. Sarah said, "What of trial and confession, the chance for the truth?"

"There will be a moment for the confession before she takes him to the church, and he will have drunk of the divine potion."

"And what of his realness?"

"I think we both will be astounded ... but just watch."

After the goat became still, Joan retrieved the bucket and handed it to Plough. "Now, Reverend, do as Moses instructed the sons of Aaron."

"What?" asked The Reverend, "What was that?"

"Ahh. You have forgotten your Old Testament."

"What?"

"Dip your hand into the blood and sprinkle it upon the horns of the altar."

The Reverend took the bucket in his left hand, dipped his right into the blood and sprinkled the first horn, then walking around the altar, sprinkled the other three. Blood splattered on his gown, on his face, and on the altar. He came back to Joan. She said, "Now pour the remainder around the altar."

Plough poured blood onto the wall of the altar. It ran down, seeping into the ground. He continued around the wall until he had emptied the bucket and again returned to Joan, who spoke again. "Now, as the sons of Aaron did, open the offering."

The Reverend took the stiletto and ripped open the goat's body, and removed the organs and the fat. The heart lurched spasmodically and muscles rippled along its surface as The Reverend cut its moorings at the throat level. "What do you see, Reverend?"

"A heart ... the quavering, beating heart."

"Now you have sacrificed to God."

"Yes ... ahhh, yes, yes, yes."

"Reverend, lift the parts and place them on the fire."

He lifted them, blood streaming down his arms, soiling the gown, intestines uncoiling over his elbows. He marched around the wall of the altar to the rear and mounted its one step, walked across to the middle, and dumped the mass upon the fire. Sizzling steam and the stench of burning flesh rose into the night. Exploding intestines blew excrement upon his gown. Burning fat sent sparks arching upward. Joan spoke again, "Ahhh Reverend, you have brought the realities of the old testament to life as the priests of old, but now place the remainder of the offering upon the fire."

Plough went back to the goat, cut its rope and lifted it in his arms. He plodded around and mounted the altar again, goat head and limp neck dangling and bleeding, and dumped it on the fire atop the burning organs, and stepped back. Singeing goat hair flared up, and goat flesh began to scorch and cook.

Joan clapped her hands for more wine. In the shadows beyond the torchlight, Dr. Marion, with Sarah at his side, continued his supervision of the drugs. He had watched the effects of his mixtures all evening. The heavy doses of tranquilizers, the traces of lysergic acid in the Wild Turkey at Eric's house, and finally, Marion's own special mixture in the wine here in the woods, using the peyotl drug of religious experience, had brought The Reverend Plough to a high pitch. This time Marion produced another bottle and handed it to a man without a torch. Into it Marion had mixed *the cocaine of Africa,* ibogaine from the West African plant, iboga, the shaman's magic, to levitate The Reverend's spirits and hallucinate his visions.

Joan poured a glass full and handed it to Plough He emptied it in one swig. She filled the glass again. The Reverend drank ravenously. An hour passed as the drugged wine brought Plough into a wild state of acute hallucinations. Keyed to a maniacal pitch, any suggestion now sent him into frenzied craziness. She waited. When the peak became obvious in the drugged madness, she said, "Reverend, what do you see?"

Running in circles, vaulting great exhilarated leaps within the circle of light, his arms up and outstretched, his multicolored gown flopping below his knees, the blood-blotched blemishes on the ephod dark within the darkness, The Reverend Plough screamed, "I see trumpets blaring, I hear bright colors ... The angels sing ... Glory be to God! Ahhhh, HA! HA! HA! ahHaaaaaaaaa. HA! HA! HA! Joan held a torch high. The light flared. The Reverend laughed, running by, while tears streamed down his cheeks, the pupils of his eyes fully dilated, his visage wild and mad, his face flushed red, his sparse hair standing on end, erected like an angry dog bristling, and the arteries in his neck pounded full and furiously. "I am watching me now I so clearly understand! I see it ... I am outside me watching me ... watching me, watching me, AhhhHAAAAAAA, HA! HA! HA! HAAAAAAAAAAAAAA!"

Joan spoke again, "Eat of the goat, Reverend. Partake of the anointed flesh."

Plough turned in his running circle and trotted to the fire, knelt beside the steaming burning goat, and cut off a large chunk of flesh with the stiletto. He tore a piece loose with his fingers, and stuffed it into his mouth. Bloody grease ran down his chin and dripped onto the bright gold of the ephod.

"Ah Reverend, just as Moses and Aaron and all of his sons, you have eaten now of sacrificial flesh."

"I hear the bright colors ... I see the angels sing ... glory be to God ... I understand ... so clear ... so clear ... I am complete!" He stood beside the blazing fire and the charring goat, arms down stretched, his palms open forward, head raised and reared back, face to the ceiling of brush, in a state of exaltation, weeping.

"Reverend, you are not a real priest ... not yet."

"Ahh, but I have sacrificed real blood."

"But Reverend, you have sacrificed nothing but goat blood, only animal blood."

"Only animal blood?"

"Yes, and your own altar is not real, your own pulpit thirsts for this atonement, the real blood of contriteness."

"My pulpit has known all the real sacraments."

"But you have never sent through the fire to Molech..."

"What?"

"Child sacrifice, to appease a god, Reverend."

"What? ... What, what?"

"I Kings, Reverend; II Kings; Genesis; Leviticus; Isaiah; Jeremiah; Exodus; Judges ... do you need more?"

"No."

"Not of thine own flesh, Reverend."

"I have sacrificed the blood and the flesh."

"Not human flesh, not your very own kin, Reverend. You have never been the real thing."

"I have fed the blood and the body to the hungry mouths, the quaking souls."

"Spoiled grapes are not real blood ... broken bread not real bones ... a dry wafer not the sacrificed, quivering heart. Reverend?"

"Yes!"

"Your pulpit thirsts for real atonement."

"The blood is all gone."

"Reverend!" She commanded, and the hum of the forest seemed to diminish as The Reverend turned his face toward her, his head wavering, his eyes drunken. "Reverend, let us discuss beliefs."

"Ah, yes. Beliefs. I believe."

"Do you believe blood has to flow from the innocent and guilty alike to atone for the sins of man?"

"Either or," The Reverend quipped, suddenly arch and snide.

"Now Reverend, this is your confession and your soul be damned for lying!"

"I believe!"

"Reverend! Give me your full attention!" Plough seemed to sober; he grew still and quiet, watching her, his head weaving. "Do you upon the sanctity of your soul, truly believe the Almighty god in all his wisdom and mercy demands the blood and the quivering heart of the terrified and helpless victim in the most violent of pain?"

The Reverend's face changed as Joan's words struck to the true limits of his intelligence. He seemed to struggle for an answer, then escaped the responsibility of truth with another quip. "The wine and the bread bring them into my power!" Then he chuckled. "Blood and bones, blood and bones, blood and wafers." And he laughed again.

"Let us go, Reverend, and make amends."

Joan summoned another bottle of wine and gave Plough a full glass. "Come, Reverend." They followed a torchbearer across the woods and entered the church through a rear door. The torch, held high near the pulpit, filled the nave with flickering shadows. Recesses of the church lay in darkness. Joan led Plough up the steps into the pulpit. "Blood, Reverend, sprinkle blood upon the pulpit."

"I have no blood."

"You have plenty of blood."

"The animal has bled. I need another animal."

"No, Reverend. The animals have suffered enough. For Moses, we need the real sacrifice. Reverend, your pulpit deserves the real, the original."

"Another animal."

"Ah, yes Reverend, indeed. Raise your left hand."

Joan moved to his right, and the bearer lifted the torch. Plough raised his left hand, staring up at it in the flickering light. The hand cast a magnified shadow against the dark recesses of the nave. Joan commanded, "Now, Reverend, give us the Cahanim blessing."

"What?" said Lotte, "What ... what?"

"Ahh. You don't know your own religion."

"What?"

"Oh, Reverend, such a pity."

"What? What?"

"Let the light in, Reverend, to keep ... in gracious peace."

"What?"

"Oh, Reverend ... then give us the Vulcan greeting."

"What?" said Plough, still perplexed, "What?"

"Lotte, you are so ignorant. You don't even know your Star Trek."

"What?"

"Lower your ring finger, Reverend."

The ring and little fingers dropped and hung down and the shadow looked now like the cast of an animal head with mouth open.

"Now, stick up your thumb, Reverend." The thumb came up in shadow.

"What do you see, Reverend?"

"My hand ... a head, a head, a goat head ... with ears."

"The ears are too long for a goat, Reverend. It's a jack-ass."

"A jackass," intoned The Reverend.

"And what is on the head?"

"Blood ... Yes, blood."

"The animal, Reverend ... hold its head."

"Yes. But blood, we need more blood"

Joan moved to his side. The Reverend stood entranced, staring out across space, the great shadow still on the church wall. She offered the stiletto handle first. The Reverend took it in his right hand. He stood statue-like, frozen in this cata-tonic posture, the left hand still raised, waiting.

"Cut its throat," she said, in a clear, commanding voice.

The right hand flicked, the stiletto flashed, the left wrist flared open, and two geysers of bright red arterial blood pumped across the space and showered down on the pulpit.

"Ahh, Reverend you have plenty of blood now ... take the donkey around your pulpit and sprinkle well."

The Reverend Plough dropped the stiletto, grasped the left hand with his right and holding it up, walked around the pulpit spraying blood on its sides and around its base. When he completed the circle, Joan approached him and said, "Now Reverend, come let us go to the last of your sacraments, a real baptism," and she led him out of the chancel and across the nave and out the rear door into the churchyard. The pumping arteries left a double trail splattered on the church floor and down the steps.

"Baptism?"

"Yes, let us wash away sins."

"Wash?"

"Wash in the blood of sacrifice."

"Ah, yes."

They approached the concrete baptism pool a few yards behind the church. Joan hesitated at the sight of it. SamuelS had filled this grave-size pit brim full with water, but without first cleaning away the collected debris. Sticks and leaves, paper cups and paper fragments, crushed beer cans, and other trash floated on its surface. It looked as though someone had filled it at a moment of madness in a great careless rush.

The Reverend's hand dropped, and blood poured from the severed arteries, but the pumping had stopped. He had become pale and sweaty and he staggered. She steadied his right elbow and guided him to the steps descending under water. Plough obeyed Joan's command and went in, docile as a child. She stepped to one side along the concrete edge, and holding Plough's extended right hand, guided him forward to the middle of the pool then turned him to face the church. He stood in water up to his belt. The left hand dropped under the surface, and a smoky cloud roiled upward and swirled through the pool. Plough stood dazed, his ephod billowing on the water. Joan handed him another glass of wine. He took it with his right hand and drank. The glass fell, plunging out of sight. The Reverend looked dizzily upward at Joan standing on the wall. The clinging miniskirt had worked its edge up to crotch level. He tried to focus on her legs, but his eyes wandered off, his head began to sag, and his body sank deeper into the pool. Joan said, "Reverend!"

"Yes," Plough muttered, his face bent down toward the water.

"Baptize the sinner."

"Who?"

"Who do you see?"

"I see me, standing beside me."

"Then baptize you."

"I have been baptized."

"But not in real blood ... not in the real blood of the real sacrifice."

"In blood?"

"Then you will be complete ... all sins washed away in real blood."

"But I hardly know how."

"Reverend, lie down on your back ... now."

The Reverend obeyed. He let himself go, leaned backward supine on the water and sank beneath its surface. The ephod skirt flared up, a great bolus of air plopped out, and the cloth collapsed. Joan and the torchbearer stood above, waiting through a long silence. Then a bubble burst among the debris, emitting a muffled cough from beneath the water. The pool overflowed, carrying trash into the weeds.

After another ten minutes nothing else had disturbed the surface. Plough lay obscured, hazy in the diluted cloud, his arms and legs invisible in the depths and his body outline blurred anonymous and dim beneath the amnion of murky water. Swirling blood from the opened wrist ebbed languidly upward. Joan raised a hand to the torchbearer and signaled toward the brush arbor.

Dr. Marion and Sarah stood just beyond the edge of light cast by the fire and the torches. Cautiously out of sight in the darkness while the action took place in the church, they had watched the procession go from the rear door to the baptismal pool and waited until Joan signaled. When a torchbearer applied flame to the brush arbor and the fire flared skyward, Marion and Sarah went deeper into the woods and joined the SamuelS men who had surrounded and guarded the area during the ceremony.

At this moment, Herman Hodder returned to the scene in a SamuelS automobile. He waited beside the driver while Joan retrieved a small valise from the back seat, stepped into the shadows of the woods, removed the trappings of drag, and transformed into a sulking Crain in sports clothes. He threw the clothes of Joan into the spreading fire, and returned to the waiting car. Herman's driver whisked them to the airport, Herman paid in cash, and Crain waited two hours and caught a six a.m. flight to New York. He still wore the kidskin gloves when he boarded the plane.

SamuelS continued the watch. The woods burned to the edge of the churchyard. The horns of the altar turned to ashes. Only the goat skeleton remained to mystify curious people who in subsequent days walked in the soot of the forest: some luckless animal, perhaps a deer caught in the frenzy of the blaze.

SamuelS monitored the public reaction, wary of an investigation. The report on television and in the newspapers said the sexton opened the church doors the next afternoon to the peculiar odor of dried blood. He found the splattering on the pulpit and the bloody knife, and followed the blood-sprinkled trail through the back door out to the bloody baptismal pool. The Reverend lay floating face up amidst debris on the surface, the slit wrist still leaving a faint red trail in the undulating water. Suicide. The Reverend Plough had gone mad, dressed himself in the raiment of Old Testament Israel, slit his wrist in the pulpit, ran into the churchyard, got in the baptismal pool, and bled to death. The investigation produced no other conclusions. Fingerprints on the stiletto belonged to The Reverend alone.

Herman reported to Kahan. "Man, what a realistic mess Crain made in Dr. Stuart's house ... gelatin and yogurt oatmeal brains and tomato juice all over the chair and rug and living room ... A balloon full of tomato juice inside a balloon of yogurt and gelatin and cooked oatmeal... all inside the plastic skull ...! Mounted on a manikin, it exploded just like the real thing. I have to admit he is a nasty little genius," said Herman.

Other SamuelS men, wasting no time, entered the parsonage before daylight and removed all records, and found the three million dollars stashed behind loose bricks within the chimney wall. The safe contained only a few thousand.

Ralph Green visited the funeral home the next day and got his first glimpse of The Reverend, a bloated, pallid, cyanotic visage surrounded by a jungle of flowers, and a misbegotten and ineffectual harem of weeping matrons. So he had seen at last The Reverend Lotte, or Plough, who had paid him so much money, and never granted a view of himself? Now Ralph could only await the return of the real Joan. And Joan or no Joan, The Reverend had paid him, for donors, enough in cash to relieve the tedium of having to supplement his income at the Athletic Club. He hated the damned fat overindulgent frauds lackadaisically wanting to be Samsons without effort. He would retire to Key West as soon as he settled the matter of Joan Pully.

CHAPTER 40

SamuelS watched the inexorable happen to The Reverend Plough's house. Near the end of June, with the moon full, a violent northeast storm struck the coast and lasted two days. The wind-whipped tides rose several feet above normal, bringing the sea over the burned site of Legation headquarters. Surging water ripped into the charred cellar, and washed away the remaining burned debris.

The flood covered the parsonage yard and the street. The streaming force of relentless water began to bring a muddy stain from the parsonage cellar out into the inlet. Then SamuelS knew the water had infiltrated and weakened the bolus of mud blocking the tunnel into the parsonage basement, slowly crumbling the dam the explosion had formed, and washing it out to sea. The rising and falling water ceaselessly seeped and sucked out the pool of mud beneath the floor of the parsonage. SamuelS increased its surveillance.

The parsonage changed hands. SamuelS continued to monitor and to listen. A new preacher moved in with his wife and family. Two days later the minister's wife, while searching for the source of a rotten odor filling her kitchen, became curious about the locked door. She found the key on a large ring in a cupboard. With her husband's help she got the lock open and the hasp undone. When the door swung outward, a dank smell, then an overwhelming stench came up the stairs. Forms on the basement floor, draped in wet slime and rubble, appeared vague in the gloom below. The wife's groping hand found a light switch, and the mud-splattered globe sprang to life. It took a minute for the minister and his wife to see through the sediment; then they slowly comprehended the secrets the tides had uncovered. The woman lay nude on her back, one stiff arm raised in a gesture of desperation mimicking defense. Her face already had given to encavement and the somber haunting rebuke of naked skull sockets. The man lay fully clothed across her pelvis, the top of his head missing, his skull fragment full of muddy slime.

The new preacher considered himself honest and forthright, and called the police at once. Gladys and Fred were identified, to the satisfaction of SamuelS and all it represented. Now the news media had a reason for The Reverend Plough's suicide — guilt from a double murder. Speculation pointed only to a mental aberration: The Reverend Plough had been insane all along until things caught up with him and he took his own life.

On the twenty-sixth of June, another man in coat and tie met Eric in the hospital hallway, and they walked out together across the grounds. He said, "Kahan plans to deliver Joan Pully into your hands three days from today, but he wants her to return with you to Xanadu in July."

"In July?"

"Yes. He wants to see you"

"About what?"

"The future."

"Oh."

"Kahan says you may return home now. The place is safe. The house has been thoroughly inspected, the bugs and wiretaps removed, and the pantry restocked with a good supply. We have carefully checked your car; we removed the bomb someone had installed. We later had a man drive the car fifty miles. No trouble, now. The bomb was very powerful. We set it off in the woods and it shattered the trunk of a live oak two feet in diameter."

Eric turned pale and quiet, then asked, "Where did you find the keys?"

"We didn't, but we have our ways."

"Oh, I see," said Eric.

"Kahan wants you to know he appreciates your patience

and considerations."

"Tell Kahan I am most grateful."

"Of course."

With no good-bys, no formalities, the man turned suddenly at a sidewalk intersection, and strode off in another direction. Eric shook his head and returned to the hospital.

Kahan said his good-bys to Joan at breakfast on the last day of her visit. He told her about the double identity and the fate of The Reverend Plough and the Legation organization. Then he said, "I do not wish to unduly change the lifetime plans of young people who have paid the price of intense training. But we need Eric Stuart here in Xanadu. Coming here would not be like selling his soul to the devil. We don't wish to make him a Faust. He could leave anytime he might choose to try something different. Once here however, I think he and you would want to stay. Here he can do more good for fellow members of the human race with less frustration than he could in any other place in the world."

Joan said, "I know, and I will present the matter to him in a neutral manner, but the decision has to be his. He may have decided already, July being only a few days away. Your offer is very generous, and we both appreciate it."

"Not at all. We are moving toward a global society, and Eric with his unique talent and dedication would be an ideal citizen of the world."

"It's hard to imagine a better place."

"Thank you. In the meantime I am concerned about the safety of you both. One of our jets is in your country every day, and a phone call will bring the plane to you immediately." He handed her a slip of paper, and continued, "Our satellite phone number."

"I hope it does not prove to be so urgent."

Kahan said, "Be vigilant, nevertheless."

The ambience of home returned with Joan, the pleasant odors of cooking food, the champagne flutes waiting beside the dinner plates. During the ten days since his last night in Xanadu, Eric had despaired of ever seeing her again, and feared she could never lead a safe life. In her presence now he just wanted to look, and savor his good luck. He held her in his arms a long time, then helped her serve dinner.

During the meal, the conversation became very serious. "Eric, Kahan wants you to come to Xanadu to work. Gambela has more than he can possibly do."

"I know. And I wonder what you think of the life you would lead there?"

"I have never known such peace and tranquility. The place is unearthly, and there is no strife," said Joan.

"Certainly, a surgeon could work without having to worry about trivia and incompetent help, and shabby, second-rate equipment."

"Yes."

"And nobody would ever be denied treatment for lack of funds, and no family would have enormous debts to pay later."

"An ideal situation."

"But would the atmosphere keep a surgeon honed to a fine competitive edge?"

"Kahan would never choose anyone not already committed to excellence. The place teems with distinguished visiting doctors. Its research laboratories are second to none. Support of every sort, financial and otherwise, for any research you might want to do is the best imaginable. There is no impediment in your way, no trivia to steal your time. But you know already."

"I believe you want to live there," said Eric.

"Where I want to live, had I chosen a place, does not matter. Where you want to spend your surgical career takes first place above all else."

"I thank you for your unselfishness. I have offers from

Boston, New York, Chicago, San Francisco, to name only the best."

"All great cities, and each a fascinating place to live."

"But wherever I might go, in any of those cities, there would always be the struggle for live organs."

"Yes, and the struggle against the inertia of the system."

"And now the maddening restrictions of the HMOs, and the intrusion of the insurance industry into the practice of medicine. And Xanadu offers total freedom to be professional with no third-party interference."

"And, of course, no street violence and a perfect pastoral setting in which to raise children."

"Well, we have a day to make a decision, unless I want to be unemployed after July first."

"Temporary rest, I think, would be better than the wrong decision," said Joan.

"Would you really give up everything here to move to remote Africa?"

"I am giving up the same amount of myself here anyway, and I am gaining all of you wherever we go. And Eric, no place is too remote in the modern world."

Eric said, "Kahan's offer includes generous sabbaticals and travel to other centers about the world. All of it is very tempting. And before I left him on my short visit he said something very cogent to me. He is quite astute, you know, and sees the trends in medicine worldwide before the changes arrive."

"I have come to understand him. He is astute in other fields, too."

"He said the day is near when reputable doctors will not build a practice. On the contrary, the patients will be concentrated in specialty hospitals and clinics of one sort or another, and these centers will demand the doctor of a particular type. Thus, the highly trained specialist will no longer be a captive to his practice. He would be able to move about the world without losing his livelihood and his professional position."

"A deliverance of a kind."

"Indeed it is. And he made another offer. He said — and I agree entirely — the days of homographs are numbered; the use of animal parts will be perfected and a mechanical heart, and other mechanical organs, will be perfected someday, body-compatible machines built to outlast any human heart or organ."

"Perhaps imaginable."

"And he thinks cloning and DNA manipulation will produce hearts and other live organs, in the meantime, for transplantation."

"Is it possible?"

"My imagination says yes. And he wants to push stem cell research to a maximum."

"Infinite possibilities."

"Yes, and he wants to build and finance a research foundation to work on these advances, and he offered me the position as director, with unlimited money to hire the best researchers, and the most competent managers."

"I'm not the least surprised, but it has to be your decision."

"I have to say now, I have this fear, whether well founded or not: If I went to Xanadu, would I always feel second-rate, like I had not met the challenge of the needs in our own country, like I had not met the challenge of competition, and I was not the real thing?"

"Eric, you know I am with you whatever you decide, but I must disagree with your sentiments about your duties in the American system. I cannot understand why the leadership lost its power."

"It has been ruined by too much inside politics, by strutting its vanity in the election of a different president every year in every single organization, by incestuous mediocrity passing the incompetent leadership among themselves. This weakness, this long sleep, has allowed the exalted medical profession to be swallowed by a true monster, an out-of-control insurance industry," said Eric. "Even the teamsters knew better."

"Yes, I'm afraid you're right."

"And too liberal interpretation of the laws intended to guard our everyday safety now renders us very weak if not helpless in the streets. We would be joining a society where such behavior is not tolerated," said Eric.

"Could you live within such strictures?" asked Joan.

"Do you want your oppression to be autocratic from the top down, or barbaric in savage insurrection from the bottom up? Which system of society truly protects citizens' rights?"

"The first, as long as you are not the underdog."

"Yes, how right you are."

"You realize, of course, with your experience at Xanadu you would be even more in demand should you decide to move on."

"Perhaps with a certain taint."

"There will always be political enemies, whatever you do, even in medicine."

"Especially so, I have come to think."

"Oh Eric, we have very important decisions to make."

"Yes, indeed we do."

"And you should know Kahan is concerned about our safety, so concerned he gave me his satellite phone number. A call would direct a plane to us immediately."

"I hope we won't need it."

In bed, Eric drowsed fitfully. The fatigue of another forty hours without sleep pulled him down, but the worries about Joan and the excitement of her presence kept him from solid sleep. Out of respect, and out of concern for her stress and emotional exhaustion, he did not touch her. She lay awake, ten hours off her circadian cycle. He dozed again and awoke with a flinch, and found her gazing at his face and laughing.

His erection stood across the space between them. She reached and pulled him over ... a slow and gentle entry, a drowsy rhythm, and he knew at once what most husbands come to know. A difference — there can be no mistaking the sensation. The entire chemistry has changed. This turned his passion to gentleness and concern, and he stopped and drowsed into sleep again, still erect, and awoke and moved, and drowsed again, half awake, half asleep, until after a long time his somnolent rapture climaxed.

In the languor after love, Eric snuggled against Joan, asked, "Why haven't you told me?"

"What, my love?"

"You are pregnant."

"Yes, The urine test is positive, but how did you know?"

"I can tell. There is a different sensation."

"Oh! Eric, I didn't know that marvelous thing was a diagnostic tool, too."

He laughed. "It has never before been used for that purpose."

"Too bad ... what a talented gynecologist you would have been."

"Oh, stop it!"

"I intended telling you in a day or two."

"Well, now I know."

"This is what you wanted."

"Yes, you know my sentiments. And you?"

"A completion."

"This makes all the difference in the world. Now I have a family. I will have a son to clasp to my heart. Imagine the movements of his little body, his searching hands against my chest, his little wobbly head resting on my skin."

"I love the thought."

Drowsing, she asked, "Do you have to go to work tomorrow?"

"Yes, I'm doing a heart transplant, the last I will be allotted before leaving."

"You have a donor waiting?"

"Yes, a brain-dead, thirty-two year old father of five children, on the respirator until we can take his heart."

"What happened?"

"Gunshot wound of the head."

"Accidental?"

"Deliberate, and not only deliberate, but evil, premeditated, and senseless."

"Who shot him?"

"No one knows. He met an oncoming car at nine in the evening, with its lights on bright. He flashed his own to let the other driver know what he was doing. The approaching car made a panic stop, turned around, gave chase, pulled alongside and the front seat passenger took deliberate aim with a handgun and shot the man, and sped away. The victim's wife in the front seat witnessed the shooting, but in her fright got no information useful to the police."

"How awful! Eric, it could be you or me. I've done the same with my headlights hundreds of times."

"Yes. But we have entered a different age. Road rage murder has become commonplace in all cities. The slightest provocation sets off explosive acts of violence."

"Why have we come to this?"

"The explosive release of pent anger, the only freedom these little minds ever reach, with nothing to stop them but democracy in reverse, justice leaning over backward."

"Will it get better or worse?"

"Worse."

After a pause, she said, "Eric do you know what happened to Legation?"

"Destroyed, I hear. Do you know the details?"

"Yes. All the major players, including The Reverend Lotte, are dead, and the operation is out of business."

"Kahan saw to it?"

"Yes."

"And you too?"

"A minor role only."

"I can imagine," said Eric, and he gave her a knowing look, and continued, "So everybody is safe now?"

"Seemingly. Kahan's men in SamuelS have combed the area and have found none of the old employees."

"Do you feel safe?"

"Eric, I have the strangest feeling, like there is a void in this whole picture."

"Something missing?"

"Yes, a sleeper, a factor yet unaccounted for."

"Who or what could it be?"

"Someone who did not die in the fire and explosion at Legation headquarters, or an unknown ... someone we perhaps have never suspected, if we even know him or her."

"Doing what?"

"Hiding and waiting, for revenge or to collect ten million dollars. I am sure there are those who think the reward is still good."

"You are giving me cold chills," said Eric.

"Well, I still am not afraid."

"Joan, for God's sake be careful. Stay at home until I get off duty, then we can go together, wherever you need to be."

"No. I'll lead a normal life, and not be frightened into seclusion. Is tomorrow your last day at Sentara?"

"Yes. Our goodbyes will be over at noon."

"Great. How about lunch downtown?"

"Okay, The Harbor Club. I never get enough of the view in the daytime ... I'll come home for you."

"No. I plan to be out anyway. I'll pick you up in front of the hospital at one o'clock. Okay?"

"Well ... fine. This will give you the chance to come in for a few minutes to meet the chief, Foster Kemp. I've been promising him. You can park at the curb."

"Oh, yes. I would love to meet him."

CHAPTER 41

Eric arrived at work before dawn on his last day of training, just as he had on the first morning of his internship. At seven o'clock surgery he performed the heart transplant with Foster Kemp first assisting. At ten-thirty he went for one last time through the cardiac ICU and kidney wards. The pall hanging over these desperate scenes had not changed in his eight years there. Most of the patients would die waiting for a new heart or kidney.

As they stepped into the hallway, the chief dismissed the entourage of students and residents and nurses, and took Eric aside. "Eric," he said, "I've not been in a position to say this until today, but I can say it now. We want you to stay on, and if you will, we can guarantee you a research laboratory, the rank of assistant professor, a handsome starting salary, and faculty housing until you wish to build or buy."

Both astonished and pleased, Eric hesitated. He really wanted another service and another city for the sake of experience and to broaden his concepts. He said, "Well, Dr. Kemp, I did not know."

"Yes, I know only too well, but my hands have been tied. Wallace will not be with us after this summer, and he let me know only at six-thirty this morning. He has a damned good excuse, of course. He is tired of medicine, applied to Harvard Law School in January, and much to his surprise was accepted, provided he could start the fall session in August. He was notified only yesterday. So he is going, at his age, fifty-four. Imagine it. Talented as he is, he was only half-interested anyway, and you could double his income and patient load easily."

"I'm grateful and humbled by the offer and I would like to have time to think about it."

"Oh, indeed."

"I'm having lunch with Joan today and we will talk."

"And I have to be very fair to you."

"Dr. Kemp, you have been more than fair and very generous."

"I'm speaking of your future."

"I would appreciate any advice."

"From a selfish standpoint I want you here. From the view of the best thing for you, I lean toward your going out into the world, see the techniques others are using, then settle wherever you like. And you must recognize the changes occurring in medicine. You no longer have to stay in one place to build a practice. In the modern world you go to the patients in one type of center or another. They will be there waiting."

"Precisely what Kahan has told me."

"I am eager to meet this man."

Eric's beeper called him to a phone. The senior neurosurgery resident, Dr. Finlay Swift, wanted him in the emergency room at once. Eric always responded promptly to this message because it meant the resident could not leave a patient to make the call himself, and almost surely there would be donors. Even at the last minute of his training period he would respond to lend a helping hand.

In the emergency room he went to Swift. "I'm afraid we have five donors on our hands, maybe more."

"A wreck?"

"No, a greater tragedy ... let's have a look."

The father, already on a respirator, still wore his petty officer's uniform. The neighbors had told the story. He arrived home from a fifteen-month tour of duty, found his children alone, half-starved, beaten and bruised, and his wife gone. She had been out all night with other men, and still had not returned home by midmorning. With his .25 caliber pistol he calmly shot each of four beautiful little boys in the head. Then he sat in the bathtub and shot himself, with equally effective aim on his own head. The others were dying too. Each had dilated pupils, agonal breathing, unconsciousness, bleeding head wounds at the sites of bullet entries and exits, all spouting destroyed brain.

"Dr. Swift, the intern needs you back in cubicle three. One has stopped breathing!"

Swift watched the stilled face for a second, the pounding neck, and the heart visibly thrusting against the chest wall. "Intubate him and start a respirator. We can prolong his life only for the purpose of giving him to other people who are quite beyond desperation."

"God, I wish we could do something!" said the intern.

"So do I," said Swift.

A nurse entered the cubicle and said, "Dr. Swift, they have found the last child. She was in another room of the home."

"Is she all right?"

"Yes. Well, at least she has not been shot. Come see for yourself."

They entered another cubicle, Eric following. From his insular place in heart surgery, he had forgotten about battered children. This one brought it all back. Five years old, and already the child had a street look, dirty and unkempt, the blond hair matted, the hands and fingernails dirty. Her clothes, in a heap on the table beside her, were shabby, ragged, and soiled. Blue, green and black bruises covered her limbs and body. She sat on the side of the table, hunkered over with the apathetic torpor of malnourishment, staring down toward the floor. Swift spoke to her kindly then pointed to a reddish dark knot on her chest and asked, "What caused that, sweetheart?" She responded to the note in his voice, and turned her dirt-blotched little face up to look at Swift. *My God, the eyes,* Eric thought, *hope and all trust gone long ago.* Tears welled up over the sick watery whites of the weakened globes and she said, "Mommy hit me."

"When?'

"Last night."

"And this one?" Swift asked, pointing to a greenish blue bruise.

"Mommy hit me last week"

Her ribs showed through the bruised dirty skin, the scrawny neck appeared too weak to support the tilting head, the large eyes sank far into their sockets, and she sat on the table edge slouched in the potbellied, swollen belly posture of starving tribal children. Infected insect bites, bruises and cuts, and frank sores, marred her legs and arms. Swift completed his examination and stepped out of the cubicle. The nurse with him shuddered and said, "My God, the little boys look the same, too!"

"Yes, starved and beaten."

"Why? Why would a mother treat children this way?'

"Men are just as bad when involved, and I don't really know how a human being can stoop to such depravity. But I have noted in almost every instance, the children have been innocently guilty of standing in the way of an adult's sexual freedom. I will wager you the boyfriend contributed his share of the physical abuse also, but under the guise of discipline. Big daddy steps in. He can handle unruly children when poor little mommy reaches her wits end, which is not a great distance. The child is miserable for one reason or another, it frets, it cries. Lover calls it spoiled. He proceeds to show his real manhood in the absence of the father. Spare the rod and spoil the child, he reasons. Strike a suffering child and it cries more, which calls for a larger dose of the same stupid brutal discipline. Stubbornly pursued, this approach comes to what you witness tonight. Bolstering each other in their illicit behavior, they commit atrocities neither would dream of alone."

"Jesus!" the nurse said.

"Dr. Swift, another one has stopped breathing."

Swift watched the stilled face, the blank face of death, and moved quickly to intubate and start the respirator. Beyond the drawn curtains the sighing, irregular, agonal gasping of the other two were louder than the hissing regularity of the three respirators.

"Dr. Swift, they have brought the mother in."

"Where was she? "

"Half drunk in a bar downtown with a bunch of sailors. She is hysterical, wild with grief, and completely broken."

They stood over the mother, who sat bowed over in her chair, weeping. The nurse said, "Mrs. Bea, I've brought Dr. Swift to see you." The mother glanced up, wiping at a teary eye, and Eric became furious at the tawdry mess: beaded blue mascara on long false lashes, lipstick painted beyond the vermilion borders and half eaten away, bleached hair growing black roots, flowing rivulets of ruin — streaked paint and powder and mascara — following the lines of gravity and early myriad wrinkles, the face haunted by an uncontrollable hunger, a taste for depravity never assuaged, a ferocious feline wanton sensuality. *Wild as Hell! Capable of complete abandon,* thought Eric, and intuitively he knew the superficial wildfire of her passion would burn as furiously and as briefly in grief. He braced for the reaction.

She said, "Doctor, I know you can save my babies."

Impulsively Swift laid a kind hand on her thin shoulder. Eric saw the dress too tight across scrawny muscle and the ridged bone of her taut leanness, the shivering tremor of her terror and dread. He read the signs and his anger disappeared, and compassion returned. He felt sorry for this woman, this person whose passions had burned out of control and who paid with the destruction of her family — lust and sloth and ruin. He fell back on the self-control imbued by his training, and his own self-imposed oath to never judge, to treat all people alike, from whore to queen with no preferential for social standing. After hesitating, Swift said, "Mrs. Bea, I am sorry I could not." And from the tones in his voice, Eric knew Swift had felt his same emotions.

She stopped sobbing and in the sudden quietness turned her gaze up to Swift, then toward the curtained cubicles, at the white drawn drapes hanging down in each entrance. The new stillness, the hush now behind these rebuking barriers, punctuated by the sibilant sonorous mechanics of the respirators, held the room in ominous awareness. Then she screamed, "No! ... My God! ... No! ... Not my babies!" She leapt out of the chair and lunged toward the curtains. The nurses and orderlies gently and firmly stopped her. She kicked and screamed and struggled against the restraining hands and screamed into space, the echoes reverberating throughout the emergency room, and sent another scream tearing into the echoes, and screamed again and again. Swift and Stuart, and the nurses and orderlies, backed off and waited. Then the screaming stopped and she sat in stony silence, the muscles of her jaws clamped, her lips white in anguish and anger.

Swift approached again and gently said, "Mrs. Bea, we need to make some urgent and important decisions."

"What kind of decisions?"

"Since we cannot save your husband and your boys, we could help other people desperate for hearts and kidneys and other ..."

"No!" she screamed, "No! No! No!"

"But they do not suffer and never will again and this is so important to desperate people who do suffer."

"No! You cannot cut up my beloved husband and my precious little boys into spare parts for the undeserving."

"But, Mrs. Bea."

"No," she said, "and I mean it."

"You positively won't let us try to help others?"

"Under no circumstances, and don't try to talk me into it. They have suffered enough."

"We could have social services come and talk to you."

"No. I refuse to discuss this further with anyone, especially social workers ... and that is final."

After a brief silence, Swift, in the kindest tones, said, "I am sorry you feel this way, and I regret your having to bear this grief."

She responded to the tone in his voice and looked up then at Swift and said, "It's my religion, Doctor. I believe in the afterlife. I believe all men will be raised from the dead, and I believe no one can be raised up if his parts are missing. What would a life in heaven be like with no heart? I cannot let my little boys go to heaven without their hearts, Doctor. What good would heaven do them then? Isn't that what heaven is all about ... the heart?"

Swift rose, touched her on a shoulder, and said, "God bless you," and left the room.

Out in the hallway he turned to Eric and said, "I apologize, Eric."

"Oh no. On the contrary, we are very grateful to you for trying, and for thinking of our predicament with our own dying patients."

"If we were in certain other countries, they would have to become donors by law."

"Such a law I'm sure is a good idea, provided the diagnosis *brain death* is a hundred percent correct."

"And has no hidden motive."

"Oh! My God, how right you are," said Eric.

Swift turned to leave. Then Eric remembered the arrangement made with Kahan, and said, "Just a minute, Finley, I know of another possibility. Try to keep Mrs. Bea here a few minutes while I make a phone call ... be right back."

Ivan Prescott had left for Xanadu again but Walter Exum knew to okay the arrangements: as much as fifty thousand dollars for each donor. Stuart returned to find Swift waiting in the hallway, and gave him the details. Swift said, "God! Are you damned sure about this?"

"Without question." He didn't say anything about guaranteeing the amount himself. Swift did not need to know of Eric's wealth.

"Okay, this puts a new light on everything. But let's try for twenty-five each." They returned to Mrs. Bea. There, the narrow and intemperate countenance of obstinate resistance softened as Mrs. Bea slowly came to realize the significance of a hundred and twenty-five thousand dollars. Finally, she rationalized her acceptance with: "I reckon I ought to do what I can to help others."

Out in the hallway again, Swift said, "Well, Eric, the refusal was a purer sentiment."

"Yes, but only if you dismissed all its hidden resentments and hostilities."

Finley hesitated, then said, "Ahh, yes. For the moment I was disarmed."

Eric returned toward the main event in the office of the cardiac pavilion. Marcus Mann stopped him in the hallway. "Eric, you have a moment?"

"Of course." They stepped aside into an alcove.

"I want to tell you first, before the news gets out ... I've accepted an offer from Kahan. I will develop at Xanadu an international organization similar to LifeChain."

Eric hesitated in astonishment. Marcus had developed LifeChain in the States with such energy and dedication. "What has happened?" he finally asked.

"The courts handed down a permanent ruling against us. Worse, my own board has voted to sell LifeChain to the biggest hospital chain in the country, or the world. I will not work under such management, such pressure, or such danger to quality control."

"Well, I think you are to be congratulated, and it wouldn't take much to bring me to the same decision. Kahan is most tempting."

"And another deciding factor. I'm sick of Virginia politics. Norfolk is like a city without a state. The damned backward legislature recognizes nothing really significant to their academic snobbery except Charlottesville and Richmond, while the most populous area by comparison goes wanting. I don't think it will ever change, despite Thomas Jefferson's advice two hundred years ago — the Tidewater Area is the place for the major state supported medical school, the real Mecca."

"I've come to the same conclusion myself."

"Good. And I hope you accept Kahan's offer. My family is very excited about the move."

"We'll see." Eric turned and entered the waiting room. Well-wishers and admirers surrounded him.

Joan awakened at midmorning. After leisurely coffee she decided to walk to the doctors' parking ramp at the hospital where her own car had been parked for a month. She had plenty of time before lunch with Eric.

At a quarter to one she walked up the first level to her car and hesitated. An eerie feeling enveloped her, perhaps a misgiving for neglect. A shroud of dust coated the car's long, sleek, dynamic beauty, but something more drastic nudged for attention. What, she wondered? She stopped and looked into the cool dankness and the deep corner shadows behind concrete buttresses. The garage hovered silent and empty of people at the noon hour. She stopped at the car door and turned to survey the ramp descending to the street below. A sensation of hollow misgiving swept over her, and she stiffened, and turned to look again. Without the sound of movement a breeze stirred across her face and a presence in its own shadow materialized at her side. She gasped in surprise and stepped back. All her premonitions had been correct, the worst of them. Pitifully hideous, the man stared vacuously beyond her gaze, and she looked into a wide-mouthed grin exposing widely spaced jagged tooth fragments. His sparse hair lay awry on a head deformed with irregular potato-shaped swellings beneath bulging scalp, the eyelids swollen and inflamed. He stood shoulder high to her. He said, "I want to operate on Joan Pully."

Joan stood still. The man reached and grasped her wrist in a cold grip as strong as steel, the skin contact rough and calloused. "You are Joan Pully ... I am going to operate on Joan Pully."

He had to be the infamous Chiron, Legation's surgeon. So the fire had spared this evil. An impulse surged to kick and chop, but emotions interfered: the revolting vision of the little man rupturing into something vile and putrid. And now she had to be careful because of her baby. She no longer could be reckless and daring. Charm might work. Smiling, she said, "You are Chiron."

"Yes," he said. "I am Chiron, and I want to operate on Joan Pully."

"Why Chiron, you can't operate on me. I don't need surgery. Besides, I am standing up."

"I'm Chiron. I'm a chimera. I have the heart and the liver and the lungs of a convict, and the kidney of a little girl. I want to operate on Joan Pully." He reached into the bulging pocket of his jacket and extracted a handful of shiny operating room instruments. He held a scalpel, a bone cutter resembling tin shears, and a ratcheted retractor. With the other hand he pulled on her wrist, trying to bring her down. In a moment she would be forced to hit him. She knew his reputation. In two minutes he could have a chest open and the heart cut loose from its moorings, and half delivered from the body while still beating. With a little more effort he would defeat her strength.

As she began maneuvering for attack, the sound of running feet slapping concrete echoed through the structure, approaching, growing louder. At once the Buddha-like form of

John, the head orderly, jiggling in a heavy run, rounded the corner of a dank concrete buttress, his bronze skin glowing with sweat. He leapt forward. Joan looked into two huge brown eyes, a concerned gaze, soft and apprising. John took Chiron gently by an arm and pulled him away, "Chiron, we will have to lock you up if you don't behave."

"I want to operate on Joan Pully."

"I'm sorry," John said to Joan. "He escaped when I turned my back to see after a patient."

"Where did he come from?"

"He sleeps in the doctors' lounge now. I keep an eye on him during the day. But this can't go on forever."

"Thanks for the rescue, John."

"Be careful. He is wicked without knowing it."

John firmly led Chiron away. As they receded down the structure, Chiron chanted, "I want to operate ... I want to operate on Joan Pully," his voice ricocheting in hollow reverberating echoes through the concrete caverns, the instruments still gripped in one hand. Joan listened to the retreating steps. In the past, she had delivered many live organs into John's waiting hands at the operating room entrance. People knew and respected him for his kind ways.

She turned again to her car. As she moved with a key toward the door, her hands trembled ... and in a moment of almost panic she knew something had neutralized her ways and had taken the upper hand, something out of control. A little regret somewhere struggled frantically for attention in a void of thinking, the silence too profound, Chiron a mere murmur fading in the far reaches of the garage, John's reassurances controlled and kind ... What had she left undone? What hovered unrecognized *there* waiting to catch her unaware ... She whirled as a masculine voice said, "Miss Pully." She came about to confront Ralph Green almost in her face. The cue ball haircut, the short, thick muscular build, the intense look out of pale blue eyes set wide apart in a large flat face —a somber, alert, threatening appearance, revealing a mean and cruel streak. She knew in a flash he had been creeping up on her and he had witnessed the aggression of Chiron, waiting for the right moment to make a dramatic rescue, ready to take advantage of an eerie coincidence. This one carried a deadlier and utterly serious threat, she knew, and had always known. What could he be doing in the hospital parking ramp?

She said, "Well hello, Ralph." She felt fright and concern, and quelled an impulse to chop him hard. The thick mass of neck muscles and his alert stance would make an effective blow doubtful, and from his build low to the ground he would be too quick. And he had been her master in judo. He could do her harm; he could kill or ruin her child. She bided her time, and turned to unlock the door. She pulled it open and turned again with the door between them, and waited.

"You have not been to the club for a Karate lesson in weeks."

"Yes, and I'm so sorry to have missed them, but events have been beyond my control."

"Too bad ... you might lose all your wonderful skills."

"Oh, I'll get back to it sooner or later. What are you doing here at the hospital?"

"To tell you the truth, I was looking for you. You simply disappeared and I thought I might find you at work ... then I spotted your lovely car."

"Well here I am, in good health."

"And a splendid sight indeed. I was wondering, could you possibly find time for lunch with me today? We could talk about arrangements for your lessons."

She almost sighed with relief. Eric would be waiting less than a block away in the hospital lobby. Now she could get to him. "Why yes, Ralph, having lunch with you would be so nice. Tell you what ... why don't you drive my car out to the main hospital entrance, and wait at the curb. I've got to run up to the operating room for a minute to meet Eric's boss. I'll just cut through the ramp. Then we can be off to lunch. What an exciting surprise!" This character would get a surprise all right, the surprise of his life when she returned to the car with Eric.

Ralph took the keys, got in the car, backed it out of the parking place, and eased forward down the ramp. In his moment of triumph he chided himself for not knowing all along his charm could take Joan Pully as easily as it had taken numerous other women, a piece of cake.

The Jaguar went down in the swag of pavement and started up the rise to street level, its slick beauty gliding away, its elegant polish, despite the coating of dust, glinting in the noon sun, and Joan knew a twinge of regret as she peeked from behind a concrete pillar at the disappearing tail lights.

Eric's friends and admirers: the teaching staff, the residents, the nurses, orderlies, maids, and a few ambulatory patients, came to him with hearty handshakes, hugs, kisses, and tears. They all loved him. But in his happiness a worry hung in the balance, a preoccupation. He felt not quite oriented on reality and uneasy about something he could not define. He wanted to join Joan as quickly as possible. But what incomplete thing gnawed at his awareness? ... Then he knew, and his belly lurched down in a tailspin. Joan! Her car! She had not been near it for more than a month, and only the caution of SamuelS had saved himself from being blown to smithereens. But had SamuelS or anybody checked Joan's? He had failed to think of it. And she would be on her way to pick up the car now, if not already in it. Had SamuelS relaxed its vigil with the elimination of The Reverend? He spun among his startled admirers, and bolted for the door and the hospital entrance. As he dashed into the street, the explosion shook the building and the fireball obliterated the parking ramp exit. He raced on, his heart pounding, his mouth dry with grief and regret.

As Joan turned to move from behind the concrete pillar toward the hospital entrance she caught her last glimpse of the tail of her beautiful car disappearing up the ramp. In this second it exploded, the concussion rocked the building, and the lid of the trunk blew through the entry and struck the pillar behind which she stood. The blast knocked her onto the concrete floor but she landed sitting. A second explosion sent flames shooting up and blocking out her view. The flames evaporated and she stepped outside. The car had been blown to bits and the remainder of the chassis rolled down the street in a ball of fire. Debris fell upon her. She looked at her bare arms and clothes speckled with raining fragments, red in tiny flecks along with salmon-colored pieces. She reentered the ramp and descended the stairs toward the outside sidewalk leading to the hospital entry. Eric ran ahead of the people swarming toward the sound of the explosion and the burning remainder of her Jaguar.

Eric reached for her. Soot splotched her face and the edges of singed hair. Blood and flesh and pieces of fiber and tiny slivers of metal clung to her clothes and skin. She extended her trembling hands toward him. "Oh Eric, that was my car."

"What happened?"

"I told you they were not gone, not all of them. First Chiron, then on his heels, Ralph Green, behind a barely veiled presence of danger, invited me to lunch. I fooled him and asked him to drive to the front to meet me. I didn't know a bomb had been planted. It blew up just as I started into the hospital to find you. He looked so evil, and now I'm wearing him in little pieces."

"Thank God it's only a car and you are all right."

"Eric, let's get out of here."

At home Eric and Joan entered his kitchen as they had the first night. He crossed his living room to open the Venetian slats. Something across the street caught his attention. There at the curb, two men sat in a van, attentively watching his house. He turned to Joan and said, "Do you have the satellite number Kahan gave you?"

"Yes." She reached in her purse and handed him the slip of paper. "Why?" she asked.

"We need a ride to Xanadu."

"Oh Eric, " she said, and after hesitating for a moment dashed for the shower.

The phone rang. Eric picked it up, wondering in mingled curiosity and presentiment of consequence. Who could be calling his home at an hour like this? Kahan himself spoke at once, wasting no words. "Dr. Stuart, where is Joan?"

"Here with me."

"Is she all right?"

"Yes."

"We have been trying frantically to find her."

"Why?"

"Her car, Dr. Stuart, her car. Something has fallen through the cracks ... we fear it has not been checked for a bomb."

"Yes, how well we know now. How stupid of me not to think of it."

"On the contrary, how stupid of me, and how unlike SamuelS, not to double and triple check my orders. We sent a man to inspect your car and another to check hers, but the latter one got himself killed in a traffic accident en route to Norfolk and no one caught the error."

"Well, your instincts were right. The car exploded just a few minutes ago."

"Was anyone...?"

"Yes. Another and the last, I hope, of Joan's mortal enemies, Ralph Green. You remember, her Karate instructor ...?"

"Ahhhh, indeed, and The Reverend's death pimp, the procurer par excellence of donors, the mastermind of befitting destinies, the night cat of the underworld. What a relief to know he ... he was ... was he not?"

"Joan is now in the shower washing off a coating of his splattered remains."

"Destiny came full cycle. What happened?"

"She used her head once again."

"Will you bring the details to me?"

"We need a plane now, this afternoon, and my house is staked out again by unsavory characters in a van parked across the street."

After a moment of silence, then the sound of shuffled papers, Kahan said, "Piedmont at three o'clock, and Herman Hodder himself will accompany a black Ford to your door, one hour from now." Then Kahan said, "We have reserved the same quarters you loved so much on your visit here."

"By the sound of running water ... we are grateful."

"Your coming here is a great boon to us, to our plans for the greatest of all hospitals. Marcus Mann is joining our staff, and with his expertise we will have the greatest tissue bank and live organ source in the world."

"Marcus just told me of his decision. Congratulations."

"Thank you, and I am very happy to tell you also Ivan Prescott is here with Teresa — what a team he and Marcus will be — and John Marion with Sarah. Both couples were married three days ago. John's favorite shaman performed the double ceremony. The same shaman, incidentally, is aboard the plane picking you up at Piedmont."

"Well, how delightful, and appropriate. Could you arrange a date?"

"Why not something unique, Dr. Stuart? How about a wedding aboard the flight, in the stratosphere above international waters, entirely appropriate for a man and woman of the world, where your talents belong."

"Could it be arranged, legitimately?"

"Indeed." Kahan talked on a few minutes about arrangements and said goodbye.

When Joan cut off the hair dryer, Eric said, "A SamuelS plane will be at Piedmont by three o'clock."

"Then there is no time to pack"

"Kahan says to bring nothing. SamuelS can crate everything and ship it later, but right now your place and mine will serve as distractions to anyone who tries to find us."

"We simply just disappear?"

"Yes, a SamuelS car will get us to The Piedmont Airport in safety. Of course, we will have a lot of phoning to do from Africa."

"Eric, are you really...?"

"Yes. Yes I am, for the time being anyway, and maybe for always."

Herman Hodder phoned into the house as his driver parked at the curb. Eric and Joan descended the front steps and took the back seat. As the car pulled into the street, the men in the van pretended to look elsewhere, but after a brief wait, followed nearly a block behind. Herman's driver kept well ahead but did not lose them.

As the party boarded the plane at Piedmont field, the van came into sight along the cyclone fence; then parked at the edge of the tarmac. Herman went to the copilot's seat and trained binoculars on the van. He called Joan to have a look. After a moment she handed the binoculars back and said, "I don't know the two in front, but my God, the man behind them, leaning forward between the two seats, and eagerly watching the plane is Chiron ... grinning. I would know that mouth anywhere. Who, I wonder, has picked him up to *operate on Joan Pully*?" Eric caught her by an elbow and guided her down the aisle to a seat. She had turned ashen and she trembled. "Oh Eric, their persistence is unreal."

The plane began charging down the runway toward the

Chesapeake Bay. "Well, they can't follow us now," said Eric.

"I have a notion to go back and fight."

"No, not anymore."

"Why not? I'm no coward."

Eric glanced out the window as the plane lifted above the Chesapeake Bay Bridge-Tunnel, and out over the bright Atlantic. "Because you might miss your wedding."

"You haven't asked me."

"I'm asking you now. Will you stop the fighting and marry me?"

"When?"

"As soon as the plane levels off ... about ten minutes."

"Eric, what do you mean?"

"The shaman is aboard, and Kahan says he can marry us in the stratosphere above international waters, as befitting true citizens of the world."

"Does he have the authority?"

"Yes. Last week it was Ivan Prescott and his Teresa, and John Marion and his Sarah at Xanadu."

"Will they be living there?"

"You know it, and so will Marcus Mann and his family. Kahan is very clever at getting what he wants."

"More like what the world needs. The answer is yes, right now, right this minute; this is going to be a great life."

The shaman stepped forward, holding a handful of papers. He stopped in the aisle, and bowed to Joan and Eric. He wore a white linen suit. Eric caught a whiff of cologne. "You wish to be married ... please stand up together in the aisle and hold hands."

Eric stood and Joan moved to his side and took one of his hands in both of hers. The shaman spoke of man and woman sharing equally in duties and dedication, in love and devotion, in the motherhood and the fatherhood of children to be brought into this world. Then he spoke of magic and medicine, and of the support of wife to the medicine man and the man-of-medicine in the realm of human suffering. He then pronounced them man and wife.

The shaman opened the papers in his hand and asked for signatures. While signing, Eric said, "How did you manage to do all the legal work so quickly?"

"Oh, Kahan had it done two weeks ago."

"Well!" said Joan.

And the shaman said, "The Kahan knows."

The darkness of night in Africa closes like a blanket caressing sleep behind the guarding walls of shelter. Only a week has passed since his arrival, and within the cloistered and gracious atmosphere of Xanadu's majestic rooms, Eric, royally relieved of all tedium by the best of all assistance, has transplanted fifteen hearts into kings and servants, and beauties and the ugly, the ordinary and the exceptional, and all sorts from around the world. And today, his mandatory day off duty, he hiked with Kahan and a guide to the top of the mountain in the morning hours, across the vast field of frozen scree. At high noon from the peak they viewed the plains stretching below.

Now Eric lay awake, Joan sleeping quietly beside him. From the mountain top in the afternoon sunshine, the guide had commented on the peculiar behavior of animals and birds on the mountain and plain below, the wild erratic screaming flight, the strange running away from the western horizon. *Storm's coming,* he had said, glancing up at the clear sky. As they hurried home hours later, black clouds gathering in the west, moved across the land. The storm struck after dusk, with great flashes of lightning and crashing thunder and sheets of driving rain, leaving in its wake the quieter sounds: the slow rhythm of dripping eaves, the whispers of rain-washed land out in the night, the distant sporadic roar of lions, the other animal noises. How strangely alike to the rainy evening when Joan appeared out of the mist hardly more than a month ago, bringing him wife and a new freedom, and a new country where night cocoons with its danger the sensible sanctuary of home. The darkness hides the predator, the lurking death, along with the genitive and secret prowl of love. And in his own bed an inner cryptic darkness harbors and husbands the brooding beginning of family. In the drowsiness of early sleep he knows the bright faces of patients rescued from certain death, the pressure of other hands clasping his, the erumpent heart relieved of agony and grief. Through the night, the river runs rapid across the rills and rocks, its plunge singing toward the sea. And beside him, his wife breathes quietly around the silence of his son, inchoate now in the stirring of new life.

END

EPILOGUE

Early in the transplant era, the editors of the official scientific journal of the American College of Surgeons, SURGERY *Gynecology and Obstetrics,* (now the *Journal of the American College of Surgeons*) published my editorial, The Donor and His Physician. At the time, I wrote these opinions out of concern for the changing and often erroneous concepts of death, the danger of these concepts to patients who were misdiagnosed and were not really brain-dead, and the innate distrust created by the deceptive and misleading new terminology. I thought then, and still think, people can handle open and candid explanations better than the hypocrisy of veiled language couched to obscure a double meaning. And under these circumstances they will respond generously when they understand the true and irrevocable meaning and the finality of brain death, when they understand the opportunity not only to save an organ itself from death, but at the same time to let a part of their relative live on, when they feel the desperation of the person who will die without the gift of a live organ, when they come to recognize and respect the life of an organ itself with its own silent intelligence working below the level of human awareness to create and sustain the miracle of life with a brilliant alchemy still largely beyond the realm of human understanding. The legal guidelines have changed since 1972, but not the controlling emotions. The editorial is reproduced here in toto. *The Wafer* evolved from these concepts over the years.

****

THE DONOR AND HIS PHYSICIAN

Joseph T. McFadden, M.D., F.A.C.S.
Norfolk, Virginia

Cleo ... is he dead?
Dio. His death's upon him, but not dead.
Anthony and Cleopatra, Act IV, Scene XV, 1, 7
William Shakespeare

By universal concept, death occurs at that moment when the heart ceases beating. No other sign ever has been considered valid to identify this final irreversible event for which death is recognized by layman and physician alike.

Resuscitation of the severely brain-damaged patient often protracts an insensible iatrogenic existence until the heart finally becomes exhausted and quits. Prior to the transplant era, there was no controversy about these patients: one was dead when his heart stopped. Fortunate was the physician who knew when not to resuscitate and intrepid was he who stopped the respirator supporting an apneic patient in seemingly interminable irreversible coma.

Now, however, a real need exists for propitious intervention to obtain live organs which otherwise would be ruined by the final throes of cardiovascular collapse. Although there is no real doubt among physicians about what to do nor when to do it, there is nevertheless, much semantic confusion about the terminal neurophysiology and the legality of intervention. The respirator-supported comatose patient, known to house officers 25 years ago as a "heart-lung preparation," now goes under the name, brain death, cerebral death, coma depasse, respirator brain, irreversible coma, and others. Armed with these neologisms, there are those who say that a patient is dead while his heart still beats. This is begging the question and, indeed, to what purpose except to avoid involvement in the forbidden practice of euthanasia. While the intent is not literally euthanasian, an overt act, nevertheless, is committed to end the only function sustaining life, albeit artificially supported. When performed on a patient in true irreversible coma, with the informed consent of the relatives, to obtain a needed organ, there can be little question that the public accepts it and the law abides it. However, the sensational term brain death, along with the already widely disseminated but erroneous idea that it can be identified by an isoelectric electroencephalographic tracing, has created a complacent, but no doubt well meant, collusion, too often between the lone clinician and the approbative encephalographer, in which the margin to err both medically and legally is significant.

For identifying irreversible coma, the electroencephalogram falls precisely where it does among the tests used to study surgical intracranial lesions. It is the least important of diagnostic procedures and as a practical matter could be eliminated from the armamentarium of the neurosurgeon if he had to choose to do without one. It should never be forgotten that an isoelectric electroencephalographic tracing is an isoelectric electroencephalograpic tracing and nothing more, occasionally found in such conditions as sleep, fatigue, and, when correctly recorded, uniformly found in the stone-dead. The diagnosis invariably depends upon other information. A correctly recorded isoelectric electroencephalographic tracing corroborates only in that it does not refute the diagnosis of irreversible coma.

The laboratory and clinical differential evaluation, resolved according to established principles, identifies the donor. He is dying from severe cerebral damage caused by trauma or spontaneous hemorrhage, and in this state, he is comatose, totally areflexic, totally apneic, and totally mydriatic without electrolyte, blood gas, or metabolic abnormalities which contribute to either the coma or apnea.

After all the proscriptive evaluation has been repeated sequentially to identify this condition beyond a doubt, the clinician still should be aware that, except in the state of Kansas, he goes beyond his legal rights when, according to published directions, he declares the patient dead and stops the respirator.

There is now a welter of published medical, religious, and legal opinions, leaving the physician fully responsible for defining death. When treating the donor with a beating heart, the physician, at present, is called upon to assume a role ethically abhorrent in his Hippocratic dedication to all mankind: to judge, and thereby to assume responsibility which belongs not to him alone but to all of society. Certainly, it is doubly abhorrent to be asked to change age-old tradition and legal concepts of death arbitrarily for the real purpose only of circumventing a deplorable void in established law. The neurophysiologic state of a life ebbing away in irreversible coma, by any of its names, is nothing new. Call it what you will, but to name it expediently is to fail to take the problem with full seriousness. Urgently now, the physician needs, for the management of irreversible coma, legal standards set within limits pliable enough to encompass medical advances in transplanting live organs, and in treating those formidable maladies responsible today for the donor's tragedy.

Reprinted, with permission, from
SURGERY, Gynecology & Obstetrics
June, 1972, Vol. 134, 999-1000